IVORY FROM PARADISE

Ivory from Paradise

DAVID SCHMAHMANN

Academy Chicago Publishers

Published in 2011 by
Academy Chicago Publishers
363 West Erie Street
Chicago, Illinois 60654

Printed and bound in the U.S.A.

Library of Congress Cataloging-in-Publication Data

Schmahmann, David, 1953–
Ivory from paradise / David R. Schmahmann.
p. cm.
ISBN 978-0-89733-612-3 (hardcover : alk. paper)
1. Jewish families—Fiction. 2. Jews—South Africa—Fiction.
3. Memory—Fiction. 4. South Africa—Fiction. I. Title.
PS3619.C44I86 2011
813'.6—dc22
2010036954

for

My Beloved Sister and Brother

'Who knocks?' 'I who was beautiful
Beyond all dreams to restore,
I from the roots of the dark thorn am hither,
And knock on the door.'

— "THE GHOST" BY WALTER DE LA MARE

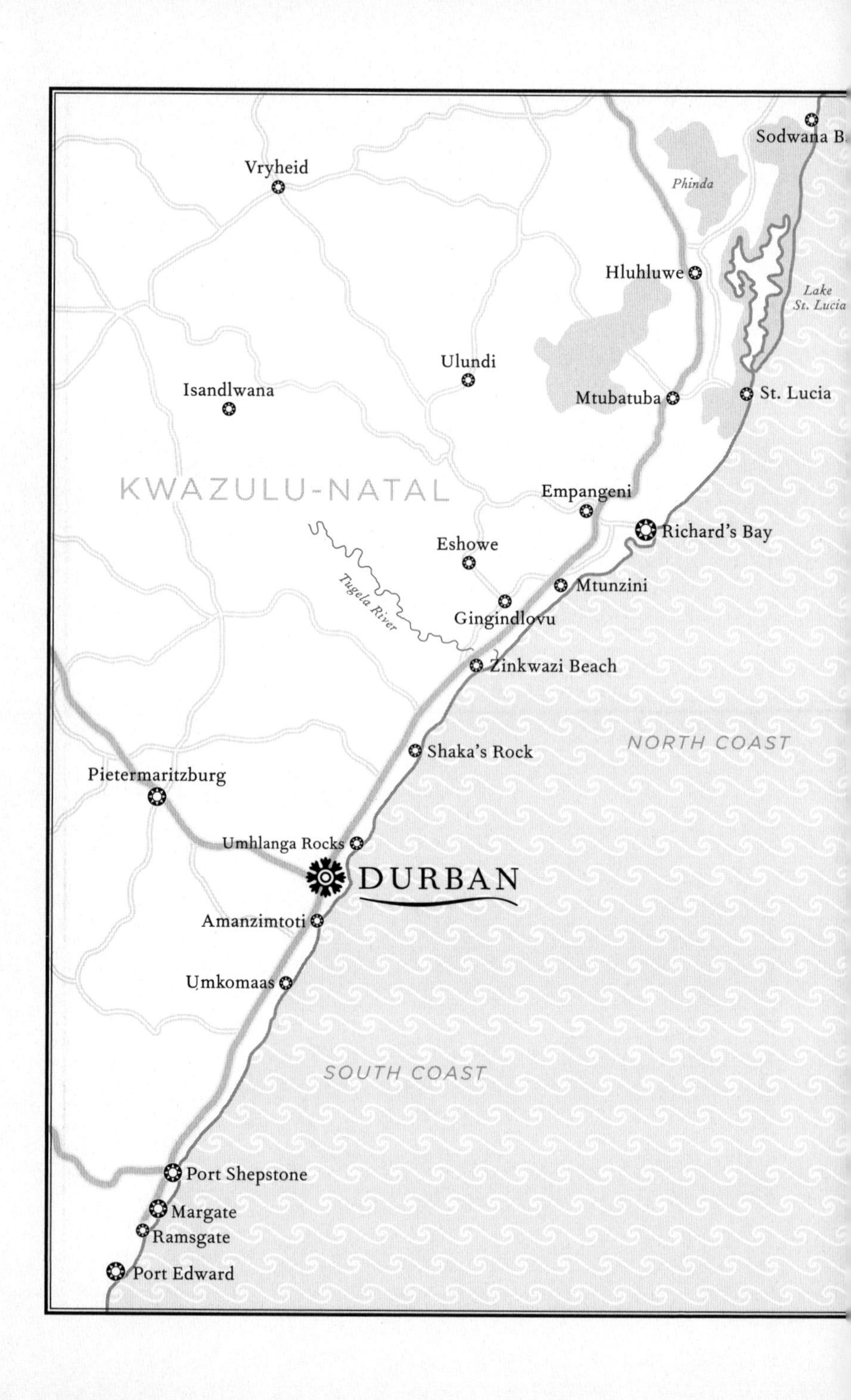
Vryheid
Sodwana B
Phinda
Hluhluwe
Lake St. Lucia
Ulundi
Isandlwana
Mtubatuba
St. Lucia
KWAZULU-NATAL
Empangeni
Richard's Bay
Eshowe
Tugela River
Mtunzini
Gingindlovu
Zinkwazi Beach
NORTH COAST
Shaka's Rock
Pietermaritzburg
Umhlanga Rocks
DURBAN
Amanzimtoti
Umkomaas
SOUTH COAST
Port Shepstone
Margate
Ramsgate
Port Edward

INDIAN OCEAN

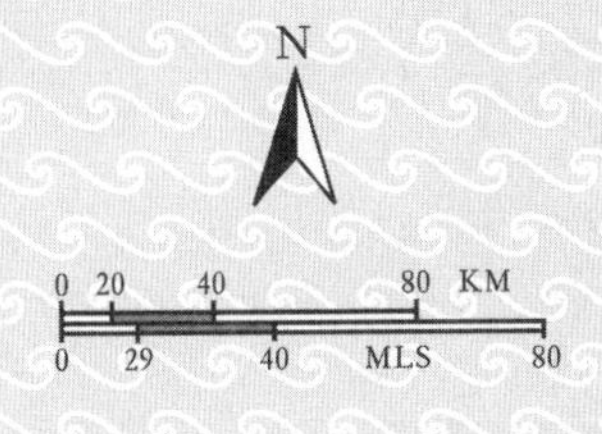

LONDON

1

MY MOTHER LIES in the ornate master bedroom of Arnold's penthouse flat. The room overlooks Hyde Park, and from other windows in the apartment you can see Wellington Arch and even the tops of trees in the gardens of Buckingham Palace. The bedroom is peaceful and clean and smells of flowers and talcum powder.

Bridget brushes my mother's hair and applies touches of moisturizer and make up to her face. If you stand outside the door you can hear them talking.

"Here, Mommella," Bridget says. "Today we're putting on eye shadow. A little here. A little there."

"I don't feel good," my mother says.

"Don't you want to look beautiful?" Bridget says.

"For whom am I supposed to look beautiful?" my mother asks wryly.

Bridget smiles. My mother has not completely lost her sense of humor.

"For me," Bridget suggests. "And for Danny. He's visiting, don't you remember?"

"Danny's here? In Durban?"

Bridget is taken aback, but just for a moment. She could say, may be tempted to say, "We're not in Durban, Mom. We're in London," but she doesn't.

"Of course he's here," she says instead. "You saw him yesterday."

"I don't remember," Helga says. "I don't remember anything. I feel like shit."

"Don't swear now," Bridget says, a mocking firmness in her voice. "And hold still. How am I supposed to make you beautiful if you bob around all the time?"

"Where's Arnold?" Helga asks meekly, and not for the first time.

"He's in the next room," Bridget says, not wholly convincingly. "He'll be in later."

"Why doesn't he spend time with me?" Helga asks.

"He does, Mommella," Bridget says calmly. "He'll be in soon."

He won't, of course. He may be her husband—her second husband that is, not Bridget's and my father—but while our mother lies day in and day out in a large carved bed in the room she once shared with him, until Bridget arrives to be with her she spends most of her time alone.

What has made Bridget stay so much longer than she had intended is the thought of my mother lying alone in that large, airy room.

THE NEWS THAT MY MOTHER had cancer came in the middle of the night. I took the call and then sat on the edge of the bed with my head in my hands. Though Tesseba, my wife, did not understand why—tried to stop me in fact—I left the house at two in the morning and waited for dawn on a bench at the airport. I landed in London and rushed from Heathrow to Arnold's home, but even as I walked in the door I realized that something more than a change in my mother's health had taken place. She had always served as a buffer between Arnold and me—Tibor, my sister Bridget's sturdy Bulgarian husband, once called my mother Arnold's "human shield." Her well-being demanded that we avoid open conflict—but it was immediately clear that those days were over. Arnold met me at the front door, a rare event, and insisted on detaining me in his study while he "prepared" me for what I was about to see. When I was finally permitted up into the bedroom I found my mother changed, newly fragile, as if in shock, almost absent.

My secretary had made reservations for me and Bridget, who arrived later the same day, at a nearby hotel, but leaving my mother's side once she had seen her condition was unthinkable for Bridget.

"Are you sure you want to do this, Bridgie?" I asked. "Staying here means exposure to an awful lot of Arnold."

"As sure as I am of anything," she answered, and yet the next morning she was not so sure any more. That first night, after a long flight and hours of panic, she received a preview of what lay ahead.

"Time to leave Mom alone now," Arnold had said shortly after dinner, even though Bridget and my mother were involved in some discussion or other, talking about the things they always did, engrossed, as was often true, in each other.

"She's fine," Bridget had said. "Quite peppy, in fact."

"Out, out," Arnold had insisted as if she had not spoken, pretending to be acting with good humor but quite determined nonetheless. "My Helgie needs her sleep."

"In a while," Bridget had said, but then, almost inevitably, the betrayal: "Perhaps I am tired," my mother had said. "We can talk in the morning."

3

ARNOLD'S HOME IS, by any measure, a grand place. The building is white with bold pillars in front and a circular drive, has a large, well-kept garden complete with a topiary and several fountains, and you reach Arnold's apartment through a lofty entrance hall hung with portraits and a wide marble stairway. The apartment is all Arnold's, of course, the *faux* Edwardian grandeur and suitably worn Persian carpets, but another, not altogether congruent presence is there too. My mother has brought to her new home my late father's collection of Africana, and to me, at least, this almost restores a balance, prevents the place from being entirely Arnold's domain. My father's collection is embedded in the public rooms without much attention to ownership, to the origin of things, and over the years the house's contents might have come to seem to others to fit together, to be part of a single seamless construct, like a marriage, perhaps, but that was never so for me. I was always acutely aware of what was Arnold's and what was once my father's.

It is unsettling, to both Bridget and to me, but especially to me now that my mother is so weak, to watch Arnold act as if he has become, by default, the custodian of everything, including, of course, of my mother. She has lost her independence, and because she is his wife, like it or not, and we are in his home, there is a fine line to tread. Most of the time Arnold does not seem to care what we do, but if he did care, if he were to challenge us on something, it is not clear whose word would govern. My mother is no longer walking about the house, her perfume filling its rooms, arranging the flowers, answering the phone, and a balance has quite tipped. Arnold's presence, his old man's scent, is everywhere, and everything in the house has become, if not inaccessible, somehow unfriendly.

This is true of little things too, things like plates and the knives, even the television set. We touch Arnold's buttons, when we have to, with an edge of distaste.

4

BRIDGET DOES NOT STAY in Arnold's house very long. She tells me she has considered moving from the top floor, where my mother's bedroom is, to another part of the house, and the place is certainly large enough that you could get quite lost in it. The downstairs rooms, for instance, even though they are no longer occupied by servants but rather by a wine cellar, exercise equipment still in its original packaging, and a "media room" that nobody, so far as I can tell, has ever used, are spacious enough. But it would be a futile gesture. What Arnold exacts for his hospitality is insidious and persistent, and for Bridget remaining under his roof is impossible.

"He keeps asking me how long she has," she says to Tibor when he calls from Boston. "I try to avoid him but tonight he posted himself outside the bathroom door, waiting for me. It's like he's counting down."

"What did you say to him?" Tibor asks.

"I said that she was stabilizing and might even get better."

"He can't believe that."

"He tried to talk to the doctor, but the doctor can't abide him and says whatever I ask him to say."

"But why? Why the subterfuge?"

"If you have to ask, you don't understand Arnold," Bridget says. "If he got the sense that she was about to die, he would taunt her with it, in his inimitable way rub it in as if it were some sort of weakness on her part. He would make her feel like a fool."

Tibor listens, may raise an eyebrow, does not pass judgment.

"There's one other thing," Bridget adds. "He would lose no time telling Mom she was dying, and if she thought it were true she would give up the ghost. It's hard enough motivating her to eat and talk now. Can you imagine how it would be if she lost whatever remains of her will to live?"

"She knows she's dying," Tibor says

"She doesn't know she's dying."

"She knows she's dying," he repeats.

"No, that's not true," Bridget insists. "And even if it were true, how would you like to have it confirmed in the snide asides of a spouse who wants to discard you?"

Bridgett finds a small furnished flat not far from Arnold's, but what was to have been a rental of several weeks stretches into several months, and Tibor finally takes a leave of absence from his job as a high school counselor to be with her. Their daughter Leora, back in Boston, is living with the family of a friend and she does not take her desertion gracefully. She is seventeen and a senior in high school. There are proms to plan for, social crises of one sort or another, colleges to think about.

"I want you to come home," she says on the telephone. "I need you. There's so much going on."

As she speaks Leora can picture her mother's face. When Leora broaches a subject that Bridget does not want to discuss, it is as if the words themselves have not been said, as if Leora has spoken in a foreign language.

"Did you remember your dentist appointment," her mother might reply or, "Uncle Danny says he took you to dinner last night."

Leora can almost see the face, the blank, uncomprehending face.

"You can't just move somewhere else," she repeats. "You live here."

I keep an eye on my niece, speak to her each night, see her at least once during the week, but I begin to find her increasingly monosyllabic. ("I'm fine." "School's fine." "Yes, she called.") In a restaurant she looks into her plate, twirls her hair, can't help but smile when I am particularly provocative.

"What happened to that boy Mumbles who couldn't take his eyes off you?"

"His name is *Barry*."

"It should be Mumbles. I didn't understand a word he said."

Still, she keeps to herself, particularly about what is most important in her adolescent life.

I cannot drop everything and move to London as Bridget has done. I also wonder whether that would be a normal thing to do, for an adult, a man in his forties with a wife and more than his share of responsibilities, to put everything on hold and to move across the world to tend a dying parent. There are people who count on me, for one thing, people who have entrusted their money to me and who rely on my judgment in a variety of quickly changing markets. And there is my wife, Tesseba, tolerant but critical too, tolerant but evaluating at the same time.

And yet, yet, backwards and forwards, the exhausting jet travel, a manic pace. I have decided that I cannot drop everything, but I have also decided that I cannot *not* drop everything. As my mother's health worsens I find myself careening between Boston and London until it seems as if I am constantly in motion. At first Tesseba and Leora travel with me, and they quickly fall into habits like seasoned travelers. Leora does her homework at the window. Tesseba reads. I work on my laptop until I fall asleep with a black velvet mask over my eyes. And then, just as I think things have settled into a pattern that works well for everyone, they surprise me. Tesseba says that she finds it too exhausting, the time changes, the long flights, the seemingly pointless hanging about once we finally arrive, and decides to stay home. As for Leora, I had assumed this was something of an adventure for her—what teenage girl gets to fly, first class, to London every weekend?—but there I am mistaken too.

Leora, who at first accepted without comment the arrangements I made for her—"The plane leaves Logan at seven, Lee. The limo will pick you up at four thirty."—now begins to find excuses not to accompany me.

"You don't want to come?" I ask, surprised.

"I can't just leave town all the time," she says. "I have things I need to do here."

6

"BRIDGIE," I SAY TO MY SISTER on one of my trips. "May I raise a sensitive subject?"

"What could possibly be sensitive?" she asks.

"Are you and Tibor okay?" I ask. "I mean, moneywise. This has all got to be something of a strain."

Bridget looks at me with that blank face I am so used to.

"We're okay," she says, and leaves the room.

I was a teenager when I left South Africa. I arrived in Boston without the right papers and in the dead of winter and struggled for years to find my footing, but those days are long gone. Tesseba and I live in a gracious house west of Boston, and while we do not live lavishly, this is a matter of choice. Bridget and Tibor, on the other hand, have never had money. You could say that they have never wanted money, but an outsider can never be too sure of things like that. In the early days, as I found my feet and worked my way up the business ladder, my sister seemed to become particularly vigilant not to let any balance be tipped by this, by the growing disparity in our circumstances.

It was an uphill battle. My mother, when she was still a frequent visitor to Boston with Arnold in tow, used to make the invidious comparison relentlessly.

"You and Tibor live on the smell of an oil rag," she used to say and Bridget, hearing her say it, would seem not to hear, would let the words drop away as if the comment had somehow not been made at all. "It makes me sick, watching you struggle when my father's money sits in South Africa doing as much good as a *toytn bankes.*"

And that was the odd part of it, that this apparition of wealth had followed us to Boston, no more real or useful or accessible than ever, but almost a generation later continuing to haunt us.

FOR MOST OF OUR LIVES my mother's privileged background has wrapped itself around us like some smothering golden fleece, and yet in all important ways my grumpy, parsimonious grandfather's money has always been irrelevant. It certainly made no difference to my poor father when we were children. It was of no help at all when Bridget and I first came to Boston. It's simply a distraction, or worse, a point of contention, now.

I have tried more than once to explain it, to Tesseba, to my business partners, but in the end I always give up. People tend to ask questions as if I haven't thought of them myself, questions for which there are no easy answers. The short of it is that when my grandfather died we learned that he had set up a convoluted trust designed to last for years and years, and then when that was done—we had all long since left South Africa—the money continued to be unavailable, trapped by laws that prevented people from taking their money out of the country if they left. It's just the way it was, a system put in place to protect *apartheid,* carried over long after *apartheid* was gone. In the end it seemed simpler, and more realistic, simply to ignore the whole thing and to start over.

"It's your money, Mom," Bridget would say when my mother pressed the subject on her. "And we're fine."

"Millions," my mother would spit, not letting up. "Not for me but for you kids. One day, when things come right in South Africa, it'll all be yours. Danny's done well for himself, thank God, but I just hope it isn't too late for you to have a little comfort as well."

Tibor didn't even know the money existed, honestly, until two years before Helga became ill when I was persuaded to go back to South Africa to see about smuggling it out in an elaborate scheme that had Arnold's fingerprints all over it. While I was away, and for the first time, Bridget did begin to talk about it, about how the money might change things in her life, and in Leora's. When I came back empty-handed her disappointment quickly turned to anger.

"Why didn't you go through with it?" she demanded. "Arnold says it was all arranged, that you could have gotten the money out once and for all."

"You know why I didn't," I said.

"No," she had insisted. "You tell me."

"It's illegal to take money out of South Africa," I said. "What Arnold arranged was illegal."

"But you knew that when you agreed to go," Bridget said, and of course that was true too. "Everyone does it and nobody gets caught. Who knows? I might have gone myself if I'd known you'd lose your nerve at the last minute."

I would not respond to this, would just sit in her kitchen and listen, but something changed between Bridget and me after I came back. I could not have explained it to her in any event, although there was an explanation. I could not have explained it if I'd had a million years to do so. How could I tell her, how could I begin to tell her, about Santi, about the real reason I went back to Durban, how I lost my nerve, why I lost my nerve?

It surprised me how angry she was. I had always assumed that the money was unimportant to her.

Now she asks: "Are you sure none of Mom's medical bills can be paid from South Africa?"

"We'd have to petition the Reserve Bank to release it from our frozen accounts," I say, and she responds, barely pausing: "Why don't you?"

"Nerpelow says it would be a long process with an uncertain outcome," I say. Morton Nerpelow is our lawyer in Durban.

"Why don't you try anyway?" she asks. "It doesn't make sense that she can't use her own money to pay for all this. And what would happen if you couldn't pay? You saw what shabby treatment she got when Arnold made her go through the National Health Service. You saw the waiting rooms, the overworked nurses, the ridiculous paperwork."

"I can't see us getting much help from the Reserve Bank in the new South Africa to pay a white expatriate's Harley Street physicians," I say. "But I am paying, and she is getting Harley Street physicians, so it's all academic."

"It's not academic and I'm not sure that isn't condescending," Bridget says. "It's our money," and she has never referred to it as this before, probably never thought of it as this, before. "*Ours.* If it can't help her in this situation, what possible use is it to anybody?"

She asks—demands, really—that I pay for whatever my mother needs, and this comes to include the air tickets, the flat she has rented, the around-the-clock nurses, the private doctors. The bills run well into six figures.

"I have to have four hundred pounds for the night nurse," Bridget might say, and almost reflexively I will reach for my wallet.

"Arnold delights in creating discord," Tibor says. "He sows dragon's teeth."

"This has nothing to do with Arnold," Bridget responds.

ONE OF HELGA'S PRIVATE NURSES, by coincidence, is South African, a Coloured woman, part white, part Xhosa, or so she says, from the Cape province.

"Why are you in England?" Helga asks her.

It is afternoon, the room is bright, Arnold is gone, Bridget is in the kitchen.

"I mean, why would you leave South Africa now that things are beginning to look so promising?"

"How promising?" the nurse says. "Things are terrible where I come from. No jobs. Crime everywhere. It's hard here, but at least here you know where you stand."

"Surely things are better for you now," Helga says. "Or at least for your children in the new South Africa. Here you're a nobody."

"I'm not a nobody," the nurse says.

If it were not Helga, if things were not what they are, she might be angry.

"Look," the nurse says, "I come from a part of the Cape called the Flats. Do you know where that is, near Cape Town?"

"Of course I do," Helga says, but despite her emphatic tone the nurse is not so sure, or certain even that Helga is following the conversation. There is a faraway look in her eyes, as if she is focused on something very distant and complex.

"When I was a girl it was hard, true," the nurse says. "The government pushed us into the Cape Flats because they didn't know what to do with us Coloureds. But it was home anyway, and we always believed that things would get better. Now, it's like the Wild West there. Horrible. There's no respect for anything."

Helga purses her lips and nods, but she looks perplexed.

"You don't like what's happened?" she asks distractedly.

"Of course not," the woman says. "I even voted for the National Party in the last election before I left."

Helga raises her eyebrows, keeps nodding, says nothing.

"I know you think I must be crazy, a Coloured woman voting for the party of *apartheid*," the nurse says. "But the National Party carried my part of the Cape Flats and there's only Coloureds there. The whites have all the money, and the blacks think they own the place, but for us who aren't one thing and who aren't the other things are not simple. The quality of life's gone downhill every day since that Mandela got out of prison."

"I'm surprised," Helga says. "Nothing is turning out as it should. And we worked so hard for change."

"Were you involved in politics, Helga?" the nurse asks, suddenly much gentler.

"Was I involved?" Helga repeats. "Of course I was involved. I ran for Parliament."

It is the nurse who is now confused. She knows Helga wafts in and out of dementia, sees no trace now of a person who can have done such a thing.

"That's nice," she says.

Helga pauses, looks around the room, appears confused.

"I never took much interest in politics, to be quite honest," the nurse says at last.

Bridget comes into the room.

"Are you comfortable, Mommella?" she asks.

"Why wouldn't I be?" Helga says. "With all the care I'm getting." And then she adds, wistfully: "Yes. Those were they days. They certainly were."

"What days?" Bridget asks.

"Nothing," Helga answers.

Later the nurse, troubled by it, corners Bridget in the kitchen and asks: "Did your mother run for Parliament?" and Bridget, busy preparing something or other, answers off-handedly: "Twice."

Yes. Twice. Picture this. Durban City Hall, March, 1970. There is an election in the offing and the Prime Minister has flown to the city to debate several local figures on the correctness of the government's *apartheid* policies. My mother, who is an opposition candidate, has been selected to present the opposing view. The Prime Minister goes first and makes his points ham-handedly and at length. Who hasn't heard them by now? South Africa is not one nation but many, an accident of history in fact, and to correct the accident each nation must now be given its own autonomous region, the whites theirs, the Zulu's what is historically theirs, the Xhosa theirs, *ad nauseam.* Each group can have all the civil rights in the world, but only after it has been consolidated in its own place.

And then it is my mother's turn. She wears a navy suit, has waving auburn hair, cuts an unbearably elegant figure on the auditorium's ornate and massive stage. She starts softly, points out that this so-called white nation of the Prime Minister sits, by coincidence, on all the country's mineral wealth, encompasses all of its factories and cities and good farmland and ports and universities, and that even so it cannot function, not for a day, not for a moment, without cheap black labor, lots and lots of cheap black labor, and thus is an apparition from the start. "And so I ask the Honourable Prime Minister," she says, her voice rising, "how this grand scheme of his can ever work, how he will ever accomplish this unscrambling of a long-cooked egg without causing dislocation and suffering, and in the process creating anger and resentment on a scale we can scarcely imagine tonight in this lovely hall? Why is it so hard to acknowledge the obvious, the common humanity of all who are blessed to live in this country, to acknowledge that we are all South Africans, all entitled to basic rights and freedoms and regardless of the color of our skins? Because the solution to the problems history has handed us will only be found in this acknowledgment. Mark my words. *Time will prove them to be true.*"

The applause from the faithful begins before she is finished. It continues long after she is done.

WHEN ARNOLD IS IN THE HOUSE he is usually in his paneled study watching television or checking his investments on a computer. When the telephone rings he answers it instantly and Bridget, increasingly curious, finds herself edging into the hallway to eavesdrop. Standing several steps from his open door, she is aware that he might stick his head out at any moment and she dreads this, but at the same time she feels that she needs to know what he is saying.

Most of the time his conversations are boisterous and inane, filled with supposedly good-natured taunts. Occasionally they are vulgar.

"I thought at some point in their lives men stopped finding jokes about blonde women who get tricked into having sex funny," she says to Tibor. "In fact half his conversation is sexual innuendo and suggestion. It's disgusting to think he once laid hands on my mother."

The people who call for Arnold, it seems, often from South Africa, call to tell him jokes, to offer him stock tips, to ask for advice. Often they want something from him, to sell him shares or to have him join in some venture or other. He leads them on, pretends interest in their various projects, requests more information or further paperwork. In all the weeks she observes this, however, Bridget does not once hear him agree to invest. "You're too thinly capitalized," he might say or, more likely: "If you'd have come to me just three months ago I might have considered it, but as it is I'm committed to something quite similar."

"Do they have a capital gains tax in America?" Arnold asks, and however you answer the question it is simply a pretext for some self-aggrandizing monologue he wishes to deliver. You listen, search for an exit, try to pry out an opening at which you can turn or walk away.

Sometimes someone does call for Helga, one of her few English friends, several people who call regularly from South Africa, me from Boston. Arnold, if he answers the phone before the nurse or Bridget can reach it, tells everyone who calls that she is asleep. He does this even when she is awake and lucid and could easily take her calls. Only when she is confused, sitting in a fog all her own, does he put callers through, even invites them to visit.

Sotto voce he adds: "We're having a terrible time."

Some people, undeniably, find Arnold entertaining. Helga once did. I find it hard to see how this could even be possible.

"How did this cretin come to be inside our family?" I ask, but the question is rhetorical, not deserving of an answer. Each of us, Leora included, believe we know, but it is not clear whether, if pressed, any of us would say the same thing.

10

I WAS EIGHTEEN when I left South Africa. I came to America as a visitor, but knowing that I would most likely want to stay. I learned the hard way that this was not how things worked. Immigration was an elusive and lengthy process and when someone suggested—a secretary in a government office, as I recall—that perhaps because of the situation in South Africa I might qualify for political asylum, I fastened on it as a path to salvation. In retrospect, of course, a white South African boy, a privileged white boy, did not stand much of a chance, but in the end it was never put to the test.

My mother was still in Durban then and it was to her that I turned for the documents I needed to support my asylum application. This was before she and Arnold connected, before all the wealth descended on her, the travel, the important friends. Back then it was just my mother in her rented apartment near the North Beach, attended by Baptie, the Zulu woman who had worked for us since I was a baby and who became, by default, though only after we were gone, our family too.

My mother, to my surprise, took a very dim view of my plans, was openly embarrassed that I should be doing this.

"What danger of persecution were *you* ever in?" she blurted on the phone. "For heaven's sake. I don't approve of this course of action, not one little bit."

I tried to explain. There was no other course. If I did not succeed I would have to leave.

"First, I don't believe it," she had said, her voice on the long-distance line echoing. "And if it's true that you're not wanted in America, then go somewhere you are wanted. Go to London. Bridget didn't have these kinds of problems."

She was unyielding and also, in the end, uncooperative in getting me the papers I needed to support my application. Bridget had been arrested under the security laws several months before I left South Africa, and although she was by then free and living in London, I planned to present the case that I would be in a similar peril if I returned. Perhaps my mother had a point in refusing to get me written confirmation of Bridget's imprisonment, but her obduracy extended even to getting my birth certificate from the registry, or a copy of my membership card in her supposedly liberal political party. She didn't say she wouldn't. She just didn't. Some evenings, waiting, working menial jobs (People refuse to believe it; I was a busboy. I cleaned floors.) and being paid trivial amounts under the table by unscrupulous employers, I was reduced to tears. I would open my mailbox, find it empty, and find myself weeping from frustration and anger.

Even so I found it hard to sustain any anger toward her. Her life too, after all, had fallen apart, and so recently, and of course at that point I knew nothing of Arnold's insidious campaign to possess her. My father had died, on a dime so to speak, and so pointlessly, my sister had been arrested by the security police and thrown in prison, we had lost, once and for all, Gordonwood, our stately home high on the ridge and brimming with my father's distinctive African treasures. Helga, alone in her little flat on the beachfront with Baptie as her sole comfort, was not someone against whom I could nurture a grievance.

That is where things stood on the day I met Tesseba. We were on a bus and I saw her right away. I saw a tall, attractive girl with full lips and shining hair, watched her as she fiddled with something in her purse alone by the window. Tesseba has a gift for drawing people out, is disarming because it is always so clear that she does not know how to dissemble, and I found myself that first day telling her, a stranger, things I considered private, describing a kind of hardship that embarrassed me, the threadbare rooming house where most of my possessions had been stolen, my immigration problems that prevented me from working, divulging things to a girl on a bus about which I had not even been able to write to my mother.

She took me that first day, Tesseba did, from the bus to her little loft in South Boston with its worn bricks and warped oak floors. We ate cross-legged on her bed, me in my gray stovepipe trousers and socks, my thin cotton shirt, she wrapped in a shearling blanket, and it was then that we began to hear, each of us, the names and notions that were to become the new themes of our lives. When it was quite late and the sporadic sounds of laughter and doors banging and the hoist's hum had closed into silence, without discussing it further she built me a bed from pillows and blankets, and later she joined me there. When she asked me to marry her—I had said that marriage to an American would end my immigration problems—my mother's cooperation was no longer necessary.

WE ONCE LIVED, in the old days, Bridget and I and our parents and a small army of African servants, on top of a ridge overlooking the city of Durban. We weren't the ones to call the house Gordonwood—we would almost certainly have called it something else if we had even thought to name it, something humorous, something with meaning to us—but that was the house's name when we came to it and somehow it fit, as much as a person's name begins to fit and with no debate down the road as to whether the name is the right one or should be something different. Gordonwood, simply, rather than home: I left it at Gordonwood, I'm going to Gordonwood, before we came to Gordonwood, if such a time, so dimly recalled, had even existed.

The house, my father's house—acquired, I would have to say, impetuously in a way that was typical of my father—was a tangle of Victorian stone and iron, turrets, balustrades, a grand, slightly crooked, slightly corroded place wrapped in verandas, with lime-washed walls and half-stuck windows, overrun by dark green creepers and teeming with red ants. From the upper balconies the view swept out into the distance in all directions; straight ahead past the Bluff and the old whaling station out to ships waiting to enter the harbor, north over the trees and mangrove swamps and all the way to Zululand if the thick air hadn't blocked the view, and south to Isipingo and Amanzimtoti and Umkomaas. There was a hotel in Umkomaas, the Lido, an hour away, where we went, occasionally, on weekends to swim.

My father, Silas, owned a shipping company that imported exotic objects and exported South African ivory and spices and woods. The company was started by his father when he arrived in South Africa from the Baltic city of Liepaja, and though by all accounts it had once been prosperous, when we were children it was already well into a slow decline. This part of it, the subtext of my father's struggle to make ends meet while married to an ungenerous rich man's daughter and living in a grand but falling down house, is missing from the stories we tell about our past. To the perceptive, I imagine, to Tibor I expect, and to Tesseba, hints of it were always there. Even if we said nothing, the photographs would suggest it, that nothing was ever renewed or replaced, that things were simply frozen in place, paint allowed to peel in the dense, wet air, window casings to drip rust down the walls, nothing relinquished but nothing replenished either. In the photographs that lie curling in an album there is an air of melancholy, birthday parties, a bar mitzvah, a boy clowning with a dog, all set against a backdrop of decline and decay.

I know that no matter how discreet we try to be, occasionally we reveal things we do not intend to reveal. This has happened several times when we were discussing how my father built his African collection. Once Bridget was remembering how he came home one evening with a chewed up piece of leather and told us that it was a Zulu warrior's sandal, straight from Isandhlwana, a relic of the Zulu War. ("I know which one," I had said. "It's in the case in Arnold's entrance hall, right at the back on the left.") We made fun of him, ostentatiously refused to touch something that had once been on a Zulu man's foot, and our adolescent hysteria had only increased when we discovered that he had bought not one but two of them, two dusty sandals carefully preserved in small canvas bags. But then, at the same moment, Bridget and I remember something else, my mother asking what they had cost, these fascinating artifacts, and my father fencing about and trying to avoid the question.

The longer he did it the more fraught the conversation became.

"Mom wasn't happy," Bridget says.

"Why?" Leora asks.

"It's a long story," Bridget says.

I, too, am left to wonder, as an adult, how it can be that if a person cannot choose between two things he buys them both, so that when a bank needs to be paid or a car breaks down there is something that resembles heartache. "Opportunity knocks but once," my father used to say. "He who hesitates, is lost." An impractical man, in short, the kind of man who shows childlike enthusiasms, a man about whom one has to wonder, from time to time. An honest man too, one would say. One would like to say.

12

I REALIZED ON MY FIRST VISIT to Arnold's house, the first time all those years ago when I heard Arnold refer to my father's collection as "curios," as if they had been picked up at some roadside stand, that he was among those who found the entire notion of owning and displaying anything African absurd.

"They're not curios," Helga would snap as if on cue, back in the days when she had the energy for it. "Silas's art collection is incomparable."

"Art?" Arnold would say then, an undertone of menace in his voice. "You think this is *art*?"

On an early visit to London, the first time I visited that house, my mother carved out an evening, an entire evening, for Arnold to describe his accomplishments to his new stepson.

"Tell him all the things you've done," she encouraged. "Danny will be very interested."

There was once a time when, once upon a time, my mother was robust, coiffed, tailored, bristling with opinions, a matriarch in every sense. And then my father died and everything unraveled, or if it didn't unravel the whole scheme of things, who we were and where we were headed—Bridget, my mother, me—became quite jumbled inside the mystery that we soundlessly conspired to build even while blood was still on the walls. The very morning he died my mother, who taught history at the university, has told us that she wondered whether she wasn't ready for a change. She thought, as she drove home, that perhaps she might enroll in the law school and add a law degree to the others she already held, and then several hours later the shame was on us and nothing was the same again. We hadn't, any of us, paid much attention to my father when he was alive. We thought him naive, ill-informed, too enthusiastic about his latest hobby, but we did not know that without him we would all become nothing, and remain nothing. We did not know it.

To cap it off, of course, to enshrine the changes before anything had time to right itself, Arnold came along, busting in on us like an ill wind and swamping my mother with his bombast and his wealth and a persistence that under almost any other circumstance one would have to admire. He wanted her and would stop at nothing until he got what he wanted, and in the end she relented. She thought, I know she thought, that marrying Arnold was her way back to normality, a turn that would help all of us find our way back, but of course it did nothing of the sort. And on the day my mother left South Africa with Arnold—my father had been dead just one year—she left behind who she was and became someone quite different, irrationally assertive, increasingly vague. She didn't even look the same, what with the ostentatious jewelry and the flamboyant new clothes, though in the end the jewels were taken back (They were loans, not gifts, Arnold said.) and she tended to wear the same few outfits over and over.

So it was that when she became ill everything was already in chaos and had been for a long time, up to and including the spectacularly foul mouth she had developed and the strange throwback speech patterns peppered with Yiddish vulgarisms and obscure pieces of Afrikaans slang.

"He can go fuck himself," she might say, through tears, sitting in that opulent house in London, about Arnold. "He can *voetsak* and *vrek* for all I care. *Gey in drerd.*" A moment later, of course, she would be worrying about him, wondering where he had gone and when he might be back.

In my view Arnold was a bully, a swaggering, alcohol riddled, blustering bully who smothered much of what made my mother engaging and admirable. He was also my stepfather, and there is of course now this lawsuit to color things further so even I would have to concede that whatever my views are, others should probably take them with a dollop of salt. But mention Arnold Miro to anyone who knew him in Durban and you will notice, especially in those who are aware of the Divin family's connection to him, a reticence to respond, a hesitation.

An evening for him to describe his accomplishments, indeed. What possible purpose could be served by having Arnold try to impress *me?*

13

When I was a boy, African artifacts held little interest for most white South Africans. People sniffed at the eccentricity of my father's hobby and visitors to Gordonwood accepted invitations to examine his collection with politeness but distance, reacting perhaps as one would to a child wishing to show off to a stranger. From time to time there were articles about him in the Durban newspapers, and reading them as an adult—my mother kept them all—the condescension is palpable. The reporters focus rather too much on my father and his untrammeled enthusiasms, rather too little on the contents of his collection. There is a sense of their amazement in the writing. "Why would you be interested in this?" they seem to be asking. "Why would anyone?" The articles are not disrespectful but they are determinedly lighthearted. *"Businessman's Zulu Obsession,"* one of them is captioned.

Of course, time changes everything. After Mandela, after the change in South Africa, Zulu history acquired its own cachet, and at some point Arnold began to take quite a keen interest in my father's things. I began to notice that some of the pieces were being moved to places of prominence, and that Arnold's own absurd and random groupings of smeary modern art and *faux* antiques were becoming noticeably neglected. One sensed that Arnold had concluded that my father's collection had become, stealthily, quite valuable. He acted in a very proprietary way. He was constantly touching, dusting, rearranging.

Sometimes I would catch him looking into one of the old stinkwood cases filled with carefully cataloged pieces, even once running his hands over the great ivory tusks standing on either side of his fireplace, as they had once stood beside Gordonwood's in Africa, and a shiver would run up my spine. I had regarded my father's collection casually for a lifetime, but with my mother's half absence it all seemed threatened, on the edge of being spirited away.

"Wherever Silas came across these old things, they do fit right in here," Arnold said once. "I've become quite used to them. The place wouldn't look the same without them."

"It's all too convenient for him," I say to Bridget. "Too much is assumed."

"Do you have any suggestions?" Bridget replies flatly.

"Well for one thing," I say, "I think we should take some of the stuff out right now."

Tibor, who has been listening, raises an eyebrow.

"Arnold would notice it in a moment," he says. "It's his house. You can't just pick things off the shelf."

"They're our things," I say.

"You can't just pick things off the shelf," Tibor repeats, "but I do have a suggestion."

Bridget and I wait as Tibor weighs his words until Bridget says, at last: "Listen Hitchcock. You've created enough suspense. If you have something to say, please say it."

"I think you should take out some other things, things that are really important to you," Tibor says, ignoring her remark. "Things like photograph albums and papers. These he wouldn't notice. The rest you should leave for now."

He is right, of course. Tibor usually is. In one of the cabinets my mother has assembled several generations' photograph albums, some of them very old, hand covered in fabric and with each photograph held on the page by delicately placed cardboard corners. There are also folios with birth certificates and diplomas, even high school reports. Bridget and I have spent hours looking through them on past visits.

We begin to spirit these away, each time reorganizing the remaining volumes like a surreptitious drunk topping off liquor bottles with water. The enterprise feels underhanded, sordid even with my mother fading on the other side of the wall, but it must be done. It must be.

"I want to take some of my father's pieces out too," I say when, ten days later, I return to London from Boston and see that the cabinet is now almost empty and the task completed.

"I wouldn't do that," Tibor responds. "Arnold looked into the cabinet one day while you were gone. He lingered for a very long time just looking in at the empty shelves. In fact he walked away for a while leaving the doors open, and then he came back with a Scotch in his hand and stood there some more. He just stood there. Finally, after what seemed like a week and a half he closed the doors very slowly and without comment."

"He said nothing?" I say.

"Nothing," Tibor says. "I was sitting right here pretending to read and the longer he stood there, not moving, in total silence, the more threatening it felt. If it had gone on much longer I might have gone into cardiac arrest. Don't tempt fate."

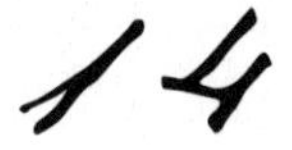

TIBOR HAS TIME ON HIS HANDS in London. He once lived here, came here as a young man escaping problems in his own Bulgaria, and London is where he met Bridget, one afternoon at a gymnasium where he was earning pocket money coaching soccer. He had seen her standing in the vestibule and hesitated to approach her, not because he lacked the confidence to do so but because she was so much younger than he was, but he went up to her anyway, and in the end it was a split-second decision that changed everything, including where he ended up living his life. I was already in America then and on my way to citizenship, and when I suggested that I might petition for them in case they ever wanted to join me, it seemed a practical idea, something to keep open. Then somehow, after the fingerprinting and the headache of getting birth certificates from Bulgaria and South Africa, and the x-rays and the police letters, when the approval came through it was as if the decision to move had already been made.

According to Bridget, each morning when I am not in London Tibor follows exactly the same routine. He goes for a walk along the Brompton Road and stops in at the same tea shop. When he gets to Arnold's Bridget will have been there for a couple of hours already, supervising my mother's breakfast and morning bath, and while there is not much he can do to make himself useful Bridget wants him close by in case she needs him.

It is while sitting in the quiet flat, interrupted only by the nurses coming and going at the changes in their shifts, or by Bridget walking to the kitchen, that Tibor begins to wonder what we will do with Helga's possessions when this is all over. It is not that he wants anything, far from it, but he is a practical man and he has no doubt that when the time comes the task of sorting out, of packing and wrapping and shipping, will be his.

"Do you know for sure what is hers?" he asks Bridget, gesturing around the room.

"Of course," Bridget says. "Every last piece. Danny can even tell you where they once stood at Gordonwood."

"And we're taking it all back to America?" Tibor asks.

"You're more convinced than we are that Arnold will part with anything," she says. "Danny's convinced he won't. I don't know what the heck to think."

"But they're yours," Tibor says, and his wife looks at him with an expression that suggests he is either too logical or too innocent.

Tibor wasn't sure whether what he saw justified our concern. The massive tusks were imposing, of course, in a league of their own, but beyond them my father's collection seemed to him to be both odd and oddly random. It consisted of things like leather sandals so worn they defied appreciation, bits of spearhead, animal skins decorated with crusty brown baubles, pieces of beaded cloth, dozens of strange little statuettes.

"Do you even know what all of this is?" Tibor asks. "Or why anyone would want them?"

"Danny does," Bridget answers. "My Dad used to go on and on about it."

KING SHAKA'S TUSKS, sheathed at their bases in silver and standing on either side of Gordonwood's fireplace on mounts of ebony, were the centerpieces of the collection. The day my father brought them home there was an enormous argument with my mother, but they remained nevertheless. They were never moved, never indeed touched except occasionally when someone might run a finger along the grain of one or the other of them under my father's watchful eye.

"These tusks are history itself," he used to say. "They were a gift from King Shaka to the first white men to set foot in Zululand, one of whom was a Jew, Nathaniel Isaacs. Isaacs sent them to his uncle on the island of Saint Helena for safekeeping, and there they remained until I learned of them from one of my agents. These tusks played a part in the founding of the city of Durban, and of all white settlement in Natal. It's only once in a lifetime one comes across something like this."

"They must be worth a fortune," someone might observe, polite, perhaps skeptical, looking at the tusks with curiosity.

"They are priceless," my father would respond. "I once wrote to the British Museum about them, and someone wrote back asking for photographs and documents, but I don't need to prove anything to them."

"How *do* you prove what they are?" he was asked.

"They are easily authenticated," he would say. "For one thing I have a letter from Nathaniel Isaacs to his uncle describing how he acquired them and asking his uncle to take good care of them. There's a description of the tusks in the letter," and here my father would always point to a series of chips in one of the tusks and add: "They are described in great detail."

"Someday you'll wish you'd paid attention," he used to say to me. "These stories are important, and someday you'll wish you knew them. Without the stories the objects are just chunks of ivory and leather, but it's the stories, the provenance, where each piece comes from, and why the person who collected them thought they were worth having, and also what happened to them after that—that makes them so interesting. Just imagine," he would say, holding a mask, a spear, a piece of bone. "One joins the chain of title, don't you see? One takes one's place in history. They'll be yours someday, and then you'll be part of the chain too."

"*Oy*," I once heard someone saying, out of my father's earshot and unaware that I was listening. "Such *meshugga* notions."

"You, of all people, should know these stories," my father would repeat. "They're your stories too. One day they will be your stories *only*."

He was oblivious, my father, to a subtext of his little anecdotes, that whatever started with those swashbuckling white explorers ultimately led, one way or another, to *apartheid*. For me there was no part of any story that ended in *apartheid* that could hold any interest. Anecdotes about Nathaniel Isaacs and his various adventures smacked of the endless meanderings of the Boers in their filthy canvas wagons, anecdotes that passed for history at school and in which I had no interest even as I was compelled to memorize dates and other notions in order to pass exams. I was not about to learn more of this parochial drivel as an extra-curricular activity, no matter how intriguing my father found it. ("I mean, how much are the Elgin Marbles worth?" my father once asked as part of a dialogue about value and I had winced. How could he make such a comparison? How could anyone?) I picture my father talking, a tall and lanky man in a white safari suit, one hand in his pants pocket, one hand on his pipe, a trail of smoke wafting above his head. As I hear his voice I am able to smell again the humid air in the room, the smoke, the always present Durban mustiness, whiffs of the brandy the guests are drinking, but now too I see the tusks being carried by Zulu bearers through the coastal scrublands, see Nathaniel Isaacs examining his bounty in a dark wattle hut on the shore of Durban harbor, hear the waves lapping against the giant iron ballasts that today line the harbor wharves. Outside are dark green bushes, their leaves thick and moist, night air as black as soot, the unified scream of the crickets, the mud spattered walls, the lush lawns of dense Kikuyu grass. Across the garden the servants are in their quarters. Everything is frozen, everyone is still alive, nothing is yet ravaged.

Now of course their provenance includes that my father bought them, that they stood in Gordonwood, witness to everything that happened there, to youth and heat and struggle, to a family that came apart at the most unexpected moment, to my father's violent death. His life ended without warning, left us, me, wondering for a generation what had happened, and why, and seeded a mythology all its own that has now come to enfold him and his wispy silver hair and his tusks and his sandals and the clammy evening air of a city we all left long ago.

And now, when it is my mother who is dying and my father more than a quarter century buried, their provenance keeps growing. It includes how Baptie, the Zulu housemaid in her pink pinafore uniform and starched white head scarf, would dab at them with a feather duster each morning, and how my mother, alone in Durban after we all left her behind, had seen them wrapped and crated, driven by lorry to Durban harbor, lowered into the hold of a ship, brought to London, and placed in this house.

But back then my father's thin hair was ruffled, his eyeglasses had slipped down his nose, his eagerness intruded too keenly.

16

ON THE RARE OCCASIONS that Arnold does come into my mother's bedroom the peaceful atmosphere changes instantly. For one thing, she perks up. Even if she has been groggy all morning, drifting in and out of lucidity, Arnold's presence awakens her.

"How are you, darling?" she asks mildly.

"Fine, fine," he says.

He stands beside the bed for a minute or two, flexing his wrist or his knee and telling her how stiff the one is or how his doctors say he will soon need a replacement of the other.

"When all this is over," he adds knowingly.

"When all what is over?" Helga asks.

"Oh, nothing," Arnold says and then, as if subtly to change the subject, adds: "Esther asked after you. And also Rosemary. And Denise."

"Did they call?"

"Yes."

"Why didn't you put them through?"

"I didn't want to disturb you."

"I'd like to speak to them."

"It's too much," Arnold says.

"I think it would be nice for Mommy if she spoke to some of her friends," Bridget says.

"What? Are you the doctor now?"

"No. But she would enjoy talking to her friends."

Arnold ignores her.

"Gold prices are up, Helgie," he says. "We're going to make a small killing this week."

"That's nice," my mother says.

"Didn't I say this would happen?" he says. "I said it would hit $400 this month."

Helga nods slowly, smiles, raises her eyebrows. It is unclear that she has listened or understood.

"Isn't that something," she says.

Later, when the nurse asks Arnold for a few pounds to buy a supply of adult diapers, he says, without looking away from the computer screen: "Ask Bridget."

One evening Bridget finds Arnold at the safe in my mother's dressing room. He has not heard her coming, but as soon as he realizes she is in the room he turns so as to block her view and launches into a disjointed description of Helga's evening as if Bridget, who has only been gone for thirty minutes, doesn't already know it well. She sees what he has been doing. He has taken from the safe all the jewelry he has ever given her. Bridget thinks she sees, perched on the shelf, several things that were my father's gifts too, but she decides to let it be.

"Helga and I have given each other rights to each other's possessions," Arnold announces in my mother's presence, not long after the probable outcome of her illness has become clear to him. "So if I should die first she has the full use of this house for as long as she lives. And if she dies first, I have full use of the things she brought from South Africa that are now in this house, and for as long as I live. It's only fair."

Helga looks down blankly, rolls a corner of her sheet into a tight ball, unrolls it again.

"Nobody's dying just yet," she says.

So what are we expected to say? That someone is, and that it is her.

"We are not going to be allowed to take anything out of here," I hiss at Tibor when we are alone. "Can't you see it?"

"I'm not convinced," he says. "Maybe, if you like, we could raise the subject with him."

"Are you nuts," I say, suddenly angry. "Are you naive? Are you blind?"

"I'm none of those," Tibor says. "I do try to be practical."

I STRAIN TO APPEAR KNOWLEDGEABLE about my father's Africana, but the truth is that I do not know much about any of it. Some of the pieces have labels stuck to their undersides with yellowing tape, but the labels are cryptic and uninformative.

"That's a Zulu assegai," I say when Tibor asks about a broken spear in one of the cases. "Designed by Shaka himself. It dates back to 1818. My father told me it was called an *iKwa* because that's the sound it made when a warrior pulled it out of his victim's body. Before this they used to throw a longer version in battle, and until the other side threw a bunch back they were basically out of ammo."

I feel a bit like my father as I say this, aware that I am overreaching.

"They fought the Europeans that way too?" Tibor asks. "Did they ever win?"

"Not often," I say. "They may have had guns too. I actually don't know."

Tibor lifts one of the sandals from a case.

"And this?" he says.

"It's an oxhide sandal that Zulu warriors wore before Shaka made them go barefoot. My father said that Shaka prepared his warriors for the change by making them dance in a field of thorns. Whoever winced was killed."

"Come on," Tibor says.

"No, really," I assure him. "When his warriors returned from battle he would execute all those who he believed hadn't been brave enough. His armies were celibate until their forties, and each soldier needed to wash his spear in enemy blood in order to be regarded as a real man. And for his enemies he reserved the special death of being made to sit upright on sharpened staves until, if he was merciful, they were dispatched by his executioners' clubs."

I know my brother-in-law, how his face changes when he is skeptical but his better judgment, that almost endless leveling in his character, kicks in and tells him to be silent. At some point then, I learn, he decides to find out for himself what it is he is looking at. He copies everything he can from the yellowing labels taped to the backs of the display cases, carefully reproduces in a notepad the symbols he finds scratched into carvings and masks. He makes his excuses to Bridget, and then he repairs to the British Museum and parks himself in a corner near the Africa collection. I am relieved to hear that he finds what he calls an "incidental accuracy" to some of what I have told him, pinpoints of information that are correct, even if enclosed in narratives filled with holes.

Tibor comes to believe that if any parts of the collection now in Arnold's home are authentic, then my father has preserved a trail of history that might otherwise have disappeared.

TIBOR FINDS WHAT HE SEEKS, easily enough pieced together from the handful of overlapping narratives on the shelves of the museum's library. There is a forbidding coast, rocky outcrops, miles of brown sand ending in muddy vegetation, clouds of steam that unroll slowly and endlessly from the sea over the land. Even as Europeans venture inland from the Cape of Good Hope a thousand miles to the south, the east coast of South Africa, first seen and named "Natal" by Vasco da Gama on Christmas Day in 1497, remains inaccessible and treacherous. There are shipwrecks and overland expeditions to be sure, but all Europeans who reach Natal perish quickly or disappear without a trace.

In 1822 the coast is chartered by an English naval ship which makes tentative contact with coastal tribesmen. These are scattered and puny, the sailors report, impoverished and living in terror of a powerful interior tribe and its savage king whose ferocity threatens to leave the country empty of all but his own people. He is the warrior king Shaka Zulu. Tibor is surprised to learn—I am relieved to hear—that my descriptions of his tactics and his prowess, stories I continued to repeat even after I had reason to wonder about the veracity of their source, have been, for the most part, accurate.

A year later some English traders, mad for the ivory they believe to be teeming inland, scour the coastline in a rickety sailboat looking for an anchorage. Desperate in a storm they scrape across what they believe to be a sand-barred river mouth, and, to their astonishment, once they clear the sandbar, they find themselves in a swampy, primeval bay. The harbor they have entered, they see when the storm passes, has calm waters, hippopotamuses soaking in the reeds, an inviting shoreline lined with mangrove trees and heavy vegetation. Like a great green arm, a whale-shaped peninsula protects the harbor from the roiling sea. There is, they find, beside the calls of the birds and an occasional lowing of a hippopotamus, an uncanny silence about the place. And so it is that what was to be Durban has been discovered by Europeans.

They stumble ashore, Lieutenant Francis Farewell, in his twenties, later called "Febana" by the Zulus, James Saunders King, the ship's captain, one or two others, and their imaginations take fire. It is a rich park, they can see, a paradise almost, empty but for the few terrified remnants of Shaka's massacres. Farewell and King hear from these survivors, or they believe they hear for this is how they repeat it, that ivory is so plentiful, that the cattle *kraals* of the Zulus are built entirely of tusks. They return to the Cape raving about the commercial prospects of Natal. Farewell tells his investors that here is a place where an enterprising person could make a quick and easy fortune.

The next year, 1824, with the Cape Governor's blessing, Farewell returns to Port Natal, this time with a larger group. It includes the young adventurer Henry Fynn, the simpleton Thomas Halstead, Henry Ogle who will live the longest in Natal, and most importantly for Tibor's research, Nathaniel Isaacs. He is the only Jew on the ship, the only Jew in this part of Africa. The ship makes its way through the greasy waters to a beach with coarse yellow sand and harsh humid air. Several of the men row ashore and spend the night fending off hyenas. The next day they begin to build huts, and the others, Isaacs too, join them.

For three days they see no Africans and then, almost by accident, they encounter one, Mahamba, terrified and hungry, and bribe him with beads to tell them how to find Shaka (just the word "Shaka" and Mahamba trembles, points, gestures) and what to expect of him when they do. Fynn leads the expedition northward, along the beach, past what we know as the Blue Lagoon, across the crocodile infested

Umgeni River. Twelve miles north of the harbor they encounter, quite by accident, one of Shaka's regiments returning from a campaign, a huge army of men, like a black sea, moving toward the little group along the beach. As the warriors approach, on the run, twenty thousand muscular and gleaming black men armed with assegais and shields, a different breed from the coastal Africans they have encountered, they are sure that their ends have come. But Fynn, believing who knows what, expecting who knows what, stands his ground on the beach and the whole army stops as it reaches him. What strange, pale, ragged apparitions they must have seemed. They have come, Fynn says through an interpreter, from across the sea to see the great king Shaka. His saying the name alone seems to act as a talisman and the army passes on in silence, or so he later writes, leaving the pathetic little expedition untouched.

Following its trail, and watched now by Shaka's spies, they continue on to Shaka's *kraal.* Soon enough they are approached by an emissary, given cattle and ivory as gifts, and told to await Shaka's summons. Preferring to await his summons at Port Natal, as they have named the place of their landing, they return to their companions filled with enthusiasm. That night, at their little settlement, they celebrate. Farewell fires a canon and raises the Union Jack and then the half dozen men, poorly clothed and fed, barely armed, surrounded and spied on by perhaps the greatest and most disciplined army in African history, solemnly declare that Port Natal and its surroundings are British territory. They do not feel this is presumptuous.

When later Shaka's messengers arrive at the bay to summon Fynn and his party for an audience, Farewell, as the expedition's leader, elects to dress in full naval uniform so as to impress the savage king, but it is Farewell who is impressed. Shaka's messengers, by design, take the little group of adventurers on a roundabout route through Shaka's vast dominions, displaying the discipline of his armies, the obedience of his vassals, and the richness of his tributary *kraals.* The journey, which can be made now by car in two or three hours, takes them thirteen days.

At the edge of the royal *kraal, kwaBulawayo,* the Place of the Killing, they pause. They are aware that elaborate preparations are under way for their visit and they know that it is unlikely any white man has ever seen anything quite like this before. Shaka's *kraal* covers several square miles, encircles a huge cattle pen filled with animals separated by color, and is filled with animated and chanting people whom Flynn estimates to number 80,000. The white men are instructed to ride their horses into the *kraal* and to gallop around the cattle pen, and Fynn, realizing that the Zulus have never seen trained horses before, knows how impressive this spectacle must be. Some in the crowd, until he dismounts, think that Fynn and his horse are a species of bird, or so he later says he was told.

More impressive is their introduction to Shaka. As soon as they have circled the cattle pen they are led to a spot where the crowd is thickest and an old man begins to make a long speech. He is, so Tibor reads, standing before a group of elders and Fynn and Farewell are led to understand that their role is to respond occasionally with "*yebo,*" or yes, to affirm that the man, whatever it is he is saying, speaks the truth. This they do.

Fynn begins to wonder when they will finally meet Shaka, and then he sees in the crowd a tall, powerfully built man dressed like the other warriors in a kilt of monkey tails with circlets of white oxtail fringes on his arms and legs, but with the long tail feather of a blue crane in his headband.

"Farewell," Fynn is said to have whispered to his near sighted companion. "I believe that man is Shaka."

Farewell begins to screw his monocle into his eye but the man, having heard Fynn, wags a knowing finger and then, with a giant leap and brandishing a stick, leaps forward and the crowd falls back. Any doubts the two adventurers may have had as to who he is vanish. There is no mistaking the authority of the man with the quivering blue crane feather.

From the crowd come bearers carrying elephant tusks. These are laid before them, one before Farewell, the other before Fynn. Shaka reassures them that they have nothing to fear from him, and gives them permission to build a settlement at Port Natal. The air is hot and rich with the smells of cattle and grass and perspiration. They are exuberant and there is cause for celebration. The history that lies in front of them is irrelevant. Judged by the history that they know, they have accomplished something heroic.

Could it really be, Tibor wonders, that it is these tusks, these very tusks, that have ended up on either side of the fireplace at Gordonwood, mounted on stands of ebony, their bases sheathed in silver?

19

"Ah, Mummy," Helga says as Bridget enters the room. "This is such a lovely hotel."

Her head moves to the side, her eyes roam about the room in wonder, take in the drapes, the cabinet with its familiar ornaments, the pictures on the wall.

"I needed this break so badly. So badly. Gosh."

"How do you feel, Mommella?" Bridget asks. "Are you okay?

My mother looks at her, her face at once bewildered and perfectly at ease.

"They are so nice to me here," she says.

Her eyes close and she begins to sleep again. Bridget stands desolate by the window. The nurse moves to clear away some dishes.

"She's fine, love," the nurse says. "You're lucky."

We know, though we are not doctors, from the mounds we feel along the side of her head, from the pallor, the dry skin, that it is almost over. But Bridget does not accept this. There is still the beautician who comes in every few days to wash and set my mother's hair, the manicurist who keeps her nails meticulous and massages cream into her frail hands, the new nightgowns Bridget keeps buying and that she makes sure are always fresh and fragrant.

"Look, Mommella," she proclaims. "I bought you a nightie in your favorite colors."

"How nice," Helga responds, looking only vaguely at the garment and then past it.

Bridget stands in the kitchen, all but one of the cans of Ensure I have sent from Boston still in their Federal Express box, and makes drinks of ice cream and egg yolk, sugar, protein powder, anything she can think of that my mother might tolerate and thus stave off by hours, moments maybe, the inevitable.

"Let her go, Bridget," Tibor says.

"She was like this last week and then she became lucid again," Bridget says.

"You must start thinking about letting her go."

They are not a physically demonstrative couple. Now he folds her in his arms, and she weeps.

Perhaps this is the moment at which Bridget must realize the end is very near. Helga's health has sunk gradually, but the tumors that seem to want to throttle her in increments rather than branch out and settle their business once and for all, are now everywhere. There have been little remissions, little descents, plateaus, but this is now different.

"Danny needs to be here," Bridget says. It is midnight in Boston.

20

I AVOID BEING IN THE SAME ROOM as Arnold, but this is not always possible. In fact, Arnold seems to hang around my mother more when I am in his home as if to force the point that this is his right, that Helga is his wife as much as she is my mother and that Bridget and I are in his home, as entirely his as Helga is his, on sufferance.

"He's not going to let us take our leave of her in peace," I say. "That's the part that's the hardest to live with. I wish we could just take her somewhere else."

"She can't be moved," Bridget says. "And in any event, where would we move her?"

"I could rent an apartment for her," I say. "Something really lovely."

"What?" Bridget asks incredulously. "You're going to set up house for her at this point?"

"If that's what it comes to."

"It's not practical," Tibor says. "And in any event, while Helga's conscious she won't allow it. Arnold would just have to ask her, and she'd say she wants to stay."

"I know," I have to admit.

"It really bothers me that he spends so little time with her," Bridget says. "But for whatever reason, she does perk up when he's there."

"Where is he all day?" I ask.

It is then my idea to have Arnold tailed. It just seems implausible to me that Arnold, a retired old man, should spend so much of each day, and almost every day, at his bank, his stockbroker, his tailor, and then at the "men's club" he has recently joined. Indeed, on the pretext that he can no longer stand the activity at night—the night nurses, the halting trips to the bathroom, Helga's occasional crazed sleep talking—he begins sleeping at his new club as well.

The private detective confirms what we would have guessed if we had, somehow, imaginations that stretched to reach such possibilities.

Arnold has himself a mistress.

21

Now that we know about the mistress our enmity is white hot even as, to preserve a measure of tranquility for my mother, we dare not show it. We believe, Bridget and I of course, but Tibor too, that Arnold will marry the mistress as soon as my mother is gone. He cannot be alone, needs an audience for his prattle, affirmation that his shirt matches his trousers, needs attention like a child who cannot be sated. We cannot redeem anything then for my mother, keep her dignity intact in the face of it, do anything to correct the path this is all taking. This is all that is left of her life, and there is nothing we can do.

It is this that adds an intolerable edge to it as we see Arnold running has hands over my father's objects. We know that when my mother goes we will have no further contact with him, and we know that if we do not do something Arnold's new mistress, someone with no ties to us, with probably nothing but contempt for us, for our vulnerability, for our weakness, will sweep in to lay claim to things to which she has no right.

"Thank you," she will say when complimented. "They are lovely."

And Arnold will say, when we are long gone and denied access: "These tusks were collected by Nathaniel Isaacs, you know, the first Jew to set foot in Natal. Can you imagine that?"

"Are you ready to do something now?" I ask Tibor, my tone sarcastic, maybe angry.

"I think we should talk to him," Tibor says. "I can't imagine he will want a war with you and Bridget after your mother is gone."

"Talk to him?" I shout. "Talk to him? Are you insane?"

Tibor does not take offense. He never does where I am concerned.

"I think what you are suggesting is based on your fears," he says. "It's not a good plan to act on feelings like that."

"We're not in your high school counseling office," I say, but Tibor simply shakes his head and walks into a kitchen to make himself a cup of tea.

22

My mother's last conscious gesture toward me is one of anger. We are all there, Bridget and Tibor and I, even the nurse, gathered around her bed after her morning bath, when Arnold saunters in. As usual, I begin to walk to the door.

"What's this?" Arnold challenges. "All of a sudden you can't be in the same room with me? Is that it?"

"We can discuss this some other time," I say. "Elsewhere."

"Is it something your mother can't hear? Are you trying to hide something from her?"

"Don't," Bridget says. "Danny, just stay."

"No, have out with it, don't you know," Arnold says. "What is it about me that you find it so difficult, when under my roof, to treat me with respect."

"I'm not going to discuss this with you now," I say.

"What could it possibly be?" Arnold says sarcastically. "I afford your mother every comfort money can buy, every medical amenity, open my house to your entire family, and you can't manage to be even minimally polite?"

"You're paying for nothing," I snap. "And this is my mother's home too."

"For now," Arnold says. "But mind this once and for all. You're here at my grace. If I chose to restrict your access to this house, I could. If I chose to take her back to South Africa to be treated, I would. She's my wife, and don't you forget it."

My mother, who has been watching with half-opened eyes, her mouth set as if she were trying to follow a complex discussion, suddenly comes to life. She sits up in the bed, turns to me, her lips pursed, her eyes wide open in anger. She stares at me, raises her hand, wags her finger angrily.

"You. You. You," she says, and then slips back against the pillow.

She does not acknowledge me again, or Tibor, or even Leora. Only Bridget elicits any expression of recognition.

"Hello, my darling," she says tiredly when Bridget approaches her, runs her hand through her hair, calls her name. "Did you have a nice time?"

"I had a lovely time Mommella," Bridget says. "And now I came to visit you."

"That's nice," my mother says, and closes her eyes.

23

WHEN MY MOTHER'S CONFUSION is so constant that she can not be reached by any of us, not even by Bridget, outright hostility breaks out between Arnold and me. Bridget, Leora, and Tibor are having dinner at Arnold's dining table. Arnold comes in and sits down.

"We're still a family, you know," he says. "We have our difficulties. But when all this is over, we're still a family."

No one says anything in response. As I enter the room the air becomes charged in its silence.

"I think I can get Mom to eat a little more," I say.

"We *are* still a family," Arnold continues, ignoring me. "We shouldn't allow any one of us to create divisions."

I ignore him, in turn, begin to put some mashed potatoes and gravy on a plate for my mother.

"In my own family," Arnold continues, "we prize our closeness. All right, we have our differences, but when the chips are down, we stick together. I know in your family that's not always the case, but it should be."

His comment is met with a deadly silence and Leora, who has been listening quietly, her head down, her hands folded in her lap, decides to break it.

"Dad, I forgot to ask before," she says looking up. "Can I go to Washington with some girls in my class sometime after we get back?"

"What for?" Bridget asks.

"It's very rude," Arnold says, "to interrupt when I'm talking."

"Just to see it," Leora says. "We'll stay with this girl's brother who goes to Georgetown."

"What a rude girl you are," Arnold says.

I am standing behind Tibor, holding the plate I had intended to take to my mother. I find myself frozen with anger.

"Why don't you shut up," I say to Arnold. "Once and for all, just shut the fuck up and leave us in peace."

For a moment there is silence, broken as Leora pushes her chair back and leaves the table, and then Bridget, and then Tibor.

"The wonderful family Divin," Arnold says as Tibor leaves the room. "Even their precious father couldn't stand to live with them."

There is no pretense at civility after this.

24

THE PLAN I AM HATCHING, now that my mother is oblivious to her circumstances, is simply to sweep in at night while Arnold is at his "club" and to remove everything that is ours. Tibor listens without comment as I describe how we might do it. I am too impetuous, he seems to be thinking, especially so when Arnold is concerned, have worked up a head of steam that somehow will blow over if left to itself. Surely, he seems to think, Arnold, who has so much, will not try to hold on to things that so clearly are not his.

"In the end they're just things," he says. "Not worth taking the kind of risks you're talking about."

"They're not just things," I say, and Bridget, who normally weighs in on Tibor's side, sits silently.

"Okay," Tibor says finally, reluctantly, slowly. "Okay. But tell me this: After you've removed half the furniture from his house, then what? You're going to show up and expect to be left in peace?"

"We're not left in peace now."

"Just imagine how it will be afterward," he says. "He may not let you in the house."

"One of us can stay with mother around the clock to be sure he does."

"No matter how bad it is now," Tibor replies, "if you do this it will be that much worse. Making a grab for something, even if you're entitled to it, can often make things worse."

But Tibor changes his mind late one afternoon. Arnold returns from his club, and on discovering that Helga is completely confused and appears to believe that the nurse is her mother, he telephones an old friend of my mother, out of the blue, and invites her to visit. Bridget, strenuously objecting, goes so far as to try and take the phone from his hand.

"I've never seen anything so rude," Arnold says when he has hung up. "Snatching the phone from someone."

"How can you let people come now?" Bridget demands. "How can you be so unkind?"

"Look here," Arnold says contemptuously. "You're not fooling anyone by trying to keep this secret, and in any event her friends have a right to say goodbye if they choose to. It's you who's being unkind."

"She would be mortified," Bridget says. "You wouldn't let her talk when she was lucid. I won't let anyone in the bedroom now. And that's that."

She leaves the room and locks the bedroom door behind her. Arnold walks up to the door and begins to say something, then he thinks better of it and instead pours himself a Scotch and retires to his study to wait. His shoes squeak as he crosses the parquet floor, crepe soles for better traction. Tibor witnessing it all thinks: *What an old man, when all is said and done. What a stooped, pathetic old man.*

An hour later there is a call from the gate man and Arnold, with uncharacteristic speed, rushes to the intercom. A few moments later the front bell rings and Arnold is already there waiting to open the door.

"Ah," he says when the woman, not even a particular friend of his, enters. "I thought it would be good for Helgie to see you this afternoon, but her children have apparently decided to keep her in isolation."

Tibor rises slowly and makes his way to the entrance hall.

"Helga is not well and Bridget has decided that she should not have visitors," he says. "She asked me to apologize."

"Not a problem," the visitor says.

"She did no such thing," Arnold says. "Bridget cannot give medical opinions, much less use them to shut out Helga's dear friends."

"No, really," my mother's friend says, quite disconcerted now. "I'll come another time."

But Arnold insists that she come in, and he offers her a drink, and before long he is thickly laying on charm and taking her on a tour of the various artifacts in the flat.

"These Zulu assegais, for instance," he says. "They're known as *iKwas,* which is onomatopoeic in that it sounds like the noise the spear made when the warrior pulled it from his victim's body. Before that, the Zulus used only throwing spears. King Shaka designed these himself, don't you know."

"When would that have been?" he is asked.

"The early 1800s," Arnold says. "The 1830s, I would say."

It is at this moment that Tibor changes his mind and decides he will help me remove these things, and every last one of them, from Arnold's reach.

25

It is Tibor's idea that we move my mother, too, have an ambulance standing by so that when we are done taking the things we can snatch her away as well, out from the barbed air of Arnold's flat to where she can spend her last few days in the peace we will build around her. It does not matter any more where this is. A small room, a bed, privacy in a corner of our own rented flat is all we need. The imposing room, the bowed windows, the antique table bearing the silver gifts I have brought, the Ming dynasty vases holding Bridget's flowers, these are useless. They do not by any measure stretch across the divide that my mother has already crossed.

Before we make our plans I call my friend Rupert, who is a lawyer in London.

"The first thing I would ask," Rupert says, "is: Are the things yours?"

"Of course," I say.

"But aren't they your mother's?" Rupert asks.

"Not exactly," I say and then I add: "Yes and no."

"Why must you take them now?"

"Because we won't be allowed to later."

"You think the old chap would really stop you?"

"I know it."

"If you're convinced they're yours, I suppose you should follow your instincts," Rupert says at last. "I know Arnold Miro, though only by reputation. If she were my mother, I would take the things by all means. By all means."

"It feels illegal nonetheless," I say. "I'm not much in the mood for a spell in Wormwood Scrubs, though if that's what it takes, so be it."

"I hear the food's getting better there," Rupert says. "Or so some of my regular clients tell me." He pauses. "Sorry to be flip at a time like this. Technically," he adds, "if the stuff is yours you can take it any time you choose, and the ball is in the old guy's court. What's he to do without looking like a total *schmuck*? Just don't breach the peace."

"What do you mean by breach the peace?" I ask.

"If the old geezer wants to stop you, all he's got to do is stand at the front door with a hatchet, and even if he has trouble lifting the damned thing, you'd better leave at once."

"And if he doesn't know what we're planning?"

"I'd say that's your only chance," Rupert advises.

26

TIBOR MAY HAVE BEEN A LATE convert to my project, but when Tibor decides to do something, he sets about doing it with a stolidity and a resolution that abates only when the job is completed. Such earnestness is a signal trait of Tibor's. So if we are to burgle a home at night and take most of its contents—and its occupant too—and if he is to be complicit in the plan, then it becomes his task to ensure that we are successful.

Tibor assembles a box of essential supplies which no one, not even I, may touch, as well as a notebook with the phone numbers we may need during the evening, his list of who should be where, and when, and what each of us has to do, and how long we will have to do it. There can be, Tibor insists, no mistakes.

"The moving company will come for the big things at three o'clock in the morning," he says. "That will give us enough time to go through and sort everything first. But even so, we'll have to be quick."

"What explanation did you give them for the odd hour?" I ask.

I am drinking coffee again. The sink in the kitchenette is filled with my half-emptied cups.

"I didn't tell them anything," Tibor says. "Just that we wanted an early start."

"What if the concierge asks questions?" Leora asks. "What do we tell him?"

"He won't ask questions," Bridget says.

"What if he does?" Leora insists.

Leora is the least willing of the participants in this commando raid of ours. This surprises me. I had thought, given how she physically recoils from Arnold, that she would have no ambivalence.

"Maybe Arnold told the concierge to call him at his 'club,'" Leora says, and she draws two inverted commas in the air with her hands, "if he sees us doing anything out of the ordinary."

"Why don't we deal with that if we have to," Bridget says. "In any event, it's not as if the concierge doesn't know me."

Bridget has bought a small television set and its silent picture flickers as we make our final preparations. From time to time both Bridget and I turn to see what is being shown. Even the two young men Rupert has hired to help with the heavier lifting, standing around and drinking their tea, glance over from time to time.

Tibor pauses to examine what it is that has us transfixed.

"It's a documentary on the royal family," Leora says, noticing his quizzical expression. "They're replaying various royal weddings, for some reason."

Tibor fails to see what is interesting in it. What relevance could this have to any of us?

Leora turns up the volume.

"I thought there were going to be no hats," a woman says.

"If the Queen Mother chooses to wear a hat," a man replies, "I can't see anyone raising an objection to it."

"And here's the Queen herself," the woman continues. "I had thought she'd be the one in a hat, but no, she has a plume of feathers in her hair instead."

The reporters all turn to watch as a black Rolls-Royce with a glass roof pulls into the courtyard of the chapel at Windsor Castle.

"Will you please pay attention," says Tibor.

"Talk. I'm listening," Bridget says, her eyes still on the television set. "It's cheery. Not that what we're about to do isn't."

27

TIBOR IS NOT ONLY the commando raiders' strategist. He is also, not entirely reluctantly, our designated prank caller.

"Hello dere," he shouts into the telephone after dialing the number the private detective has identified as that of Arnold's mistress. The accent may be Yiddish, or eastern European, or Hispanic.

"Is that Moishe? Moishe Pipick?"

"No," Arnold says. His voice is unmistakable. Fruity. Ponderous. An old man's voice, but strong nonetheless. "You have the wrong number."

"But it's Moishe's number," Tibor yells.

"No it isn't," Arnold insists. "What number did you call?"

"Are you sure you're not Moishe?" Tibor says.

"What are you doing?" Bridget whispers.

"Sorry," Tibor says and shrugs his shoulders. He hangs up.

"What was that all about?" I ask.

"You couldn't help yourself, could you?" Bridget says, and she smiles. Her face is filled with affection. "The purpose was to see if Arnold was there, not to audition for *Fiddler on the Roof*."

"You have hidden talent," I say.

"I think I dislike that man very much indeed," is all Tibor says.

"But it was him?" I ask.

"Of course," Tibor says. "Do you think I would waste my performance?"

"If we're going to do it, let's do it already," Leora says from behind a book.

"And is the private detective at the entrance to the building he's in?" I ask, ignoring her.

"Yes."

"And he has your cell phone number in case Arnold goes out?"

"He won't leave. He's at his 'club' for the evening," Bridget says. Like her daughter, she draws inverted commas with her fingers.

"Well then, let's go," I say.

"Sophie Rhys-Jones, the future Countess of Wessex, steps from the royal motor car and pauses as her attendants adjust her train. Would you say it's white? Or is it ivory?"

"In between, I'd say," the correspondent says.

"Mommy would have loved this," Bridget says. "She couldn't get enough of the Princess Di thing."

"The funeral?" Leora asks.

"Let's go, please," I repeat and turn off the television.

28

WE HAVE TWO MORRIS VANS, a rented station wagon, Rupert's young men. Tibor has estimated that it should not take more than two hours to wrap everything and then rush it from the building and into the vans in one, or at most two, loads. Even if the concierge is an informant, then, the most valuable things will be on their way to Bridget's flat before any alarm can be sounded. We have no choice but to leave the big items—the furniture, several wooden chests, things we simply cannot carry or fit in the rented vans—for the movers who will take them straight to a storage facility in their lorry.

"I wish we could figure out a way to take everything now," I say.

Tibor is firm.

"No," he says. "We have enough to do."

When Tibor is done with his prank call and has confirmed that Arnold is with his mistress, we set out. The streets of Belgravia, through which the white vans and the car move in a slow convoy, are quiet and we ride in silence. Just as the procession of cars reaches Arnold's building, Tibor's cell phone rings and our hearts miss a beat. There is only one person who has this number.

"Yes," Tibor says, holding the phone so that we all can hear.

"The subject has come out of the building," the detective says, "but since he was headed away from your location I decided to follow him for a few blocks so that I could provide you with better intelligence as to his plans."

"And?"

"Well he walked for a block—he's an old chap, isn't he?—and then he stopped at a fish and chips shop and bought some fish and chips. He stood and ate them on the sidewalk, and now he appears to be headed back to the location he started from."

"Arnold stood and ate fish and chips on the sidewalk?"

"Yes, mate," the detective says. "He certainly looks harmless enough to me."

"Don't be fooled," Tibor says, thanks the man, and ends the call.

"Can you imagine Arnold eating fish and chips out of a bag?" I ask.

"In some ways he's pathetic," Bridget says. "Sometimes I find myself feeling like a bully, doing this."

"When you do," I say, "just picture for a second his floozy sitting among Dad's stuff."

"I don't need to," Bridget says.

WE APPROACH THE HOUSE and slow down. Each of us is carrying a suitcase in which we have stashed the tools we will need. I have the box cutters, tape, rope, and bubble wrap. It is a quiet night and late, almost midnight. The streets are empty.

I cannot help but wonder at our little congregation of suitcase-carrying burglars. Tibor walks slightly ahead. He is not quite as tall as I am, is older, impeccably dressed, a little gray at the temples. There is an air of deliberateness about him, but that is usual; single-mindedness is one of his personality traits, whether it is doing what we are about to do, or counseling high school students in Cambridge, Massachusetts. Bridget and Leora are a few steps behind him. They are strikingly similar in affect, in frame, in how they walk. Both are lean, neat, attractive women, with long legs, narrow waists, large brown eyes. Bridget's hair has faint streaks of gray, while Leora's is dark and curly.

And the instigator, me? Six foot and an inch or two, a fairly full head of hair, a narrow, moody face for a narrow, moody person. I am wearing a cashmere sweater, tasseled shoes, trousers bought at Brooks Brothers. I may look, then, though I am not, not by a long shot, like an American. Certainly I live in America, legally so following my marriage to Tesseba. I have a quintessentially American occupation, spend my days behind a computer screen and on the telephone. I *schmooze* well when I need to, if I say so myself. I avoid conflict, tend to work at finding solutions to problems we periodically face in our business rather than heading off into argument. I am, at heart, quite provincial, or at least I think I am, conservative, ruminative, nostalgic. Snatching things from a house in London is not my métier, in other words. I would not in the near past have been able to imagine any of this, nor begun to concoct the sequence of events that has led to this night. But the undertaking is undeniably my idea. It has Tibor's full support, Bridget's half-hearted support, and Leora's acerbic participation. But it is my idea.

The house looms above us. There are lights on in an upstairs bedroom, but that is to be expected. The lower floors are in darkness. A siren cuts through the night. The sound is coming from the Brompton Road a few hundred yards away, but it is sobering nonetheless. We pause mid-stride.

"Could it be an omen?" Leora asks facetiously. "So young, and made a criminal by her parents."

"Oh, for heaven's sake," I say. "Some idiot's probably speeding."

As we cross the threshold I do wonder, once again, how things could have reached this point. It does seem that events have careened about randomly for years, and that nothing follows logically from anything else. But this?

"I need you to pay attention," Tibor says abruptly, and then talking to me and his daughter in the same tone he adds: "You two stop making light of this."

I would respond, normally would act immediately to keep anyone who pressed on me in this manner in check, but not Tibor, not tonight.

"You're right," I say.

"Now that's a first," Bridget says. "But as a matter of interest, do we have a plan if we happen to get caught and the police are called?"

Tibor turns and looks at her. His expression is quite blank.

"We won't get caught," he says. "And if we do, we will face the music together."

That sounds strange, coming from Tibor. He is not a touchy feely kind of guy, and this is an affirmation of sorts, of our family, of the four of us.

30

We have gathered in this house on Helga's birthday each year, taken naps on the couches, paged through photograph albums at this table, sat in these canvas chairs to keep her company as she pruned the leaves of her garden. Now we are, each of us, keenly aware that we are crossing the foyer for the last time. My mother's life since leaving Durban has been here, and when the medics wheel her through the door one last time, the life she would recognize will be over.

"Who ever would have dreamed, back in the old days, the Durban days when she was so admired, that her life would end like this?" I say. "But I have to believe that the old Helga, the Durban Helga, would rejoice at what we are doing. And that somewhere, too, Dad is celebrating."

"She wouldn't want us to be doing this," Bridget says, shaking her head. "I wish I could ask her, or at least try to explain why we must."

"What difference would her approval make?" I ask, and Bridget says nothing.

Tibor, who was born in Bulgaria, was an afterthought in his family, or so he has said, and his parents are long since gone. He has a much older sister who still lives in Sofia, but she is over seventy, and widowed, and lives with her son who Tibor has met only once. She writes that she is a little less strong than she once was, but not much so. She still tends her garden, sees her friends, insists on her glass of vodka each evening. When Tibor reached America and offered to petition for her to join him, her response was: "What for?"

"You are doing the right thing," Tibor says quietly, and for a moment Bridget's face loses its anguish.

Tibor, rational Tibor, has not felt this strongly about anyone, not even the petty party apparatchik who intervened to sink his admission to the university in Sofia and changed forever the course of his life.

31

THE NIGHT NURSE, who has endeared herself to us by the care she gives my mother, is the only outsider, other than Rupert, who knows what we plan to do. When we reach the bedroom we find her ready. She has made a little parcel of the things my mother will need during the move and immediately afterward.

The television is on, showing yet another royal wedding. Tibor glances at the screen. The camera is scanning the chapel, and from up high the congregation, in its neat rows on a blue carpet, seems to fidget in waves.

"How is she?" Bridget asks.

"The same," the nurse says, stroking Helga's hair.

"Did she know who you were?"

"No, dear. She hasn't for some time now."

"Hello, Mommella," Bridget says.

My mother opens her eyes. She looks up at Bridget, and scans her face with a perplexed expression.

"Hello," she says weakly.

"How are you my sweetness?" Bridget asks.

"Fine, thank you," she says. "I'm so pleased you came. I've been having trouble with the birds."

She closes her eyes again and sinks her head back in the pillow.

"Danny's here," Bridget says. "Isn't that nice?"

My mother's eyes remain closed.

"Let's get started," Tibor says.

"May I make a suggestion," the nurse says to him.

"Please."

"It's not as if I was eavesdropping on purpose," she says, "but this afternoon I got the impression that Mr. Miro plans to give a woman friend of his Mrs. Miro's clothes. I know you have no further use for them, but . . ."

"They come," Bridget says definitively.

"It's a good thing we brought extra boxes," Tibor says, and immediately starts planning how best to pack them.

Leora, who is standing in the bedroom's doorway, watches her mother without comment.

"Do you need help in here?" she asks, her face expressionless. She is leaning against the jamb, a languid, teenage slouch.

"No," Bridget says.

"You're going to have to keep an eye out to be sure we're only taking your Mom's things," Tibor says. "There'll be hell to pay if we take something that doesn't belong to us."

"We won't," I say.

I walk around the living room turning on lamps. It is Arnold's room, and it has always felt like Arnold's room even as my mother has so many times played hostess in it. It is large and oval, with oak wainscoting, crown moldings at the ceiling, Persian carpets at each of the several clusters of seats. Although they are embedded in Arnold's decor, the things that come from Gordonwood stand out for me as starkly as if they were illuminated.

I lift one of the tusks from beside Arnold's table. I am surprised at its weight. Zulu bearers must have had difficulty bringing this unwieldy object from deep in the interior to Farewell's little settlement at Port Natal. I discover that the ivory detaches from its sheath and take it apart, lay both pieces carefully on the floor. Tibor, watching me and ready to help if the tusk proves too unwieldy to handle, hands me bubble wrap and a roll of tape.

From across the room I see one of Rupert's youngsters lifting an elaborate mask from a case.

"Please be careful with that," I say, and then add: "Maybe I should pack it myself."

"I can do it," the boy says. "What is it?"

"It's a *sangoma's* headgear," I tell him. "A Zulu witch doctor. Those yellow baubles on the top are dried goat bladders. If you're not gentle with them they'll fall apart."

I feel as if I may have sounded too harsh.

"*Sangomas* would wear them to smell out evil-doers," I add.

"Blimey," the boy says. "They smell enough on their own."

It was a signature of Zulu life, my father had said, this smelling out of evildoers. Shaka's *sangomas* in these terrifying outfits would prance and whoop and gesture, and then they would point at someone and without ceremony, without resistance even from their victims, the executioners would descend and haul away the evildoers for clubbing, or for neck twisting, or for impalement on stakes. It was a daily ritual, during Shaka's public morning bath, at meals, during dancing. You just had to look at him wrong and you'd get the finger. Heaps of bodies were left each evening for the wild animals that prowled outside the *kraal*.

Lifted from the case, the smell of the headdress and its baubles fills the room. If my father were here there is so much I would ask him.

32

EACH MORNING at Gordonwood Baptie would walk about in her pink uniform and white head scarf, feather duster in hand, touching everything lightly in her ritual gesture of cleaning. Bridget and I weren't supposed to be in the formal rooms at all and I have never, not once before this moment, done more than brush my hand across the ivory that lies on its side between my knees. Now I feel it carefully, run my fingers along the curve of the great tusk, feel the filigree of its silver sheath.

"Look at the grain," my father used to insist. "The perfect color of it, as if it has been lit from the inside. You can almost imagine the madness, why they used to call ivory white gold. Imagine where this has been, what it has been witness to. Just imagine it."

Now I roll each of Shaka's tusks around and around until it is wrapped in several layers of bubble wrap. It becomes difficult to handle and I need help to move it.

"This is worth something, then?" one of Rupert's young men says.

"It's ivory," I reply and am about to mention Lieutenant Francis Farewell but at the last moment think better of it.

"These go in the first run," I say instead.

"Of course," Tibor says.

Under his steady direction we wrap and pack, quickly but quietly, and the room with its glass windows overlooking the river and the ancient buildings is filled only with the sounds of tape being wound, subdued comments, little scraping sounds as ornaments and paintings and small pieces of furniture are moved about on the floor. The hired boys work diligently, and if they had been uneasy at the apparent secrecy, the way the wrapping paper and masking tape had been concealed in suitcases before we marched past the concierge and into the foyer, their concern fades as we make progress.

Bridget, who has been emptying the kitchen cabinets of my mother's silver services, passes through the living room as she goes to check on my mother. Leora looks up at her and then down again. A moment after she disappears into the bedroom the sound of the television increases.

"Dearly beloved," a man intones. "We are gathered here today in the sight of God and in the face of this congregation, to join together this man and this woman in holy matrimony, which is an honorable estate, instituted of God himself, signifying unto us the mystical union betwixt Christ and his church."

"Christ that's distracting," Tibor mutters.

"Pass the tape, will you," one of the hired boys says.

"I don't have it," the other replies. "Maybe," and he gestures toward Leora with his eyebrows, "she does."

They exchange a knowing smile. Leora is a tall girl, taller than most, and well proportioned. It is easy to see why men find her appealing. She flicks a roll of tape to the boy and continues working. She is used to such skittish attention.

Tibor needs Bridget's guidance on something and he finds her sitting beside my mother on the bed, my mother's head cradled in the crook of her arm, both of them watching the television. He is unable to comment, to remind Bridget that they have work to do.

"Wow," my mother says, her eyes fixed on the screen. "How lovely."

"It is lovely," Bridget says, her voice very thin.

At that moment I enter the bedroom and find myself next to Tibor, both of us standing quietly against the wall. We watch as the camera pans again across the church and follows the princess down the aisle. Neither of us say anything, and for whatever reason we decide to share a moment of relief at the reprieve the spectacle is unexpectedly delivering. The princess moves as if shrouded, wrapped in layers of white fabric and gauze and crystal, and as she does, as I watch her move down the carpet, watch as her dress catches at her knees as she steps, I am aware too, I cannot avoid it, of her body inside the dress, of her stomach and her buttocks and her perspiring feet in her shoes.

We lack a camera to pan across and to allow us to see more of the context of things. The best judgment of my entire life tells me that we need to do what we are doing tonight, and if it is not a fairy tale it is at least a sorcerer's tale and one from which I am engineering a deft escape. I cannot fathom the import of things beyond that. I cannot see from on high how things might be better ordered.

My mother, lost in confusion and sitting beside Bridget, whose arm is around her waist, watches in silence as the princess floats across the screen.

33

THE DETECTIVE CALLS past midnight to report that the lights in Arnold's room have been turned off, and Tibor tells him that he may end his surveillance. We line the boxes up by the door in the order of their importance and then, after a cell phone call to the Morris drivers to pull to the front of the house, we stream out the door and across the courtyard like a procession of native bearers. We move quickly but we do not run, affect a nonchalance we do not feel. As we reach the man at the gate we slow down even further, but he is either dozing or fails to notice that anything is awry. We pack the first van and it leaves without a hitch, and then the second. Within minutes, as Tibor has planned, the most important of my father's possessions are in the white vans and snailing back to the flat.

By three o'clock, when the ambulance arrives, Arnold's once glittering house is transformed. The rooms look as if they have been picked over by a finicky thief, with gaps on the walls and empty shelves, lighted cabinets displaying nothing, seating areas missing chairs. Bridget walks around with a broom and a pan, sweeps away dust that has gathered under tables and the footprints left by ornament stands and African ebony tables. She rearranges the objects that are left on the shelves, stands back to see how it looks, makes further adjustments.

"What are you doing?" Leora asks.

"Trying not to leave the place a mess," she says.

"The place *is* a mess," Leora says. "You and a dustpan aren't going to change that. And why do you care?"

"I care," Bridget says. "I just do."

They stand together, Bridget and her daughter, and look at the half empty shelves.

"It's going to be okay," Leora says and then, unexpectedly, she takes her mother in her arms, she is taller than Bridget already, and cradles her head against her shoulder.

Tibor greets the medics at the door and they, like the boys earlier, seem to find nothing odd in the swirl of activity that awaits them; the packing and the carrying, the quickness and the quiet, and that it is all happening at three o'clock in the morning.

"Where's our patient, then?" the man asks.

He and another are wheeling an aluminum stretcher on wheels. It has straps folded across it and bright red blankets.

"I'll show you," Bridget says, and leads them into the bedroom.

"You have some visitors," Bridget announces as they enter the room.

For a few minutes there are sounds of movement in the room, metal parts snapped in place, the bed scraping the floor as it shifts.

"Where are we going?" my mother asks. Her voice is shaky, uncertain.

"Would you like to go for a little ride, Mommella?" Bridget asks.

"I want to stay in bed," my mother says. "I'm tired."

"You sleep," Bridget says. "These nice boys will do everything."

Tibor and I stand at the entrance of the bedroom and watch as the medics prepare the trolley. One on either side of her, they lift her on her sheet and place her on the trolley.

"Why are you doing this?" Helga asks, teary now, her lips quivering.

"It's okay," Bridget says, taking her hand. "I'm with you."

"But I want to go home," my mother sobs.

As they wheel her down the passage she looks about and appears to notice that things in the house are not as she knows they should be.

She raises her head slightly, looks at the walls, bites her lip. All she says, more than once, pointing at each empty space from under the strap with a perfectly manicured finger, is:

"But . . ."

34

Back at Bridget's flat we do not go to bed. Bridget has propped several jugs with the flowers she has brought over on the windowsill, and she lays out my mother's medicines and tissues and creams on a trestle table.

The nurse sits in a folding chair and tells us to go to sleep.

"You've done what you had to," she says. "Now you must look after yourselves."

The sun begins to rise, the city to stir, and we sit, the four of us, in the adjoining room on chairs brought from Arnold's flat. I drink coffee. Tibor smokes his pipe. Leora dozes. There are boxes against the walls, furniture stacked all around us.

"Have we done the right thing?" Bridget asks.

"No," I say. "Let's take it all back."

Even Leora who is not, apparently, asleep opens her eyes and smiles.

"When do we call him?" Bridget asks.

"Maybe he'll have a heart attack and save us all a lot of trouble," Leora says.

"Don't talk like that," Bridget says, and even Leora knows not to respond.

"People like him are indestructible," I say.

"Not indestructible," Tibor says. "But it is good that he will finally understand how we feel."

35

"IS ARNOLD THERE?" Tibor asks the woman who answers the phone.

"Who is this?" the woman asks. She cannot, though she tries, disguise the extent to which she is startled.

"Tibor."

"Who?"

"Tell him his son-in-law, Tibor, is on the phone."

There is a very long silence, some muffled talking, and then finally Arnold.

"Yes?" he says, although he says this word in the nature of a question, as if he is seeking to dispel a misgiving, and then he adds, solicitously: "What is it Tibor?"

Tibor is brief with him. He tells Arnold what we have done, everything, sparing nothing, and then, with a vehemence that neither Bridget nor I could have anticipated, he tells Arnold that we do not want him to try and see Helga again.

"You have my wife," Arnold says. "And you're telling me you took things from our home."

"That is correct," Tibor says. "But only the things that belong to her children, and nothing of yours."

"I think I'm going to call the police and have them determine that," Arnold says. "And I'm particularly disappointed in you. I might have expected it from Helga's children, but I always thought you had integrity."

"That is the last insulting thing you will say to any of us," Tibor says even as Arnold is going on about lawyers, attachments, damages, and replaces the receiver.

"What have you done to my Helgie?" Arnold demands, but the line is silent.

36

My mother lies on a narrow rented bed in the flat's only bedroom. Sometimes she opens her eyes, but mostly she appears to be asleep. On the afternoon of the day we bring her over, Bridget goes in alone and kneels by the bed. She takes my mother's hand, strokes her clammy brow, listens to the rattling breath.

"You did a good job," she says. "You did everything you came to do. You must go now. We have to let you go."

"Your famous children," Arnold has said to Helga, and more than once. "So cocksure. One swipe and they'd be off their little pedestals. A strong gust of wind."

As the day goes by and we hear nothing further, no sirens, no knocking at the door, we begin to believe that maybe, just maybe, Arnold will leave us in peace. Even as I am relieved, something in me spoils still for a fight, a showdown. It is as if a giant wave has washed over us and then spilled itself onto a beach without any return, without any backwash at all. All that bombast, and now nothing.

At four the doctor visits and tells us that the end is only hours away, and as he leaves, barely has the door closed behind him, there comes from the little room the sound of a faint coughing. The day nurse comes to the door and beckons us in. She herself waits outside. There is a last faint breath, a final, inelastic exhalation, almost a whisper, a kick of the leg under the cover, and it is over.

I take Bridget's hand and bury my face in the bedclothes. From deep within this sharp new grief I hear something I had not expected. It is Tibor's sobbing, unrestrained, hoarse, primitive. It frees me into a cave of sadness of my own.

37

THE FUNERAL is an angry, divided affair. The family and Arnold do not acknowledge each other. For my mother's friends it is awkward, the need to negotiate two hostile camps on either side of the grave. Perhaps they feel there is blame to go around. Either way they divide their condolences carefully in half.

"Do you think she's here?" Bridget asks.

"Who?"

"The floozy?"

We are aware that we are being scrutinized, that what has happened has sped around this little circle with what effect we cannot tell, but that either way we are an island among people who are little more than strangers at a funeral that seems to be taking place where it doesn't belong. There are just the five of us, Bridget, Tibor, Leora, Tesseba, and me. Tesseba has arrived from Boston just this morning and stands beside me against the wall of the cemetery's gatehouse. She is wearing a black skirt and a knitted maroon shawl, and her hair is in a braid that reaches almost to her waist.

Perhaps because we are such a small group, perhaps because I feel so adrift, I say to Bridget: "We should have brought Baptie from South Africa."

Bridget looks at me skeptically. When we were children at Gordonwood, Baptie in her pink housemaid's outfit, her white apron, her starched headscarf, was as much a part of each day as my mother herself, as much a part of Gordonwood as its walls and its air and its sounds. "How I dream about Gordonwood," she writes in her letters. "But passed days will not ever return."

Baptie was hired to be Bridget's nanny, then later became mine, then learned to cook, and, after my father, after Bridget and I had left, she stayed on with my mother, more than a servant then, more like a companion, a confidante, even a chaperone in the early days when Arnold began calling and Helga wanted someone around just in case. Bridget and I write to her, reminisce about her, support her, but even so she is more a living memory than a living person, not someone who travels, has ever flown, could exist with us here in this English graveyard.

"Can you see Baptie on an airplane?" she asks. "Or on a London subway for that matter? Can you just imagine Baptie in England?"

I cannot imagine it even as, if I turned around and saw her standing at the cemetery gate, it would not be any more surreal than anything else that is happening. She will be in her pink housemaid's outfit, white apron, starched headscarf. She will be a ray of light among the tweeds and cottons of this bleak English cemetery.

"Perhaps not," I say.

We stand at the graveside and a rabbi who knows none of us rushes through the ceremony. Tibor, vaguely awkward in a *yarmulke,* is as still as a column behind his wife.

"*Yitkadal, veyitkadash,*" I begin the prayer for the dead on cue, and I can see that Tibor is momentarily taken aback, surprised to see me speaking a language he has never heard me speak, but then his life with us has been punctuated by moments like this, by small incongruities, starting on the day he met my mother for the first time, that moment in the lobby of the Cumberland Hotel in London when she had come over from Durban, in part, he had always suspected, to look over the man her daughter had suddenly announced she planned to marry. Bridget had gone alone to Heathrow to meet her and the plan was for Tibor to join them at the hotel later. So he was in the lobby, and then the elevator doors opened and he said later that he saw Bridget and a woman who could have been Bridget's older sister except that she exuded a kind of class he had not seen close-up before, a poise he could not quite place. They came across the lobby, Bridget in a blue dress and my mother, tall, her auburn hair in waves about her face, suede shoes, a camel skirt, a tailored jacket with a gold brooch at the lapel. This was in the pre-Arnold days, and back then Tibor knew nothing of Helga but the legend Bridget had created, that she was steady and powerful, that she possessed a moral clarity that distinguished her from the world around her, as Bridget described it an almost redemptive clarity down there in the cesspool of South Africa, but even so he had not expected this degree of confidence, at least not in a woman, and not in one so recently widowed, and not in one so far from her home in Africa. As Helga swept across the lobby, Bridget a step behind her, Tibor found her magnetic.

The decision to marry had been impetuous, this was true, and he was older, and of a different faith, and a refugee, and without a profession, but Helga had been charming to him, focused, intent, deeply engaged in what he was saying as they talked, and she had never, whatever her private misgivings may have been, not once, interfered in their decision once she was convinced that Bridget knew her mind. My mother was, after all, only twelve years older than Tibor, and young looking too, and when all else was said and done the truth is—how could he have said anything of this to his wife, though I am almost sure it is true—that if Bridget and my mother had been standing side by side in the gymnasium that first day, he would have been more intrigued—it is hard, it is impossible, to conceive this—by my mother.

And now this. In the shed at the entrance to the cemetery, beside my mother's open coffin, its hammer and nails to one side, I notice Bridget fumbling in her purse. She finds a comb, for a moment I am puzzled, then she leans into the coffin and begins carefully to comb the wisps of hair that protrude from the cowl of my mother's shroud.

"*Oseh shalom bimromav,*" I chant, bowing slightly at the waist. My reading glasses are perched on my nose, the words are blurred, my hand shakes. Tibor looks on with a face full of compassion.

I finish, look up, see Arnold. Arnold is an old man, walks with a limp, has a thin white beard and an almost bald head. He combs his hair across his pate, waxes his moustache, is wearing a collar too big for his thin neck so that his head sticks out like a stalk. How can such a man wreak the havoc he has?

The prayer ends and I take a small step backward, and just then, as the rabbi is about to speak, Arnold pushes forward and raises his arm like a policeman determined to create a break in a stream of traffic. His *yarmulke* is held on with a hairclip.

"I beg your pardon, Rabbi," Arnold says, "but this is my wife's funeral, and I, too, have something to say."

A silence sweeps over everyone, freezes me where I stand, Bridget too. Leora, who has been holding her mother's hand, looks at her father and then at me.

"The nature of the bond between a man and his wife is not always apparent to their children," he says. "And nothing I know of mandates that adult children have a right to be brought to understand the nature or condition of their parents' marriage."

He pauses, lifts his hand to straighten the *yarmulke* which has slipped to the side of his head.

"As many of you know," he says, "Helga and I were together for a long time and had deep feelings for each other. They may not have been apparent always, but that was our business. I will miss her, and I know that if I had been the one to go first, she would have missed me. People, even children, witnessing snippets of a marriage, do not know as much as they think they do. But I do know one thing for certain: My Helga would not have condoned the choices some of us have witnessed, and all of us know about, of the past few days."

I begin walking back along the path to the entrance of the cemetery, walking out on my own mother's funeral, my hand in Tesseba's. I turn and see that Bridget and Leora are a few steps behind me, moving quickly to catch up. Behind us the small group remains at the grave side, but of the family only Tibor is left, his head bowed, his hands at his side, his *yarmulke* still on his head. He hears Arnold's voice and he cannot fail to notice something ominous, something secretly triumphant, in his tone. Arnold is not accustomed to being bested, and while we may believe that we have purged ourselves of him, Tibor has no doubt that it may not be so simple. It is not that Arnold can impose himself on us any longer, rather that what was taken from his apartment may have acquired a new and bold significance.

The rabbi takes up as soon as Arnold concludes, chants a prayer, and then hands Tibor a shovel and indicates that he should throw the first spade of dirt into the grave. Tibor takes the shovel from him and digs into the earth. As he lifts it a sprinkle of sand spills over the sides. Nobody moves. Nothing moves.

BRIDGET HAS BOUGHT CAKES and several kinds of biscuits, and she and Leora set out teacups and plates in the event that any of my mother's friends return with us from the cemetery. That's the way it is in South Africa, anyway. Whether you want company or not, in the end the presence of others does seem to help.

Nobody comes. Not a soul. The cups and biscuits sit untouched on the tray until Tesseba and Leora, finally, take it all, as unobtrusively as they can, back into the kitchenette.

"Oh, God," Bridget says. "I hope she isn't looking down and cursing at us. Could Arnold be right, and we wrong? Have we alienated everybody?"

She gestures to the things heaped about the apartment and adds: "And for what, in the end?"

39

THERE ARE THINGS Bridget knows that she has not shared, not until, after it is all over, she bares it all in that little flat on the edge of Belgravia.

She knows, for instance, that my mother discovered a lump in her breast long before, months before, she told anyone about it, not Arnold of course, not her own doctor, not even Bridget. Apparently, so Helga told her much later, she felt something, waited, ignored it, preferred simply to let it be, and only when it had turned bluish and begun to collapse inward did she mention it, in passing, to her dentist. He, of all people, a South African and a friend of my father's from long ago, had asked a few questions and then canceled his next appointment to take her to the hospital, then and there, her half-hearted protests notwithstanding.

She refused surgery, insisted instead on a minimal procedure that even Arnold didn't notice, and then did not show up, not even once, for the chemotherapy they told her was essential. When her surgeon, who knew nothing about my mother's home life, telephoned and spoke to Arnold, told him everything, asked for his help in getting her to stick to the treatments that were essential to her survival, Arnold promised to do what he could but never mentioned the call, not to Helga, not to Bridget who could cajole my mother into doing almost anything, certainly not to me.

Bridget learned all this later, from my mother close to the end, from my mother's doctor at the funeral, still puzzled that she had refused all help, had not even returned his calls, from other things, oblique, mysterious things, that Arnold had hinted at.

Bridget is sure of all of this, and yet she was sure too that at the time there was no reason to tell any of it to me. Once the die is cast, she believed, what purpose would my fury serve? And in the end things are always so much more complex than they appear to be.

40

It is strangely disappointing, now that we have actually gone to the trouble of carrying out our heist and have even seemingly pulled it off, to have at such close range the objects that had seemed so fraught in Arnold's apartment just a week before. There is, to be blunt about it, something anti-climactic in the air. In my mother's homes, in Durban and even in London, it all had a certain context, displayed as she had wanted it on pedestals and in cases, but now, in a mound on the floor of the rented flat, it all constitutes a forlorn little community. In the light of day, my father's collections are chipped and faded and quite pedestrian, and it is hard to see, really, what it is we have been fighting about.

"Is any of this valuable?" Leora asks, holding something up to the light, a mangled leather sandal with its strap hanging down like a piece of chewed over meat.

We can guess, Bridget and I, what must be going on outside of our hearing, people we barely know speculating about things that are none of their business, about whether Arnold really does have a mistress, or whether the woman is simply, as we hear Arnold is insisting, a loyal friend, about why, if he is such a bastard, a woman as perceptive and independent as my mother would have stayed with him for all these years, about why, indeed, she married him in the first place. Dirty linen, all of it, off limits but for our own actions.

I do not know the answer to Leora's question. We have all assumed it is valuable, but the truth is that we do not know.

"Some of this may be," I say. "It is to us."

"The tusks must be worth something," Leora says, trying to be helpful, trying to find a sliver of optimism. "Ivory's valuable, isn't it?"

"First we have to find out if we're allowed to take it home," Tibor says. "The embassy tells me there are rules about this. Elephants are an endangered species."

Tibor started making his inquiries on the morning we brought all this back to the flat, spent much of the day on the telephone even as Helga lay gasping for breath in the next room. It is not that he is a callous man, just that he does not think that the two things are related, keeping a death watch and getting done something that needs to be done.

"That's ridiculous," I snap. "These things predate the laws against owning ivory. Elephants weren't endangered in the nineteenth century. People killed them for fun."

"Maybe," Tibor tells me. "But you still have to prove it, that the object is old enough that the elephant was killed before the law was passed, before you can bring ivory into the United States. I'm not aware of any paperwork that can do this, unless you have that letter you talked about, the one Mr. Isaacs sent to his uncle."

"Did you find the letter among Mom's papers?" I ask Bridget.

"I wasn't aware I was supposed to be looking for it," she answers, a trace testily, and then she adds: "Have you *ever* seen it?"

I can see in Tibor's face that he knows whatever my answer is, it will not be helpful.

"I think I have," I say, "but honestly I don't remember. Dad said he had it. It must be somewhere."

"Well with or without it," Tibor says, "it's our burden to convince them."

"And when do they tell us if we've convinced them?" I ask.

There is something condescending in my tone, I suppose, as if I think that it is Tibor who is missing the point, Tibor who has already done so much.

"You get the paperwork and you show it at the border," Tibor says patiently. "And if they don't believe you, they can confiscate whatever they think is not in compliance."

"Oh, come on," I say, and leave the room.

"You're not serious?" Bridget says to her husband when I am gone, and it's funny because if customs did take everything she would mind, but not all that much, not honestly. She does not, still, regard our mother's possessions as authentically ours. She will get there, perhaps, but for now they remain my mother's. Looking at them, she cannot shake the feeling that she has overstepped her bounds, done something wrong, and she tends, in the little flat, to avoid looking at any of it.

"Better the U.S. Customs, in any event, than bloody Arnold," she says to Tibor.

While we wait for Tibor to sort it out, everything remains stacked in the living room. Bridget drapes a sheet over it all, she says to restore a sense of order to the place, but that is not the only reason. With the giant tusks looming from one end of the mound, it looks as if we have killed an elephant and left it lying, shrouded, right there in the middle of the floor.

THE DAY AFTER THE FUNERAL my mother's hairdresser shows up at the door, and not long after that the nurse who helped us on the night of the raid ("The thought of that man makes me shudder," she says as she comes in,) and after that a slow trickle of people arrives, all of them quite tentative, as if they are not altogether sure they will be welcomed. We are relieved rather than grateful, make a mental note of how many people have come, as if there is some number, some critical mass of visits, that will tip a balance in our favor.

"I wonder who's visiting Arnold," Bridget muses, but nobody answers.

My mother's English friends, those she has met since coming to London—a woman from the library, several members of an informal club of women who attend the same concert series and meet for lunch, several neighbors—arrive, and they are meticulously polite, polite in a distinctively English way even as they are somewhat distant and palpably cautious. They knock on the door and when Bridget lets them in they make their way past the mound to the little circle of folding chairs, are careful to say nothing about the greatly reduced circumstances in which my mother seems to have spent her final hours, cast searching glances at the young people who are responsible for it and at their elephant asleep on the floor.

It is the same each time. We talk for a while, small talk, and then as the minutes pass, as the conversation peters out, their eyes begin to wander about the apartment with its plastic chairs and mismatched teacups, eventually to the pile, to fixate on a certain place within it as if suddenly they are seeing something familiar for the first time, as if the pile itself has an answer they particularly want.

"This is too bad," they say eventually, or, "What a pity."

"Does it really matter what they think?" Tibor asks when we are alone.

"Not to me it doesn't," Bridget says. "But it matters anyhow."

There is something skeptical about their reaction, something that does not hang together for those who have been in that opulent apartment and been awed by it, impressed too by the courtly manner Arnold displays when he works to ingratiate himself with my mother's female friends, something in the tone that says: "Arnold Miro? Why would *he* need your mother's things? What would he want with *this?*"

I suppose it is true, as Bridget tries to say circumspectly, that my manner does not help. As Bridget talks I can't seem to stop myself from interrupting her, from adding some detail or other as if it will make her story more credible, as if her story needs to be made more credible, and then no sooner have I started talking than I become too animated, too forceful, so that Bridget can see in people's faces that they simply want the whole thing to end. It seems possible, their manner suggests, that if I do not stop my flailing arms and clenched teeth will run out of my control, that something violent, even, will happen.

It is better, more predictable, when the former South Africans start to visit. For the most part these are people Bridget and I remember well, though it has been years, decades, since we last saw them. They are elderly, afflicted with this or that disability, gray, slow. Sometimes it takes all sorts of messing about at the front door, fussing with umbrellas that will not fold and galoshes that become snagged, before they can actually cross the threshold and step into the flat. They have not come before, they say, because they know my mother had many English friends and they have not wanted to get in the way. As often as not they just appear at the door, "popping in" they say, and are then reluctant to leave. "No, we're fine," they answer when Bridget offers them tea, "unless you're having," and then when Tibor or Leora come from the kitchen with a tea tray, they look on with a measure of relief, are quite specific in how they prefer to take theirs, chew on the offered biscuits with pleasure and determination.

There is no need to discuss the circumstances that bring the family to this tiny flat. They know from each other what has happened, have pieced the rest together, and with them, at least, there is no need to revisit any of it. They talk instead about things that happened thirty years ago as if they are recent events, about my father and mother as if Arnold never existed. Leora watches in astonishment, Tibor and Tesseba too, as they become animated, Bridget and I as well, about things so trivial, and that happened so long ago, and in a place so far away, that it's a wonder anyone could, anyone would care to, remember such details; the night someone's foot went through a rotten floorboard at Gordonwood, for instance, how Silas found a fretsaw and cut her free without so much as damaging her shoe.

"It happened," the visitor, an elderly lady with neatly brushed hair, says. "Of course I remember it, but you were a child. What a memory you have."

"And," I am off now, "do you remember the Passover Seder at your house when my father knocked over the ceramic dish with the horseradish and the bitter herbs?"

"My God," the woman says, astonished. "I'd forgotten that. He gathered up all the pieces, and a week later he brought it back mended so flawlessly I couldn't even see where it had broken."

"He worked on it every night," I say.

"You must have been a baby then," the woman says. "How do you remember this?"

"I remember everything," I say enthusiastically, and then before I know it I am off and running, blathering on about places no one in the room, not even I, have thought of in years. Almost against my will, it is that compulsive, I hear myself talking about things that have no relevance now, had scarcely more then—the Mermaid Lido and the Athlone Park Hotel, the Big Top and the Amphitheater, double-decker buses, how they once had conductors with long silver machines for making change.

"Remember Uncle Cyril from the Mermaid Lido," someone says, and in a thin voice sings:

Come to Durban by the sea
and see how happy we can be.
We'll sing and dance there
and find romance there.
So come to Durban by the sea.
The moonlight's so inviting . . . .
in Durban by the sea.

"It's how they began and ended each performance," he says beaming.

He stops himself short, abruptly aware that he is singing while on a condolence visit. There is an awkward quiet.

"Do you remember the Coo-ee Restaurant on the beachfront?" I ask, breaking the silence, and now someone says: "You couldn't possibly remember that place. It burned down in the fifties."

All eyes are on me as I collect my thoughts.

"No," I say. "I remember it. Off to the left as you came down to the beach from the Marine Parade."

"Yes," I am told, "that is where it was. But it burned down when I was a boy, and I'm a good thirty years older than you are."

"I remember it," I insist. "Vividly. Going there for ice cream."

For a long moment everyone in the room is silent, contemplates how this could be so, how someone can remember something that he has never seen. *Perhaps he has seen a picture of it,* they may think, *if it is indeed true that it burned down before he was born, and having seen the picture, his imagination fills in the rest, adds the missing pixels, completes an image seeded with something quite different.* But no, I insist that I remember it as vividly as I say I do, even though, after a few moments, I am not so sure anymore. I seem unstuck in time, my own Billy Pilgrim, there even when I am not.

Someone steps in and saves me: "I'm not sure that isn't just what time does," he says.

"Is it just our family, or do all South Africans love to reminisce?" Leora asks when everyone has left, and before Bridget can answer Tibor says wryly, looking up from a newspaper: "It's a requirement of South African citizenship."

Bridget stops in her tracks and looks at her husband with a bemused expression.

"Did Tibor make a funny?" she asks, and Tibor cannot help but smile even as he continues reading. "I think he's making fun of us."

My mother's friends are very forgiving, we find, don't seem to hold her responsible for anything in her recent behavior, not for brushing them off when she was out with Arnold, not even for lording it over them, all the flaunted wealth, while they eked by on their decaying little South African pensions.

"It is too bad we didn't see more of your mother after she came to London," is all they say. "She was always so busy."

These are political people, too, these early exiles. Most of them left South Africa in protest and long before it was clear that *apartheid* would collapse under its own weight.

"I think the country's headed in the direction of a one-party state," someone will say, and suddenly other conversations peter out and everyone, without warning, appears to be years younger than just a moment before. "I mean, there are now party cadres deputized to fill all sorts of government jobs, party activists visiting schools to proselytize, something very unkosher in a lot of what I read."

"Maybe the country has to pass through a phase," someone else says, and there are those who agree and those who disagree, words like "apologist" and "double standard" and "relativist" thrown about, and the only constant is how well informed they are, how much they have read, how much they care about the discussion itself.

"There's no precedent for this," someone else offers, "a handover of political power without any transfer of wealth. Of course it's combustible. Why would any sane person expect different?"

"God," I say, almost forgetting myself where I am and why we are together in this room. "The government was right when they banned you. You really *are* a Communist."

People laugh.

"Your mother would have enjoyed this discussion," someone says, and suddenly, at the mention of her name, people remember why they are there, and there is a lull in the conversation.

"South Africans pay strange condolence calls," Leora says. "They say they're here to console you, but once they've got a bit of tea in them all they can do is sing and talk about ancient history."

"Those were the defining moments of many people's lives, and Grandma was a part of it," Bridget says. "It's their way of paying respect."

"For all the troubles, on a personal level those old days in Durban were golden," someone has said. *"Goldene yorren."*

None of Arnold's friends, not one of his jocular circle who were once so free with their flattery when my mother entered a room, come anywhere near us.

42

We want to go home, are homesick if you will, desperate to draw the curtain on all that has happened and to be back where we belong, but there are so many details to be seen to, bank accounts to be closed, forms to be completed, (my mother is, suddenly, something different, something cold, "The Decedent," "The Testatrix," not someone we recognize, grander, more distant,) and each detail leads to more details until it seems we will never be done with it. We go through her papers, find bills, phone messages, notes to herself, things so vividly my mother's we are left marveling at how death has made everything she did and cared about seem futile, as if the next rung of a ladder had simply been chopped away without any attempt at explanation.

We discuss sending Leora home but she wants to stay, convinces us that she is missing nothing that can't easily be made up. For us this is an easy decision because we want her to stay too. Without fanfare or explanation she has suddenly come into her own, has become funny, and more than that, has become, in some odd way, the only adult in the group. It is Leora who insists that we eat proper food and then keep the kitchen clean. ("I have a rule," she announces, looking pointedly at me. "If you drink a cup of coffee, either smash the cup and then go downstairs to buy another one, or wash the one you've used. Is there anything about that you'd like to discuss?"). It is Leora who comes padding into the living room in her night gown at two o'clock in the morning to suggest that Bridget and I go to bed. She starts calling her father Moishe Pipick, and then Bridget does too, and when she refers to the mound as "Dumbo" it does seem, for a moment at least, to lift some of the heaviness from the room.

Sometimes it is easy to forget that she is still a child. When she turns on the radio and starts humming along to a rock tune, I stop what I am doing and stare at her angrily.

"Please," I say harshly, shout actually, bringing a numbing silence into the room. "It may not mean much to you that our mother has just died but do you think you can find it in yourself to curb your music for a little longer?"

"I'm just trying to lighten things up," she says.

"Someone has died," I repeat. "We don't need your constant levity."

Leora, stunned, turns off the radio.

"It's me," I say, contrite, an hour later. "I'm very volatile these days. I don't know why. I just am."

"No, really?" Leora says with a smile, and then puts her arms around me.

To Leora's dismay one of the moving boys telephones to invite her on a date.

"What shall I tell him?" she asks, horrified and flattered, covering the receiver.

"He seemed like a nice young skinhead," I say.

"If you'll come, I'll go," she says, throwing it back at me, and then she removes her hand from the mouthpiece and explains, calmly and with all good humor, that her grandmother has died and that she will not be going out while we are in London.

"He says he's sorry and that she seemed like a nice lady," she says when she hangs up.

"She was unconscious," I say, and then, though it is disrespectful to Helga, worse than disrespectful, we find ourselves laughing and unable to stop.

For whatever reason, we find ourselves able to laugh.

43

ON THE FOURTH DAY after the funeral there is a sharp series of knocks, and this time it is a man in uniform with a sheaf of papers which, it doesn't take long to see, come from Arnold's solicitor. He has sued us, said he would and now has, has gone to court on a lying affidavit in which he swears that everything in his flat was a gift to him from his wife, in effect that her children have robbed him and caused him, so the papers say, "grievous harm."

"How can someone even think to do that?" I say. "Lie through his teeth to get what he wants?"

No one answers, and the question is rhetorical. I call again on my high school friend Rupert, the lawyer, and Rupert promises to stop by at the end of the day. I have seen him a few times on his various visits, but Bridget has not seen him since the Durban days. At the funeral she had expected to see the tall, athletic boy she remembered, but that Rupert is, of course, long gone. The English lawyer Rupert is middle aged, a little paunchy, endlessly affable. Something about him inspires confidence.

"Oh, dear," he says, as he looks the papers over. "Litigation is never a good thing, though compared to what you fellows make of it in America, we may even look efficient."

"Can he win on this flimsy shit?" I ask.

Rupert looks at me oddly.

"One can win unfairly on anything," he says. "But one has to believe that right will prevail. It usually does."

There is a moment of silence.

"I mean," Rupert adds, "isn't there paperwork on any of this, some reference to possessions in her will or elsewhere?"

"No," I say. "She simply leaves everything to Bridget and me. I've gone through her papers and found nothing else relevant."

"I'm referring to other issues," Rupert says. "I mean, did he pay several thousand pounds to ship and insure all of this when it originally came from Durban? And more recently, did he hire someone from the museum to come in and restore some of the more fragile pieces, and then to coat them with preservative? It's all in here," he says, pointing to the papers.

I have to say I don't know any of this. I just don't.

"Apparently one of the tusks had a crack in it, you know," Rupert says. "The papers say he spent a small fortune restoring it."

"Well that's nonsense," I say. "It always had a crack. I can show you. It still does."

"No need to convince me, old fellow," Rupert says. "The basic question remains whether she gave any of this to him, even if in a moment of weakness."

On this point Bridget and I, even Leora, have divergent views.

"She could have, you know," Bridget says. "She wasn't herself."

"I bet she did," Leora says. "He was like a steamroller when he wanted something."

"No," I say, though without conviction. "She was never that far gone. They belong to us."

"I must say," Rupert adds, "I can't imagine your mother being forced to do anything she didn't want to."

"Thanks," I say, "but you didn't know her in the Arnold years."

"Perhaps not," Rupert concedes. "Though after you'd both left Durban and before I left, I used to stop by and have tea with her down there in her flat on the Marine Parade. It was just her and Baptie then, of course, constantly bickering like an old married couple."

"I didn't know you used to visit her," I say.

Rupert looks at me quizzically.

"What do you mean?" he says with a smile. "I considered it a privilege. She was working on her doctorate in Zulu history, and we'd sit on the balcony and chat about it. She was quite an original thinker, you know, and way ahead of her time."

"What do you mean by that?" I ask. "She was a historian. How can you be ahead of your time in studying the past."

Rupert looks at me, takes a biscuit, chuckles.

"When it comes to Zulu history," he says slowly, "there's a lot that's not settled. Your mother studied the written accounts of the early white adventurers and came away believing that their reports owed more to Victorian romanticism and Robinson Crusoe than to reality. That's old hat now, but I'm talking about twenty-five years ago. She was convinced that old King Shaka was nowhere near as brutal as those unscrupulous early buccaneers wanted people to believe he was. They certainly told a good story, but how much of it was for effect and how much of it was accurate is something no one's quite so sure of any more. Either way, I enjoyed her thoroughly, make no mistake about it."

He pauses, stands up.

"I'll find someone in my office who can handle this for you," he says. "I'm too close to it to handle it myself but I'll keep an eye on it. In the meantime there's an order saying you can't take any of this out of England, so you'll have to arrange for storage and the rest of it."

For the next day or two it is all oddly serene. Tibor's shipping plans are put on hold and he visits several warehouses to inspect their facilities and to compare prices. Bridget, Leora, and I stay in the flat, Bridget and I reading my mother's papers, commenting to each other as we do, reminiscing, trying to put things in some sort of order. Leora does homework, watches television. Occasionally we step out for something to eat or to go to the store.

It is a kind of limbo, but it is also a welcome, if enforced, excuse to defer returning to our familiar lives with their gaping new absence.

44

It's not that Bridget doesn't remember as much as I do. It's that she remembers different things. She doesn't remember which buildings stood where, or how the furniture at Gordonwood was arranged, or who was where at any particular time and said what to whom. My memories are always discrete, little settings with beginnings and middles and ends, while hers are more personal, more vague, nothing she could actually repeat or share.

She remembers, for instance, sitting between Helga's legs on the toilet and being taught to use the bowl like a big girl.

"You were toilet trained at eighteen months," Helga had said when Bridget told her how she'd tried to use the same trick with Leora. "How could you possibly remember?"

"But I do," Bridget had insisted. "I remember it clearly."

"That's nonsense," Helga had replied and maybe she was right and maybe she wasn't but either way Bridget could still feel it, how soft and rubbery my mother's thighs had been, how she had slipped a little between them, how they had sat like that, quietly, in the bathroom and waited. She remembered the feel of the carpet in the lounge at Gordonwood as she sat cross-legged and leaning against one of the giant tusks to watch my mother arrange flowers, the ones she used to bring each week from the Indian stalls at the bottom of Pine Street. The heap of flowers shrank as the arrangement in the vase became a perfectly balanced tower of color, and it used to leave Bridget wondering by what miracle she might some day be able to do things like that, whether it was even possible to do things as effortlessly, as tastefully, as flawlessly, as my mother did them. When people came to Gordonwood and Helga left the room, no matter who else was there, the air itself seemed to darken, would only lighten when she returned.

One day a photographer from the newspaper must have been passing as Bridget, sitting on the garden wall, handed a piece of candy to the postman. We found the page from the *Natal Mercury* among my mother's papers, and looking at it Bridget remembered nothing of the event but everything of the dress she was wearing, how it felt, even the day my mother brought the dress home for her. Her other memories were like that too; standing in a store and watching as my mother gave information to a clerk for entry into the accounts ledger, waiting on the grass outside the gymnasium and seeing my mother pull up in her shining maroon car, sitting on the edge of the bathtub the day my grandmother died and seeing my mother weeping, her own heart close to breaking, the tears running off her cheeks and onto the floor, incoherent memories that stirred her but would mean nothing, could hardly even be repeated, to anyone else.

A journalist overheard her saying at a public meeting that my mother had just addressed, that Helga would one day be the prime minister, and that had found its way into the newspaper too, the stylish, talented mother and the earnest little daughter, "good foils for each other" the journalist had written, and it was a phrase my mother used again and again, almost to the end. We found that article too among my mother's papers, carefully preserved in a little plastic packet.

Bridget's piano lessons started when she was five, her gymnastics and tennis coaching when she was six, and she was diligent in all of it, practiced each afternoon, competed with determination, and by her final year of school she was the captain of the school's gymnastic and tennis teams, and the only girl in the school who periodically played the piano with the orchestra.

"Sounds a little nerdy," Leora remarked once after, in small pieces, details of Bridget's accomplished youth had leaked out. Bridget had simply shrugged and said: "Probably, by today's standards."

There was nothing nerdy about it, there couldn't have been in such an athletic, graceful girl. At some point when she was a teenager the boys started calling, swaggering, confident boys when among themselves but suddenly so uncertain, so polite, so *clean*: "May I speak to Bridget please?" Even the surfer boys, the cool ones who went each afternoon to the south beach to ride the waves and were mooned over by the girls, each took their turn to call Bridget Divin. Regardless of who asked her out, though, she always said no, politely but with as much conviction as if this were her own decision.

"They can come here," my mother used to say. "You can swim and play ping-pong and talk. There's no need for teenagers to go running around the town unsupervised."

In the end, years later, when even my mother admitted that the rules may have been too strict, Bridget insisted that she was pleased they had been there. There was plenty of room for crushes and flirting, and opportunities for fun too, she insisted. Unlike me, who bridled at every rule my parents set and made mistakes over and over, Bridget remembers her childhood as lovely, really lovely, and peaceful too.

This is not to say that she took no notice of things going on around her. She could not have avoided sharing my mother's political views, her outrage at injustice, at the pernicious edge to the world outside of Gordonwood. It had dawned on her, slowly, what it was that my mother was saying, how unfair it all was, how rotten life was for Africans given the array of laws that existed to segregate and oppress them. In high school she joined the youth wing of my mother's political party (they wanted her to head the group but my mother had said she could only have her bottom in one place at a time, and how many hours were there in the day, after all?) and she broke the school rule that forbade politicking on school grounds by handing out my mother's pamphlets at election time. She had never broken a school rule before, of course, but she had the sense that this time it was okay, that this rule could be, should be, broken, that there was a rule that trumped even school rules.

For all that, the country's problems were remote. No one was being tortured or murdered, there were no Nazis shipping people off to be gassed. There weren't the rivers of blood one pictures in the Sudan or in Kosovo or in Rwanda. For the most part things had been the way they were for so long, would remain that way for so much longer, that there was no urgency to it. No matter how bad things were, over time it all blended into the scenery and became invisible, or if not invisible simply a part of the fabric of everyday life.

There were moments, of course, when it was not. One day they were driving in the car, Ambrose the African driver and my mother in the front, Bridget in the back, and it was pouring rain, sheets of it coming down sideways, a sea of cold water. They stopped at a streetlight and they saw, Helga and Bridget at the same time, that there was a tiny African boy selling newspapers on the sidewalk, shouting "*Daily News, Daily News,*" over and over. He was drenched, and his voice was so hoarse that he was barely audible over the rain. The water flowed off his hair and into his face, and the papers he was trying to sell had long since become a soggy mess.

"Open your window," Helga told Ambrose.

Ambrose looked at her suspiciously.

"Why?" he asked. "We have our own newspaper at home."

"Open the window and tell him to come over here," she repeated, and when Ambrose sat for a moment too long, his hands on the steering wheel, she added: "Or do I have to get out of the car and do it myself?"

Ambrose opened the window, but reluctantly, brushed away the water that cascaded in. The boy looked up at them hopefully.

"Tell him to come here," Helga said, and Ambrose had done so.

"Get in," she gestured, and when the boy did not understand and remained on the sidewalk, water running down his face, she added, impatient now with Ambrose's sulky silence there behind the wheel: "For God's sake, Ambrose. Tell him to get in."

"The Master will be angry," Ambrose says.

"I'm not interested in your opinion," Helga snaps.

Eventually then, and after more dialogue between Ambrose and the boy that Bridget and Helga do not understand, Ambrose leans across and opens the back door, and the boy gets in. He is dripping and Bridget can see, as he sits in a puddle beside her, that he is cold. She thinks about lending him her sweater but he is beyond that, would only wet it, dirty it, make it unusable.

"Ask him where he comes from?" Helga says to Ambrose, and whether he does or not and if he does how kindly he does it, is not clear from his terse sentence.

"He comes from a farm," Ambrose says, but the boy's delivery has been so halting, so broken with a shiver, that it is not at all clear what they have exchanged.

They take him back across the Berea to Gordonwood, several miles from where they have found him, and Ambrose brings him into the kitchen. Baptie gives him a towel, some of my old clothes, and something to eat.

But when it is done, when he is dry and fed and the rain has let up, Baptie has a question.

"What do you want to do with him now?" she asks, and that is the question that cannot be answered, of course, because none of the servants will have him stay in their rooms—"He will steal even my head if I am not looking," she adds—and where else is there for him to stay?

In the end then, there is nothing for it but to turn him back out, carefully dried, carefully fed, onto the street again, this time with a whole rand in his pocket and holding a packet with some of my old clothes. Bridget does not think of the wet boy again, not for years, not until one day in a rainstorm in Boston she sees a small black boy running across the street, and then she remembers it clearly, and though by all accounts it is ancient history, completely irrelevant, the memory plagues her and she mentions it to nobody.

Or this . . . . Did she not know better, even as a girl, from somewhere within herself perhaps if from nowhere else, the afternoon she is swimming in the neighbor's pool and the Coloured daughter of one of the servants, a girl a year or two younger than Bridget, maybe twelve or thirteen, comes over and sits at the side? Bridget is not paying attention, does not see exactly what has happened, maybe they are all distracted and looking away, but suddenly the neighbor's daughter, her friend, starts yelling and the Coloured girl who has been dangling her legs in the water has jumped up and run off and her friend is demanding that the gardener pour chlorine in the pool in that spot, in the exact spot, where the Coloured girl's legs have been. Bridget watches as the gardener pours in the chlorine while Ambrose, curious about the fuss next door, peers over the fence but makes no protest of any kind.

Gordonwood creaks in the wind, the salty air clouds the windows, the sun beats down white and plain. It would have been so easy to protest.

In the driveway Ambrose sits stoically behind the wheel of the car, his trademark white cloth on the dashboard so that between trips he can polish the fender to maintain its perfect shine. More than once she overhears him boasting to others about our cars, "a Humber, e'heh," he says, "the best, A Number One, and a Wolseley, from England, nice red color."

The Boswell Wilkie Circus is in Durban and performing in a large tent across from the Jewish Club. On the night it performs for Africans the servants are let off early and as a special treat, a gesture that is the envy of the neighborhood servants, Ambrose is allowed to borrow my father's car and to take them to see it. What Bridget remembers of it now, though, is not Ambrose in his dapper suit and feathered hat, not Baptie and Josephine in their best clothes, or Alfonse or the others, but us, Bridget and me and our parents, as we gathered at the bottom of the driveway to see our servants off, how for us this is a spectacle, and that we feel amused, even proprietary, as we watch them, all our familiar black figures, crammed into my father's shining Humber car and setting off in a plume of exhaust.

My mother sees things as they truly are, does not flinch from letting people know where she stands. Sometimes when she comes home from addressing one of her rallies and protest meetings, Bridget sits on the edge of the bed as she undresses and watches her, out of her smart clothes now and in a satin nightgown, cream on her face, rollers in her hair, and says, relishing the moment of intimacy, bursting with pride: "If only your constituents could see you now."

And if ever she saw a hint of contradiction, considered the notion that my mother may not be perfectly consistent in living out her views, my mother quickly dispelled it. There was the time, for instance, when she asked Helga why she left flower clippings all over the floor for Baptie to pick up.

"Why don't you just keep them in a little pile," she had suggested, "and then Baptie won't have to run around afterward cleaning up the mess?"

Helga had looked at her with impatience.

"It'll take twice as long," she had said. "And it's her job," and after that, as Bridget watched, she made the argument herself, the one my mother would have made, that there was nothing unusual in it, nothing at all out of the ordinary in any of it. My mother would have said, if asked, that people who could afford it had domestic help all over the world, that there was nothing to apologize for. Pointing it out, even, was absurd.

"There are things we should feel guilty about and things we shouldn't," my mother had said. "Having servants is something about which we owe neither an explanation nor an apology."

On election day when my mother ran for Parliament, Bridget was in high school then, the campaign had Ambrose driving voters to the polls in my mother's car. He would pull up at the polling station in the maroon Wolseley, at the wheel in his white driver's coat and hat and with a white campaign volunteer beside him, and then the back door would open and Bridget would see someone, perhaps an elderly white lady, poorly dressed, or a frail man in a safari suit, sitting on the leather seat and listening patiently to reasons they should vote for Helga and her color-blind society even as they were sitting behind the candidate's white-coated African driver. By then, of course, Bridget knew better than to raise her misgivings with my mother. The response would be strident, and in any event she was sure, more than sure, that there was a rationale for it, and that it would make sense to her if she heard it.

When Bridget began her studies at the University of Natal where my mother was a lecturer, it wasn't long before people began referring to her as "Little Helga," and snide though it may have been, it made her smile, and Helga too, and not only because they looked so alike, like sisters as much as mother and daughter people said, but because she welcomed the comparison. Between classes she would stop by Helga's little office near the Student Union and leave her books on the table along with a pastry too if she had stopped at the bakery on the corner. Sometimes, she would even sit in on my mother's lectures just to hear her speak, and then they would leave together and share a pot of tea in the cafeteria.

On the day my father died Bridget was at the university, sitting in the cafeteria, in fact, when someone came looking for her. There was a call at the pay phone and she was told by a friend of my mother's, trying so hard to keep her voice calm that she sounded frantic, to come home. She ran to the parking lot, jumped into the little secondhand car my father had bought for her and sped home in tears, almost frozen with fear, her heart pounding, and when she saw the cars lined up in the driveway, the dead calm in the garden on a beautiful autumn day, everyone packed inside, she feared the worst, the very worst, the end of everything.

But it wasn't, for her, the worst. It wasn't my mother who had died. It was my father. It wasn't the worst.

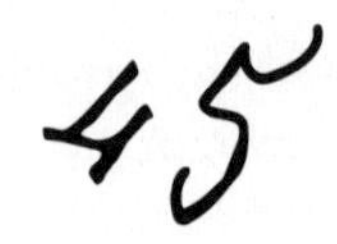

BRIDGET MET TINI MAKHATINI at a party my mother allowed to happen only three months after my father's death. The party violated so many rules and conventions that one couldn't even begin to list them, and indeed it almost did not take place because when the parents of the girl who was supposed to be having it found out that Africans had been invited they forbade the whole affair. Bridget asked my mother if it could be held at Gordonwood, and of course my mother said yes. Bridget sometimes wondered how things would have been if she had said no, but then my mother was in a bind when Bridget asked her, and Bridget knew it, even at the time. When no other parents would allow such an event at their homes, it was a matter of principle that my mother would say yes. What was her political posturing about if she wouldn't?

It was the first joyful event at Gordonwood since my father's death, the night Bridget found herself sitting on the grass with a group of people and next to Tini Makhatini, a student from the black medical school on Umbilo Road, the province's only medical school for Africans. It was the first time, she has said, that she had even met an African man socially, and it was a revelation to her to be there, to be a part of it. Tini was funny, off beat and original but mostly just funny, she has said, and elegant, and like nobody she had ever known, familiar and yet completely alien too. In the end it was Tini who persuaded her to do something more than talk, to come with him to tutor black children in Umlazi, the black township, and she agreed to do it, did it with enthusiasm, if the truth be told, not out of any great idealism but because Tini intrigued her and because, as he sat on the grass next to her and they talked, all of a sudden he was stroking her foot, just lightly, just the edges of it, and it was a small thing, exciting and disgusting at the same time, yes, honestly, to her, a white girl, disgusting, but the truth of it was that until that night, until she decided to take Tini seriously, until she shivered at the softness of his touch and noticed his long, slender fingers, what was happening a stone's throw away had no personal relevance to her and she started teaching, if the truth be told, because when he stroked her foot she thought her insides would melt.

My mother usually knew what Bridget was up to, they talked about everything, almost everything, but Tini was the first subject that had ever come up that Bridget did not share, certainly not the foot stroking, not for over twenty years, and then only with me, deep in the night in that little flat in London. It was the first time Bridget had done something she was absolutely sure my mother would have disapproved, but even so she didn't stop herself. My mother knew who Tini was, of course, but Bridget knew she gave no thought to the possibility that their friendship had reached the boundaries of what was permissible, and while my mother may have mentioned repeatedly the vigilance of the security police when she asked about Bridget's tutoring, Bridget assured her that it was all quite tame, nothing to be concerned about. Bridget was sure that my mother would have been doing just the same things had she been younger.

"Just be careful, for Christ's sake," my mother had said more than once.

So figure this. From the moment Tini touched her, from that moment until the morning she was arrested and thrown in jail, those were the most magical, the most exhilarating, the most idyllic times of her life, or so she has said. They would drive together to the African school, she and Tini, stop in the same place each time to eat the fruit and sandwiches Baptie had packed, (there was of course, nowhere else they could go to eat together,) and as they ate Tini would regale her with stories, stories about growing up dirt-poor in Zululand and yet being happy notwithstanding, anecdotes about outsmarting township teachers who knew almost nothing, about skirmishes with every kind of authority figure, and almost unbelievable stories of police ineptitude that allowed him time after time to slip through their fingers, and somehow he would also find a way to make her laugh, to turn it into a kind of comedy. Later, after she had dropped him off, her heart pounding, in some deserted spot where no one would see them to ask questions, she began to think of how her life had suddenly become, how else to put it, exciting, fun, filled with a daring and a commitment and a usefulness, and of a passion she had scarcely imagined.

It all came to a crashing stop, of course, on the day she was arrested and held without trial. Although the security police had no obligation to explain why they arrested anybody, they did tell her, and even our lawyer Morton Nerpelow who was allowed to speak to her, that it was a crime under *apartheid* for whites to teach blacks, and for anyone to teach African children things that might expand their horizons too far, but the truth is that Bridget had no idea that what she was doing was illegal, and that's the point, really, as she sees it, that although my mother's friends in London treat her as something of a comrade at arms for having been involved in the struggle, she was arrested because she had no inkling that *apartheid's* crushing laws could ever actually reach her.

"Did you know Nelson Mandela when you were growing up?" Leora asks.

"Of course not," Bridget answers. "He was in prison for treason. It would have been like knowing—and here she searches for an appropriate comparison—"Sirhan Sirhan."

When Bridget was released from prison my mother—this is old history already—drove her straight from prison to the airport, and without asking for Bridget's views put her on a plane to London and after that, looking back from overseas, first from London and then from America, the world around her had seemed quite flat and cold, quite uninteresting, and the crummy weather, the smallness of people's concerns, everything, had seemed irrelevant and for a very long time. What was the point of it, she used to wonder, of life now, of saving to buy things, of polishing a car, of planning a holiday in some cramped little bungalow by a moldy closed-in lake? How does one pretend to be interested in things that are trivial, whether taxes are seven percent or three percent or five percent, whether children must recite some pledge or other at the start of the school day, whether one's house is green or blue or small? My mother's lifelong bereavement thereafter is something Bridget has always understood perfectly. And the point is, for Bridget, that there is the smell of failure in it too, her own failure of course, how grievously she had let down my mother when she should have known better, how the consequences of her indiscretion had just gone on and on for a lifetime, and without reference to the point at which they had started.

Now my mother is dead, and it seems to Bridget that the casket that closed on her and her newly combed hair has closed on a part of Bridget too, that, like my father's collection, she has been marooned, lies inert, lacks, like my father's collection, all sense of context.

46

BRIDGET GOES THROUGH my mother's clothes, had started to do so even before the funeral, as Leora and I lounge on the bed and watch her. She wants to send the clothes, all of them, to Baptie in Zululand, and she folds them and places them carefully into a box.

"Do you think she'll wear these?" Leora asks.

"Of course," I say.

Bridget finds herself, as she lifts things and shakes them into some kind of shape, recognizing outfits, imagining that she recognizes others, wondering again what my mother would say about how things have all turned out. She sees labels she knows, Stuttafords at Field Street, Ansteys on West, shoes from Cuthbert's and the ABC, finds things in the pockets, a used Kleenex, a mint, a safety pin, that bring my mother right back into the room.

"I wish we'd packed these more carefully," she says. "We've made such a mess." With her incredulous daughter for company, Bridget goes off in search of special packing boxes for Baptie's clothes, a steam iron, tissue paper, so that when Baptie opens the box she isn't greeted by an avalanche of creased fabric.

"It's going to get creased anyway," Leora says as they begin their expedition.

"It would be disrespectful to send it that way anyhow," Bridget says. "I'd like it to start out pressed."

"You're giving her the clothes," Leora insists. "What's disrespectful about that?"

"It just would be," Bridget says.

It's hard for Bridget to believe, really, that what has happened is even possible. It seems so outrageous that larger-than-life Helga, bundle of contradictions though she may sometimes have been, can simply be no more. But her clothes, at least, with Baptie inside of them, will come to life once more, will be walked through the streets of Durban and will see the light of day, and that is something she can hold on to and look forward to.

But they must be pressed, folded, made to look like new.

47

AT HOME I HAVE a recurring dream, one in which Bridget and I are standing on the grass somewhere unfamiliar and a car pulls up, a shining maroon Wolseley just like my grandfather used to own, the one he gave to my mother when it was already quite old and faded, except that this one is owned by Morton Nerpelow, my father's adviser, my father's friend. He has come to drive us to Durban, and we know this and are waiting for him, though why it is that Morton Nerpelow is going to drive us there I cannot say. I am worried, though, that when we get home there will be nothing left, that Gordonwood will be empty, and that we may not be allowed to go inside to get our things.

Nerpelow stops the car by the verge and we get in, Bridget in the front and I in the back, and then, without saying anything, Nerpelow starts to drive, out of the city and up the highway, climbing all the while as we pass the little settlements, clusters of huts, animals, chickens, African children, some of whom wave as we go by. We drive and drive. Inside, the car becomes quite warm. We are hungry.

"How much farther?' I ask, and Nerpelow, intent on keeping the car safe on its course, does not reply.

We pass towns that I know lead away from Durban, not toward it, but I am resigned to this interminable trek, safe in the knowledge that Nerpelow knows where he is going, how to take us home. I sit back in my seat and breathe in the aroma of leather and pipe smoke.

Finally, though, I can stand it no longer.

"This is not the way to Durban," I say. "I know that for sure."

Nerpelow does not reply, his manner remains resolute, and now it is not easy, I find, in this dream, to find anything else to say. I watch Nerpelow carefully, the silver hair curling just slightly over his collar, the clouds of smoke that rise from his pipe, and realize that I do not, in fact, either trust or recognize him at all.

"I'd like to get out," I say, but then, to my regret, I see that it is my father to whom I have said it, not Nerpelow, and that my father, even as he slows the car, looks pained.

The car pulls to a stop on the side of the road and the three of us sit in complete silence.

"Why did you go away?" I demand, and sitting in the back of the maroon Wolseley I feel heartbroken, not only because we have been abandoned but because the question means that our journey has ended, that we will never get to Durban, that the illusion that we are going there could have held if only I had said nothing, gone along with it, that then we would have reached Gordonwood and everything would have been okay.

The dream in its subtle variants always leaves me restless. Usually I leave the bed and go to sit in one of my breezy white rooms. Often I remain there until signs of sunrise gleam through the walls of glass.

Now, in London, Bridget has a dream too, and it is this . . .

Finally, finally, there is nothing more to be done and we can go home. It feels so strange to her, so impossible, to be walking through Heathrow with Tibor and Leora and me. She looks down at her new shoes and she feels both surprise and shame. We have been trapped in a strange country and suddenly she has succeeded in freeing herself, but even so she knows that in time she will look back on this, on the day her confinement ended, on the memory of her feet as they cross the shining floor tiles, and that it will have an ambiguous feel, triumphant but still humiliating, filled with relief, but also wrapped in secrecy.

She is at a loose end, lacking direction, has no idea what she will do when she finally reaches home, if there is any food there, if she even has the keys to her own house. Now she imagines herself there in Boston, sitting at a table with nothing to do, no medication chart to update, no nurses to supervise, and she knows she must go out, anywhere, if only she could focus on it and make her decision. She cannot call her mother—the telephone will not work—and this makes her, even as she sleeps, breathless. She shows her passport, checks her baggage, chooses her seat, and then she waits, alone now, for her flight to be called. The wait is endless. The hours pass, the lounge empties and fills, flights leave and arrive, and still she waits.

We once lived, or should I say that once upon a time we lived, at Gordonwood, a tangled tower of stone and brick and wrought iron high on the ridge, our parents and Bridget and I, looked after by five Africans who lived in a shed at the bottom of the garden, protected from everything outside by our color, by my father's supposed steadiness, by the illusion of wealth, by the sparkle of my mother's short-lived but tangible celebrity.

"How odd to feel orphaned at forty-five," she says to my mother, lying unwell under the covers in the dimly lit waiting room.

It is like a dream to think back on it but it was all once quite real, everything happened just as she remembers it, and yet time has made her memories seem absurd and has turned the act of remembering itself into an embarrassment.

"Tell Baptie I won't be down for dinner," my mother says and pulls a blanket high about her face. "You play Mummy at the table."

Worse yet, even the most absurd, the most appalling, the most shameful of her memories, has taken on a new cast, has taken on, oddly, surprisingly, irrationally, indeed, a *goldene* shine. When she looks back on it, indeed, on being cast out in the manner she was, on how she and then our whole family was forced for one reason or another to leave Durban behind, it does not seem any longer to be simply a matter of being cast out of Africa, but of having fallen from grace, of having been thrown out of Eden, unceremoniously and with no hope of redemption.

ZULULAND

1

Eben pulls up in front of his mother's house—the small brick house with its corrugated iron roof that the Divin family built for her when they left to go overseas—and finds her sitting in a chair on the veranda. She is fast asleep. Her blue hat with Kangol printed on the front has tilted to the side.

She keeps chickens in her yard. They scurry about, pecking at the ground.

"Wo, Mother," he calls as he steps from the car. "Are we going to Durban today or are you going to sleep until the sun goes down?"

It has become a ritual, almost, this waking his mother each time he visits. She lolls in her wicker chair, starts at his voice, straightens her hat.

"I can sleep until the sun goes down next year," Baptie answers. "Now that I am old, that is what I do best."

They both laugh. It is warm, will be hot, the air at her house smells of old wood smoke, earth, the chickens scratching about in her yard.

"As true as God," she adds. "If you do not wake me I will sleep my whole life away, sleep until I die."

"But not today," Eben says. "Today you are going to Durban for this thing, this white people's thing. Today you will not sleep at all."

"No," Baptie answers. "Today I am happy. Today I will see them all again, all the people from the past days."

"And this time," he says, "you are not staying at Umlazi with Aunty Mabel in her room there?"

"No," Baptie answers firmly, her voice strong as if she thinks he is doubting her. "This time I am staying at the Beverly Hills white people's hotel in Umhlanga Rocks."

"There is no more such a thing as a white people's hotel," he says quickly, though he knows what she means. "Do you know what a place like that costs?"

"They will pay," she assures him. "They will pay for everything."

"Do you know what that place costs?" he repeats.

"What do I care?" she insists. "They will pay."

"Three thousand rand a day," he tells her.

"What nonsense is that?" she exclaims, and then she sits heavily back in her chair. "Yo, yo, yo," she says. "For one day?"

"Yes," Eben says.

"These white people who live in the overseas, I think they have a lot of money," Baptie says. "Before there was always not enough."

"Who said you were staying at this hotel?" Eben asks.

"Danny and Bridget told me this," she answers. "In a letter."

Baptie has, and this astonishes Eben, a servant woman of her own. For a few rand a month she has hired an old woman, a dark, shuffling, skeleton of a woman, who sees to her needs, makes her tea, sweeps the bare cement floor of her house. This woman, Balekile, which in Zulu means "ran away," also sits on the veranda, the two of them in chairs drawn side by side, dozing in the shade of the trees.

She wakes now too.

"*Sawubona,* Eben," she says.

"Good morning, Baba," Eben replies. "Does my mother still pay you while you are both asleep?"

"You stop your rubbish questions," Baptie says.

Even Balekile smiles.

"It is good to have sons," she says. "I am sorry I do not have a son."

Eben has sons, two sons, or he had two sons because now it is almost as if one of them does not exist at all. Eben had a son named Danny, or, as this Danny now insists on being called, Mgobozi. Baptie chose her grandson's name when he was born, Danny, after the son of the white household where she worked for almost her whole life, but now this Danny has rejected his name, renamed himself. His name is now Mgobozi, he says, Mgobozi, like King Shaka's greatest warrior.

"And who is this Danny anyway?" the new Mgobozi challenges his father one evening. "The settler son of a family that bought and paid for my grandmother's life as if she were a slave? What else, that I should be named for him?"

Eben sits like a stone to take such insolence from his son. He, and not only he, a whole generation of fathers, is becoming used to it.

"You know nothing of that Danny," Eben replies. "Maybe he is a great man there in the overseas."

"It is shameful to be named for a settler," Danny says, anger filling his face. "I must choose my own name, and it will not be in memory of a settler."

Eben lets it pass, lets it pass for months and months. Eben thinks it will pass and then be forgotten altogether, but that does not happen. Now the anger is a part of his life, of Mgobozi/Danny's, even of his mother's. For Eben it is the source of a deep, raw sorrow, like a constant pain in his chest. Neither Baptie nor Eben talk about this Danny in front of Balekile. They do not need to.

She, like everyone else in Gingindlovu, knows everything, the whole story, from start to finish.

EBEN WORKS FOR the KwaZulu-Natal government in an office in Eshowe. He is head of the office now, promoted after the white man who sat on the position for years was made to retire by the new government. He earns well, enough for himself and for his family, needs to ask his mother for nothing. His house is sturdy, like hers, and larger too, and his wife Julia too has a good job working as a nurse's aid. He would help his mother if she needed help, but her needs are so simple, her life is so slow, that she seems to have almost no needs at all.

If Eben were to be absolutely truthful he would have to say that he does not work hard. When he first started out and had to prove himself, he did more than his share of the work while his white boss, Hans Theunis, an Afrikaner, pushed papers around his desk and returned from lunch ruddy-faced and smelling of tobacco and beer. Now he sees no reason to do more than is necessary. Things work—or they don't—in Zululand, and he could set himself on fire in the courtyard and nothing would move any faster than it was going to anyway. So why do it? Theunis, he has heard, after he was pushed out from this job, took the only work he could get, driving overseas visitors in a minibus.

The son of a domestic servant, Eben is well aware that he has made a journey to be here. And more is to come. With luck, and of course with God's blessing, his daughter Bridget, almost twenty now, will go even further. Bridget wants to be a doctor, and she will be one too. Baptie's granddaughter will be a doctor. He has already visited the medical school in Durban and spoken with the people who run the place. Coming to this point in life, being where they are, Bridget going to the university for sure, Silas and Helga, his other two, working in Durban and doing well, and with a little money for the things they need, for more too, has allowed him, forced him really, to think about the past. Before it was all too rushed, too much of a struggle, too vivid in the present, to spend time just reading books and sitting on the veranda, a cigarette in one hand and a cup of tea in the other, doing nothing.

Perhaps it is because of his Danny that he has been forced to think so much, to try and understand things that can defy a father's understanding. And how does a man enjoy his good fortune when he has caused his son to suffer as he has done? Anger such as the anger he once had, even quiet anger, can filter down, sink, like blood in water, to those who are there to receive it.

"So what great thoughts are you having?" his wife will ask as she comes up the stairs to the veranda, still in her white clothes from the nursing home, pausing before she goes inside to change and to prepare the dinner.

"I am wondering," Eben says, "how things got to be the way they are."

The veranda has a polished red floor, a cement wall that he himself has painted white, and three chairs made of wicker bought from a man who came door-to-door with about twenty just like it, all tied together and balanced on his back.

"And this is interesting to you?"

"It is everything to me," he tells her.

She stops halfway through the door.

"Would you like some tea?" she asks.

"Yes please," he says. "I would like some tea."

Eben, married to Julia in her orderly, well-run house, sits on the veranda and drinks his tea. He has come so far, pulled himself up so far from where he started, but the further he travels the more interested he becomes in things that have already passed. Sometimes he asks himself why it is that his mother has such power over him, why the thoughts of this frail old lady count for so much in his world. When his children were born and each time she made her suggestion for their names—more than a suggestion, really, in the hospital she just said it, said what each name would be—he had accepted it almost without thinking. Even Julia, in so many ways a modern woman but deep down traditional too, did not argue too much.

"Why is it," she had asked, "that your mother thinks she will choose the names of all of our children?"

"It is something I offer her out of respect," Eben had said. "We have discussed this. Many Zulu sons do that," and he proceeded to list other families where other grandmothers had chosen their grandchildrens' names.

"That is all from the old days," Julia, so old-fashioned herself in so many ways, had insisted, but in the end she had let it go. Why pick a fight about something so important to her husband and so unimportant, really, to her.

So now they have a Silas, to be kind, his mother had said, and a Helga, to be clever, clever and also loved by people, a Bridget, because Baptie said that she would one day grow up to be beautiful, and she has, and a Danny, to be lucky and also to think for himself. Julia had hoped, finally, with her fourth, that she might choose the name herself, but her mother-in-law had been adamant, and Danny was a nice enough name after all, like Daniel in the Bible, Daniel who survived the lions with Shadrach, Meshach, and Abed'nego. As for him being lucky and thinking for himself, the problem with this Danny of theirs was that these two things, it seemed, luck and thinking for himself, had canceled each other out.

Baptie is fussy and old now, of course, but still she is powerful, much more powerful with him than he is with his children. His children, not only Danny but the others too, treat him more like a companion than a parent, agree with him, disagree with him, and then they go and do whatever they want while he, who is much older than they are, finds himself with no choice but to respect his mother's wishes. Perhaps it has to do, he thinks, with how old you are when the world around you changes. If you are young enough you can change almost completely. If you are not, if you are old, you do not change hardly at all.

He thinks these things as he sits on his *stoep* and drinks the tea that Julia brings him. Like Theunis and the whites for whom he once worked, he has acquired a taste for tea.

EVERY SECOND MONTH Baptie takes a taxi to Durban to collect her small pension from Mr. Morton Nerpelow, the Divin family lawyer. She says she does not trust the post office but Eben suspects that she goes to Durban because she enjoys the trip into the city. Usually Eben drives her to the taxi rank, waits until she is safely in the little white minibus, and then, once the bus has rattled off out of the parking lot, goes on to his job. Sometimes, after she has climbed on board and taken her seat there by the window, he looks at her slim figure and is saddened by how frail she looks. Those minibus drivers nowadays are an aggressive lot. They drive too fast, fight about passengers, carry guns more often than not. But mostly he does not worry. His mother is a survivor.

Today Eben is driving his mother to Durban in his own car. He will take her to the hotel to see these white people, but first he himself has business with Mr. Nerpelow, and because he does not know this man, his mother must take him there and say who he is.

"This is a nice car," Baptie says. "It is not good to eat all your money, but it is good to have a car."

"I do not eat my money," Eben replies.

He has never, not even as a boy, asked his mother for money. He could not have anticipated, though, that when he was grown, when every tradition dictated that he should be supporting her, that then, from the heavens, she should have her own money, her small pension which makes her independent even of him, there on the outskirts of Gingindlovu.

"You eat your money," Baptie says firmly. "And your wife eats your money."

"Okay, mother," he says. "I eat my money."

Eben is driving a white Toyota, a thirdhand car or maybe a fifth-hand car for all he knows because he knows almost for sure that it has been stolen. He has not had it for so long, bought it a year before from a man who swore up and down that he had owned it for his whole life but who did not have paperwork stretching back even to yesterday. Eben can easily see this car in a driveway, in the home of a white family, ready for a white woman to take her children to school. He can just as easily see a young man, a black man with a knitted cap and a stocking pulled over his face, slipping over the electric fence, cheating the lock to open the door, beating all the other tricks the whites now have to save their property.

It is not that Eben thinks crime is a good thing, in the long run. Theft, you can say, is also a kind of violence, and he is opposed to violence. Especially now, he is opposed to violence. But in South Africa there has been so much crime that has gone unrepented.

"Tell me again, Mother," he says, gently now, and also he is curious about this thing, has not been able to explain it even to his wife. "What is this thing these people have come to Durban for?"

"Honestly, I do not know," she says.

"What did they tell you it was?"

She is wearing clothes that have been sent back for her from overseas by the dead woman's children, but the blue hat is her own. He cannot see the dead woman wearing a floppy blue hat with the word Kangol printed on the front, to cover her hair.

"They said it was something for my Madame, but they did not say what."

He lets this go. The dead woman was her Madame. Nothing he can say will change this.

"But she is buried already."

"She is buried already. But in the overseas."

"So what are they doing now in Durban?" he asks again.

"I told you," she says impatiently. "I do not know. I think that something is not right with them since my Madame died, that they are doing this. I think that something is wrong."

"What is wrong?" Eben asks.

"I do not know, but I see it in their letters. I am an old, stupid woman, but if I can help them, I will help them."

"What can you do for them?' Eben finds himself asking. "They are rich. They have everything."

"God has blessed me with these people," Baptie says. "God has a reason for what he does."

She is tied to these people, this white family long gone from South Africa. They write letters to her, send her pictures, money, always money, and when she speaks of them her voice is wet with longing. They are generous for sure but they are also rich, for sure, so rich that they must not even notice what they give to her, or he doubts they would give as they do. They could not have changed so completely in one lifetime.

"What did you do to these people," someone has asked her, "that they treat you this way? I worked in Durban too, but the family I worked for, I don't know where they are, even if they are dead or if they are alive. But these white people of yours, they don't leave you. They don't forget."

Eben has the same question. What makes them so generous, from so far away, and after so much time? He saw it all once, back when he was watching his mother washing and ironing and cooking, running up and down the stairs with trays of tea and food. Sometimes these people would see the tray arrive, keep talking, say nothing at all as if nothing had happened, as if a tray had appeared in front of them out of the air.

Sometimes they complain, even the children, about something that has happened on this tray that has come to them from the air.

"Why orange juice? I said apple."

His mother lived then in a small room at the bottom of the white people's garden. To get there you walked across the grass and down the driveway, past the swimming pool, a swimming pool for this one family only, through an arch, down a dark little passage. There at the bottom of the passage were all the servants' rooms, including his mother's. He can see this room as if he were still in it, were still a young boy in short pants visiting her, the spiderwebs under the rafters, the smell of paraffin from the little stove, the cracks in the walls. On bright nights the moonlight would shine right in.

"Why don't they fix this broken wall?" he had asked her. "Maybe this whole room will fall down soon?"

"You ask too much questions," she had replied.

"And why can't I stay here with you always?"

"You know nothing," she had insisted.

Now, all these years later, for three thousand rand, one night in that expensive hotel, his mother could live like a queen in her village for months. But what would happen, he wonders, if they offered her the money and then let her stay with Auntie Mabel in the black township of Umlazi anyway?

Honestly, he does not know what she would decide.

4

BAPTIE IS NOT A PERSON who dwells on the past, her own past that is. Eben knows this, although these days, after she hears that the white woman has died in England, she spends a lot of time dreaming about her days in Durban. Of her own past, of the years before she went to work in Durban, she says nothing. Before, if he had asked her anything about those times she would have shaken her head, looked at him in exasperation, replied by wanting to know why he was asking such foolish things. And now, now, he thinks, she simply would not remember.

She looks so old, wrinkled like she has been folded into the seat. When she got into the car for this journey he watched with sadness to see how she struggled with the seat belt. She pulled the shoulder belt under her armpit instead of over it, and then across her chest, and if he had not leaned over to untangle her, knocking her hat into her lap in the process, she would have tied herself in a knot. This simple thing has never been a problem for her before.

She is in her seventies, his mother, seventy-two or -three she says, always with an odd laugh as if not knowing for sure will expose her as ignorant.

"I think maybe seventy-five," she says. "The same exactly as my Madame."

"Did nobody write it down?" he asked once. "In the hospital? In a book? Somewhere?"

"What rubbish hospital? What book?" Baptie said, laughing. "You know nothing about how it was."

"How was it?"

"There was no hospital and no book."

"And if you were sick, or something went wrong?"

"Then you died, for sure," Baptie had said, and wandered from the room.

He has tried, Eben, to picture what it must have been like in Dikinyana, his mother's village in Zululand, in nineteen thirty-something, with no hospital and no book, not even within contemplation. In the little villages even now, the clusters of black people's houses that he passes as he drives to his job in Eshowe, it must have looked then as it does now. More roads now, and paved, and towns like Eshowe and Empangeni with their whites and Indians that have grown and grown, but you didn't have to go far, just a stone's throw really, to see how it had once been. No electricity even now, no stoves or refrigerators or televisions. No indoor plumbing. No indoor anything.

"Did you go to school?' he asks his mother.

"Do you think I am so stupid that I did not go?" she replies suspiciously.

She tries to make it clear to him over and over that she simply does not have the time for this inquisitiveness.

"I don't think you are stupid," he says patiently. "But was there a school here then?"

"Of course," she says. "Same as now."

When he was very young, first when they were all at home and his father was dying of black lung disease from the coal mines, and then afterward when his mother went to work for the whites in Durban and he was sent to live with his grandmother, there was no real school even then. There was a place they called a school, a room with a mud floor and an iron roof, but it was not a real school.

"What school was it?" he presses her. "The same one there by the big *umKhuhlu* tree?"

"Not that one," she says. "Before that."

There was nothing, he is sure of it. He thinks of the children who were his friends when he was a boy, the ten or fifteen of them in their mismatched uniforms, cross-legged on the floor of that room, reading a single textbook in turns, puzzling at its meaning, examining everything as if it held a clue of some sort, as if it offered answers to questions they did not even know how to ask. He sees them sometimes when he drives by Dikinyana, his old friends, trudging, in torn clothes, single file, by the side of the road, laborers, farm workers, laborers home from the mines in Newcastle or Johannesburg, unemployed.

These straggling lines by the side of the road, they are part of the scenery of Zululand.

"Sawubona," he shouts, recognizing someone, lowering the window, slowing to a stop.

The cars shoot by him.

"*Yebo* Eben," his friend will respond, dropping his bundle, his wood, whatever, to the ground. "How does it go with you?"

So they will talk, glad to be meeting, but each time, soon, Eben becomes aware that his friend is looking carefully at the car, wondering, sizing it up. There is, he sees, an edge of deference in his friend's manner, not a real respect but a grudging, made-up thing. You have crossed over, is in his old friend's manner, with your car and your suit and your job inside a building. You have become a *baas.*

He finds himself, thinking of this as he sits on his red-floored veranda, tea in hand, becoming quite agitated.

Gingindlovu is just one street, really, Indian traders in their shops, white farmers in their pickup trucks, Africans in their broken huts on the outskirts, all of them swept by rainstorms and heat and dust and breathing the smell of animals and the smoke from fires in the grass. It is, for the most part, old government, new government, quite unchanged from the days when he was young.

THE OLD ROAD from Gingindlovu to Durban, not the new one where you must stop and pay toll money to a booth in the middle of the road but the one that was always there, the one that didn't even have tar reaching to the edges until a few years ago, follows a bumpy path from the low hills, through the cane fields and clumps of trees, south and away from the smokey villages of Zululand.

Eben has traveled this road many times but even now, even in his own car, an employee of the government, a taxpayer, a voter, as they approach the Tugela River where Zululand ends and Natal begins, he gets an old feeling, a sense of being on edge, a hangover from his long-ago trips to see his mother at her work. He knows of course that the police are not waiting for him, that nobody can stop him and demand to see his Pass, that these feelings of being a trespasser should long ago have been put to rest. But it is not so easy, when something is made so much a part of you when you are young, just to flick it away.

His mother, there in the seat beside him, clasps between her knees a shopping bag with clothes and the things she will need for her stay in the city. She leans forward as he drives, watches the road as if she needs to do something, maybe to peel it away, before they can go forward.

"Sit back," he says. "Relax. Perhaps you want to stop and get something to eat. Perhaps at Zinkwazi Beach. There is a restaurant there near the sea."

"I have brought sandwiches for us," Baptie says. "Balekile made them."

"We can go to a restaurant," Eben suggests.

"And eat my money?"

"I will pay."

"You. Me. It is the same thing. Eating your money in a restaurant is for white people."

They used to come by taxi to visit his mother, back in the old days, Eben and his grandmother. Back then it was not like it is now, or even like it was with his own children who had to be in school every day. Back then when he was a boy you could go or not go to school and nobody cared, and so whenever his mother sent the money for him they would go, he and his grandmother, just leave for a few days or for a week and the teachers didn't care.

There was just one rickety van then, the same driver making the trip down to Durban and back in one day. He would collect his fares in front of the bottle store in Gingindlovu and then they would set off down the bumpy road, stopping only when people on the side of the road waved them down, whether there seemed to be room in the van or not. When they reached Durban the driver would go straight to the market on Berea Road and drop everyone off, and then he would load up for the return trip and leave before he attracted too much attention with his cargo of rumpled passengers fresh from Zululand and Gingindlovu license plates. Hurrying out of the taxi, standing there on the sidewalk surrounded by crowds of Durban people, Eben always felt very simple, almost ashamed among these cocksure Africans that he was just a country boy who knew nothing.

"One day I will live in Durban too," he told his grandmother.

"No," she had snapped back. "You will stay in Zululand. There is nothing for a boy in Durban except to work in a garden or to carry things for white people in a factory. In Zululand, even if you have nothing, you do not have to sell your life to the whites."

She had paused, watched for a moment the crowd moving around them.

"Amakhafula," she said.

Those who have been spat out by Zululand, the word meant, were homeless, gone to work for the whites far from where they belonged. *Khafula.* Like Kaffir. Even the whites didn't use that word much any more.

No matter. She was old and knew nothing. He would get a Pass, he dreamed, a job too, stay in Durban for as long as he wanted. He would earn money of his own, buy a car, have nice clothes, be a part of all the bigness, the buying and selling and colorful language and immodest behavior.

Having glimpsed it, he could not be stuck forever in the red mud and backward ways of Dikinyana.

6

HE COULD SEE IT ALL from behind the hedge, the huge Divin house, the swimming pool sparkling in the sun, flowers everywhere, cleanly cut grass, canvas shades flapping slowly over the windows. Even the hedges are decorated with flowers, orange creepers that drape across the top and spit their yellow petals down onto the grass. Birds splash about in a concrete bowl, monkeys climb from the trees and scamper about in the garden, an unused raft floats in the swimming pool.

Ambrose, the driver, when he is not taking someone or doing some errand in the cars, works the machine that cleans the pool. Eben leaves the servants' quarters and walks across the grass to him.

"Can I try that?" he asks.

Only Ambrose and the whites are allowed to touch the swimming pool machines.

"What will you do if you break it?" Ambrose asks.

"How can I break it?"

"People fresh from the farm can break anything," Ambrose says, but he passes Eben the handle of the machine, a giant plastic broom, and holds his arm as Eben sweeps it through the water and along the swimming pool floor.

"Have you ever been in this thing?' Eben asks.

"It is for the whites," Ambrose says, hardly hearing.

Ambrose is a ladies' man, meticulous in appearance whether he is wearing his white driver's coat or, on his afternoons off, on his way to

Umlazi in a suit and a hat with a feather in its band. He is always polite to Baptie, flirts with Emily, the housemaid, wears cologne. When he passes Eben he spars with the air, invites Eben to land a punch, avoids it easily, leaves only a trail of fragrance. Ambrose is saving his money so that one day he can buy a used car. He has pictures of Peugeots taped to the wall of his room.

"Peugeot cars are the best," he says. "You can drive to France and back in a Peugeot car."

Sometimes, in the evening, carrying his pail of hot water to the servants' bath—there is no hot water there; if you want hot water in your bath you must carry it in a bucket from the kitchen—Ambrose jumps in the air and swings his leg over Eben's head, all the while carrying his bucket of water so that for a moment it seems as if he will kick Eben and scald them both, but then, always, he is past, still carrying the bucket, like a cat even, with not a drop spilled.

The Master Silas asks for his advice.

"Do you think we should trim those hedges back?" he will ask and Ambrose, examining the thing carefully, will say whether they should or whether they should not. The Master will usually do what Ambrose has decided is best.

On most mornings when Eben is in Durban, he passes the time sitting in the sun and thinking, or wandering about near the concrete path that goes past the servants' rooms and leads to the toilet. He cannot leave the property because he is not supposed to be in Durban at all, and in any event there is no place to go. The bus that comes to the bottom of the hill is red, for whites only, and it is a long walk to Umbilo Road, where the green-colored busses for the rest of the people are. It would be better too if there were people there his age, boys or girls, but there are not. None of the servants, not in this house and not in the others nearby, are permitted to have their children with them.

Each morning his mother and the others go up, across the grass, to the house, and they stay there doing their jobs. Only Ambrose, whose duties leave him with time to sit and talk, to watch things, to nap in the sun, comes and goes between the house and the servants' quarters. Around eleven o'clock each morning he comes to the path behind the hedge, folds his white coat and driver's cap into a neat pile, and then he squats, his bread and tea in front of him, and eats his breakfast. As he eats he talks, about cars, about women, about how much things cost. He is saving for his car but still he wants to buy a hi-fi for his room, a new suit, a gold watch.

"What is the whites' school like?" Eben asks.

"Like everything white," Ambrose says, laughing. "Very nice and filled with money."

Of the whites in the house, the Master and the Madame, the boy Danny, the girl Bridget, Eben thinks very little. His life and that of the whites might as well be on two different planets whose orbits touch, and only slightly, at the kitchen door. Eben watches them through the hedge sometimes, the Master leaving for work, the Madame, always in a hurry, the children in their school uniforms getting in the car with Ambrose, and in truth he doesn't think much of it. You cannot compare yourself to a bird that flies when you have no hope of wings, or to water, or to the sun.

On some weekend days they all come down to the swimming pool in their bathing suits, even the Master with his bony, white legs, and Eben watches, from back there behind the hedge, as they lie in the sun. They talk and they laugh, friends come and visit, they read their books, they fall in the water, and then they come out shining. The girl's legs are gold, like honey, long and strong, and her hair, as she twists it to squeeze out the water, shines like a sheet of gold. At lunchtime his mother and the others come from the kitchen carrying trays of watermelon and salad, sausages, chops, cold drinks, ice cream, everything. The boy and his father stand at the *braaivleis* to cook the meat, but Ambrose has already lit the charcoal, laid everything out on a tray, waits in case he is needed. Everyone has their backs to Eben hiding there behind the hedge, but Ambrose sees him, knows he is there, may even wink.

When the food is cooked, the whites help themselves.

"You have hidden talents," someone says to the Master as she tastes the food.

"Baptie's job isn't in any danger," the Master replies, and they laugh.

Smoke from the cooking meat lifts in the air and reminds Eben of home.

Eben crouches behind the hedge for a whole afternoon as the white boy plays soccer with his friends. If just once the ball rolls in his direction he will stand up and kick it back, show that he can play soccer as well as any of them, better even. When they are done they jump, all of them, into the swimming pool, in and out, diving and bombing, sending sheets of water onto the grass. A large spray rises over the hedge and rains on him. He feels the coolness of the water on his skin.

TWO TIMES IN HIS LIFE, just two times, Eben finds himself, as if he is dreaming, standing on the inside of that house.

This is the first time.

He is watching from behind his hedge as Danny hits a cricket ball into the air, and then walks across the grass to get it back.

"You can throw it," Danny says, talking in Eben's direction.

He knows Eben is there. It has made no difference to him. Eben could be there or not be there. It is as if there is just a pot behind the hedge, a pot or even a monkey.

Eben stands up and walks slowly around and onto the grass. He waits to catch the ball when Danny throws it. They do not play cricket in Gingindlovu. No bats. No expensive balls. Eben does not catch it. The heavy ball falls through his fingers onto the grass.

"Just throw it, like this," Danny demonstrates.

Eben tries, and the ball sometimes goes where it should but mostly it does not. After a while it is clear that the boy is bored.

"Come," he says, and starts walking in the direction of the house.

"Why?" Eben asks.

It is the first time, really, that they have talked to each other at all.

"I'll give you a cricket ball to practice with."

Eben does not want this cricket ball and his mother will kill him if she sees him where he is not supposed to be, has made this clear more than once. But he follows anyway, keeps a few steps behind, sees with dread that the boy is leading him in the direction of the kitchen where his mother will almost certainly be.

When they reach the house Eben stands at the door as Danny goes inside. He hears him opening the refrigerator.

"You coming?" Danny calls.

Eben steps into the house. This feeling, the feeling of being where he should not be, the one that persists even to this day, that maybe his arms will fall off for the size of the transgression, that it cannot go unnoticed or unpunished, floods through him. The inside of the refrigerator looks like a picture.

Danny fills two glasses and hands one to Eben.

"Here."

The servants do not use the white people's plates and glasses. They use enamel mugs without saucers, enamel dishes with black painted rims, steel spoons and knives, all from their own drawer. Not even the same food.

"Come," Danny says.

Eben follows because he does not know how not to. His legs just carry him then, across the kitchen, through the doors that the servants use to take food to the table, along a passage covered in a thick red carpet that catches your feet as if it were mud. Everything is so clean and new. As he walks he sees pictures and chairs, more things than these people could possibly need, all the richness he has imagined, more than he has imagined. And he is surprised to see, these things are so out of place, things that are familiar to him, a spear and a cowhide shield on the wall, drums, a beaded shawl, a knobkerrie.

The white boy sees him lagging, turns.

"Do you want to look at these?" he says.

"Why do you have them?" Eben, daring, asks.

He does want to know this, and it overcomes his shyness, the feeling that he is in hot water. Why would this white family have Zulu things all about their house when they could have so many other things, good things, rich things? These are not beautiful. They have no value.

"My father collects them," Danny says.

The white boy doubles back and walks slowly with Eben along the walls lined with shelves and chests, explains what is there, tells stories, all these stories about Zulus as if Eben is a visitor, not to the house but to the whole place, someone from far away. The stories swerve in and out of what Eben knows, has heard before, are very strange to hear from the mouth of this white boy.

Eben, startled, sees a witch doctor's headdress, complete with its goat's bladder.

"What are you doing with this thing?" he asks.

"I told you," the white boy says. "My father collects them."

"But when the *sangoma* dies," Eben says, "this must be buried with him. This has his power."

Danny looks at him blankly.

"We don't believe things like that," he says.

Eben can see in the boy's face that he thinks his questions very primitive. He feels very primitive as they make their way across the house and up the stairs, wide stairs covered also in a thick red carpet with handrails on each side. Eben has never seen wood so polished that it gleams like water. Upstairs he stands at the balcony railings and looks down on the houses, the buildings, the ships floating in a line at the harbor entrance. This is the city, then, as the whites see it, spread below like a toy on a tray, something they can lift up and put down any time they please. He has seen nothing before in his life now that he has seen this house.

The boy takes an old cricket ball from a shelf, and then they are going down the stairs again, the big wooden stairs with their thick carpet, across a room and another room, so many rooms except that this one is the biggest of all, huge paintings on the walls and there, at the other end, a giant fireplace. Towering over it on each side, curving up like huge white arms, are elephant tusks.

Danny sees him staring.

"Do you know what those are?" he asks.

His manner has pride in it, Eben sees, as the white boy, the cricket ball in his hand, looks first at him and then back at the tusks. Eben knows what they are. But why, of all things, would white people want elephant tusks in their house?

"They come from Zululand," Danny says, "and they are very old."

"How old?"

"Hundreds of years," Danny says. "Do you know who used to own them?"

"Who?"

"King Shaka."

Eben stands, will remember forever how he stood at that moment, and watches the tusks as if they might move on their own, rise off their stands and float across the floor. That King Shaka, that one, the father of the nation, the one his grandmother goes on and on about, still mourns, who once owned everything? That King Shaka, who is almost too big to have lived at all? Even that, his things, the whites have, here?

"Why did he give them to you?" Eben asks.

And then Baptie, passing by on some errand or other, spots her son through the open door.

"What are you doing here?" she demands.

"I brought him in," Danny answers.

"Get out," Baptie yells. "I don't want you in this house."

As Eben, cowering, begins to leave, Danny moves toward Baptie and confronts her.

"What are you doing?" he demands. "He hasn't done anything."

"You shut up," Baptie shouts and, roughly now, pulls Eben forward. "You don't understand anything."

So Eben leaves, and for the moment he is glad to be leaving. Something in him has been changed, even he knows that, and some part of him regrets that he has seen what he has. He does not know either, then, for how long, and how strongly, he will remember that afternoon. Only later, long after he has passed across the grass, under the arch, down the bleak passage, gone back into the world of the servants, does he find the questions that insert themselves still, still today, today as he is driving his mother through the countryside on his way to Durban.

How can it be that his people's things have been lifted away like this, that in the dark servants' quarters the Africans live with brick walls and empty cupboards while pieces of their past are held above them in the white people's house like trophies for display? What can be the stories these people believe as they look at these things, all no more remarkable to them than a dead animal's head mounted on a plate, while the people who once made them drift quietly at the edge of the room in white uniforms, serving soup and carrying plates?

"Baptie, your dinner was delicious."

"You can clear the table now, Ambrose."

"Emily, are the children in bed yet?"

Here is how Eben comes to be in that house a second time.

He has never broken the law before, never defied a white person, but he knows because he has heard them talking in the servants' quarters that the house is not properly locked at night and he is drawn back, must go back. Ambrose has said more than once that if someone really wanted to they could carry out the whole household, the family too, before anyone, even the dogs, knew what was happening.

He asks Ambrose about the tusks. Is it true? Were they Shaka's?

"I heard the Master say this many times," Ambrose answers. "And in his business in Maydon Wharf he has things like those tusks, things you cannot imagine. But something is not true because you say it many times. I don't know where they come from."

"Danny said they were from King Shaka."

"Maybe they were," Ambrose says. "But Shaka was not an elephant. If they were his, he had a thousand more like those. A million more, even. It means nothing to me."

His mother undresses and lies in her bed, but he stays in his clothes and on top of his mattress. He has found a flashlight in Ambrose's room, and it is hidden behind the door. His eyes are wide open.

"You can't sleep?" Baptie says.

"I'll sleep," he says.

"How will you sleep?" his mother demands. "You are going to lie in your clothes all night?"

"I will change," he says. "Later."

An hour passes, maybe two, and then he rises quietly, stands, takes the flashlight. His mother is breathing deeply, on her back, her face to the wall. He steps outside, into the passageway with the cement floor, walks alongside the wooden fence with a gate that leads into the neighbor's yard. The cement slopes and it is wet and cold to his bare feet, but he edges along the fence and towards the archway that will take him from the servants' quarters.

"How much do the elephant teeth weigh?" he has asked Ambrose.

"More than you can carry," Ambrose had answered, looking at him strangely.

Everyone is asleep, he is sure. He believes he can sense this from the quiet shimmer of the grass, the black gape of the windows spread across the face of the house, the perfect stillness of the shadows that line the swimming pool. Only the nightlong crying of the crickets breaks the silence, but as he crosses the lawn his heart begins to beat loudly, to hurt even within his chest, drowning out even that. Sometimes Ambrose, who thinks of himself as the protector of the family, equal in function to every person there except the Master himself, will prowl about if, late at night, he hears a sound that he thinks is out of the ordinary. Hopefully tonight he will sleep like a tree.

"What are you doing?" they will say if he is caught. And what will he give as an answer? Even he does not know for sure what he is doing.

One set of windows rattles when he tries the handle, but they are locked. One hard pull and they will open, he can feel it, but then he will have broken the latch. Are these people not scared of burglars? In Gingindlovu there are burglars. This house would be empty in one night if it were left there. Upstairs they are all sleeping, the Master and Madame, Danny, his sister Bridget. They sleep as if there were not a thing in the world that could ever harm them, and maybe they are right.

He tries another handle, this one to a tall door that leads from the room to the veranda outside, and almost to his regret it turns and the door swings open, just opens as if someone were on the other side pressing. Thick curtains press on him as he goes in and, carefully, he moves them aside. He is in the dining room, velvet chairs, a table with carved legs and a big silver bowl standing in the center, walls lined with pictures and statues. If the white people wake and come downstairs they will call the police and he will go to jail for sure. They will come and see him standing surrounded by all the things, the silver and the paintings and a sleeping white girl upstairs, and he will be finished. They will not believe him, not even Ambrose.

He does not turn back, walks past the chairs and the statues, sees on the wall a bracelet made of leather and beads, sandals like they still sometimes wear on the farms, a case filled with blades from the heads of assegais. Some of them are broken. Others are so old they would be useless, are not even clean. And then he sees, to his right, all the way at the end, through the open doors that lead from the dining room, what he has really come for. They gleam in the dark as if a light is shining on them. He walks slowly, quietly, until he is right there, sits on the floor, safe now because there is no more movement, no more creaking boards, and holds his hands out to them.

It is here, as he looks back, that Eben loses track of what he knew then and what he knows now, what he thought when he crouched on the floor of that great room and what he thinks as he sits and daydreams on the veranda of his house in Gingindlovu. Either way he has come to see the man with perfect clarity. Shaka is tall and his skin is smeared with grease and ocher so that he glistens like a rich and polished wood. He stands in the sun as they bring his herds before him, animals so numerous they cannot even be counted, a rolling sea of wealth moving slowly and in perfect harmony. Behind him is his royal enclosure, his *isigodlu* with its women, the most beautiful in Zululand, the great kraal *kwaBulawayo* where he exercises power over life and death, over who breathes even, a place bristling with regiments of men, strong, vigorous, trained to perfection and filled with energy. Everything is his, the land, all the land, all the rivers, the Tugela, the

Umlali, the Umconte, north to Delagoa Bay, every elephant in creation, every plant, every animal, every person.

He is still in the house when the sun begins to break into the sky, the sounds of the birds to sweep in waves through the silence. Majesty and pity flow together in his veins.

THE ROAD FROM GINGINDLOVU to Durban, the same road that comes from Ulundi, the last Zulu capital, and passes through Eshowe, once *kwaBulawayo,* cuts through the sugarcane fields like a river. Driving along it can make a person feel like he is surfing on sugarcane, just floating along under the sun on the endless hills of cane.

"You drive very well," Baptie says. "I don't know where you learned to drive so well."

Eben feels it each time he drives along this road, this feeling of floating on the cane. He feels too his closeness to the things that are buried in the cane, bones and spears, private treasures, somewhere, too, the lost *Inkata* of the Zulu nation. King Cetshwayo, the last real king, the last one with power, had this *Inkata* with him when the English arrived to take him captive. Eben imagines this *Inkata,* that secret throne watched over by the king, the nation's magic coil filled with the essences of dead kings and vanquished enemies, with particles of wild animals and the blessings of special potions. When the king enters and takes his seat on the *Inkata* his body fills with the strength of the past and he becomes empowered to act with all of history on his side. Mgobozi would be able to tell it all, to recite the whole thing, chapter and verse, as if it were the bible itself, this story of a stolen Zulu kingdom.

And Shaka? Shaka is a theme park now, there off to the side of the road from Gingindlovu to Durban.

"Have you heard of Shakaland, Mother?" he asks.

She looks at him as if he is delirious.

"Why should I think about that white people's place?" she answers.

When the English took Zululand they divided it up and then handed it over to the settler government in Natal, left the Zulu sacred places, even the bodies of kings, to molder like old tires under farms given to white people. People who had been living on the land for generations had to pay rent to these new white farmers. Even the king's son Dinizulu had to pay money to stay in his own royal house, and white farms with their white names were brought to cover Zulu history like a blanket.

It once made him so angry, these thoughts, but Eben's anger, he would have to say, is now also covered, subdued under a blanket of years. He wishes it had always been like this, that his anger could have been set to one side earlier, covered over, because if there is any one thing that he would have done differently in his life, any one thing he would change about how he had raised his children, it is this: When his own children were young, babies even, back in those *apartheid* years when everything about him seemed to have been designed by the devil himself, he did not watch what young ears were hearing. His son Danny, this Mgobozi they have raised, is in jail, this boy who was supposed to be lucky is in jail, and Eben is convinced that this is his fault.

Just driving now, looking at the fields on either side of the car, the cane, the huts, the footpaths trod down hard into the red mud, reminds him of this, of the things underneath, of the things he said, how they may have been heard.

"Now why is it," Julia asks over dinner, all the little ears lined up around the table, "why is it that this *Inkata* is so important to you? It is finished, the past, gone by."

Eben looks at her over the table. They are eating a meal of samp and beans, staples almost every night, and a chicken, not a luxury for them any longer but when he was a boy, back then, chicken was as rare as a holiday.

"It is who we are," he says simply.

"No," his wife insists. "Who we are is where we live, in this house, who our children are, what we do each day. That is not who we are. It is not who I am."

"No," Eben says. "We have been robbed, and there must be redress. The robbers will never agree to give back what they have taken, but one day it will be taken back from them whether they are willing or not."

"So what are you saying?" his wife demands. "That you want now something that belongs to white people because a hundred years ago they took it away from someone you do not even know."

"Perhaps," Eben says. "Not me myself. I have enough. I have everything, I think. For other people."

"No," his wife insists. "People have moved on. What was taken cannot be restored. There is no more peaceful, herding country life any more, not in Zululand, not anywhere in the world. That is where these people who dream of bringing back the past in South Africa are wrong. Maybe one day there will be freedom here, but it will be freedom for all people to live their lives in peace, not one freedom for us in Zululand, one for the Xhosa people there in the Cape, one for the Venda, one for the Tswana, one, one, one, in bits and pieces. That is what the whites have tried to sell us, what *apartheid* wanted, to separate us out into little groups. But we are not little groups with our own dead kings and past dead glories. We are South Africans and that is all, and freedom is freedom and that is enough. A person cannot go through the world combing through history and making right every wrong. It is too late, and too tangled, and people want just to live their lives."

She pauses, suddenly bashful at how brazen she has been.

"I want just to live my life," she says, softly, conciliatory.

And then he had answered, certainly, and all along all the little ears were drinking it in, chewing on it, thinking on it, taking their sides. His four children, all of them, had listened and learned, but only three of them do what Julia has always wanted them to do, live their lives. The fourth, his son Danny, this Mgobozi of theirs, though he has come to disdain his father in the process, took in every word nonetheless and when the people with their fiery talk of a reborn Zulu nation, not one big colorless South Africa but a new and vigorous nation of Zulus, when they came to Gingindlovu, they made sense to him. They were saying things his father had said for years, after all, and when Eben tried to revise this, to say to him now that no, things have changed, freedom is freedom, there is no Zulu freedom separate from the freedom Mandela is bringing, it was too late, it fell on deaf ears, as if Danny could not accept that back then his father had spoken in anger only, more to let anger free from his body than to be believed word for word.

Danny is in prison outside of Durban and Eben feels every day of his life that it is because of him that his son is there.

"But you yourself are not guilty of anything," Julia has said, and more than once.

"You yourself did not hurt anybody."

Julia's family are devout and hardworking people. Her trim, orderly simplicity was what drew him, a clumsy country boy, to her in the first place. Her great-grandparents left Zululand for Pietermaritzburg almost a hundred years before, were *Kholwa,* early converts to Christianity, almost middle-class city people with city tastes. Her grandfather, Julia has told him, would have been a lawyer if he could have been, would have had an office there in Pietermaritzburg, become a successful man, but the white government stamped on the dream back then, even before the *apartheid* days. That isn't what they wanted. They wanted labor, hard labor in the gold mines and in the cane fields and the factories. If things had been different, Julia's people would long since have been like the English, English in every way except for their color.

Julia leads the choir of the Zionist church in Gingindlovu. Sometimes, when she sings her gospel songs, it is possible, Eben thinks, to believe in God.

10

Eben pulls into a clearing on the side of the road. They have stopped at a stand to buy fruit to eat with Baptie's sandwiches, and it is almost midday. Now they can hear the sea but it is hidden behind thick rows of trees.

As they eat Eben notices, not for the first time, that his mother is missing several teeth. She chews on one side only, moves the food about, washes it down with tea. She eats like an old person, concentrates, doesn't talk much.

"When did you lose those teeth?" he asks.

"They just fell out," Baptie says, and laughs. "One day I woke up, and they just fell out."

"If you ask the Divin family, they will pay for false teeth," Eben says.

"They will pay for everything," Baptie says. "For everything. If I ask, they will pay. And I have my own money too. I can buy my own stupid teeth if I want."

"Why don't you, then?" he asks.

"Stupid teeth," his mother replies.

She chews her sandwich, takes a sip of her tea.

"I have a question for you," Eben, watching her, says. "Are you not ever angry about things in this South Africa of ours, how it used to be, and how it still is mostly? Are you not angry with the people who made it like this?"

"Made it like what?" Baptie says without looking up.

"Who took most of Zululand for the whites, the whole of South Africa, and made us servants in our own place."

"You are not a servant," Baptie says. "My people have been good to me. God has blessed me. God is very good."

"But for your whole life, until Mandela, everything was so bad," Eben says. "Everything was there to make your life difficult."

"The Dutchmen did this maybe," Baptie concedes. "But the others, the Madame and the Master and their children, and their friends, they always treated me well."

"But they didn't," Eben says and he is about to add things, to add his litany of their shortcomings, when she interrupts.

"You know nothing of how it was," Baptie says. "I do not like barking dogs, but I am not angry at people for nothing either. They were not perfect, but God did not make any person perfect. I am not angry at people for nothing."

It is a warm day, and bright, and also a lazy day. He leans against the wheel of his car and watches the water in the river below as it rolls slowly toward the sea. A gull flies overhead. A truck rumbles across a bridge several hundred yards away.

"Look here, Eben," she says suddenly. "I am not a stupid. I know what I have seen and how things have to be. But Mandela is gone now, and these other politicians they are selfish bloody fools. Everyone in Zululand is dying of this AIDS and they do nothing, just drive fancy cars, live in big houses, make speeches. The hospitals have no medicine, the people are dying like flies, there are *tsotsis* waiting to rob you everywhere. And the nice white people have all gone now. What did my family in Durban do wrong? For what I should be angry to them? Only children think that life is so simple, black and white, not that there is anything in between."

Their sandwiches are finished, their wrapping paper refolded, the thermos back in the little wicker hamper.

"I have a question for you," Baptie says, "for the person who is so filled with questions this morning. These are questions that Danny, the white Danny, wrote to me from America. I thought I would just forget them—I am an old lady and I can forget anything I want to—but you ask, so I will ask."

"What questions, mother?'" Eben asks, curious.

"Danny said in his letter that his mother told him that once, when you were boys, he and his friends locked you in the Master's shed and you were crying and shouting and they would not let you out again. I don't know why, after all this time, but Danny wants to know if you remember this."

"After all this time?" Eben says, puzzled. "But in any case, I don't remember."

"You don't?"

"No," Eben says, but he is not being fully truthful. "Maybe it happened," he adds, "but I don't remember."

"He said one other thing," Baptie says.

"Yes?"

"He told me that he thinks the reason why he never saw you again after you went to school, that proper school in Eshowe that the Master paid for you to go to, was because one day you came to the house in Durban and saw him in a soldier's uniform. And that you were angry for him being in the Boer army. Is this true?"

"I saw him in his soldier's uniform one time," Eben says. "But that was nothing to me. He can do what he wants."

The water in the river is brown, turbid, slow moving.

"Let's go mother," Eben says. "Or we will be very late."

11

AMBROSE IS STANDING at the entrance to the servants' rooms and calling his name.

"Eben," he shouts. "Come on, man."

Eben hears him, waits to be sure he has heard correctly, comes out of his mother's room and up the dark cement passageway. Ambrose has not called him with a note of urgency before.

"What?" Eben says as he reaches him.

Ambrose, standing there in his driver's coat, has a look of enjoyment and mischief in his face.

"The Master has brought something home. You must see it."

"What?"

"Come," Ambrose repeats.

Eben follows him across the garage, out into the sunlight on the whites' side of the hedge. He is startled to see, standing there in front of the house, next to the swimming pool, not only Danny but the Master too.

"This is Baptie's son?" the Master asks.

"Yes," Ambrose says. "He is the same age as Danny, and also the same size too."

The Master looks at Eben and nods. And then Eben sees that Danny is wearing a set of shining boxing gloves and holding two others by the laces.

"Ambrose said you might want to try these with Danny," the Master says.

It is the first time he has spoken to Eben directly.

"They're my birthday present," Danny says. "It's my birthday tomorrow."

Eben says nothing. He knows boxing. Every Zulu boy knows how to box. It is something they do in Gingindlovu.

He looks at Ambrose. Ambrose is smiling broadly.

"You can try them," he says to Eben. "I said to Danny, you are the same size."

Eben doesn't move, looks at Danny standing there pulling on the strings of his gloves, at the Master smiling, at Ambrose.

"No, it's okay," he says, and steps back.

"Go on," Ambrose says.

Eben has boxed a thousand times in his life, has boxed with boys who are big and small and tall and short, but in all his life he has never boxed with a white boy, has never even touched a white boy.

"It's okay," Eben says.

"I won't hit hard," Danny says. "They're new."

"If he doesn't want to, don't force him," the Master says.

"Go on," Ambrose, insistent now, his lip curling, repeats.

The sun is shining directly overhead. It is a very warm day and Eben is perspiring. Danny has taken off his shirt and it lies in the grass and Eben takes his off too, drops it so that it doesn't touch any part of Danny's. He steps forward and takes the gloves. They are soft and smooth, smell like the inside of that house. He slips one on, and then the other, and Ambrose, standing right next to him, his chest touching him almost, ties the laces.

"I want to see how well you fight," he says to Eben in Zulu. "Whether you are a man."

"Okay," the Master says, and at this point other people, Alfonse the house boy, Emily the maid, are standing at the bushes that lead to the kitchen, watching.

Eben, his gloves now tightly laced, turns to face the white boy. Danny, hopping as he pops the air with his right, protects his face with his left, moves in, lands a blow on Eben's ribs. Eben feels almost nothing. Maybe the Master sees this now too, but everyone stands, just watching. Danny steps in again, punches again. Again Eben feels almost nothing.

And so they go on for a little while, Danny stepping in, hitting with his right, bouncing back, protecting his face, Eben taking the blows, still unsure what the nature is of this permission to hit a white boy.

"Come on, Eben," Alfonse calls from the bushes. And in Zulu, "*Bulala,*" kill.

The Master understands.

"Watch it," he says turning, and sternly, and Alfonse giggles.

Eben turns to see what Alfonse will do and that is when Danny moves in with a left, hard to the jaw, knocks Eben's face sharply backward. The leather stings his skin and for a moment he sees only white.

"You can hit him," Ambrose says. "You don't have to worry."

"You can," Danny says, breathless, dancing, landing another blow.

There is a splash. The white girl, uninterested, on the other side of the garden, has dived into the pool, begun to swim quickly backward and forward. Danny lands another punch on Eben's face.

"Hit him, dammit," Ambrose says.

But now something is happening inside of Eben's body. He looks at the white boy, lean, smiling, standing there in front of him, and something close to hatred rises in him, contempt, fury even at the white body darting in and darting out, punching in a flash of red and black, pulling back. Slowly, almost blindly, Eben steels himself, waits for an opening, and then when it comes he opens up, punches with his left, his right, again and again until he sees blood on the boy's face, a scared look in his eyes, and how easy this has been enrages Eben even further until he is raining blows on the boy and the boy's gloves are simply now held over his head as Ambrose and the Master step in, each taking an arm, tearing him away from his carnage even as Baptie comes running, apron flying, from the kitchen.

Eben sees the Master only one more time after that afternoon, and Danny, who must go to the hospital for stitches, he avoids with a sense of dread and apprehension.

12

WHEN THE TROUBLES CAME, back in those days before Mandela was released but when it was clear that the young people would pull the whole house down if something did not change, Gingindlovu was not the worst place to be, but it was not removed from the troubles either. And trouble came upon the town so suddenly, Eben thinks, like a strong wave from the ocean that slams at the beach without any warning at all. Trouble came so quickly, the young people became so angry so fast, so irredeemably, so unreachably, that no one, least of all his Mgobozi, was left untouched. The elders, Eben too, could only stand back and watch in awe.

"Why are you not angry?" his son Danny asks him over and over, his voice brimming with contempt. "You, and your parents too and even theirs have been like mules in your patience, and for what? Look at you. You have nothing. White people come from Europe and take everything, and you act as if that is God's way and it makes me ashamed. Ashamed for you."

To this Eben does not know how to respond. All the children talk this way to their parents. Sometimes when Eben directs his son to do something, Danny replies, an edge of surliness in his voice: "Yes *baas*."

"Do you know what Shaka should have done with your bloody ivory?" Mgobozi on another day yells at him. "I am sick of your stupid stories about it and that bloody house. He should have used it to buy a cannon, one box of ivory for one cannon, I think, and then one shot and boom, all the wagons, all the Boer wives in their bonnets, all the ignorant, flat-faced Dutchmen who think we are little more than animals, and also the red-neck English in their red jackets, no business here, flying in small, white pieces through the air."

He pauses.

"Boom," he says again, his face inches from his father's.

He is right, the children are right. But for Mgobozi even freedom from the whites, the end of *apartheid,* is not enough. Even this new South Africa does not, in his eyes, restore what was stolen, and so he sits stuck there in the past—Daniel Dhlamini on the court docket—stuck to rot in a stinking jail cell in Durban, in a jail cell even now that the country has changed and black men instead of white are running things. Perhaps Mgobozi heard something different when Eben was talking because otherwise how could he take the story of the tusks, the story Eben loved to tell about how he had stolen into that house to see Shaka's tusks for himself, and bend it all out of shape? How could he take a bedtime story about King Shaka and build on it and build on it until it led him to kill a man, a black man, because he thought it would make him free.

This is what haunts Eben, the thought that it is his own reckless talking that has caused all this trouble, that it is for *his* anger that Mgobozi believed that the cause of Zulu freedom required him to kill one of Mandela's African National Congress men. The man, so Eben read, though only later when it was much too late, had come to Gingindlovu to ask the people to let go of their dreams of a reborn Zulu kingdom, to leave their *Inkata* movement, and to join this new South Africa of Mandela's, to ask for votes. Just to ask for their votes.

"Don't you see, Eben," Julia says over dinner, there in the old days, before the trouble even, but with Danny listening to every word, "that your anger is based on romance only. The past is not the paradise some people like to think it is. This was not a Zulu paradise spoiled only by the whites. These kings were tyrants. Many people left Zululand to live with the whites because it was better there than here under the rule of the kings. People did not even own their own bodies in that Zululand of yours. And, of course, they did not know Jesus at all."

"They did not need Jesus then," Eben answers, and Julia looks at him harshly, and then at the children.

"Everyone needs Jesus," she replies.

When the African National Congress man came to Gingindlovu to ask the people to vote for Mandela, Mgobozi and two other boys hit him about the head and neck with the blades of their hatchets, at night, outside of a restaurant where he had gone to eat. Eben can see it clearly, the man filled with food, wiping his hands on his trousers, walking to his car, three boys waiting, hatchets.

"Come to dinner," Julia calls and he sees the man again, lying on the ground with blood all around him. "And wash your hands first."

13

Now the road begins to widen, to become smooth. To their left are the big hotels, rising from the far-off line of bush, hazy in the wet air of the sea. They pass a shopping center, new and bright, see the clean signs pointing this way and that, Umhlali, Umhloti, Glen Ashley, smart white places. They see the roofs of rich houses with views of the ocean, more and more buildings, the hotels closer together, gardens like parks.

"So Eben," Baptie asks as they approach the city and the road widens further into several lanes, the tall buildings of Durban right before them. "Why do you think that Mr. Nerpelow can help us to bring Danny home from jail?"

Eben has told her that this is why he wants her to take him to the lawyer, but still she does not know what can be done. There was a trial, many pictures in the newspaper, and then nothing, years of nothing, bits and pieces of news about her grandson who sits day in and day out in the dark of a jail cell until one day he will die. She knows Eben has been thinking about his son the whole way down, and so has she, but she has not asked this question before now because sometimes when Danny's name comes up, when they are eating, once after church, even if they are just sitting somewhere talking, Eben becomes very silent, and even the air around him becomes dark and heavy. Even now, though it is the first time either of them has said his name in this car, he has been with them all the way, in the car, in the air, on the road.

"I don't know, Mother," Eben says. "This Truth and Reconciliation Commission, this thing of Archbishop Tutu, they considered cases like Danny's, and if they decided that if what happened was part of the struggle, not really a crime at all, there was a way out for people like Danny. A long time has gone by, but maybe there is still a chance. If others did a crime but it was part of the struggle for freedom, if they told the Commission everything, and were truthful, they were pardoned. That is what they tell me the law says. Danny did not come forward then, but maybe there is something that can be done. That is why we must talk to this lawyer. Bygones are bygones. Danny must confess, and then if he does, if he confesses to this and apologizes too, maybe he will come home."

"Bygones are not bygones," Baptie says. "I want Danny to come home too, but a man is dead. For his family there is no bygones." She pauses and looks across at her son. "In any case," she says, "why do you think he will confess? He has never confessed to this moment."

Eben pauses.

"I think there is a lot of paperwork that will have to be done," he says. "And that it is not easy to do it without help."

"But will he say yes?" she asks again. "He said before he would not."

"That is what I will find out today," Eben says. "I think he must. What he did, it was wrong, even if so many other things that were going on were wrong too. Many white people from within the system, who did terrible things, have confessed and gone free. It is time for Danny now."

So many white people had confessed and gone free, but for this to happen for his Danny, for Mgobozi, he is going to need help, and that will cost money. Eben has an idea where this help and money will come from, even as this does not seem to have been a problem for anyone else. In fact everyone, it seems to Eben, has confessed and gone free. He watched this on his television night after night. They asked their questions and the witnesses answered, and with each question and each answer he winced, shifted in his chair, wondered what it meant for his Danny, for the future.

"Why do you torture yourself?" Julia had asked.

"It is something I must do," he said and he found himself shrugging, as if he did not know exactly why he must do it. "Not everyone suffered equally for our freedom," he added. "At least we should know about those who suffered more than we did."

He used to watch this thing of Archbishop Tutu on the television. The hours would pass and he would stay riveted to the pictures, but it was also unsatisfying, left him groggy with too much television watching and deeply unsettled. Such hideous things, really, and then when the questions were answered, the worst of crimes revealed, the worst, really, murder and torture, of women and of children, the perpetrators went free, and simply because they said they had told everything. Why did telling about it let you go free? Who will pay? How will the people get their land back? Why, when it was over, did everyone just go home again, the rich to their rich houses, the poor to their poor ones? What will have changed?

"Come and see this," he says to Julia. "This one you must see too."

She sits on the sofa beside him. One of the lawyers on the television is asking questions of a man who was on one of the *apartheid* death squads.

"How many people did you kill that day?" the lawyer is asking.

Julia sits quietly beside him.

"Eight Bantu," the white man replies, defiantly, in Afrikaans. *"Ag Bantu."*

"Bantu" was how the System referred to Africans. It meant "people" only, denied Africans any identity but that of a living thing.

"Maybe nine," the man adds. "I don't remember."

"You don't remember?"

"No."

Now the television camera shows a picture of the people who are in this chamber listening, pans over black women with scarves on their heads, young children. Some are weeping.

"So tell us then," the lawyer asks, "when you were finished killing these eight or nine people that you do not remember exactly, what did you do with the bodies?"

"We burned them," the white man says, "in the *veld*."

"Where in the *veld*?"

"About fifteen miles outside Vereeniging," the man answers. "In the *veld*," he repeats.

"So tell me then," the lawyer asks, almost matter of factly, "how long, constable, does it take to burn a human body?"

There is a slight rustling in the room where this is happening. Eben and Julia sit in silence.

"It takes about seven hours," the man answers, and then he adds, helpfully. "Some of the body goes quickly into ashes, but the rest of it, like the skull and the leg bones, these take longer."

"And you, what did you do while you were waiting for these bodies to burn away?" the lawyer asks.

The white former policeman pauses, thinks for a moment.

"Well," he says, "we played cards."

There is a pause, the whole television set is frozen as the lawyer stands there, the witness stands there, the crowd sits so still the screen looks as if it might be a photograph.

"Seven or eight hours is a long time," the lawyer says at last. "Did you get hungry? Did you eat?"

The policeman looks at him as if this is a stupid question.

"Yes," he says. "Of course. We were there a long time."

"And," the lawyer asks, "what, constable, did you eat?

The white man answers: "We made a *braaivleis*."

A barbecue. Julia is beside him. His shirt rubs against his back. A shuffling sound comes from the television. He pictures a body on fire, the skin peeling off, the muscles curling as they burn. He finds himself wishing that Danny were there on the couch with them because there is something he would like to say to him, something he plans to say to him, something that is more important than anything he has ever said to his son, to his son or to anyone else. There is a time for anger, he would like to say to Danny, even for fury, and he understands his son's anger, is proud of his son's anger even if he does not agree with how he has expressed it. But Julia and his mother are right as well. There must always be a time for forgiveness. It is the only way to think. It is the only way to be civilized.

It is the simplicity of this equation, that some things can never be put right, that has made it clear to Eben, and he plans to tell this to his son when he sees him, that a person cannot spend his whole life being angry. Life cannot be only a big accounting with wrongs remembered and carried forever. When Mandela came from prison with no anger after all those bad years of sweat and exile he showed no anger at all. And this is not only Mandela's lesson but someone else's too. Even the sacrificial lamb has to forgive. Without forgiveness there can be no salvation. There cannot be a constant reshuffle of everything, a carrying backward and forward between people as history, all on its own, changes the rights and wrongs of all things.

Perhaps then Julia is right also that it is only God, really, in the end, whose judgment counts. Either way, whatever it is that Danny has done, whatever violence he is capable of, it is time for him to come home.

14

Eben and Baptie are almost there, turn onto West Street where Mr. Nerpelow, the lawyer, has his offices. Baptie has led him this far, left here, right there, but now she is confused. The street signs are missing, and she cannot be absolutely sure that this is the right corner.

"This is West Street," she says. "I am sure of it, even though I have not driven here in a car for a very long time. But where are the signs?"

Eben shrugs, waits for her guidance.

"I don't know," Baptie says, but this is the building. I am sure. This is the one."

Eben pulls to the curb and looks up at the tall building. He can trust Mr. Nerpelow, he thinks. The Divin family would not have handed their affairs, everything they have in South Africa, to a man who was not fair and did not know what he was doing.

He finds his heart beating quite hard now, as if he is going in for an exam or standing outside a courtroom where someone's fate is being decided.

"I have decided something today," Baptie says, as they sit in the idling car. "I have decided about something I am going to do."

"What is that?" Eben asks. "What have you decided?"

There is a note of resolution in her voice.

"You know this Baptie rubbish," she says. "My name. Baptie."

"That is your English name," Eben says.

"No," Baptie says. "It is not my name. My English name is Beauty. My parents called me Beauty. My Zulu name is Ntombifuthi, which means 'a girl again,' but my parents called me Beauty in English."

Eben is confused. His whole life he has heard her called Baptie by the whites, Baptie this and Baptie that, even in the white stores in Gingindlovu.

"It was Beauty," Baptie says. "But then when Bridget the first born of the Divins, came, she could not say this. She called me Baptie and it was funny, and everyone, the Madame and the Master, they laughed and they called me Baptie, and soon everyone forgot my name was Beauty and called me Baptie. It is the Divin's name. Before that time, no one called me that."

"I didn't know that," Eben says, looking at her, amazed, and then he adds: "Is this one of your secrets then, mother?"

The look on her face suggests that she thinks his question is very foolish. Her glasses have slid down her nose, are perched at an angle as she looks across at him.

"I have been thinking that I must have my name back," she says. "My parents called me Beauty in English. That is my name. That is what I have decided."

"Who will call you Beauty anyhow?" Eben says. "Everyone in Gingindlovu calls you Aunty, or by your Zulu name."

"I must tell them, the Divins," Baptie says. "Bridget and her little one, and Danny, and the others in Durban, that my name is Beauty. It is not Baptie. You should not spend your whole life with the name given to you by a baby who cannot speak."

"No mother," Mgobozi's father agrees. "You should not."

IN THE AFTERNOON there is a strange thunderstorm, rain while the sun is still shining brightly, what they call a "Monkey's Wedding" in Gingingdlovu. They have left Mr. Nerpelow's office not sure if they are satisfied with what they have been told, and then Eben has decided, since he is in town and it is the right day, that he will go and see his son too, go and visit Mgobozi in that living tomb he is trapped in. He drives to the prison in Westville, tells his mother to wait, and goes inside.

When he returns to his car he finds that his mother has fallen asleep, is slouched to one side with her mouth wide open. The car's windows are foggy from the rain and the humidity, but he can see, standing at her door, that she has taken off her shoes, made a pillow of her sweater, that there are small beads of perspiration on her lip and forehead.

He taps on the window and she stirs. He sees her searching for the handle, tries to open the door himself, sees that it is locked.

"There," he mouths, pointing, but it is futile. "Wait."

He opens the door with his key, and she looks up at him, her face suddenly anxious.

"What did he say?" she asks.

The Durban-Westville prison is a stark place, all chain fence and dirty cement, heavily guarded.

"He is growing old in there," Eben says, not because he meant to say it but because this is what has struck him most forcefully, what disturbs him most each time he sees his son, how much older and thinner he looks. "He is a young man and he lives in a cage. He does not look well."

"What is the matter with him?" Baptie asks, something suspicious in her tone, something she remembers about people in her village who had become suddenly old and thin. "Is he sick?"

Eben shrugs.

"I don't know that he is sick or not," Eben says. "But I think that his heart is sick, and there are no doctors in that place who can take care of that. I gave the guard fifty rand just to be sure he gets the food he is supposed to get, but whatever I do, nothing will be right until he can come home again."

"What did he say about that thing of Archbishop Tutu?" Baptie asks, fear now in her face. "Did he say he wants to do this?"

"He said he is ready," Eben answers and then he runs his hands over his face, over the top of his head, stands for a moment looking upward as if the branches of the trees above him, the birds that are beginning to gather noisily for the evening, the sky itself, have the answers to all his questions.

16

THE SUN IS SETTING when they reach, at last, the road to Umhlanga Rocks, pass by the new shopping center, approach the tall bright buildings that stand along the edge of the ocean. Eben is tired, more preoccupied than he has been all day, must still drive back to Gingindlovu, but as he coasts slowly downhill to the Beverly Hills Hotel, to the white people who are waiting to see his mother, the clean buildings, the colored lights in the little village with its restaurants and shops, intrude to remind him that outside of his little bubble of worry life must go on.

"These people," his mother says suddenly, "they all left and then they did not come back. And now they have come back."

Inside the car it is dark. He waits at the stop sign as several people pass in front of them. There is a black man in overalls carrying a paper bag, a suntanned white couple holding hands, two domestic workers in pink pinafores and white aprons. There was a time when his mother wore clothes like that every day and he thought nothing of it.

"What are you saying?" he asks.

"I don't know what they want," she says. "Perhaps now they are ready to come back."

Eben releases the brake and the car starts to coast down the last stretch of road to the hotel. Up ahead he can see the parking lot, even a doorman standing in front of the hotel in his smart khaki uniform and helmet. He does not make the mistake some people make of thinking that just because a person is white therefore they have everything always easy in their lives, but he cannot even begin to imagine what life must be like for these people. He does not know, even at this stage in his life, what things are like inside that hotel. Why look when you cannot afford to touch? Why think about things that are out of your reach? There are blacks there too now, he knows it, the newly rich ones, profiting from this Black Economic Empowerment that means a small group of people connected to each other can grab big pieces of what used to be owned by the whites, just for themselves, for themselves alone, with no sharing even though they say the right things, talk of sharing. There once were rich whites and poor blacks. Now there are some poor whites, and a much smaller number of very rich blacks. For him, not much else has changed.

But he can go into this hotel, if he wants, and that is something. He pulls under the portico of the hotel and a doorman steps forward to open his mother's door.

"Good evening," the man says, so politely that Baptie does not for a moment realize that he is speaking to her.

"Sawubona," she says.

"Are you Mrs. Dhlamini?" the man asks.

"Yes," she says.

"Welcome," the doorman says. "Mr. Divin asked me to keep an eye out for you."

"He is here?" Baptie asks.

"Inside," the man says and he adds, looking at Eben: "May I park your car, sir?"

Eben is anxious to get back on the road, to leave without a fuss and to make his way home, back to Gingindlovu, back to Julia.

"No," he says, and to his mother: *"Sala gahle."* Take care.

She leans over and looks across at her son sitting so resolutely behind the wheel.

"You're going?" she says.

"Julia is waiting."

She looks at him for another moment and her face is quite without expression.

"You're going?" she repeats.

And then, just for a moment, as his mother straightens her dress and the doorman holds out his arm to steady her, he is visited by a memory of everything from that place and all at once, of the slippery touch of the polished furniture, the feel of curtains, the fragrance of the dust and the moisture on things, of the dried flowers in their bowls and the thick carpets underfoot. He remembers suddenly his mother's dark room with its cracked walls, her starched pinafore hanging behind the door, hints in the air of paraffin and grass and smoke, and the dreams of ox hides and the giant ivory tusks and others things well out of reach, of how things used to be and how they are no longer. He is surprised by the tiniest pull of a strange and unfamiliar longing.

He will stay, but only for a few minutes.

DURBAN

1

MORTON NERPELOW, on his way back from lunch, catches a glimpse of himself in the window of Stuttafords department store.

"God," he mutters. "I'm so bloody old."

One moment, he thinks, you're a schoolboy in a blazer and short pants, and the next an antique hobbling through the traffic.

"Am I a caricature?" he asks his daughter. "One plays the game, mixes with those one feels comfortable with, obeys the rules, and suddenly, without warning, one is told that one's whole life has done nothing but give offense."

"You're too sensitive, Dad," she answers. "You can't take any of this personally. It's the times."

The times, good and well. Here's what he sees in the storefront glass: An old man in a rumpled suit, a sheaf of papers under his arm, going about his business as if all were just hunky-dory, business as usual, one white face in a sea of brown ones. Too sensitive indeed. Must the whole place fall over, he wonders, before anyone acknowledges that something is awry?

To make matters worse, very soon he will face something of a moment of reckoning. Soon a little secret of his, something that is quite at odds with the way he has conducted himself as a person and as a lawyer for almost five decades, is doubtless going to be aired. He does not actually regret what he has done.

Everything else has changed. So has he.

EACH WEDNESDAY, as he has for years, Morton Nerpelow lunches at the Durban Club. As he walks from his building on what was once West Street, crosses Smith at Gardiner, turns briskly onto Durban Club Place, he looks about as if he were taking inventory. Less than a hundred and fifty years ago there was nothing here but sand dunes and mangrove trees. As he sits on the Club's veranda and looks out across the grounds he still marvels at it. Just forty white families then, and the idea that the makeshift little settlement could one day grow into a great city must have seemed preposterous.

Just look what had been achieved. From a few huts on the Point, Farewell's little settlement at Congella, Fynn's on the Bluff, to the day they laid out the first streets of the city was just sixteen years, a heartbeat really, but once civilization took root it was unstoppable. Mud huts were replaced by houses of iron, and then by sturdy buildings of brick. Where there had once been a dusty postman's shed there now stood an architectural masterpiece, a great hospital flourished on the very ground where all there had been was a crude infirmary.

Bridges, power lines, highways, all of it, by any standards, a wonder.

Could anyone disagree?

And yet when he tries to convey this, his pride in it, to a luncheon companion, he has the sense that he is barely heard. It is at these times, more than ever, that he has the sense that he is a caricature, ineffective, fulminating, perfectly obsolete.

"Did you know any of this?" he asks. "The history of it. What an achievement it's all been?"

The Club's Indian waiters stand against the wall, able to hear everything but expressionless.

"Didn't really," his guest answers.

Once the harshest of it was behind them, the worst of the wildness contained, the early settlers found elegance and time for the pursuit of leisure. There were balls held in emptied stores, bathing at the new safety enclosure on Back Beach, money was found for a theater, a botanical garden to rival the best in England, an impossibly ornate City Hall modeled after the one in Belfast. Even the problem of the harbor sandbar, when the engineers put their minds to it, was solved with dredgers and specially outfitted tugs.

"Very few natives in Natal in those days," Nerpelow says. "Mostly refugees from the predations of the great Shaka and his half brothers."

A waiter approaches and offers second helpings. He knows, it is his job to know, Mr. Nerpelow's preferences. Nerpelow pays no attention as food is placed on his plate.

"Of course it's all being revisited and revised," he says. "But facts are facts. Can one dispute documented facts?"

"Things change," his companion says.

Nerpelow sees himself in a mirror across the room, watches as his moustache rides up and down. No one would guess that he makes the most of this because it is his only hot meal of the day. His African *factotum,* his one remaining servant, as old as Nerpelow himself and increasingly doddery, has long since stopped preparing meals.

"Pathetic old man," he thinks.

3

As advancing age, an edge of forgetfulness, force him to think of retirement, in the quicksand of things he finds himself quite unprepared for it. Already he is in the uncomfortable position of having one client who pays most of the bills, one family that keeps the doors to his law practice open, so to speak. This is not a happy circumstance.

Who would have thought, forty-five years ago, back on the day when Silas Divin first walked into his office, that at the end of his career his days would be filled with this family's problems, that he would end his professional life on retainer to the wife, answerable to the children, on call, so it sometimes seems, to its former domestic servants? He knows what they say in the legal community, the newcomers who have long since stopped referring matters to him, that he is past his prime, out of his element. There is some satisfaction in knowing that it must perplex them that this family, which owns so much of the city center, would choose to leave their affairs in the hands of a relic.

"Divin?" he had asked that first day a lifetime ago. "What sort of name is that?"

"Anglicized from something quite different," he was told. "That you can count on."

Over the years he had come to like Silas, found him resourceful, if a little too quick on the draw. Silas could have easily have been English, Nerpelow had always felt. There was nothing showy about him, no sense of swank. As it was, of course, their backgrounds were rather too different to allow anything of a social nature between them. He had not been invited to Silas and Helga's wedding, for instance, and that was as it should be, and indeed he knew nothing of the wife until he started reading about her in the newspapers. He had wondered at the time—this must have been in the mid-sixties—how a person came to believe the sort of tripe she apparently did. One would have to come from another planet, he had said more than once, to see the world the way she did.

He was careful, though, on those few occasions when he raised it with Silas, to do it lightheartedly, as if he were asking about some excessive shopping habit of hers or a suffragette-like escapade about which men were entitled to smile.

"What's this I keep reading about your wife?" he had asked. "Oppose the government by all means, but make your case without giving offense."

"She feels strongly about these things," Silas had replied. "It's her right to speak her mind."

"It's all going to take years," Nerpelow had added, hoping somehow that the logic of it would make its way back to her, "generations, a slow bringing up to civilized standards of the black masses, before anything of the sort she's after will be a possibility. Giving Africans a vote before they are ready to exercise it would be a recipe for disaster. One has only to look at the Congo and other places north to see that."

"Perhaps," Silas had replied with a smile. "Though I'm not sure I'm up to the task of persuading her of it."

One thing led to another and it came as no surprise when the political party she'd had a hand in founding put her up for Parliament. The seat they gave her to contest was, ironically he supposed, his law partner Percy's. Percy was a member of the official opposition and had done yeoman work representing the constituency for years.

What was the sense in targeting Percy, for heaven's sake?

"Making him waste his energy fighting an election against this new lot of your wife's is complete folly," he had said to Silas. "He's doing a good job in there and they should leave him to keep doing it."

"What twaddle," was Helga's response. "He and his party stand for white rule in South Africa and white rule is white rule however politely you phrase it. He should join the government and say it honestly, or if he has no new ideas he should get out of the way for those who do."

Unduly strident, but so were they all, in his opinion, those of her mindset. And then there was all this goading of the students, planting unrealistic ideas in a whole generation of youngsters not old enough to realize that what might look good in theory may not always carry through in practice. His own daughter, a student at the university herself then, told him, the admiration obvious in her tone, that students flocked about Helga Divin like acolytes, even as she daily irritated the government, pressing it, surely, to within an inch of its limits.

"There's something compelling about her," his daughter, mercifully level-headed, had said. "It's not that everyone agrees with her, but there *is* something very logical about her argument."

They did not have the answers to South Africa's problems any more than anyone else did, these supposed clear-thinking creatures of the left, though they certainly acted as if they had some unique insight, a vision of the truth that evaded mere mortals. And even if people did not think alike, they were still obliged to act with a measure of civility, weren't they? What was the sense in being so irredeemably strident? Water under the bridge now, of course.

All that aside, it had always been Nerpelow's experience that on the important issues of the day most of the people he knew *did* think alike.

Here's an example.

The tea girl, any one of a number of native women who did chores about the office, had the job of bringing in the tea tray at the same time each afternoon. As often as not, in fact he would say almost invariably, something was missing from it. Like day follows night, tea in a teapot without water, or a tray without milk.

Occasionally she'd even bring in a tray without cups.

"And the sugar?" he might say.

"Master?"

"The sugar," he would repeat, gesturing to the tray. "No sugar."

Even then whether one actually got sugar remained an open question, but that was how things were and to some extent, though on a much vaster scale now, it was how they remained. You could not change a sow's ear into a silk purse, he would say, no matter how devoutly you might wish it.

Among lesser men it could have been awkward when Silas Divin ran into Percy in the office, but there was none of that.

"One can disagree without being disagreeable," Percy used to say.

Of course, she lost the election handily.

4

IT WAS AN ODD SITUATION, representing Silas Divin in his constant struggles with banks and creditors in light of what everyone knew was his wife's enormous expectancy.

"Why doesn't the old man just step in?" he was asked more than once.

"You know his reputation," he would reply.

"But we're talking about a son-in-law."

"All the more reason, for all one knows," he would say.

Nerpelow sometimes had the sense, though it was never said, that there was a waiting game going on, that Silas thought that if he could just outlast his father-in-law he would somehow redeem all the juggling, all the ups and downs and failed schemes. It wasn't that Helga's father was old—he must have been then in his late sixties—rather that Silas seemed to believe that if he could just keep the balls in the air long enough everything would be okay. That was not how Nerpelow tended to see things. To him, at times, Silas sounded a bit like Mr. Micawber.

"You need to trim your staff," he might say, standing with Silas in the gloomy warehouse. "This place looks like the Pass Office at the end of the month."

"These people have worked here for years," Silas would reply. "Two of the older chaps began in my father's time, and I paid the *lobola* bride-price for most of the others. One doesn't discard people when one has no further use for them. No," he would add, looking vaguely about, "we'll have to think of something else."

The something else, of course, never materialized, and therein lay the problem. It would have been better, in the end, if Silas had simply thrown in the towel, sold the things that had value, the warehouse and the trucks and the cranes, and moved on. There was only so far one could go with loyalty to the past, how much one could prudently sink into an enterprise that was more a romantic notion, more a nostalgic indulgence, than a business. In the end, of course, things reached a point where there simply was no further hanging on.

"What we need is a new investor, someone who can capitalize on our good name," Silas had said. "Arnold Miro comes to mind."

Nerpelow had heard before that in the Jewish community businessmen did, on occasion, go out of their way to help others, but he doubted Arnold Miro was one of these. Miro was seldom a subject of conversation in Nerpelow's circles, but what was said of him was not flattering.

"I can't imagine he does much from altruism alone," he had replied.

"It's not altruism," Silas had insisted. "There's a revolution in electronics going on in Asia, and with the right financing we could bring it to South Africa. We'd all make a fortune."

"What do you know, if I may ask, about electronics?" Nerpelow had asked, cautious but blunt at the same time.

"I import things, Morton," Silas had said simply, as if this were obvious. "Whether it's these new television recording machines or jade and sandalwood, I have long-standing relationships on the ground. Ships are ships. Containers are containers."

"I wouldn't be so sure Mr. Miro will see it that way," Nerplow had muttered.

"It's letters of credit I don't have," Silas had added. "And to be perfectly candid, I'm not certain I have other options."

Whether Nerpelow became convinced that somehow this was all plausible, that somehow it was reasonable to approach one of the city's richest industrialists with a proposal of this nature, or whether Silas simply wore him down and he acquiesced against his better judgment, in the end he went along with it. He knew, though, every instinct told him the moment they walked into Arnold Miro's ostentatious reception hall, that it was a mistake. As they waited in leather chairs too far apart to talk, he almost suggested more than once that they simply leave, just get up and leave, but inertia prevailed and he said nothing. Looking over at Silas he wondered what it was that allowed him so calmly to read a magazine, to inspect the chair's carved arm, to chew on a piece of toffee.

"Nice," Silas had said, gesturing about him.

Miro's office looked more like a living room than a place of business. There were Persian carpets on the floor, two groupings of couches, several lamps on tables, and the walls were covered with photographs that had Miro in each of them, Miro with David Ben-Gurion, Miro with President Nyerere, Miro with Prime Minister Vorster, Miro with others who had no conceivable connection to each other except the dark-haired man in the well-cut suit smiling beside them.

The office overlooked the bay. It was low tide and the sandbanks were visible.

"Haven't seen you since who knows when," Miro had said to Silas. "Your wife still at it?" and then, without waiting for a response he had added: "I voted for her, you know, though if I'd thought she might win I'd have thought twice about it."

The notion made him laugh, and at the time it seemed as if they had no choice but to go along with it, to act as if they saw humor in it too.

"The country's not ready for her," Miro had added. "One doubts it ever will be."

He led them to a cluster of chairs and began talking, told them about a business trip to Zambia, about power outages at his factories, about advice he'd given President Kaunda.

"What is it you'd like me to do for you?" he had said at last.

He heard Silas out, read the papers he was offered, said little. Immediately Silas was done he stood up.

"This is a fly-by-night scheme," he said roughly, almost angrily. "I mean, you don't seem to have the vaguest notion what you're talking about."

"Now that's unfair, I'd say," Silas had said, mumbled really, his face ashen. "There's nothing here that's not been researched."

"No," Arnold Miro had said, standing and moving purposefully across the room as if he were going to get something until it dawned on them, as he stood by the door, that the meeting was over, that he resented the time they had already taken.

Outside, waiting for the elevator, Silas looked as if the blood had been drained from his body, and Nerpelow, though no more than a spectator to what had just happened, felt the humiliation so thickly about that it became his too. He had assumed there was some social context to this meeting but apparently he, or Silas, was quite mistaken about that too.

"My wife and children wake up each morning confident that the day ahead will resemble the one that's just passed," Silas had said. "How does one tell them?"

"Things are seldom as bad as they seem," Nerpelow had replied, and he wanted to say why that was so, why things were seldom as bad as they seemed, but in this instance he could not, could not himself see what lay ahead.

For a moment they waited in silence.

"Do me the favor of not mentioning this to my wife," Silas had said and Nerpelow had replied: "Not a word," and he had not, though he had been sorely tempted, tempted beyond anything he could have anticipated. A few weeks later, of course, Silas met his end. It was a body blow, and not only to Morton Nerpelow. What happened should not have happened, could not have happened. And yet it had.

To compound things, within weeks of Silas's death Helga's father, that sputtering foreign scavenger who had steadily been buying up bits of the city for years, died too, of a stroke. Nerpelow's first thought, on reading it in the newspaper, was how unfortunate the timing of it was. If Silas had only held out a little longer, how different things might have been.

As it turned out, of course, it wouldn't have made much difference. Helga's father was as relentless in death as he had been in life.

"I've seen men tie up their estates," he said to Percy at the time, back when he first read the trust that had now lasted for decades, first saw the thirty pages of detailed instructions about how it was to be invested and managed and disbursed *("twice yearly, on the first of July and the first of December, providing only that . . . .")* "but I've never seen one come so close to taking it with him."

Oddly enough it was then, though she barely knew him, that Helga began to lean on Nerpelow as if he had long been her confidant. Perhaps he offered her a measure of continuity, a sense of stability, and that was his answer to the question how he of all people had become, and then remained, the principal lawyer for the one of the largest Jewish estates in the city.

Later that year, coincidentally, Arnold Miro had applied for membership in the Durban Club. Without explaining himself, without saying a word to anyone, Nerpelow had sealed the matter by casting a blackball although, of course, blackball or no, Miro would never have been allowed to join. One had only to picture him sitting in the most prominent chair in the room, smoking cigars and telling lewd jokes, to see why the club's members would have seen to that.

Ironically the only Jew Morton Nerpelow could picture fitting comfortably within the confines of the Durban Club was Silas Divin, and it would never have crossed Silas's mind to apply for membership in a place he was not wanted. That, for no better way to state it, was the measure of Silas's mettle.

After Silas's death something at the center of the Divin family failed to hold. At first it was the children who ran amok, Bridget arrested for violating the security laws and then held without so much as a hearing, Danny stopped in his tracks by an indiscretion even worse.

Bridget's arrest had, of course, shocked him. Who wants to see a young girl thrown in prison even though he felt instantly that what the girl had done was foolish, any parent would have known that, meddling in the black townships after hours when the government was quite explicit that such interference was not permitted.

The apple doesn't fall far from the tree, he could have said, though he did not, and he did what he could for her although there wasn't much he could do. The security police meant business, and it was their job to maintain order in difficult times. In any event she was released after three or four months, and he hoped she had learned her lesson.

"I need to get her out of the country," Helga had announced. "Somewhere safe."

"This country's as safe as any," he had said. "Provided one watches one's p's and q's."

Helga had looked at him sideways.

"She's twenty. Could you tell your daughter what to think and do when she was twenty?"

"As a matter of fact," he had answered, his tone acerbic, unfamiliar with all this unbridled outspokenness, this refusal simply to follow a few simple rules, "I could."

"Well I can't," Helga had snapped. "And I'm pleased of it too. Let her see things clearly and say what she thinks."

"From a prison cell?" he had answered, equally tartly, instantly regretting his tone.

The son Danny, in his turn, was pushed off to America, and though at the time his mother gave no reason for it, brushed off his inquiries, she did not hold out for very long.

"Who," he had asked her one afternoon, a ledger page with Silas's obligations on his desk before him, "is Santi Ndlovo, and why are you obligated for her schooling?"

To his surprise she had blushed, Helga Divin, quite red.

"You have to tell me the truth, now," he had added.

"Really?" she had said combatively, but the fight wasn't in her.

It was then that he learned of the boy's escapade. Midnight sessions with the daughter of a Zulu domestic servant, indeed, and under the sleeping noses of the family. Had the boy quite taken leave of his senses? There was no pregnancy, or at least so Helga had said, and the vice squad had obviously not heard of it or there would have been a host of other problems. Why Silas should have felt himself responsible for educating the girl when all was said and done was another matter entirely and remained quite unclear to him. *Ndlovo* meant "elephant." Sophisticated system this crowd had for naming themselves.

And then, worst of all, something that tested every measure of his self-control, came the rumors about Helga and Arnold Miro.

"Malicious muck," he had said. "What would a woman of her caliber see in a boor like that?"

"Apart from the money?"

"She has enough of her own," he had said in her defense, but of course the rumors had become persistent, specific, not easily dismissed.

When she was in his office now he sensed a new tension, but she said nothing and he did not pry. They indulged in the same give-and-take, but suddenly it had all become somehow rushed, done without her full attention, surrounded in a vagueness he could not finger. He noticed things too, a blonde streak in her hair that had not been there before, a precipitous loss of weight that left her with a thin, some would say girlish, waistline, costume jewelry unlike anything she had worn before. She was often out of town now, away so much that he read in the paper she had been made to forfeit her position in her political party, on a barge through Europe, on a plantation in Mauritius, on a cruise ship in the Mediterranean where, she told him, world famous musicians had been brought in by helicopter each afternoon to perform.

"You should do it sometime," she said as if this now was all quite normal.

"I certainly will, when I win the Irish Sweeps," he had replied.

Perhaps it was her way of telling him that something out the ordinary was afoot, of cajoling him into prying, but he was equally determined that he would not. One must let things take their course, is how he would have put it.

And then, on one of her trips, so a terse postcard informed him, she and Arnold had been married at a registry not far from Arnold's London apartment.

"You may know Arnold," she had written, as if this had all come as a great surprise, even to her. "Certainly you would know of him."

Still he kept his counsel, and when after she returned and her conversation began to be peppered with "Arnold says" and "Arnold advises," he felt genuinely heartsick but said nothing.

"He's been very successful," she said once, trying to go behind the doubt that sat like a mask on his face.

"So they say," he had replied, moving a paper on his desk.

6

AND THEN HELGA left the country as well.

"Arnold has a beautiful house in the best part of London," she had said. "And there's nothing here to stay for."

"Nothing here?" he might have said, but he checked himself.

"Perhaps you'll be happier elsewhere," he said instead.

Leaving South Africa was not a simple matter for someone with Helga's newly acquired, if largely inaccessible, wealth. As an emigrant everything she owned had to be put into special accounts that were then frozen by the South African Reserve Bank, and there were all sorts of rules that governed how and when disbursements could be made. There were even rules about how much of her money she would be allowed to spend *in* South Africa if she were to visit.

"This is unbelievable," she kept saying as he tried to explain it to her. "If I come back to Durban they'll tell me how much of my own money I can spend."

"If you come back to live, they'll unblock the accounts," he had said. "While you remain resident abroad, that is the rule."

He didn't much care for the rules himself, of course, but there was no doubt as to their logic. If everyone could take their money and go, given the uncertainties, the obvious advantages of keeping one's assets in a place like England or Switzerland, there'd be none left. What good would that do anyone?

"Arnold says," Helga would sometimes begin and Nerpelow would blanch, know that she was about to repeat, innocently on her part for sure, some sharp or legally impermissible suggestion. He did petition—it was Miro's idea, he was sure of it though Helga denied it—the Registrar of Wills for greater flexibility in managing the trust after her emigration, but the attempt failed and Nerpelow was relieved. Helga's father had not been a fool. His protections stood even if the person he had sought to protect didn't want them.

He found himself spending as much time on the trivial as on the important.

"I'd like to give my maid Baptie a pension," she had said. "I've promised her."

"Why on earth do you feel you need to pay her a pension?" he had asked. "Far better to encourage her to find another position. When eventually she does stop working her children will take care of her. They bloody well should. It's their way of life."

Helga had shown him a side of herself others rarely saw, indecisive, insecure, constantly doubling back on decisions she'd already made, but now she flared up, the old Helga.

"Oh come on, Morton," she said impatiently. "She only has one son, and in any event would you like to depend on your children when you're old?"

"I am old," he said, "though not Zulu."

"Would you?" Helga had repeated, refusing to be deflected.

"I have taken care of my retirement," he said. "She, in all likelihood, has not."

"On the tuppence we paid her," Helga had scoffed. "Oh, come on. Be realistic."

"Let me just give you a final piece of advice, then," he said, his tone now conciliatory, "unsolicited though it may be. Be moderate in this gesture or you will risk isolating her in her community. I know these people. Give her too much and you'll make her something of a freak up there in," and here he had to check the paper on his desk, "Gingindlovu, wherever, God help us, that may be."

"I think building her a house and giving her a small stipend is far from excessive," Helga replied. "And she can still work if she wants to, though after the habits she's acquired working for us I'm not sure anyone will have her."

She meant it as a joke. He waited to see if she had anything to add but she did not.

"By all means," he said at last. "By all means. I mean, the money's there. But I would still be careful that you don't let your generosity cross the line. These people tend to take things for granted very easily, you know."

Helga, across his desk, smiled.

"These people?" she said. "Are you trying to get into a political argument with me, Morton?"

"Do you take me for a masochist, old girl?" he had asked.

"Well then just tell me how to do it, and make sure it's done properly, and I'll leave your political views alone," she responded.

"By all means," he said with alacrity. "What's the woman's full name?"

"Baptie," Helga said and then, surprising herself, paused. "And do you know, after all these years I'm not sure I know her last name?"

"Why would you?" he asked.

He buzzed his secretary, and when she appeared at the door instructed her to call Helga in the morning.

"Care for some tea?" he asked as the secretary turned to leave.

"I thought you'd never ask."

It is this issue of the maid's pension, of course, that has now become the bane of his life.

7

THOSE WERE HALCYON DAYS, indeed, shortly to end. Not long before Helga Divin left South Africa he had bought a beach cottage at Shaka's Rock, thirty miles or so up the north coast. The town was small, bucolic, built around a promontory from which the old king was rumored to have thrown his adversaries. The house was on the edge of the sand, open, facing the sea, and with a veranda running the full length of it. The air there on summer days was thick and muddy, heavy with salt and water, the aroma of the mangrove trees, of the sun beating on the rocks. Those had been perfect moments, sitting there on deck chairs facing the waves, drinks in hand, cold crayfish, corn, fruit.

On a weekend before she left he invited Helga up for dinner. She came in Silas's Humber, and as he watched her pull into the driveway, heard the sound of the gravel beneath the wheels, he felt something for her he had not felt before, not pity exactly but a sense of hollowness, as if he were seeing a shameful reminder of a mishap that he had in some measure caused, or if not caused, failed to avert. The sight of her sitting alone behind the wheel of the inappropriately large car, dust from the dirt road on the doors, was somehow disturbing to him. She was, all else aside, quite lovely to look at, no question about that, flawless in her clothes and grooming, but more than that she still exuded a kind of certainty, an unwavering sense that her views would prove to be correct, a woman ahead of her time perhaps, and one, when all else was said and done, of rare substance.

It was late afternoon but the sun was still high and from the upper lawn one could see the sea and the sun trilling over the waves. He greeted her warmly and then somehow found himself with his arm about her shoulder as he led her into the house. It was the first time he had touched her other than to shake her hand, perhaps to tap her sleeve, and he noticed how smoothly she moved, how firm her shoulder was, how graceful were her manners.

"Isn't it strange," his wife had said to Helga, "that after all these years we only meet now?"

No matter how hard she tried to disguise it with polite questions and interested conversation, it was clear that she was preoccupied, he might even have said nervous, and he couldn't help but wonder what lay ahead for her. "Widow Loses Party Post," the newspaper had read when, because of her frequent absences, or so they said, the young Turks in her political party had forced her from her position. The "widow," he had thought, meant more here than a woman without a husband. Could anyone have read it differently? He remembered thinking that perhaps, ironic though this would be, Arnold Miro with his wealth and power and seemingly endless self-confidence could help mend some of the damage that had been done. Perhaps something in it all did, in some strange way, make sense. Helga was no fool.

"Won't you miss this?" he had asked as they sat on the veranda at dusk, the sounds of the waves crashing in the air, steaks on a barbecue, an African maid setting plates on a table nearby.

For a long moment she said nothing, watched the sea, sipped from her cup. He regretted asking, had meant it largely rhetorically, knew it was a question without a real answer.

"What will be, will be," was all she had said.

His daughter, then a teenager, crossed the veranda with a friend, both in their swimsuits, and walked slowly across the sand for an evening swim.

"Watch the undercurrent," he called.

What possible need was there to roam further afield when everything one could possibly wish for was so close at hand. As the two girls faded into the twilight, sitting there on the veranda with the sound of the sea in the distance, people talking inside the house, a drink in his hand, a breeze ruffling the bougainvillaea bushes in the garden, he remembered thinking that at that moment, all else aside, his life was as close to perfect as it would ever be.

And that, then, was that.

HE HEARD ALL ABOUT HOW supposedly well they had done overseas. Occasionally, signing a check, making some application or other on Helga's behalf, he found himself wondering about her there in London, what it might be like to be married, after Silas, to a man like Arnold Miro. Someone who had visited their place in London told him that it was ostentatious beyond measure.

"Africa on Thames, though," the person had added. "Poor Silas Divin's menagerie scattered about the place as if it were the Imperial Museum, tusks and all," and hearing it he had remembered Silas repeating how his father-in-law had dismissed that same collection, quietly agreeing with the sentiment: "Good money squandered on primitive rubbish," Helga's father had apparently said.

One thing hints at what else Helga's life in London may include.

"Have to get off the phone now, Morton," she says each time they speak, and only minutes into the call, her manner rushed, harried. "Arnold will be back soon and he makes all sorts of ruckus over long-distance bills."

There remains, loosely speaking, one relic of the Divin household in Durban and that is Mrs. Ntombifuthi B. Dhlamini. Even after Helga has been so long gone that most of the office staff know her only by reputation, this same Baptie makes the trip each month to collect her pension at his office, becomes, indeed, something of a familiar figure to the staff. She presents herself like clockwork at the beginning of every month, waits while the check is found, departs with scarcely a thank-you.

"Now nobody's touching this money but you?" he says to her once, early on. "I'm not going to all this trouble to write a check for you if some boyfriend or your son with a sob story comes along and takes it as soon as you get it."

"Hawoo," Baptie answers, laughing, her hand shielding her mouth. "There is no boyfriend, Master."

"There'd better not be," he says, bluff, smiling, but deadly earnest nonetheless. "An old lady like you."

She keeps laughing. The Indian clerks in the office, listening carefully, smile.

"And your son?" Nerpelow asks. "What's his name again?"

"Eben," Baptie says.

"Yes, Eben. He leaves your money alone?"

"Yes," Baptie answers. "Eben is a very good son."

"I'm pleased to hear it," he says and instructs his secretary to give Baptie tea before she leaves.

"Ran into your old housemaid this morning," he reports by letter to Helga. "Retirement, to all appearances, suits her. Apparently her dentures have broken, or so she says, and she seeks a *bhansela* for the purpose of securing a replacement. I'm not sure exactly what she's done to have earned her *bhansela,* but one way or another your instructions are invited. You know my views, of course, not that I have anything against dentures."

As the currency slips, riots, devaluation, sanctions take their toll, inflation eats into the value of everything, Baptie informs them that she will be coming to Durban once every two months rather than once every month. Her one hundred rand stipend, as things turn out, once rather too generous, has begun to seem, if not a paltry sum, an amount not significantly greater than the cost of the trip from Zululand.

"Why don't you tell her we'll mail it to her?" he suggests to the clerk. "I'm not aware that there was a problem when we did that in the past."

"She's afraid it will be stolen," he is told.

"Did you tell her that no one can steal a check?" he asks and the clerk, standing on the other side of his desk, stares at him without expression.

"I tried," he says.

"And?"

The reply he receives from the clerk makes no sense to him. Fine. There's nothing more to be done.

9

CHANGE IN DURBAN came slowly, each small difference almost imperceptible in itself, but the change had been deliberate and purposive, irrevocable, nonetheless. The streets of the city had been transformed so that there was never one particular day on which he began to feel unsafe walking on them, but a process in which a hint of unease became something more until he simply stopped doing it, ended his lunchtime strolls, when he did go out moved in swift and deliberate strides and wouldn't have dreamed of stopping, of lounging among the monuments in Francis Farewell Square.

"One takes life and limb in hand," he said, "if one dares."

When he first read, years back already, that the government was considering releasing Nelson Mandela, he had felt a sense of forboding, that the writing was on the wall, and even if he had not supported things as they were in all their excess, he had a sense that what came next would almost certainly be worse. Sometimes he stood at his office window and looked down at the line of minibusses below, at the young black men hanging from their vehicle windows and yelling for fares, brutal, coarse, dangerous, and he realized again that the city in which he had lived his whole life had become unrecognizable.

A city inspector, now an African gent, when Nerpelow calls to get a routine permit on behalf of a client, asks for a bribe and Nerpelow hangs up, speechless.

But it is, after all, simply another step down.

"This was inevitable," someone says, but he does not accept this.

He does not accept that it was inevitable that the city's landmarks should have become dangerous to visit, that there should be prostitutes at every corner, that almost half the police force must always be absent for one reason or another, that there are predators roaming the streets at night with white teeth and shining bloodshot eyes, carrying knives and sticks, guns too, out only to do you harm. At any moment there might be a flash, a movement as you approach your car, and if you are lucky only the car will be stolen, you yourself left unmolested.

They are changing the names of the city's streets too now, streets that would not even exist but for the men whose names they bear, rechristening them with the monikers of minor political functionaries, this one a Communist who died thirty years ago in Moscow, that one who may have blown up a railway station, all in the name of the struggle. Lord Chelmsford who led the advance into Zululand, his street will be gone, its name changed to commemorate some party official, and even grand old Berea Road, the highway that first led in a meandering trail from the city as it grew on the Point up onto the ridge, was about to go too. King Dinizulu Highway, they say it will be called, as if King Dinizulu could have conceived of such a structure, could have bothered himself to build a permanent way through the jungle. And what, exactly, did these luminaries do to build this great city, what role did they have in it other than as hewers of wood and bearers of water? This is not by any stretch theirs, their creation, their city. It is something far different, the fruit of something far more subtle and slow in its creation. It would require an act of amnesia, a great erasure of history, to believe any of this tripe about legitimacy and redress.

But no matter. It is all now something other than what it is, and there is nothing to be done about it. Such is the state of affairs. He has himself twice now been forced to surrender his watch and wallet, wears a cheap plastic contraption with blinking numbers instead of hands, and carries a few rand only on his person, enough, perhaps, to satisfy a mugger if he is mugged, nothing more. He will not soon forget the faces of the young hooligans as they stood before him, just stood and watched as he removed the gold watch from his wrist, a wedding anniversary gift from his late wife, his wallet from his pocket. The faces are dark, blank, expectant, lacking in overt malice but endlessly threatening nonetheless. They are young, matter of fact, remorseless.

The days when he would stroll carelessly down West Street, (whose street signs have now been removed, will shortly be replaced by others bearing the name of Dr. Pixie KaSeme, whoever she may or may not have been), spend a few moments in the sun by the Cenotaph, amble along the Esplanade, are so far in the past he can barely recall how they had felt. There are no white people to be seen on the street outside after the sun sets.

That is now normal, wholly unremarkable.

10

"THERE'S A BIT OF A PROBLEM out here with Mrs. Divin's girl," his secretary tells him one morning, half in and half out the door.

"I'm afraid to ask," Nerpelow says.

"She came in to get her pension this morning," he is told, "about an hour ago actually. Now she's back because she says she was robbed on the street."

"What was stolen?"

"Two months worth. The two hundred rand I'd just given her."

"I thought we gave her a check," he says.

"Not lately," the secretary replies. "Apparently she has to pay some shark to cash it out where she lives—that doesn't seem fair to me but it's the way it is—and so now she just takes it in cash."

He finds himself pulling on the edges of his moustache. It is a habit he seems lately to have acquired. On some evenings, catching himself in a mirror, he looks as if he has been caught in a rainstorm.

"So now we have to decide if *we're* being mugged or if she really did lose the money."

"Oh no, Mr. Nerpelow," his secretary says quickly. "I'm sure it was stolen."

"I don't know how you can be so sure," he says, "but there's no question what the good Mrs. Divin would want us to do."

He asks for the checkbook and writes another check, careful to debit the Divin Trust, and the secretary then takes the money out of petty cash and leads Baptie into the ladies' room, where she makes her lift her dress and tapes the notes to her stomach.

"Are there many thieves in Gingindlovu?" the woman asks as she smooths the money into place.

"A thousand," Baptie answers.

"Do you remember," he asks someone, "what it was like to visit Europe in the old days, after the war, when Jan Smuts was Prime Minister? It was an honor to be a South African abroad then."

"That was a long time ago," he is reminded.

"The good sense of things doesn't change simply because of the passage of time," Nerpelow replies.

"What stank in the past is the present's perfume," he reads a labor leader saying in the morning newspaper.

He sits in a leather chair at the Durban Club and nurses his drink. The room is almost empty but still it is not quiet. Time was when he would have called a waiter over and complained, but it would not be worth it now.

"Good evening, Mr. Nerpelow," they still say as he walks in each evening.

It is their training to know the occupations and personal details of each member so that when they perform their duties they do so with a particular and meticulous attention to detail. They take pride in it, he is sure, sure too that the Club's old-time African and Indian employees yearn for the old days as deeply as does he. Simply because someone was victimized in the past does not make him any the purer when the tables turn and he becomes the victimizer. The group of corrupt thugs, murderous alumni of the Spear of the Nation, that rogue army of Mandela's in exile who killed and butchered their own as readily as their enemy, are now in charge, siphoning off billions in arms deals and no bid contracts, living high on the hog in colonial palaces built by real empire builders who really built, really were trailblazers, not a ragtag bunch of carpetbaggers pretending virtue that is not theirs.

"The usual?"

On the stairway wall there are pictures of a city that is the same as the place outside but that even so is barely recognizable. The same is true of the Club itself. With its curved windows and elegant stairways, its pruned gardens, it has always been a place of tranquility and refuge, has offered something the world around it lacks, but even that is now gone so that, like the city, it is the same place still but not the same place at all.

"The Durban Club, one of the city's colonial landmarks, is set to join the list of casualties among old-style British gentlemen's clubs in South Africa and may become a Hindu community center," the world was free to read in the newspaper.

Yes there was an offer, and though the members had rallied around and found the funds to hold on, once the possibility had been raised, the unthinkable—women in saris, yelling children, the smell of curry, overweight brown men in ill-fitting suits smoking in chairs, the beginnings of an overwhelming shabbiness—the seal had been forever broken. It has been hard to stomach.

He cannot help but wonder, though, what it is that has excited such destructive malice. Yes, the Club was an exclusive place in many respects, but then its members never intended any harm, never did any harm, indeed, not a one of them asked anything of anybody. If you didn't like the Club or what it stood for, or didn't approve, you didn't have to have anything to do with it, after all. For all he knew, indeed he was sure of it, there were Hindu cultural centers all over the place, a Jewish Club on Old Fort Road, all sorts of organizations in which he would not be welcome, would not deign to suggest he be invited.

But why go out of one's way to tear something down?

During that United Nations affair about racism held of all places in Durban, as a revenue raising measure the Club was rented out for several functions.

"Only ten years ago the Durban Club was exclusively a white man's domain," a journalist had crowed. "Reclaiming this space by a meeting such as the World Conference Against Racism was perfect."

Reclaiming!

But then, when the Club was gone, when they had succeeded in ripping it apart, he wondered what these people would feel. Would it be a victory, to stand gloating over nothing, to feel vindicated because something had disappeared not ever to be replaced?

"The Club," Helga Divin had scoffed once when he had invited her to join him there for lunch. "I wouldn't set foot in the place if you dragged me in with a forklift."

If she were alive, the old Helga, if she were here, he would ask her to sit with him and to explain it all.

NERPELOW HAS LIVED for years in the same house on Musgrave Road, not inelegant in its own way with its floral patterned furniture and fraying carpets but so tired-looking that, on seeing it for the first time, a visitor, if he had visitors, would not know what to make of it. With the collapse of standards and the need for extreme security measures it has come to resemble a fortress from the street, but back then, when his wife and he first saw it, there with its tiered gardens and verandas opening out at the city, it had all the charm in the world.

Since his wife's death everything has been firmly set as it was, nothing changed or replaced, and the gardens have lost their exuberance. His African man tries to keep it all somehow going, but in the garden the wild growth of things has outrun him and inside the humidity, the sunlight, the hours of rain and the years of wear, show in everything. He notices it, of course, though he professes not to. Either way, there is no money for indulgences now.

"I wish you'd sell the house and move into something smaller," his daughter keeps saying, but she knows as well as he does that even if he could he would not.

The house, despite its high walls and expensive new electrified fence, or so he has been told, is almost unsaleable except to a speculator or perhaps to one of the newly minted native bureaucrats. No one will buy an old house standing alone in so large a garden. It is too easy to infiltrate, and there are too many places to hide. Death and emigration are relentless in the damage they do to the familiar, and his life, he would be the first to admit, has shrunk, but even so he cannot move now, in his declining years, to a cramped, newly built, unfamiliar little flat.

He finds one night that a squatter has built a hut at the bottom of his garden. He calls the flying squad police in order to have her evicted. They respond languidly, three hours after his call to them.

"You must start a court action," he is told.

"But she has built a shed at the bottom of my garden!"

"You must start a court action," the black constable repeats. "We can't just throw someone into the street."

"But this is private property," he insists, and the constable, wearied by the argument, repeats: "We can't evict her without it."

His daughter, so tentative in telling him this—she insists on coming over to his house one evening in the middle of the week, brings biscuits and makes tea before sitting him down in the living room to talk—has put in for papers to go to Australia.

She asks him to consider going with her.

No.

He cannot see himself living in a dingy flat in some strange Australian city, friendless, rootless, a maundering old man perpetually lost. But he cannot see himself staying either, a prisoner in his office, a prisoner in his creaky house, nattering on about history to unwilling listeners. And, of course, there is this matter of the Divins, of the maid's pension, of his stubborn and unethical decision . . . .

Yes.

He will go. He will need to tell the young Divins when they arrive that they need to find new counsel, that is if they do not tell him first when they learn what he has done.

12

It was at about the time that the nature of the country's transformation was finally sealed, so-called democracy at last, freedom, the past covered over by a great big patchwork quilt embroidered of amnesia and optimism, that the Divin Trust finally came to an end. He began receiving inquiries from the Reserve Bank about the intentions of the beneficiaries and that was the beginning of his reimmersion into the Divin family and its personal affairs.

Morton Nerpelow had never paid much attention to the value of the buildings he oversaw for them—Helga's father's will had ensured that nobody could sell them—but now the process required that he get them appraised. He had no preconceptions on this point. They were office buildings, to be sure, and therefore of a certain value if fully rented, but the center of the city had already begun its journey downward, its transformation from a place where businessmen came to conduct their affairs to a lawless outdoor market with vendors selling vegetables and noisy hawkers carrying cheap curios right on the plazas of once exclusive venues. The value of the properties, he knew, had been damaged, but the final appraisal came as a shock nevertheless.

"Seventy million rand," the clerk had reported. "That's what all the buildings together are worth."

"That is a great deal of money," he had said, "even in English terms, several million pounds. Mrs. Divin needs to pay attention to it."

He had called her in London and, as luck would have it, Arnold Miro had answered the telephone.

"Is Mrs. Divin in?" he had asked.

He may even have tried to disguise his voice but he had no experience in such things.

"Who may I say is calling?" Arnold had asked, and even if he had been prepared to assume a rasp that might change his voice, outright deception was beyond his powers.

"This is Morton Nerpelow," he said. "Calling on a private matter."

"Ah, Morton," Miro had said, as if this were a usual occurrence, a call from an old friend. "We've been wanting to talk to you."

"Really?" Nerpelow said.

"Yes," Arnold had continued. "Helga and I have been discussing this business of her father's trust. We were anxious to get started on some of the details of it, liquidating it and so forth so as to be prepared for whatever it is that Helgie and the children decide they'd like to do."

Nerpelow had not heard her called "Helgie"before. In his estimation her image did not carry a diminutive well.

"I'd be glad to discuss it with her, if she's at home," he had said.

Arnold acted as if he hadn't heard, began prying for details, asking questions the answers to which he simply was not entitled.

"If necessary," he said, "we can get my own people involved in all of this."

That was not a happy prospect from any angle.

"I'd be glad to discuss it with Helga," Nerpelow had insisted, unwavering.

Finally, from Arnold Miro, a measure of vitriol.

"Now listen here," he said. "This is not a lot of money as far as I'm concerned, and I have no interest in any of it in case that's what's worrying you. But my wife has asked me to monitor this to ensure that things are handled in what I would consider a businesslike manner, and that is what I intend to do. Are we quite clear with each other?"

"May I speak to your wife?" was all Nerpelow could think to say.

When eventually Helga Divin did come to the phone she sounded as if she were caught in the middle of something, as if her lawyer and her husband were antagonists pulling in opposite directions. Even though the money must still stay in South Africa when the trust was over, everything was her call, but it had somehow moved beyond her, rather than empowering her seemed to have left her quite befuddled. He tried to picture her there in London with the receiver to her ear, and it proved impossible. He wondered if she was unwell, whether it was only her husband listening in or something else that accounted for a vagueness so complete it verged on incoherence.

He was relieved, then, to receive a call from the boy Divin, Helga's son, from Boston in America. You could say from the nature of his questions that he appeared to be a bit of an upstart, one of those American chappies who seem to know all the answers and are keen to sue when things go wrong, but Nerpelow was prepared to keep an open mind.

HE HAD EXPECTED a period of awkwardness when the boy first arrived, but the problem went well beyond that. From the outset he found the boy unfocused, and over a meal at the Durban Club he was so obviously not engaged in their conversation that his conduct verged on ill-mannered. Daniel Divin was a businessman of some sort, apparently quite an experienced one if his mother was to be believed, who must have had some passing knowledge of business etiquette even though he lived in America. Nerpelow tried to ignore his misgivings, was too old and too withered to take offense easily, rattled on instead about the city's past, about history, tried to establish a rapport, and in return heard polite but disjointed questions suggesting something else was on Daniel Divin's mind.

Later that evening a light went off in his head and he understood everything, even berated himself that he had not come upon it more quickly. Whatever else Daniel Divin may or may not be, he was Arnold Miro's stepson and it did not have to be spelled out what was on his mind. Indeed when the boy called in the morning and began spelling it out, Nerpelow interrupted him. He did not need to be told the details, he had said, to have it explained to him why there would be new accountants, a lawyer in Johannesburg, several businessmen from Durban with mixed reputations.

"I am an old fool," he had said, "but not a complete fool. Arnold Miro is not the first nor will he be the last person to smuggle money from South Africa against the law."

He chose not to be in his office when the messengers arrived to remove the files, went to the Club instead, gave instructions that he was not to be disturbed, and when he returned the files were indeed all gone, their dusty outlines on the shelves the only reminders of a half century of something that had overnight become nothing.

But that was not the end of it.

A day later there was another about face, Daniel Divin on a plane home, all instructions rescinded, no hint of an explanation and no apology. If nothing else Morton Nerpelow was a good soldier. He fielded the telephone call informing him of the change, listened without comment as Arnold Miro's unsavory business associate made statements laced with insulting innuendo, remained silent, demurred. The twenty-four hours of turmoil he had just witnessed was small potatoes against the years of steadiness that had characterized his relations with this family.

When the files arrived back in his office his secretary simply dusted them off and replaced them on their shelves as if it had all been nothing more than some sort of excursion, a mistake in routing that had been caught in the nick of time.

"The Divin boy has a good deal of experience yet to come," is how he phrased it later, visiting his former partner Percy, quite unwell, now resident in a home for the aged on Windermere Road.

14

WITHIN MONTHS it was the daughter's turn. She telephoned from America to let him know that her mother was not well and that she now would be handling matters. Her initial inquiries were basic enough, but while they were talking he realized that she too had something else in mind. Must everything with these people, he wondered, be cloaked in pretext?

Eventually, of course, she got there.

"My understanding is," she said suddenly, her voice dropping as if she wished no one else to hear, "that if my Mom were to pass away we would be able to take her entire estate out of South Africa."

"They can't keep the money indefinitely," he told her. "If she were to die you would indeed."

"Everything?" she asked.

"Everything," he said, and there she let the subject go.

"There's something else I want to ask you," she said as if this was an afterthought, though it became soon clear that a decision on the matter had long since been made. "We've been following the South African currency, how it's been sliding in value. I can't imagine a hundred rand goes too far any more."

"Things have changed," he said.

"Back when Mom left a rand was worth a dollar and a quarter and now it's worth twelve cents or so," she added. "We'd like to increase Baptie's pension."

"You can't convert things quite so easily," he said, still trying to be helpful. "Basic items are substantially less expensive here."

It was as if he hadn't spoken.

"My brother and I would like her to have fifteen thousand rand a month," the girl had said. "It's only a bit under a couple of thousand dollars, but we understand this would make her quite comfortable."

"I would say," was all he could find to say.

Fifteen thousand a month! It was exorbitant. It was an outrage. The destruction of the currency, the collapse of property values, the dishonesty and decay evident in every institution, had wrought havoc on his retirement planning. When he was finally compelled to stop working the good Mrs. Dhlamini's income would be greater than his own, and that was why he had not paid it, not once. He had not. He could not. He would not. The money was still there, of course, but they would have to find someone else to carry out this instruction. The girl Divin would doubtless be irate when she learned of his faithlessness; her instructions and intent were clear, but so be it. There were some things that were too much to ask a man to do.

Perhaps at the bottom of the world, down in Australia, the topsy turviness of how it had all ended would begin to make sense.

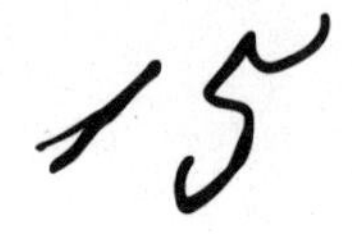

THEY WILL SOON BE HERE to express their displeasure, what is left of them. On the second anniversary of Helga Divin's death, so her children have told him, they are coming to Durban, they and their spouses and offspring, to hold a memorial service for her, though for whom to attend, and on whose account, he is not yet clear.

"If you don't mind my asking, Bridget," he had said when Bridget first telephoned to broach the idea of this ceremony of theirs, trying to couch his question as politely as was possible, "is this a Jewish ritual?"

No, she had answered, it was simply something that she and her brother had decided to do and had no religious significance.

"But why have you chosen to do it in Durban?" he asked. "You've been gone rather a long time and I'm sure your mother had many friends in England."

The line falls, for a moment, silent.

"There are people in Durban who meant a great deal to my mother," she says finally.

"Very well," he says. "It's none of my business anyway."

What he is trying to remind Bridget Divin is that many years have passed since her mother left this city, that although it may seem to some as if time stands still, in reality it does not. For whom is this memorial to be held, he would like to ask, and what is it that she would like remembered? In your mind, he would like to say, the past is a frozen tableau. The reality of it is that nothing stays the same.

He thinks something else too, something he will not be drawn into saying on this phone call. On some matters people do have long memories, and these are mostly of the uncharitable sort. Her father's end, so sudden and accompanied by all sorts of speculation, was not a happy one, and over time people have had a thing or two to say about her mother's marriage to Arnold Miro.

"Anyone who marries that braggart for his money," he had once overheard someone saying, and the person who was speaking had been a friend of Helga Divin's, or so he had been led to understand, "will certainly spend the rest of her life earning it."

But fine then, okay, even if he is not altogether sure Helga's children have taken into account everything they should. If it is help they want, help he will provide. He has made a career of being a good soldier, has achieved, when called upon, the close-to-impossible for the family Divin. When a lifetime ago Silas set his heart on buying Gordonwood, that monstrosity on the ridge, and he discovered a clause in the deed forbidding its sale to those of the Jewish faith, he had devised a way for them to buy it nonetheless, his own misgivings aside. When Silas asked him not ever to mention this little historical detail to his good wife, believing probably quite accurately that it would influence her view of the place, he had obliged there too. His approval now is neither sought, nor is it necessary. He will make the requested telephone calls, write the necessary checks, do what he can, within reason, to enable this venture of theirs, this memorial to the vaguely remembered, to proceed.

He wonders about something else. He has not quite been able to fathom the reason for the flurry of requests he has received of late from the son, urgent letters with questions about receipts that haven't been in existence for decades, affidavits, if you will, about Silas's collection of Zulu knickknacks. He knows enough about the legal process to guess at what is going on, and a fight between siblings for a parent's belongings is as unseemly as human conduct can become.

Things have a way of unraveling that no one in their right mind would have dared forecast. Silas for one would, he is sure of it, have had a chuckle at how it had all turned out.

Silas was one of nature's gentlemen, no one would dispute that.

His children are a different story.

16

IRONICALLY AS HE SITS in his office working on Divin matters, paying bills, preparing financial statements for the family to review, he receives a visit from the doubtless soon-to-be affluent Baptie herself.

His secretary buzzes and informs him of an unscheduled appointment.

"Who is it?" he asks.

"Yes, Mr. Nerpelow," she answers, "they're standing right here."

"Who?" he insists.

"Mrs. Dhlamini and her son Eben," she says.

"Who?" he repeats.

"Mrs. Dhlamini. You know, Mrs. Divin's former domestic worker."

"Oh?" he says. "What does she want?"

"They won't tell me," his secretary informs him.

Somewhat to his surprise, although he has not seen her for some years, he recognizes the old woman the moment she comes through the door. She wears an oversized suit, a little hat, carries a handbag. Her son is a tall man with a shaved head, lean, surprisingly well-dressed. They do not, of course, have an appointment. Did they not think for a moment, he wonders, that he might not be so easily available to them?

He gestures them to chairs, offers tea. They decline and he returns to sit behind his desk, rests his chin on his closed hand, a gesture that he is listening. He has an inkling, just an inkling, that he is about to be asked to do something he will have to decline.

"This is my son, Eben," Baptie says.

He has conducted many business meetings in this room. This one does not resemble any of them.

"My son is in trouble," Eben says. "I have come here because only you can help him now."

"You must help him," Baptie adds.

Well, of course, he says, always courtly, always courtly, he is not what one might call a criminal lawyer if that is the kind of trouble his son is in, but he is sure that there are criminal lawyers who might be able to help, perhaps in their own community.

"My son has already been convicted," Eben says. "But it is not *that* he has committed the crime that is important. What is important is *why* he committed it. That is the important thing."

Nerpelow is not following.

"What exactly did he do?" he asks.

"There is a person who has been killed," Eben says carefully.

"A person?"

"A man, a black man, who came to Zululand," Eben says.

One reads too, every day, about black-on-black crime. Whatever problems exist in the white suburbs have always been endemic in the native reserves.

"And your son committed this murder?"

"Yes," Eben says, his voice very soft. "We think he did."

"What does he say about it?" Nerpelow asks.

"He says that he is proud of it."

Nerpelow says nothing, waits with his chin on his fist.

"And what do you say?" he asks finally.

"I asked him how he could be proud of such a thing?"

"And?" Nerpelow says.

Pulling teeth, this is.

"He said the man was from the African National Congress of Nelson Mandela," Eben says. "He said that the man he killed did not care for anything that matters to us as Zulus, that with his ideas we are as good as dead."

For a moment there is silence.

"I see," Nerpelow says when it is clear Eben has nothing further to add. "Well then, if he is convicted already, what is it that I can do for you?"

"It was a long time ago," Eben says. "During the struggle. We have waited too long, but even now we think that maybe you can help us."

"The Mandela people also made trouble," Baptie adds vehemently. "And the white security forces too. People did not care if it was someone's mother who was in the house they burned, or if someone had worked hard to build what they destroyed. They only cared if you were for them or if you were against them."

The newspapers had been filled with stories like this, though Nerpelow can't claim to have read them all. Not all people are able to settle their disputes in an orderly manner. And it was all so long ago already.

"We want to talk to you about the amnesty program," Eben says. "The commission of Archbishop Tutu. We need to get my son under that program. We want amnesty for him."

Finally then Nerpelow understands what they are after, but he has no appetite for it, for the self-abasement, the regurgitation of old acts, the resurrection of grievances real and imagined. When he had seen it on the news he had changed the channel. And it was all over, the Commission long since disbanded.

"What took you so long?" he asks. "I think the time for all this has passed."

"No," Baptie says, angry, vehement. "What is fair for one is fair for all."

Nerpelow weighs this, looks her carefully in the eye, decides to try a different tack.

"You know, of course," he says, "that there are lawyers who are trained to handle matters such as this. I am not one of them."

"I think," Baptie pipes up, "that the Divin family would not have you as their lawyer if you were not clever."

He can't help but smile.

"I may or I may not be clever," he says. "But the fact remains that I know nothing of these things. And as far as I understand it, that Commission has long since gone out of business."

"The Divin children are coming to town now, to Durban," Baptie says. "I will ask them to tell you to help. They will pay. They have the money."

This is presumptuous, of course, but he lets it go, and for several reasons.

"You can't just barge in on whatever may be left of the Commission and say you have a murderer who deserves to be set free," he says instead.

"So what must I do?" Eben asks.

His face has begun to show a measure of anger. His nostrils flare as he talks, and his lips become quite thin. Without responding to him Nerpelow lifts the telephone and summons one of the Indian clerks.

"What do you know about the Truth and Reconciliation process?" he asks when she enters the room.

"A little," she says. "Not much. I followed it like everyone else."

"I have great confidence in Miss Patel," he says. "I will have her find some answers for you."

He has read in the morning paper about a meeting protesting rising electricity rates: "We will occupy the homes of city councillors who do not vote to roll back the increases," someone has said, "and form action groups to race to houses where the electricity supply is being disconnected to confront and chase away the city's technicians. We believe that to deprive us of the right to electricity is an act of violence."

And so, he wonders, how then is this going to work, with murderers being let out of jail, with nobody paying electric bills, with hawkers in the lobby of his building who cannot be removed, how is this going to end? But he does know. It ends with blackouts and potholes, corruption and stagnation, it ends with everyone expecting something for nothing, not paying their fair share, becoming enraged at those who are better off, becoming violent when they do not get what they demand. It ends in lawlessness and crowds of poverty stricken people on the sidewalk. It ends in an avalanche of unfettered crime, in a tidal wave of AIDS, in a break down of routine and of law, in a revision of history. It ends in famine and decay, indeed in life as it is being lived every day in Zimbabwe, the old Rhodesia, where rather than have white farmers on the land the whole nation is about to starve to death.

Indeed, he has a squatter in his own garden who has rights equal to his own.

He stands, and they stand too, and then he leads them, his hand on Baptie's shoulder, to the door and watches as the three of them walk down the hall, the short Indian woman with her long hair in a shining braid, the two Africans.

As they reach the end of the passage Baptie pauses and then turns to face him.

"You have become very old," she says.

Another little matter that he has not shared with Bridget Divin is that there has been quite a bit of traffic in Baptie over the past week. Arnold Miro of all people has telephoned with a host of questions Nerpelow has simply refused to answer, questions about the Divin Trust and the childrens' intentions, even about the provenance of some of Silas's possessions.

"I'm not at liberty," had been his refrain.

"Well perhaps you'll tell me this, then," Arnold Miro had said, surprisingly coinciliatory under the circumstances. "I'm trying to get in touch with Baptie, you know, my late wife's Zulu maid. Would you happen to have her address on hand?"

Nerpelow had no idea why Miro would want this information, but even so he had no intention of providing it.

"I'll find it one way or the other," Miro had said at last. "I'll be in Durban myself shortly, and I do have other resources."

"I'm afraid I'm not at liberty," Nerpelow had said once again, and the line had gone dead.

NERPELOW HAS NOT BEEN in the City Hall for months, years even, but with the Divin buildings about to be sold and the family due in town there are forms, certificates, waivers, all manner of paperwork he needs from the city's clerks. Trying to explain on the telephone what he wants to a newly minted African bureaucrat would be pointless, he believes, and the City Hall is just a block from his office. He decides to walk over himself. In the bright light of afternoon, even with the groups of sullen men waiting at each corner, the risks of it seem inconsequential.

He crosses Francis Farewell Square, passes the Cenotaph, is about to walk up the steps and into the building when he decides, for old time's sake, to visit the Council Chamber. He continues walking past the building's main entrance and down what was once West Street, goes in the side door, climbs a curving stairway, and makes his way to the great hall. New government or no, it all looks pretty much as he remembers it, but as he reaches the third floor he senses that something is different, that the singing, the thumping he seems to hear, are out of place. Curiosity, a sinking sense that he is about to see something he would rather not, draws him onward. People hurry by as he approaches the doors to the visitors' gallery.

The gallery is mobbed but there is one face offering comfort in it all, a white man taking notes, and he moves in his direction.

"What's going on?" he asks.

He must shout to be heard.

"Half the opposition has just defected and joined the governing alliance," he is told. "I'd say it's the perks that sealed the deal."

Nerpelow looks out into the chamber with its green leather chairs and its carved wooden balustrades and all he sees is pandemonium, wet-shirted men stamping in place, singing, yelling, thrusting their fists rhythmically into the air as they perform the *toyi toyi,* the Zulu victory dance. The once sedate air, witness to a hundred years of reasoned debate and civil discourse, thunders, and the floor shakes. There is laughing, taunting, ululating. It is, all of it, suited to a tribal council or to a jamboree under a tree, to a battle on the side of a dusty hill, but not to this room, not to this poor musty room built with such pride and within some people's living memory less than a century ago, not to this room built for careful debate and rational decision making.

The stench of sweat fills the air. You cannot say it, of course, dare not say it, but the country is being run by a bunch of venal incompetents who cannot even kept the lights on and who you dare not criticize on pain of being found guilty of that most violent, that most odious, of all offenses: on pain of being called a racist. So you endure things. You endure the crime and the chaos, the belligerent rhetoric, the decay, the menacing street vendors, the mattresses piled on the sidewalks. You endure the motorcades speeding about, sirens blaring, carrying all manner of minor officialdom, police who fire at cars that have the temerity not to drive off the road and out of the way. Competent white managers are replaced by so-called "Struggle Veterans," people with no discernible training or skills for the task at hand other than that questionable political credential. Institutions are stripped of everything by kleptocrats. Things run down. Breakdown follows breakdown. A place once filled with shining structures now has broken streetlights, broken windows, broken plumbing, dark and shattered buildings. There is crabgrass on the medians.

Fortunately he is old, and for him it is almost over. Soon he, and all he remembers, will be dead. Then it will not matter. The bush has fought back and reclaimed for itself the small clearing that was made, and wildness infiltrates the monuments that were built to cement its taming. Randomness, brutality, nature in its unaffected state, will no longer be fenced out by the civil structures of city life but are inside of them, in possession of them, making their way into the very mortar that holds things together. A final irony: In the last election Nerpelow voted for Helga's old political party, the only group, it seemed, still sticking to some principles that made sense, a voice of reason still saying, wonder of wonders, the same old things, and now, wonder of wonders, making perfect sense. Civility. Merit. Discourse. Order. Europe in Africa.

He thinks of Silas as he returns, empty-handed (the clerk he needed to see was at lunch, in mid-afternoon, needless to say,) to his office.

When the English army reached the king's hillside corral at the end of the Zulu War and opened his treasury they found it filled with mirrors, velvet gowns, beads, the worthless junk of Europe. Officers took their pick and brought it all back to Durban for display, laid it out on tables in the city's ornate public buildings.

How does one compare that cache of childish trash, the trivial primitive artifacts his old friend Silas was so fond of, with the best of Europe that was being assembled so fastidiously, so relentlessly, on this spot, even as the king was executing evildoers and gathering beads and masks?

How does one?

One cannot.

No matter. That has been the trade.

The vanquished have turned the tables, and now they will have their pick.

PARADISE

1

My offices in Boston are in a tall building on Atlantic Avenue. From my desk I can watch the airplanes as they take off and land at Logan Airport. Sometimes they come in from the right, cross my window slowly, trace a line from the silhouette of the Hingham cranes to a runway just at the edge of the water. Sometimes, depending on the wind, they seem to come straight at me. A tall palm tree stands in the corner of my office. Its leaves dip each time the air moves.

When I was a boy we lived in a house high on the ridge and we could see, from the veranda upstairs, out over the entire city. In the foreground, looking down, was the swimming pool, and then a stretch of grass and some scrubby bushes, and then the servants' quarters, and then beyond that everything stretched out down the nape of the ridge to end at the ocean. In the distance, unreachable but also unable to reach back to us, were the buildings and parks of a stolid, humid, slightly shabby, seaside city. That's how we saw Durban every day, through the white columns of Gordonwood's balconies, drifting below us like a hazy painting for all the years of my youth.

I bought my first property in Boston using credit cards and a collection of overdrafts offered in the mail, and then worked feverishly at night and on weekends to fix it, sold it at a profit, bought another. After that first success I repeated the process and then did so again and again, seven or eight times until one day I found the *one,* the house I now own. When I first saw it I was awed as much by its grandeur as by the possibility that I could make it perfect, turn it into the perfect house after which no more searching would be needed. It was built in a different era for a family whose name people would still recognize, and it reflects in its details an age long lost. Many of its rooms have no practical use. Perhaps that is why no one else seemed to want it. But I restored each room nevertheless, and each room, in its own way, serves a purpose. It required a lot of work to do all this, of course, long stretches of paneling to be scraped and stained, floors gone over with special pastes to restore their original gloss, antique appliances replicated and made to function. I did much of the work myself, built something from nothing, brick by brick, inch by inch, from a mattress on the floor to the catchment of my dreams.

My home is in one of Boston's near western suburbs whose rustic air belies its proximity to the city. Isabella Stewart Gardner once had her summer house here, as did the Cabots and the Lodges, but now new economy investors and lawyers are liberally interspersed among the old money types, and there are several orthodox synagogues within an easy Sabbath walk. I knew the first time I was brought here that some day I would live here, that I wanted a piece of the solidness and the tranquility that has settled so grandly on these quiet rural lanes. I have it now, drive home each day under a canopy of ancient trees to a house hidden behind iron gates and set in a secluded patch of oldest Boston.

When I bought this house the seller, an unmarried woman in her eighties whose grandfather had himself built the first rambling clapboard house that stood here, offered to give me pictures that had been taken over the years of that first house, the land, the little lanes that bound it, and I gladly accepted. It is not hard to imagine the days when people came out here in carriages from their homes on Beacon Hill, or to feel in the loamy ground the decades of fallen leaves, or in the ledges and gullies the crusty winters that have given them contour. You think, especially in the fall, of pilgrims and Indians, of colonial ladies in their bonnets, of a variety of things all doubtless interesting but none of them, no matter how hard I try, of interest to me.

Perhaps that is an immigrant's lot, that no matter how committed he is to the ideals of his new home, his points of reference lie elsewhere.

But perhaps it is a personal matter.

On either side of the fireplace at Gordonwood were two large tusks that my father told us had once been King Shaka's and which he had given to Nathaniel Isaacs, one of the earliest white settlers in Natal. When my mother died we were concerned that my filthy stepfather would steal them and so one night we simply took them from his home in London. We are now involved in a fight to the death with him in the English courts. In time, and after spending a whole lot of money, I expect we will win. I believe our solicitors who tell me that, to a lesser or greater extent, if we choose to fight on, we will ultimately win.

But here's something I know that Bridget, who hints of all sorts of things behind the scenes that I am better off not knowing, does not know.

The tusks, I have discovered, Nathaniel Isaacs's mythical tusks, are fakes, worse than fakes, not only not genuine but not even ivory. There is no letter from Isaacs to his uncle describing how he came to own them, and this is a good thing because if there was, if there were this letter my father had always said existed, it would be a forgery, a foolery, a paper written to deceive and that did, in fact, succeed in deceiving him. When I learned this, and I learned it quite early in the process, I decided instantly—quicker than instantly—to tell no one. It would make my father look so weak and so gullible, so completely quixotic, make junk of a generation of stories and transform our raid on Arnold's flat from a success, something about which my friends still laugh, to a laughingstock. All that, and in the end crushed bone and epoxy. The irony is too rich even to contemplate.

To make matters worse, we are being urged by the solicitors in London to consider settling Arnold's lawsuit.

"Most cases are settled," Rupert faxes me. "I've said many times that I believe in the end you will probably prevail. But whether you want to keep at it depends on what you want to achieve. Perhaps there is some compromise you can live with because there is always a risk in litigation. I don't need to tell you that."

"Exactly," Bridget says when I share this advice with her. "We've proved our point. Let him keep the stuff until he drops dead and then we'll take it back. He's almost eighty. He can't go on forever."

"After what we went through you could live with an outcome like that?" I ask.

"What if we lose?" Bridget says. "All they're suggesting is that we have everything valued and have him post a bond to ensure that we get it all back when he croaks. This grudge match must be costing you a fortune."

But I have decided that I must have the tusks. I must have them not because of animus for the loathsome Arnold, though I have plenty of that, and not merely because of some empty desire to win. Oh, no. If it is possible I want them even more now, even more than if they were truly valuable, objects of such historic importance that they are beyond appraisal. I want them more now because what I want is to have them in my house where no one will ever discover the truth about them. I will allow no appraisals, no mediation, no settlement. I will pay, and pay, and pay.

"It was never about money," I say.

Tesseba was half right, then, when she said all those years ago that my whole family, but mostly me, live in an ivory tower, but a strange kind of ivory tower, one without foundations, one that wobbles, one that we see as likely to fall at any moment.

"As you describe poor old Gordonwood," she said once, "it could not have stood on its own. It defies architectural logic, all those balustrades and towers and crenellations, don't you see it? You have embellished it beyond recognition."

"No I have not," I say. "Ask anyone."

"There is no one left to ask."

"Write to Baptie if you're so interested," I say. "Ask her."

"As if she would remember," Tesseba says. "More likely she'd add a flock of angels and a chorus."

I see again in a fading photograph that I keep above my desk, one taken from Gordonwood's second floor veranda thirty years ago, the old buildings of the city center, squat, tawny, stretching to the oily waters of the bay. There are the hoops of the sugar terminals, the green oval of the racetrack, the harbor with its glistening sandbanks, and the mossy, whale-shaped Bluff. When I was a boy I went fishing every Sunday with my father from a little boat in that harbor. Sometimes we chugged our way clear across to the Bluff and anchored just off shore to eat the sandwiches Baptie had packed for us in a straw hamper. On the far side of the Bluff is an old whaling station. People used to say that in the summer the smell of rotting blubber drifted up as high as the peak of the great ridge.

I was seventeen when my father died and sometimes it feels as if my life is divided into two parts, creased in the middle, on that day. Things fell rapidly apart after that. His death was followed by a cascade of uncertainty and change, but whether it was his death that *caused* the cascade or whether it is just some sort of coincidence, tectonic forces that had been building and that happened to come together so shortly after he died, I cannot say. My marriage to Tesseba, even my marriage to Tesseba, a marriage of necessity at first but then later something quite different, seems to flow without interruption from that moment. Perhaps my mother's death will be a *coda* to it all. It feels as if it should be a *coda* to it all, but there is still something in the air that smacks of unfinished business.

"In fact I would say it's more a dinghy than a tower," Tesseba had added. "It's as if you're adrift in an ornate dinghy made of ivory."

My hands are large and clumsy. My ears obtrude. I lack finesse. There are barnacles on my teeth. I will scrape them off with an ax.

"But life is not as fragile as you believe," Tesseba insists.

There are clay bells on my toes.

And the question remains, of course, the granddaddy of them all: I have seen, Rupert has shown me, the receipts from that restoration specialist in London whom Arnold paid to restore a crack in one of the tusks. He must have seen instantly what I later learned.

How is it possible that Arnold has said nothing too?

2

AFTER MY MOTHER'S DEATH I try to pick up where I left off but it surprises me how tedious it all seems, the calls to be returned with their fake cordiality, the decisions I have to make, the trivial way I spend my days. I spend hours drafting and redrafting papers for the English litigation, am on the phone with Rupert constantly.

I distract myself with these things, and also with our affairs in South Africa. These have assumed a new immediacy. My grandfather's money is not only now ours, but with my mother's death it may even be taken from the country. At last, and in it entirety, what was my grandfather's now belongs to Bridget and me, though it is not all that much money by today's standards. He was rich when he died, my grandfather, but over the years and under Nerpelow's tremulous care the estate has shrunk, ossified, so that what we now own consists of several buildings that have aged badly in areas of the city that time has left behind. Even so our crumbling little empire still has value, life-changing value for Bridget, something less than that for me.

It is Bridget to whom Nerpelow now reports, but Bridget has no frame of reference, no training in this sort of thing.

"We have an offer for the building on Mona Road," he calls to tell her. "We put out a few feelers to test the market, and a group of Indian businessmen came out of the woodwork."

"How much are they offering?" she asks.

"Well," Nerpelow says, and he is equivocating though she is not sure why, "I do think you should consider the offer and talk it over with your brother."

"How much?" she repeats.

"They're offering thirteen million rand," he says. "The figure may seem low, but these are not usual times."

"Because?" Bridget asks.

He pauses.

"Things change," he says. "The center of gravity in the city has moved away and up the coast. There's not a whole lot of interest in property in the central city these days. It's a little rough, in patches."

"I can't tell what anything's worth," she says when she reports all this to me. "Nerpelow apologizes for bringing me offers that sound so high they make me dizzy, and then he apologizes because they're so low."

"The rand's worth twelve cents, not a dollar thirty like it used to," I say. "A million and a half dollars for a ten-story building in what was once the heart of the city is pathetic, but then everything's relative. If that's what property's worth there, then that's what it's worth."

"Nerpelow also says that you can't just convert rand into dollars," Bridget says. "That a rand buys a whole lot more in South Africa than twelve cents does here."

"How would he know?" I say dismissively. "The last time Morton Nerpelow left South Africa was in the Crimean War."

"You're not helping," Bridget tells me.

"It's a no brainer," I say. "Sell. Get the money the hell out of South Africa. If Nerpelow's right and the money can come out, take the best offers and sell everything. What decisions need to be made beyond that?"

"Maybe things will improve," Bridget says.

"We've spent a quarter of a century wondering if we'd ever get the money out of South Africa," I say. "You want to invest there now?"

"Why not?" she asks. "People sound quite optimistic."

"How should I put this to you Bridge?" I say. "It's a Third World country with tremendous problems of corruption, wealth inequity, and crime so bad a fifth of the white population has emigrated. It has unstable neighbors, huge unresolved questions of land ownership, and an AIDS epidemic the government refuses to concede is caused by a virus. What more would you like to know?"

"You're painting a very one-sided picture," she says. "Even I know that, and I know nothing about business."

"Bridgie," I say, "if you want to stay, stay. I don't mind. We'll ride it out together. But let's do it without illusions."

"Look here," Bridget says, losing her temper at last. "Things may or they may not be as bad as you say they are, but one way or another there's no reason to yell at me."

"I wasn't yelling at you," I say.

"Well you were yelling at somebody," Bridget says, looking around the room.

3

I HAD BEEN WORRIED about Bridget given how closely bound up she was with my mother, but my worry is misplaced. There is a flip side to it, she has apparently discovered, to feeling at a loose end, and it is the sense of being suddenly, almost perfectly, free. The sense of release is undeniable and grows over the weeks as her life resumes its routines. After Tibor and Leora leave each morning she finds herself beginning to exercise on a patch of grass behind her house, and then after a week or two she leaves her own yard and begins to run, something she has not done since the Durban days. She tries on jogging shoes in a local sports store, buys an exercise bra, clears a shelf in her closet for her new sweats and the little weights she has bought to velcro to her wrists.

She joins a gym, buys a book on macrobiotic cooking, does not understand why she feels so transformed, so renewed. It is as if something that bound her has released, as if her point of reference has shifted, as if she is free at last to be frivolous. She ambles through the Ann Taylor store and wonders what she will do, what she will buy for herself and for her daughter, when the money finally arrives.

"We're going to get a check and it's going to be for four million dollars?" Leora asks, and Tibor looks at her across the dinner table, frowning, a look of the deepest skepticism on his face.

"Nothing is going to change," he says.

Bridget sees an advertisement for a triathalon in the vestibule of the supermarket and tears off the contact information.

"You look great," Leora says one evening. "I can't remember when you looked so good."

"I feel good," Bridget says, and it surprises her.

She says it, and then she feels shame. Helga has been gone for only a few months. Jews aren't supposed to resume their full lives for a year after a family member dies, but she's already looking forward to Tibor and Leora leaving in the morning so that she can limber up, go for a run, try gymnastic routines she hasn't tried since she was a teenager.

She notices that Tibor and Leora are exchanging one of their many glances.

"What?" she says.

"Nothing."

"Oh come on?" she demands.

"I think," Tibor says, slowly and carefully, like he is giving bad news, "that you should not be afraid to feel grief."

Bridget is floored.

"Is that what you think this is?" she demands.

She is sad, true, stunned even, but there is nothing more she can do, nothing more she could have done. When Helga needed her she dropped everything to go and be with her. She made sure her mother's end was as comfortable as she humanly could have made it. But now Helga is gone, and while Bridget is sad beyond description that she is gone, and misses her beyond description, none of this is any different than she knew it would be. She knows that whether she can be happy each day is suddenly in her own hands, and that without warning all the "if onlys" that have dogged her since her earliest adolescence have simply and without notice evaporated. She is not responsible, not any more, for trying to repair the damage, does not need to try and make things right when she hardly knew, hardly understood, what it was that had made them so wrong. It is now impossible. She can affect nothing. She is free.

In all the years she has known him, leaned on him, she has never known Tibor to be so wrong. Even that she finds liberating.

4

WHAT BRIDGET is not interested in, and despite all that we went through in London, is my fight with Arnold.

"Do you know what the judge decided in London this week?" I ask her.

I am having tea in her kitchen, have left my office in the middle of the morning, too restless to work.

"No," Bridget says.

"That Arnold has a substantial likelihood of winning. He has required us to post a bond for a million pounds in order to keep the things in storage, otherwise he's going to release them and let Arnold use them."

"A million pounds!" Bridget exclaims. "Where on God's green earth did he come up with that number?"

"It's the value we placed on the stuff," I say.

"You've got to start letting this go," Bridget says softly. "If he ends up with the things it's not the end of the world. In the end they're just that. Things."

Bridget does not want to know what Arnold is alleging in his papers, and I stop trying to force the information on her. It's when I learn, for instance, that he has spent lots of money repairing and restoring my father's treasures, and that he has the receipts to prove it, and somehow I suspect this should change how I see things but it does not. He alleges that he had an agreement with my mother, one he says we ourselves heard her ratify one morning in her bedroom in London, and that he is simply trying to enforce it. And he alleges, and this is news, hard to digest, that he has grieved her, and does still. "Defendants have removed each and every trace of more than twenty years of domestic life, leaving the plaintiff a home as cold as it is picked over."

"I will not permit Arnold to end up with Dad's collection," I say to Bridget. "We've been damaged already, as much by Mom's appalling judgment in choosing him in the first place as by anything else, and I won't stand by and see it compounded."

"This is pointless," Bridget says, angry, turning to face me. "You can't spend your whole life placing blame and nursing anger. For one thing nothing's ever black or white, and for another it doesn't do any good. What's done is done."

I am taken aback by her vehemence.

"They aren't done with Arnold," I say. "This lawsuit is an affront to us and a threat to the memory of our parents."

"Look," Bridget says, her patience wearing thin. "What happened between Arnold and Mom is something you can't change."

"Perhaps none of this would have happened," I say at last, "if we hadn't abandoned her in Durban in the first place, simply cut and run when it suited us, and so soon after Dad died. Maybe we are responsible too."

Bridget looks at me astonished.

"We were kids," she says. "We were just kids. We couldn't have saved her from anything. She had to live her life, and we had to live ours. We were just kids."

I slump in my chair, shake my head, twirl my cup.

"I sometimes think of the moment I left," I say. "Looking out the airplane window and seeing her standing there at the edge of the tarmac. Back then you could come all the way to the edge of the runway, do you remember, and stand behind that rolling white barricade?"

"What does any of this matter?" Bridget sighs. "She's dead Danny. It doesn't matter."

"I went up the steps of the airplane—do you remember the old planes, with orange tails and a blue springbok emblem?—and right at the top step I realized for the first time that after the plane took off she would be all alone. The house would be completely empty, except of servants. I wanted to turn round and run back down. I still have that feeling, even now, this second, sitting in your kitchen."

Bridget says nothing, takes a cup to the sink.

"I don't have the energy you do for this stuff," she says. "You are to blame for nothing, not for leaving Mom alone, not for her choosing to marry Arnold, not for anything."

Her kitchen, she has begun to notice, makes her claustrophobic. If only it extended another ten feet or so it would be much more convenient. The counter, that old smoky-colored green Formica, chipped at the corners, is really beginning to bother her.

When the money comes out she wants to redo the kitchen, redo her whole house, indeed.

5

THE IDEA THAT WE should go to South Africa descends on Bridget at a charity function she attends. She doesn't tell anyone she is going—it is just a whim, something that descends on her—and she is even a little furtive in her planning. It is a fundraiser arranged by a Boston group that assists South African causes, and Archbishop Tutu is speaking. Bridget buys a ticket at the door, enters the ballroom, finds a seat at a table of strangers and watches as a choir from a local black church escorts the Archbishop into the room. He is a tiny gnome of a man in a purple robe, bobbing about in time to the music. She listens to the speeches by a parade of black celebrities, Harry Belafonte among them, and watches as they claim South Africa as their own. There is something jubilant in it, but something threatening too: she has no part in the bright colors, the yellows and greens, the braided hair, the triumphant singing.

"I sat there in the hearing room of the Truth and Reconciliation Commission, up there on the platform, raised up, you know, above the room, and watched things happen that I never in my life thought I would see happen," the Archbishop says when it is his turn to speak. "I saw a policeman confess to the most terrible crimes, to murder and torture, and he did it in the presence of the families of those whom he had murdered and tortured, and then I saw him turn to them, to the people sitting in the audience, and ask for their forgiveness, ask to be taken back into the community of decent people, and I saw the family members without even a moment's thought stand up and applaud, tears still on their faces, and I said nothing for a while, and then I said: 'We are in the presence of something holy.'"

He ends his talk with a joke about himself, something that he must know will—is intended to—lighten the atmosphere. Someone had given him a hat that did not fit.

"My wife, if she was a nice wife," he says, "she would have said that the hat was too small. But *my* wife, she said instead that my head was too big."

Everyone laughs. She likes him so much, this little church man with his endless good humor, his willingness to dance along with the children even as he must have known it made him look comical, his seemingly endless compassion. He would humor her if she approached him, she is sure, but she is equally sure that he is not here for her, for whatever purposes have drawn her. This is about something else, something larger, something she is not a part of. Over dinner a woman at Bridget's table, a South African woman from a village near Johannesburg, tells a story. She is very dark-skinned, she says, and so is her mother, but she has a Coloured sister who is very fair, and one day when they were young they were out with their mother when her sister started crying and had to be fed. Back then, she says, breast feeding in public wasn't favored so her mother went into an OK Bazaars department store, and in the privacy of a niche under a stairway started feeding her baby. An African woman came by and then scurried away, and a few minutes later a white store manager showed up, anger all over her face.

"Does your Madame know you're feeding the baby?" she asks.

The women at the table, all Africans, start to laugh, and they don't stop until tears are running down their cheeks.

"Does your Madame know. . . ." they keep saying, and each time they find it funnier.

"My mother, I tell you," the woman at my table says, "she still tells that story though the baby she was feeding is now a mother herself."

"That was some country," another woman, wiping her cheek with a napkin, in control of things now, so poised, so self-possessed, says. "All these bad things, but sometimes you can only laugh. You just have to laugh."

A choir sings as they eat, youngsters flown in from Soweto for the occasion, and Bridget finds herself surprised by the emotions that overtake her. She does not live in the past, as she accuses me of doing. She is not obsessed with the details of our history. But something in the music does bring it back, the children's singing reminiscent of other singing we once heard drifting up from the servants' quarters each night when we were ourselves children. It is then that Bridget realizes what she wants to do. She wants to go back, yearns to go back, to see for herself what has happened and what remains, and if this money is real, is finally to materialize, to leave a portion of it there, to make a gesture that might repair some of the damage that has been done to everyone, ourselves included.

"We probably need to go anyway," she says, "to finalize things. Why not combine it with a party, a ceremony to honor Mom's memory, with all the people she used to talk about, the people who loved her and who remember her as she was? I think it will do us good."

Bridget combs through my mother's address book and makes a list, has Nerpelow's secretary send a telephone directory by Federal Express, collects the names of caterers, florists, venues. At some point, I can't say exactly when, it strikes me that this is all real, that it has moved beyond my humoring Bridget's daydream, and that from the copious lists of people and speculations something is going to happen. She wants as well to make our memorial service a charity function and she selects several charities my mother would have supported for very sizeable gifts in our parents' names. I want to ask why, I want to ask what for, so far away when there is need closer to home, but discretion is the better part of valor. In any event, I think I know the answer.

6

A FEW DAYS BEFORE we leave, Tesseba and I have a houseguest, my cousin Janice visiting from Johannesburg. At first Janice seems determined to be upbeat, to give a good impression and be positive about her country in the company of her relatives who have chosen to leave. All the racist laws are gone and the constitution is more liberal even than the American. The economy is picking up, and the culture's on fire, she says.

She even bristles at the notion that Soweto is more dangerous than ever.

"That's just newspapers making a fuss," she says. "American celebrities visit there all the time. They're always amazed at how modern it all is."

She pauses and an impish, ironic look crosses her face.

"Sometimes they travel in Casspirs," she says. "But they go."

"What's a Casspir?" I ask.

"An armored car," she says calmly. "It's overkill," and my face must be particularly blank because she adds: "I'm joking."

I ask: "Well are the streets still cleaned, and does electricity still flow, and do the busses still run?" and she answers, nonchalantly: "What do you think? That everything's ground to a stop because Africans are running the place?"

"Of course not," I say. "But do you feel safe? I mean, I read about the crime and I worry about you."

Janice deflects me with: "What do you mean by safe?"

"It's a simple enough question," I say. "After dinner we'll go for a walk down the street. Would you do that in Johannesburg?"

"Some people do," she says, "though many of the places one used to go, like Zoo Lake or Hillbrow, are off-limits. It's not that there's constant mayhem, just that it's unpredictable. There's a lot of unemployment, you know. It'll get better."

"Can you count on the police?" I ask.

"That's another story," Janice says. She is animated now, unnerved too, I believe by a sense that has grown in the few days she has been in Boston that things in South Africa may not be exactly as she has thought. "Do you remember how you used to tell the police if you were going on holiday so that they could keep an eye on your house?"

"Yes," I say.

"Well the police are now the last people you'd want to know if your house was empty," she says. "The very last."

"What are you saying?" I ask.

"Sometimes," she says, "I think it was easier to live under the old system and to feel guilty than it is to live like this."

"You don't regret that *apartheid* is gone, surely," Tesseba says, and Janice looks at her carefully, wary of being misunderstood.

"Of course not," she says. "Things are much better for blacks, and the whites may complain, but the principal difference is that now we're forced to live behind electric fences rather than behind laws that kept poor blacks at a distance. Some of us felt terrible about the way things were, you know that," she adds. "I mean, after you lot scarpered I spent my twenties going to protest meetings and getting teargassed by the police. So if patients in white hospitals now have to bring their own sheets and food, the point is that the black hospitals were always like that, so what right do we have to complain? Maybe we deserve what's happening, maybe we were spoiled before, but sometimes one wonders how it's all going to end. There's even a fellow now who is head of the youth wing of the African National Congress and who many people think is in line to be our future President. He's rabid in how he sees whites and what happened in the past, and I sense an implicit threat of violence in everything he says. It's all racial, tinged with hatred, laced with threat. Add to it that he lives in a mansion and drives prohibitively expensive cars with no discernible means of paying for any of it, and you've pretty much summed up the future."

She pauses.

"Do I sound schizo?"

"Yes," I say. "Certifiably."

After she's come and gone, and with our plane tickets booked and in a drawer, I become concerned about our safety while in Durban.

"But is Durban safe?" I ask everyone I come across who may have an opinion.

"Of course it's safe," I am told. "You just have to be careful. And drive with your doors locked. And not walk on the streets at night."

"But that *means* it isn't safe," I insist. "If you told me I could drive downtown Boston but that I should keep my doors locked and my windows closed at all times, I wouldn't go."

"You know what I think?" Bridget says. "I think you view Durban as some sort of postapocalyptic nether zone, which is why you're so concerned about whether you can even breathe the air there. It may be less safe than it was, it may even be unsafe in parts, but there's been a change of government, just a change of government. Nothing more or less, black government or white. Deep inside I'm not so sure you see it that way."

"I don't know how I see it," I say.

I once dreamed of taking Tesseba to Durban, of driving down the coast road from the airport through the thickest, greenest vegetation and coming upon Durban suddenly, not the real Durban though not completely unlike it, this Durban filled with huge stone monuments covered in ivory, immaculately carved buildings, lawns of the smoothest green, all almost perfect.

7

PERHAPS IT IS SIMPLY THE TRUTH that emigrants are untrustworthy people. Even the trustworthy ones are untrustworthy. We can't help it, in my view. My father used to tell us that his great-uncle had been a doctor in Liepaja, Latvia, or the Duchy of Courland, as the area was then known. He told us that this great-uncle made house calls in a carriage drawn by four white horses, and it was quite easy to picture this, really, a carriage drawn by a team of white horses careening through the picturesque streets. But then at some point I began to wonder about this, just as I began to wonder about a lot of things. I mean, how many Jewish doctors were there in Liepaja, Latvia, in the nineteenth century, and how even would one fit a carriage drawn by four white horses through the narrow streets of a medieval city? He may not have been Tevya in a *shtetl,* but a Jewish doctor with four white horses? For years, after once believing the story completely, I dismissed it equally completely.

They're all dead now so we'll never know for sure, except for this. One day I wandered onto the website of *Yad Vashem,* the Holocaust Museum in Jerusalem, after I'd read an article that referred to it. I entered the Liepaja index and typed in my name, and then sat in awe as I saw that there had indeed once been a doctor there, a man with my first name and my last name. I saw that he had a son and a daughter too, but as I read on I learned that all three of them died on the same day in December 1941, something my father had not told us and maybe did not know. On Saturday, December 13, 1941, the senior SS officer in Liepaja published an official order in the pages of *Kurzemes Vārds,* the local newspaper, confining all Jews to their houses on Monday and Tuesday, the 15th and 16th of December, and on those days the Germans arrested most of them and drove them to a place called Shkede near the sea, where they were shot and pushed into a trench already dug by the town's Latvian collaborators. I was horrified to see, as well, photographs taken by some Nazi soldier, of the trench, of Jews in a line on the edge of the trench, being shot, falling in. There are naked women, thick black pubic hair stark against the grayness of the background, covering themselves without success with their hands, a boy in a cloth hat, at one moment standing on the side of the trench, at another splayed against its sides.

And the doctor, well, he was a member of the yacht club (a *yacht club?* A Jewish member? My legendary great-uncle?) and his address is there too, extracted from a telephone book that still apparently exists, and data from which has been carefully transcribed in the *Yad Vashem* log. So I suppose it is true that it may be my own conceptions that need revision, not my father's credibility. Lawyers call these things, the website, the photographs, the entry about the man with my name, *indicia* of reliability. They are all, then, *indicia* of reliability. The weight one accords them depends on their provenance.

And then there is me myself, no more reliable than my father or the website or anything else. I am weighed down by complexity and ambiguity. It is an affliction that came upon me late in life, this emigrant's untrustworthiness, this tendency both to be exact and to magnify so that in the end what is true and what is not becomes completely muddled. Exile, you see, is a form of rebirth, a moment in time when one passes through a cleansing portal and can leave behind what one chooses, select what one brings. Nothing else, after all, once one has left one's home, is ever quite real again. Bring on the white horses, two or three or fourteen, and oddly enough with time they either were or become so real that what is true is lost. I both remember clearly and harbor all sorts of illusions, no doubt, about my childhood in South Africa. The *goldene yorren,* someone called them after my mother died, the "golden years," and I can still feel in my fingertips the windowsills and door handles of the place, slightly tacky in the humid air, warm, the muddy sap of Africa in everything. I recreate without effort those days in my father's house, sometimes sit quite still and feel it all again as if I am there, as if it all still exists, as if it is quite real. For whatever reason it has become no stretch for me to place myself where I am not and have never been, to feel things that are not mine to feel. I know how it feels to line up on the edge of a trench in Shkede in the freezing December air, with women I have known my whole life standing unreally naked, shivering, about me. It causes so much pain I cannot bear to see the photographs of us on that day, the naked women, the boy in the cloth cap.

Perhaps it is simply a collation of other things, a memory of tanks rolling up Silverton Road and the soldiers marching to suppress an uprising of angry Africans in Cato Manor, of being forced to leave cover and retrieve a hand grenade that had failed to explode during my year of service in the Fifth South African infantry, of being stopped by Boston police when my immigration status was still quite ambiguous, other fears too, but whatever it is I know intimately the trepidation in Liepaja as the tanks enter the town. You rise from your bed, still warm despite the icy air, eat something even though the orders are to assemble and that tardiness will be punished. You take a last look at the cramped room into which you have been herded never knowing, not quite, when you will see these things for the last time ever, whether this is that day. Later you stand, barefoot, in the mud. The wind trips mercilessly off the ocean. The winter sun gleams horribly on the waves. Did we not once picnic right there, over there by the little dune? All these naked girls, but the air is so cold, the terror is so immediate, that their presence is no more unreal than anything else this day.

There is talking, shouting, bursts of a guttural, heartless laughter. There is a man, a skinny little runt of a soldier, his cap askew, brandishing a whip, who forces the naked and horrified women to pose, to stand in the freezing wind as he snaps photographs with his ice cold camera. There are men with guns, a light crackle of gunfire, things tumbling in the mud, a chorus of moaning. The lights go out, out with the vertiginous ease of an anaesthetic.

THE AIRPLANE IS PERFECTLY SILENT, simply floating, as we drift slowly down over the crumpled green carpet of the Valley of a Thousand Hills. Below are clusters of corrugated iron roofs, slim pillars of smoke, people who from the air resemble nothing so much as flecks of cloth as they snake down the red-earth paths. Tesseba, in the seat beside me, is reading a biography of Hillary Clinton, of all things, and I am tempted to interrupt her, to insist that she watch, with me, as the aircraft approaches Durban. She looks intent and I let her be. In the distance I see the factories of Mobeni, the foaming arcs of the coast, the tall buildings. We land in the light, but even as we taxi darkness descends like a sudden fog. There are swaths of muddy sunshine, a gloomy pause, and then deep, velvety blackness.

Our travel agent has arranged for us to be met at the airport, and for whatever reason I have assumed that it will be an elderly African man in a white driver's coat who will be waiting for us, someone like Ambrose who will sit assuredly behind the steering wheel with his back affording privacy. That is not what happens. We are met instead by a burly Afrikaner holding a sign with our names and talking on a cell phone. His name, he says holding out his hand, is Hans. He has a full head of blond hair, large hands, long, closely cropped sideburns. He is dressed in a safari suit, the kind we used to wear to school, short pants, long socks, a loose shirt with oversize pockets. His arms and legs are tanned and his shirt pockets bulge with keys, a pager, and a packet of cigarettes. He insists on carrying my bag, walks purposefully ahead.

"So are you here on holiday, then?" he asks. "It's a good time of year for it."

I wonder whether I should point out to him that on the morning I left, this airport was just a one room affair, its decor rich in propellers and linoleum and lattice dividers, that it was more interesting certainly than it is now, a period piece in fact, but also so small, so provincial. Back then it was called the Louis Botha Aerodrome.

"Durban has become South Africa's number one holiday destination," Hans says.

He says this with a measure of pride but also assertively, as if he suspects I may not fully agree.

"I was born in Durban," I volunteer for whatever reason. "I'm here for a family event."

"No, really?" Hans says. "What event is that, if I may ask?"

His manner is gentle, solicitous, but even so I do not feel like going into it with him. In any event I would have to say that I have no answer. Bridget has arranged everything. Whatever happens will happen. It is hot and humid. My shirt feels bound about my arms.

I pretend I have not heard.

"How long has it been since you were here?" Hans asks after a pause.

"Not so long," I say.

"May I ask," Hans says, "why you left?"

He is driving, so I see, not even a car but a white minivan, its windshield speckled with dead insects. The air is so thick that it coats the car with a sticky film of dust and pollen.

"It's a long story," I say but what I really want to say, what bubbles inside of me to say, is something quite different. Hans steers with the tips of his fingers. He leans one elbow on the half-open window, the other on the vehicle's armrest. "I left because of you," I want to say.

Outside the car the black air cracks with menace.

"I see that they call Durban 'Thekwini' now," I say instead.

"No, yes," Hans says. It is a peculiarly Afrikaans idiom. *Ja nee*. It means yes, but it is qualified. "They're changing a lot of names, you know. Around here they choose Zulu names. They're thinking of calling the new airport the King Shaka. I don't know if they will."

"The King Shaka," I say, and given what is going on with Arnold the mention pricks at me. There is something I want from this thing, from this dead king. I cannot place it.

"Now that would be something," I say.

"Of course people call places what they remember them as, but the kids will get used to it," Hans says.

"What do you think?" I ask, "of all the changes."

"No," Hans says mildly. "It's okay."

"You don't mind, then?" I press on.

"What can you do?" Hans replies.

We are on a road I do not recognize, seem to be going inland to a dark nothingness I do not remember.

"Is this the way?" I ask. "We're going to the north coast."

"It's a new road," Hans says. "It bypasses the city."

"Is it safe at night?" I ask.

Hans lifts a finger from the steering wheel. The road cuts through what were once sugar cane fields, green in the day, black at night.

"It's safe," he says.

"Overseas we read a lot about crime here," I say.

"Well," he adds thoughtfully, "I suppose it depends what you mean by safe. I mean, I carry a gun, but they carry guns in New York too, I hear."

"How long have you been driving a minivan?" Tesseba asks.

"About four years now," Hans says, and then he adds that he was once in charge of a provincial government department but was laid off.

"Right or wrong," he says simply, "they have this affirmative action now."

Suddenly I know where we are. We have, Hans was correct, skirted the city, emerged onto the North Coast Road. We are, ironically now that I see it, heading away from Durban, the place I want to go toward. It feels a bit like one of my dreams.

"How does it work, this affirmative action?" I ask.

"Ach," Hans says matter of factly, "they brought in a lot of black people to do the jobs we had been doing, and we were let go. It's how it was. Some of them didn't know anything about anything but that didn't make any difference. Now they've fired all the city managers too, just because they were white, and replaced them with black people who were active in what they call The Struggle. We'll see what happens next."

"Perhaps it was their turn," I say, and Tesseba, her hand on mine, squeezes just a bit, a reminder perhaps that we are guests, that this is not the time for an exposition.

"Perhaps," Hans says. "But I don't think two wrongs make a right. So we have a choice now. Start a little business, like this one I have, or leave. There is nothing else to do."

Something in our little capsule of light moving down the dark road becomes blinding.

"Did you really think," I ask, my voice rising, "that after fifty years of *apartheid* with the best jobs and the best schools and the best neighborhoods reserved for whites, did you really think there would be no price to pay? No reparations? Nothing to undo? Maybe there is a price tag and affirmative action would be a small one at that."

"No," Hans says softly, answering my question. "I still don't think two wrongs make a right. It may look like that to those who have left the country, but to people like me, simple people who never took much interest in politics and who still have to earn a living, it doesn't look so right. Perhaps if you were here when the lights started going out, when the hospitals started falling apart, when thousands, tens of thousands, of skilled white people who could have really made a difference, left to go overseas because it was just too hard to stay, you might think differently."

I sit back in the seat. I have never seen this man before. There is nothing familiar about his face. He is not Marnus van Zyl, the Afrikaans farmer who made my life miserable in the army, nor one of the schoolboys who yelled *"Jood,"* Jew, as an insult when they played sports against us, nor one of the khaki-clad hecklers disrupting my mother's political rallies. On Sunday mornings on the way to tennis or to the beach I used to see them, dressed in their best clothes with freshly combed hair and an ominous confidence, on their way to their churches to inhale sermons laced with self-righteousness and racism, but who is to say that Hans was among them? The night my mother debated the Prime Minister on the stage at the City Hall, as we walked to our car, a group of Afrikaans teenagers came menacingly close to us, within inches of my father, fists up, and shouted: *"Jou vok. Kaffirboetie. Jood."*

And yet, against all odds, somewhat to my astonishment, this man has just won an argument with me. How could anyone disagree with what he has said?

"Ja nee," Hans repeats. Good jobs are scarce and some people are pessimistic, but he is not.

"People forget," he says quietly, "that whatever else may have happened, we turned the country over because we came to see that what we were doing was not right. We were not forced to. We chose to."

I could say that it was under duress, that the strikes and the violence and the international pressure had become too great to resist forever, but in the end he is right. There was no out-and-out bloodshed. They were not defeated. There was a quiet, a civil, realization, that change had to come, and it came from him and others like him, as unlikely as it had always been that this could be so.

"I have to believe that God has a plan," he adds.

I look at the back of his head, at his thick neck and strong arms as he steers the van into the darkness. I see no trace of the swaggering *volk* that blighted my youth and I regret my rudeness. We ride for a while in silence, and then I recognize, a few miles ahead, on the left, the dull, moist lights of Umhlanga Rocks. I know exactly where we are.

AFTER HIGH SCHOOL we were drafted into the army, Rupert and I. Having Rupert around, being able to look across at his honest, sweating face as we crawled about in the bush, went a long way toward making army service tolerable. It was on our first leave home that we started going to the Oyster Box Hotel in Umhlanga Rocks for tea. On the veranda there were wicker chairs that overlooked the ocean, a breezy lawn, Indian waiters in white coats serving tea and scones. It all seemed so tranquil, such an antidote to the roughness of the army, to the swirl of life itself, that we promised each other that someday, no matter where we both ended up, we would come back here, if only just once, to have tea together and to take stock of how things had turned out.

"You sat drinking tea with Rupert on a hotel balcony?" Tesseba has said. "On your army leave? Just the two of you boys?"

"It was lovely," I had responded.

As for Tesseba's tease, Rupert was not a ladies' man, and the only girl I wanted was barred from the hotel, would have turned it upside down had I tried to bring her. Her name was Santi and she was the Coloured daughter of Emily, who was the neighbor's Zulu cook. I met her just before I went into the army and fell for her hard, but when my father found out about it he gave me no choice but to leave her alone, and I did. I left her with a promise though, a vague, unfulfillable promise, that I would not abandon her, but twenty years went by before I saw Santi again. I was in Durban on my Arnold-inspired mission, and whatever else logic may have told me to expect, I expected to find the same girl I had left behind, Santi as I last saw her, standing in the shadow of the servants' quarters, wearing the same thin cotton dress. I found instead a university lecturer, a self-assured, worldly, funny woman, someone who had not sat wondering, as she attended conferences in London and Geneva and even in New York—even in New York, two hundred miles from where I sat dreaming—what would have been, what could have been, what of it still remained.

The truth is, if the truth be known, that I discovered when I came back and found her, came back *to* find her, Arnold's mission a pretext, that Santi had moved beyond where I had gone, had matured, succeeded, become the sort of woman any man would admire, memorable by any measure and in any place. It was I, in the end, who had been left behind.

Rupert, who at times can be quite tactless, has never passed judgment on any of it.

"I don't suppose I'll get to meet her, though," he had said one afternoon, the last day of our army leave, the two of us sitting there on the veranda of the hotel. "Not here anyway, not with your sneaky late night rendezvous and the rest of it. Maybe in a year or so we'll all meet up in London and the whole thing will seem quite quaint."

"You think so?"

"Why not?" he had said. "God knows you're not the first to encounter a blockheaded obstacle to true love. Think of poor Abelard and Héloise, or Romeo and Juliet, even the Duke of Windsor and that American tart. Of course they didn't all have happy endings, but that's another matter and in any event there's no reason why if you want her that badly you can't have her. No reason at all. The whole world's not South Africa, you know. Loving someone who's a different color isn't illegal everywhere."

Rupert tells me that he goes to the Oyster Box each time he is in Durban to see his mother, but lately he says that has given up on the idea of our someday having tea there together.

"Life goes in a straight line, old chap," he says, "not in a circle."

Bridget has booked us into a hotel just down the road. They are disarmingly cordial when I check in, deferential in a way I had forgotten, courtly without being obsequious. As I am filling out the paperwork Leora and Bridget come clattering across the lobby, suntanned already and filled with stories.

It was because of Santi, because of how arbitrary and unfair and wrong he was in forbidding me to see her, that I was not on speaking terms with my father when he died. That fact, that rift, and how irredeemable it suddenly became, underlies almost everything that has happened since. And after he died, of course, I did not have the heart to try and pick up where we had left off. I regretted that for a very long time.

10

THE CRICKETS, THE TIME CHANGE, the sudden bursts of bird song, make for a fitful night. I am up well before my usual time.

"Is it safe to walk on the beach?" I ask the concierge.

"Perfectly," a handsome Indian boy says as he hands me an access card. "This will allow you back onto the hotel grounds."

We walk, Tesseba and I, on the coarse brown sand, watch the sun creep above the horizon, see a school of dolphins swimming slowly in the shallows. The air is familiar, heavy, wet. Far in the distance I see people fishing in the breakers, casting off, pulling back, buckets beside them on the sand. Tesseba walks with a light step and a young girl's enthusiasm. When the dolphins approach the shore she yells at me, runs to the edge of the water, wades in up to her knees.

"There are sharks here," I say. "Don't swim where it's not marked."

"I'm not swimming," Tesseba says. "And it would have to be a mighty flat shark to sneak up on me here."

Tesseba walks from the water, foam from the breakers seething about her ankles. Her skirt is tucked into her underpants, her legs shine. I notice again that she has beautiful legs, long and naturally athletic. The sun streaks her hair.

"I'm not going to get eaten by a shark," she says.

The sand is gritty, an even carpet of tiny brown pebbles. In the early morning light things look pristine. I see two young men, Africans, coming toward me along the sloping flats where the edges of the waves end in slivers of water that sink quickly into the sand. My instinct is to turn around.

"You didn't tell me there were dolphins here," she says.

"I didn't know."

"How could you not know?"

"I don't know that either. No one mentioned it."

"You didn't see any?"

"No," I say. "I suppose I didn't pay attention."

Baptie told us when we were children that seawater had restorative powers. Back then the city's beaches were all "whites only," and so she couldn't come down to the water's edge and do it herself, but each time we went to the beach she'd give us several empty bottles and ask us to fill them for her, and we would, and then she'd store them under her bed for when she needed them. I'm not sure how she used them. Perhaps it was to clean cuts, or even to rub on her skin when she felt the need for cleaning or renewal.

We sit together at the edge of the water, Tesseba and I, let the waves trickle up toward us, scoop handfuls of foam as it edges around our feet and coat first our hands and arms, then our faces, then our hair too as the sun continues to rise and heat fills the air. The water is thick and sticky, warm, opaque, filled, as Baptie told us when we were children, "with many magics."

It tingles on my skin as it evaporates. Perhaps there is magic in it.

WHEN WE FIRST MET, Tesseba's appetite for stories about Africa, about my family and the life we had led, was insatiable. She would ask me questions and I would answer, aware all along that I was being incomplete, less than accurate, that my stories contained more than a hint of four white horses in the streets of Liepaja. No city could have been that quaint, its thoroughfares that orderly. The Edwardian buildings that lined the esplanade, the dense mangrove forests, the charming hillside tea rooms, these were based on something real but rested more on things that weren't, things wishful, things rueful. Gordonwood was flawless, my parents were constant, even the servants understood that we were deeply ambivalent about their servitude. She used to listen, Tesseba, to accept my answers with open, interested eyes. We did not, of course, live in a vacuum. Reference points were available. But Tesseba, living her life, painting her pictures, content in the evenings to sit with me, to read, to go for walks, was not inquisitive. So none of it was challenged, not even the more brazen inaccuracies.

Shortly before my mother became ill, Tesseba and I were visiting her in London and I decided to call Rupert, with whom I had been only sporadically in touch over the years. We were both busy. We had let things slide. We met for breakfast at the Savoy and he was clearly elated to see me, effervescent in fact, couldn't take his eyes off Tesseba.

"So this is who you ended up with," he said, and to Tesseba: "You must be a very patient woman."

We made our way to a table and ordered breakfast, and as was almost inevitable once we had caught up we began reminiscing, and as the two parts of my asymmetric life sat across from each other, a sense of foreboding crept up on me. When we were boys, Rupert and I were honest with each other.

"I remember Gordonwood like it was yesterday," Rupert said enthusiastically. "That big study lined with books. The clanky front door. I even remember how rank the servants' quarters were."

My face had warmed and I had the feeling of being suspended in midair, vulnerable and exposed. It was not only the servants, of course, how we may have treated them. Rupert knew about other things, my family's big secret among them. Rupert had been there. Rupert knew.

"They weren't that bad," I remember saying.

"They were the worst I ever saw," Rupert continued good naturedly. "Calcutta right in your garden."

"Is that true?" Tesseba had asked. "I thought your family made a point of not doing things that way."

"He's exaggerating," I had said, trying to deflect things. "They were old, rickety maybe, certainly not as derelict as he's making out," but Rupert wouldn't let it go. "I felt bad for your servants, old man," he insisted.

"You mean Baptie too?" Tesseba had asked, "Baptie who raised you?" and as I sat speechless I saw her recoiling from her own question, wanting to take it back.

"Oh, come on," was all I said.

After that she began to press me on the details, and then, I can not say precisely when, I realized that she accepted almost nothing I had said as true. Even I realized that it was all too flat, too ordered. I left out nothing of the menace, of course, the affront of *apartheid,* but under that shadow things were startlingly placid; well behaved boys in safari suits, girls in long dresses and straw hats, old-fashioned manners, cricket matches that stretched on for days. She didn't say it at the time but it sounded to her a bit too much like Mayberry in uniform, with

Africans doing the chores and Aunt Bea offering tea in the afternoon, complete with scones and jam.

Her doubts ran to other things too. As I presented it, when my father died the whole world turned on a dime and led directly to me sitting that day on the bus, cold and almost destitute, but without guessing directly she had already decided that the father I described was not quite real, too pure in motive, too civil. There was too much wistfulness, she said, too much vagueness.

"What did he die of?" she once asked.

"An accident," I said.

"What kind of accident?"

"Leave it, Tesseba," I said, but she knew, just as she knew that the Gordonwood of my stories was not real, that we were on the edge, right on the edge, of the massive secret I had conspired to keep from her, and that when my father's life ended the sadness that descended went beyond only the sadness of death. My father killed himself because he was a business failure, and because he had melted to nothing in my mother's shadow, and because Bridget and I thought so little of him, and for reasons that I am sure are not rational too, and yet that is the starting point for me, the starting point of everything, the moment of ultimate defeat from which recovery becomes less and less likely every day, regardless of how beautiful my home or how elegant my routines. In America a person can reinvent himself, start again fresh, and that's what she has said I seek to do, but there's a part of every person that can't be reinvented and that part is one's own past. One can't rewrite the past, Tesseba would say, recast things so as to filter out the parts one regrets and enhance those one wishes to embrace. My father shot himself one night and died in his study at Gordonwood, ten miles down the coast. He and I had not spoken in weeks. What's done is done.

Rupert knew. I knew. Everyone in my family, even Arnold, knew. Tesseba did not.

"Leave it, Tesseba," I repeated.

As I settled down in Boston, became moderately successful, I made sure that my mother and Arnold's visits were extravaganzas worthy of Gatsby or *Sabrina's* Larrabees. My mother seemed to delight in it, made an ostentatious show of walking from room to room when she arrived oohing and ahing like an audience at a gala show even though she had seen it all before. The floors were made of creamy stone, polished and polished until you could see your face in them, the walls were glass from floor to ceiling, there were soft white curtains, carvings from Nigeria, masks from Benin, beadwork and sandstone from Zimbabwe. All of it made for a spectacle, indeed.

"Why are you doing this?" Tesseba used to ask, and I remember thinking that the question was preposterous. "Our lives are our lives," she would add. "This stuff is a farce, all stage dressing."

But I know, knew even then, that the charade was not for my mother. I know that my father and Arnold knew each other, though I can only guess at the circumstances of it. When I think of my father's struggles I have come to think also of Arnold, his nemesis, accumulating a fortune doing who-knows-what, there on the other side of town. The redemptive role I have assumed then has everything to do with that, and it is stupid, it is gratuitous, but it is so nevertheless. If Arnold is to enter Silas Divin's son's house the place must be pristine. There must be not a speck of dust anywhere. Everything must sparkle. It is as if it is I who must wash the blood from my hands.

I did not know either, until the end, that Arnold had once propositioned Tesseba, put his hand on her knee under a table and winked in a foul manner that confirmed to her once and for all that he was simply ridiculous. Even that, had I known about it, would not have changed anything.

12

WE RECLINE IN WHITE CANVAS CHAIRS under a white canvas awning. We are stuck, waiting for Baptie who, for whatever reason, is late. So we wait, on edge, wonder how we will feel to see her again, and she to see us.

The hotel pool is large and there are about a dozen children in it. Within minutes both Leora and Tibor are in it too, treading water, Leora's arms around her father's neck. It occurs to me that I have not before seen the two of them acting with such intimacy. Tibor is lean and trim and also very fair, and he swims sideways in a manner I have never seen. People notice but they say nothing. Leora is as tall as her father and is hugging him, draping her arm over his shoulder, ruffling his hair. She has escaped, steadily and completely, the shadow of heaviness that has come to cover Bridget and me. As his daughter bullies him in the water Tibor, so straight, so unruffled, submits with a wry smile, clearly enjoying the way in which his lithe daughter treats him with a new and growing confidence.

"How long are you here for?" a woman asks.

"Just a week," I say.

"You should stay longer," the woman says and launches into the sights I should be sure to see, a description of the new restaurants that have opened on Florida Road, the new art galleries, the largest shopping center in the southern hemisphere just up the road. "It isn't all going to rack and ruin like some of you overseas seem to think," she says.

"We don't have much time," I say. "But thanks for the advice."

She keeps talking but then I begin hear another conversation, someone behind me saying, "and, of course, no provision made for them to stay anywhere. They brought them in on busses from Zululand or wherever and just dropped them at the beachfront. By the end of the day hordes of hungry black children were peeing in the sea and shitting on the sand."

"What were they doing here?" someone else asks.

"Some sort of provincial holiday outing," she is told. "A trip to the beach. Who knows?"

"They don't have beaches in Zululand?"

"I wouldn't know. In any event, they certainly made a mess of ours."

"Ours?" I hear a voice say quizzically, and I turn to see an elderly man, bald with a fringe of white hair. "Ours? It's as if for you the world started yesterday and what happened is just a figment of someone's imagination. Don't you stop and think sometimes, in between complaining about how high your bloody taxes are, how dirt-poor children act when they see the ocean for the first time, how lucky you are, how lucky we all are? Don't you wonder what the alternative was, what would have happened if Mandela hadn't been who he is, alive when he was, thinking as he thought? This conversation, this carping, it makes me sick."

"Oh, come on now," the woman says. "Nobody here supported *apartheid.*"

"These days you'd be forgiven if you thought nobody did except perhaps bloody Dr. Verwoerd," the man says.

"Sounds like my mother at a dinner party in the old days," I mutter to Tibor as he dries himself off beside my chair.

The chatter continues. Servants. The price of electric fences. Casual chatter. Bright sunlight. There is no sense of dispossession, no nostalgia, no exiles' angst in it. The children in the water are playing a game I do not understand. "Marco," the child in the middle calls.

"Polo," the others respond. A waiter brings cold drinks. I may drift off. The lawn sprinklers go "chick, chick, chick."

I wonder how the markets have moved in Asia and Europe during the night.

13

IT BEGINS TO RAIN, a driving, drenching, Durban rain and what's more a rainstorm that does not interrupt, not at all, the bright, wet heat of the sun. We are driven indoors, off the stone patio and into the hotel lounge. We take possession of a corner table, order tea and sandwiches, pull over chairs and an ottoman, and spread ourselves out.

"Where the heck is Baptie?" asks Bridget, who has half the hotel staff on the lookout for her.

The rain stops and the afternoon sun continues to shine as if there never were an interruption, as if the day will go on forever.

"Let's go down the cliff to the beach," Leora says. "It looks quite nice." No one answers and she says: "Well I'm not going on my own," and sinks back into her chair, and just as she does a bellhop comes running in as if on some urgent mission and announces that a battered white Toyota Corolla has just pulled up at the rotary and that Baptie is in it.

So how does one describe the scene as Baptie, with Bridget holding her arm and my hand on her shoulder, comes through the revolving doors and stands in the foyer of the hotel? She is wearing, we all notice it immediately, one of my mother's suits, a red plaid, too warm for this weather, and a floppy canvas hat, not my mother's, with Kangol printed in large letters on it.

"This is them?" she asks as we enter the lobby and when we say yes she puts her bag on the floor and bows her head as if she is afraid to look up, as if she is blinded by the very sight of Tibor and Leora, of Tesseba, and then she begins to clap her hands and to chant.

"Yo, yo, yo," she says. "*Nkulunkulu*," the Great One. "This is my reward. This is my blessing. I never in my life."

"This is my baby, Nanny," Bridget says and Leora, even though she wants to give her mother every indulgence, is somehow enthralled herself, tilts away.

"Yo, yo, yo," Baptie says and runs her hands through Leora's hair, touches her arm and her shoulder, her breasts too, runs her hands over her breasts, and then stands back.

We are making a spectacle of ourselves, our little group in the foyer, with our talking over each other, our laughing, Baptie's hand clapping. Eben stands to the side. He has wanted to drop his mother and to drive off but Bridget and I have insisted that he join us for tea, maybe even for dinner. He accepts the invitation to tea, says he cannot stay for dinner, and I am surprised by his manner, not exactly self-effacing but as if he has no will in the matter.

Now he watches what is going on in silence.

"You look so young," Bridget says. "You look the same as you used to."

"Ah, *Nkosi*," Baptie says. "You talk nice to me for nothing. I am old and too thin. I walk like this," and here she breaks off to mimic a hunchbacked hobble, right there on the marble floor, "and then I sleep the whole day."

"Mommy would have loved to see you in that dress," Bridget adds.

"Oh shame, oh shame," Baptie says. "When I opened that packet from you I nearly died I was so happy. All these beautiful dresses from the Madame, even some that I remember. One of the dresses, oh God, I opened and there I saw in the pocket a tissue from the Madame, smelling from the same perfume, the same one that the Madame used to wear in the old days. Oh, that was a happy day for me. I thank God every day for that from you."

When Bridget and I were children and Baptie lived in a room at the bottom of our garden she was an elder in her church. Occasionally we'd see her church outfits hanging out to dry with our own clothes, long white gowns with green trim and gold crosses, and on Saturday nights she'd hold church services in her room. Sometimes we'd catch a glimpse of her all dressed up for the service, an African shepherdess in a linen frock bearing no resemblance to our housemaid in her pink dress and white pinafore.

One Saturday night my father and I, needing a key to something or other from her, disturbed a service in process, knocked loudly on her door even as we tried not to pay attention to the singing we heard coming from inside. The service came to a stop, everything fell silent, and Baptie, in her white gown, opened the door. There were tears on her cheeks, total stillness in the dark behind her. Candles were burning on the table and the room smelled of perspiration and wax.

"Do you have the key?" my father asked, and without saying anything she turned and went to a metal cupboard against the wall and rummaged through its contents.

When she returned the key was in her left hand and she held it out without a word, her right hand resting on her forearm.

"Thank you," we said, and it was as if we were not speaking to Baptie at all but to someone else entirely, someone with whom we were not familiar. It was the only time in my life that I ever saw Baptie out of character and I suspected at the time that she was in some sort of religious thrall. "Now I have seen my children," Baptie announces. "Now I can die."

She turns to Tesseba.

"And this one, this is the one you married?"

"Yes, I say. "This is Tesseba."

"*Yo*," she says, taking Tesseba by both hands. "She is very beautiful. Maybe she is too good for you."

We laugh, and the relief we feel is palpable. Eben, his expression unchanged, looks on.

WE ARE TO BE DRIVEN, Bridget has arranged it all, to Zimbali up the coast. A concierge has told Tesseba that it is the best and most expensive restaurant for miles around, and at six we find two Mercedes-Benz cars waiting for us under the portico.

"Bridgie," I say. "I'm not sure what point you're making but we're allowed to take the money out of the country now. It's not trapped money you're spending. It converts to real money, to dollars."

"Maybe," she says, but vaguely, as if she has not fully heard.

When we were children elegance here was simple and sturdy and found in old English hotels like the Royal and the Caister, but Zimbali, when we approach it, resembles a cluster of African huts and its grounds are lit with flaming torches. Flowering bushes shroud the walls, extravagant white awnings flap slowly over the windows. As we walk from the cars through the colonnade we are surrounded by ebony wood, decorative calabashes, an air rich in colonial nostalgia.

I can't help but wonder what Baptie makes of it all, the oversized tribal artifacts, the cathedral ceilings of *faux* thatch, but all she says, seemingly unmoved by any of it, is: "This is a nice place, but the Beverly Hills is bigger," and then she adds, unaware of any irony in it: "They have things here like the Master's."

"Oh, my God," Leora says as we enter the foyer. "This is like the movie set for *Out of Africa*. Paging Robert Redford. Please see Meryl Streep in her room."

From the restaurant we look out over the pool, how it drops away to a waterfall at the far edge, one's eye connecting the crest of the waterfall with the Indian Ocean half a mile and a deep valley away. There are palm trees, waiters in white, lights illuminating the fairways of a golf course. We take in the planters' chairs, the linen umbrellas, the flapping awnings.

Baptie studies the menu and says she would like meat and potatoes, some bread.

"Wouldn't you like to try something new?" Bridget asks her.

"For what I must eat the new food?" she counters.

She is the only African eating in the dining room and our African waiter is impeccably polite to her. Bridget orders for the rest of us, crayfish from the Cape and langoustine from Mozambique, avocado salad, a chocolate bread pudding for later.

"I would like to see them all again," Baptie says, and for a moment we are unclear what she means. Then she adds: "I would like to see everybody from the past days again."

"You will see them at Mommy's ceremony," Bridget says. "The ones that are still here. We have invited them all, all the people Mommy knew and used to speak about," and then she turns to me and a strange, self-deprecating look crosses her face. "If they come."

"What do you mean?" I ask, but before she can respond Baptie puts down her fork and asks, indignation in her voice: "Why did so many of these people from the old days go away? Why did they go to the overseas?"

Bridget shrugs, thinking how to answer, and I say: "They were worried about the future."

Baptie makes an angry, snorting sound.

"This bloody South Africa," she says. "The people have nothing now. They must eat sand while the leaders, Mbeki and all of them, they are like the Dutchmen from before. I think even Malan and Strydom, those Dutchmen from the first days of *apartheid*, were better than these. Now the hospitals have no medicine," she is ticking it off on her fingers as she speaks, "the people are dying like flies, there are *tsotsi* criminals everywhere, nobody cares about anything. Did Mr. Nerpelow tell you that even in Durban they took my money, the *tstotsis,* and then that nice lady in his office had to give me some more money and stuck it with bandages under my shirt?"

"Yes," I say. "He told us about that. We were glad you were not hurt. "

She picks up her fork and begins to eat again. We are all watching her and for a few moments there is a palpable silence.

"What was Danny like as a boy?" Tesseba asks finally.

"He was good some of the time," she says, and then lowers her head. "Not so good like Bridget, but in the end okay."

"But what was he like?" Tesseba asks and there is a lull, just a moment of silence, as we wait for her answer.

"Our house was a very good place," Baptie says. "I was there every day, wake them in the morning, bring them breakfast, sometimes for this one," and she gestures toward me, "put the tray on the pillow, next to his head when he will not get up. I fix the clothes, make the lunch, when they come home clean their things, listen to their stories when the Madame was out."

"That's why I'm asking you," Tesseba says. "What was he like?"

Baptie turns back to the bread on her plate and takes a bite from it. The rest of us wait in silence.

"He was horrible," she says, and something slips inside me but at the same time it is as if an old invoice has suddenly reappeared, a forgotten score been recalled.

"Do you remember?" she asks, turning to me, "always throwing your clothes on the floor, losing things, blaming the servants, not speaking nicely to us."

She laughs, covers her mouth with her hand.

"'You bloody fool,' he shouted when I did not let him do what he wants. 'You bloody black fool.'"

This is a peasant woman, after all, rough of manner. She turns back to her plate, takes a piece of bread, a sip of her Coke.

"But then, after he had been gone for a long time," she adds, "he became nice. That is why I say it is good that he is old. When he got old he became nice. And they built me a house, these Divins, a nice house in Gingindlovu with a bedroom and a kitchen, and Danny writes me letters, and everything is good now."

She laughs again and we all watch her, aware of how she cuts her meat with strong and deliberate strokes, of her missing teeth, of how they make her chew on the side, how she wipes her mouth after each bite with the starched napkin.

"Can we come and visit you where you live?" Tesseba asks, surprising me, surprising everyone. "I'd love to see the house they built for you."

"No, no, Tesseba," Baptie says, chiding her. "Mrs. Divin did not build this house. This house was built with my Master's money. But in any event, why would you come there? For what? There is nothing. Not even a hotel, a thousand *tsotsis*, people with nothing. No," she adds, shaking her head, "this place, this Beverly Hills, is better. If you want to see me, I will come here."

"Okay," Tesseba says mildly.

Baptie takes a piece of bread, breaks it, uses it to mop the sauce in her plate. Something drips, she removes her napkin, tucks it into her collar. Her mention of my father has us on edge, Bridget and me.

"What happened with my Madame and that man she married?" Baptie asks as she eats, dominating us now, holding the table in a kind of thrall. "I have been thinking about this and I do not think that she was happy with him. I do not think a person can be happy with a person like that."

"Why didn't you like him?" I ask.

She ignores the waiter who is trying to reach over her shoulders to remove her empty plate, looks at me blankly.

"Do you think I am blind?" she asks.

"Well, he was horrible," Bridget says and then, as the waiter clears the table, refills glasses, scrapes crumbs with a small silver spatula, Bridget tells the story, or an abridged version of the story, that leaves out the floozy, the detective, the wholly passive, confused role of my mother in it all.

"Yo," she says from time to time, and when Bridget is finally finished she says it again, laughs, claps her hands loudly, causes several people at other tables to cast knowing glances in our direction.

"Why would he want my Master's things, all those stupid things that we used to have at Gordonwood, the wood cases that I made to shine, the things on the walls, the elephants at the fireplace, why would he want those things that should be for the Master's children only?" she asks. "But even so, everything you are telling me, everything, this is not news to me. I always knew he was not a good man. I knew things I could not tell anyone. I knew he was horrible from the first day."

"What did you know?" I ask, suddenly curious.

"I said I cannot tell anyone," Baptie answers. "This is something from before that nobody can know."

"Hey," I say, leaning across the table and trying to enlist Bridget's aid. "It could be very important. We have a court case against him, you know, in front of a judge in England. What you know about him from before could help."

Baptie looks at me grimly.

"I told you, Danny," she says, and it is almost as if it is the old days again, Baptie telling me that it is time to go to bed or that I cannot leave my clothes lying on the floor. "It is something I cannot say."

Leora has shown Baptie how to use the television remote, how to order room service, how to adjust the temperature, and we have noticed two empty trays lying outside the door of her room as we leave for dinner. We are determined to treat her like a princess.

"But you must," I demand.

She looks at me, everyone at the table looks at me, and then for just an instant I see myself, my face reddening. I can see, everyone at the table can see, that she is steadfast. Leora examines the dessert menu, even Bridget looks away.

I am annoyed at how smug, how complete, is her refusal, at a sense I suddenly have that our own feelings rest on a bond that may or may not be mutually felt. I am irritated too by the others at the table, by Bridget with her secrets and coy asides, by Tibor, opaque, imperturbable, Leora with her adolescent cockiness and urgent need for privacy.

"Excuse me for a moment," I say, and make my way to the restroom.

Throughout the rest of the night the crickets scream, the bullfrogs croak, the wind shakes the leaves of the dark trees without letup. A hundred yards below the waves churn at the rocks jutting from the shore.

Across there, just a few walkable miles away, down the coast, reachable, is home.

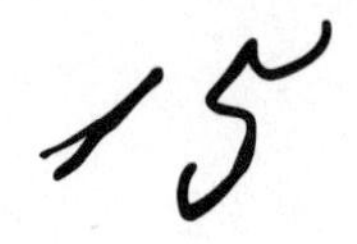

Bridget and I have an appointment with Morton Nerpelow. Leora and Tesseba want to go walking on the beach, as far up the coast as the beach will take them.

"Not on your own," I say, and definitively. "Not on your own."

"It's the beach," Leora says, and now she sounds like a teenager. "What can happen on the beach? Tesseba and I will protect each other."

"I'll go with you," Tibor says.

Leora looks at me with her head turned sideways, a hint of mockery in her tone.

"Don't you think I can take care of myself?" she asks.

"No," I say. "Not here."

"But we're with Dad," she says. "He's indestructible."

If I thought she was completely flippant I would laugh and let it go.

"Violence is random," I say instead. "No one's indestructible."

"We're not so fragile," she insists.

"As I understand it," Tibor says, his manner perfectly serious, "if we start up going north on this beach we'll be following the course your Nathaniel Isaacs took to reach King Shaka and pass the spot where Henry Fynn encountered his Zulu regiment. Maybe you'd like to come with us."

I can't tell if he's being serious. It's not like Tibor to tease, let alone to tease me.

"I'll pass," I say and then I add: "You're right though. This is the beach."

Leora is as tall as her father and is always hugging him, draping her arm over his shoulder, ruffling his hair. Our constant reminiscing, it seems, is also becoming grist for her mill.

"Why don't you send Uncle Danny to the lawyer and come with us, Mom?" she says. "If you don't you might miss something, a bird perhaps, the great-great-grandbird of a bird that once flew over Granny Helga while she was giving a speech about human rights."

They all laugh, none more heartily than Tesseba.

"Okay," I say. "Do whatever you want. But don't come crying to me if you're cut into pieces and left in a ditch."

"I won't," she says. "You have my word."

Before we leave I fill them again with cautions, not to go too far, to shy away from groups of non-white men, to come straight back if they feel insecure, to stay together, and then Bridget and I wait under the hotel portico for the car and driver Bridget has ordered.

"What is it, do you think," Bridget asks, "that's making you so nervous? Dare I say it? Don't you trust black policemen to keep you safe?"

"Don't be dumb," I say.

"No," she says. "I'm not being dumb. You go to all sorts of places on business—God knows, Detroit. Jackson, Mississippi. Camden, New Jersey—and you don't say a word about safety. Suddenly here you act as if every person's a rapist. Every black person, need I add."

I'm about to resist, to find fault in all sorts of assumptions, and then I lose the energy.

"I don't know," I say. "Things really are unsafe. It's the contrast. It just feels wrong."

"Well you're putting everyone on edge," she says. "We have our own car, by the way," she adds. "Parked right over there in the lot. But I figured you'd find something either unsafe or unhygienic in it."

No, I agree, not yet, not into the city. Once we have parked, I say, what sort of gauntlet must we run to reach Nerpelow's building smack in the middle of town.

"I think you've gone over the top," Bridget says.

Maybe she's right. A fountain puffs water into the humid air right in front of us. There are trees with leaves as big as a person's head, a rising heat so dense it penetrates the ground and raises a musty vapor that discolors the air.

"I hope he has the papers ready for us," she says as we wait, "though I don't know how they get anything done here they're so inefficient."

"What are we signing?" I ask, and this is not typical, for me to be going to a business meeting so disengaged, so unprepared.

"What we need to sign to unload Grandpa's buildings once and for all," she says. "But one thing I don't want to do is fritter away the day having lunch at the Durban Club. He invited us but the thought gives me the creeps."

"It's almost worth doing," I say. "He took me there when I was here and spent the whole meal giving me a history lesson. You should experience it just once."

"I can't think of a place I want to go less," Bridget says.

The car arrives and it's another Mercedes-Benz driven by an Indian man in a short-sleeved shirt. A doorman in a white jacket and matching helmet opens the door and we get in, and then the car pulls out of the parking lot and we are on the old North Coast Road. It is narrow, overhung with dense trees and dark bushes, and as we maintain a slow and steady speed other cars rush by us. Bridget rifles through her notebook. We pass over the Ellis Brown Aqueduct, pass the turnoff to the Blue Lagoon, drive right in front of Natal Command where Rupert and I once reported for army service. An African sentry stands guard.

On the traffic islands black women offer plastic coat hangers and bundles of wafer thin garbage bags. They lean right up against the car's windows each time we stop.

"No, no," the driver says, gesturing with his hands.

"It wasn't always like this, you know," he reassures us. "The police should just sweep them all away."

"Are they dangerous?" I ask and he looks at me over his shoulder and says: "Not dangerous. A nuisance."

"Spark plugs," my cousin Janice has said. "They smash the car windows with spark plugs, grab your purse or jewelry, and then they disappear."

I watch a man's lips moving as he shouts at me through the closed window. A piece of newspaper tumbles across the tar in the dusty wind.

"Let's ask him to go past grandpa's buildings," Bridget says. "It'll be interesting, don't you think?"

The car turns onto the Marine Parade and we snake along through the heavy traffic. African women sell curios and vegetables on the sidewalk, their wares spread on blankets that reach right into the pathway. A white couple ambles hand in hand among them. We pass a woman pushing a stroller.

"We own all of this," Bridget says as we drive up Gillespie Street toward the city center. "From there," she points, "to there. And then around the corner to the bottom end of Smith Street."

When I was in Durban last I looked these buildings over carefully, walked through each one with a manager, and then entered our tenant stores and was introduced as a representative of the owners. Nothing has changed except that it all appears more decrepit, more run down, than I have remembered. Groups of men stand about on the sidewalk. Three men seem to be waiting for something in the vestibule of one of our buildings.

There are *For Sale* signs in front of most of our buildings and several *Under Agreement* signs as well.

"I think that's the one that we've just sold," Bridget says. "There. That's the thirteen-million-rand one."

The driver, I suddenly sense, is listening. I nudge Bridget and gesture with my eyes.

"Do you think we could stop at one of these?" she asks. "Just for a moment."

The driver says nothing, begins to pull over.

"You own these?" he asks, unable to resist.

His tone is skeptical.

"My grandfather built them" I say. "Very long ago. See that building there with the name Palelga Mansions on the front?"

"Yes," the man says. "Is that where you want to stop?"

"That's short for Helga Paladin, my mother's maiden name," I say. "Or that one down the block, the blue one. Danbridge Hall, that's named for Danny and Bridget, for us."

"Just one thing, please," the driver says as we open the doors. "It's sometimes an iffy area here, you know. Take a photograph, you know, but hold on to your camera."

"Iffy?" I say.

I look up and down the street and then at the several groups of men. Their expressions range from indifference to mild curiosity.

"It's not a good idea to loiter about carrying expensive things in this part of town, " he adds. "But it shouldn't be a problem."

"Never mind, then," Bridget says and gets back into the car.

She closes the door and turns to me.

"I think you make everyone nervous," she says. "Is it safe? Is it safe? It's bright daylight, for Christ's sake. People are going about their business."

"Is it safe here?" I ask the driver again. "My sister thinks I'm overreacting."

"Not overreacting," he says. "Maybe pickpockets or something like that, but it is safe."

"What the hell does that mean?" I mumble.

A woman in an expensive car drives past us and it seems to me that her car is an illusion, hers but not hers at the same time. And we too, we own everything here but something holds us from laying our hands on it. There are things we want, but at the same time there is nothing for us here at all.

16

In any other place, in almost any other time, you would find few people, hardly anyone in fact, who would not describe Morton Nerpelow as a good man. He has all the makings of it, a sense of solidness, of reliability, a sense of personal fairness. His handlebar moustache is perhaps his only affectation, and it is a mild one for all the care he must take when he grooms it. He disdains a briefcase, carries his papers, I have seen this, edges flapping, under his arm, passes an acquaintance, nods, keeps walking. Suede shoes, firm step, leather patches at the elbow, battered black Rover car. If you were to hear that Nerpelow had stolen money, for instance, you would only be able to conclude that this had happened in some parallel universe where the impossible was possible and where, as he might have said, pigs can fly. Inside the building, in the carpeted lobby of Nerpelow & Loudon, everything seems quiet and secure.

"Mr. Nerpelow will see you now," a receptionist says. "His secretary will be right out."

As we walk into his office I am struck by how much Morton Nerpelow has aged. His hair has gone perfectly white, his moustache has become wispy, there are dark circles under his eyes.

"Good morning," he says as he comes out from behind his desk and extends his hand.

It is as if we are in for a routine appointment, nothing else.

"How are the two of you?"

I don't know what we have been expecting. The last time I was here Nerpelow met me at the airport, put himself at my disposal, but now, it seems, all that is forfeit. We exchange pleasantries, but only for a moment.

He lifts the phone.

"Send in Miss Patel," he says and replaces the receiver.

"Miss Patel is the associate assigned to stay on top of your affairs," he says.

He offers us tea which we decline, and then, almost as an afterthought says: "I was sorry to hear that your Mother had a tough time of it."

"Thank you," Bridget says.

"You know my feelings about your stepfather, I dare say," he adds. "Not a well regarded figure in these parts."

"Not in any parts," I say.

Nerpelow does not respond, turns his attention to a group of files lying on his desk.

"You'll find that everything's really quite straightforward," he says.

Nerpelow's office overlooks the bay. It is low tide and the harbor looks as if it has been drained, stranding a line of ships in several narrow channels. Emptied of water it is a maze of sandbanks and puddles and the slivers of water that remain look incapable, surely, of ever floating such great ships away. It looks like a giant saucer, flat and swampy and ringed with trees, and despite the wharves and the cranes it looks just a short step, a heartbeat, from being empty of everything but hippos and crocodiles.

"Children are swimming in the harbor," Bridget says suddenly. "Is that safe?"

Nerpelow looks up, but only briefly.

"Who knows?" he says shrugging. "Nobody's going to stop them either way. The new rules, don't you know."

"The water looks dirty," I say.

He asks, but in a perfunctory way, how long we are staying, about our ceremony.

"There's something I meant to raise with you," Nerpelow says. "You do realize—I expect someone you're in touch with has already told you—that you've chosen to hold your function on the same evening as the Durban Philharmonic has its series *finale*."

Bridget and I exchange glances.

"Why didn't you say something?" Bridget asks, and Nerpelow looks up, studies her face, returns to his papers.

"I assumed one of your family friends would have told you," he says.

"Nobody did," Bridget says, but the truth is that nobody could have. We have been in touch with nobody. Nerpelow is all there is.

"Will *you* come?" Bridget asks.

"I will put in an appearance," Nerpelow says, but his manner is not reassuring.

Now Nerpelow becomes even more aloof, there is no question of it. It is a disappointment, even uncomfortable.

There's a knock on the door and an Indian woman enters and introduces herself.

"Miss Patel needs you to look over and sign some papers," he says, drumming a finger on his desk. "Once the decision was made to sell the buildings you could have done it from America, but since you're here now we have them ready. Then it's just a matter of waiting for the Reserve Bank to approve our various applications and you'll have your money several months after that."

"I've heard so much about you," Miss Patel says and then she adds: "You're all Mrs. Dhlamini talks about."

"You know Baptie?" Bridget asks, smiling, relieved at the friendly interlude. "She's with us at the Beverly Hills."

"I know, she told me yesterday," Miss Patel says. "She was in with her son, you know, Eben, to talk about the Truth and Reconciliation process."

Bridget and I sit forward in our chairs.

"Why would she be doing that?" we ask.

"You don't know?" Miss Patel asks. "About Danny? Eben's son Danny?"

"No," Bridget and I say at the same time.

"He's in jail for murder," Miss Patel says, but there is something uncertain in her tone and she looks at Nerpelow for guidance.

"Who did he kill?" I ask.

"A senior official of the African National Congress," Nerpelow says, "or so we are given to understand."

"What happened?" I find myself asking.

"The fellow went out there to address an election meeting and our boy whacked him with a hatchet," he adds. "Why that's a political crime I couldn't say."

"It's the first we're hearing of it," I say. "Baptie hasn't said a word."

"Why would she?" Nerpelow asks and there is something now so dismissive in his manner that we find ourselves, Bridget and I, turning to his clerk, to this Miss Patel whom we have never met and whose first name nobody has told us, turning away from Nerpelow, indeed, so that our backs are almost to him.

"Is he eligible?" I ask. "I thought that process was long since over."

"I don't know," the woman says. "That's what we're trying to find out."

"New rules," we hear Nerpelow say and he is truly angry now, and with us. "Hacked a man's head off with a *panga.* These days we ask why, and then if it's expedient to do so we look the other way."

"It has to do with the conflict between the Zulu nationalists and the African National Congress in the last days of *apartheid,*" Miss Patel says. "If that is true, if it was politically motivated and if he accepts responsibility for the act, he may be eligible for amnesty. The problem is that the whole thing is long since concluded, though perhaps in the interests of fairness we might be able to make a special case for him"

"They assume, of course, that your family's footing the bill," Nerpelow says. "Why they would assume that is anyone's guess. Endless expectations all around, I would say. Some met. Some not."

I turn to Miss Patel.

"Do what you can," I say. "We'll pay. Of course we'll pay."

"It's all so very easy when you live ten thousand miles away," Nerpelow says sharply and then, without more, he excuses himself and leaves the room.

"What was that all about?' I say to Bridget as we leave the building. "It can't just be about Eben's son."

She laughs strangely, clasps her skirt against the wind.

"Children swimming in the bay, I think," she says. "Your little escapade the last time you were out here. Who knows?"

We stand for a moment on the sidewalk, both of us reluctant to return to our cocoon just yet. Ms. Patel has told us of Nerpelow's plans, that he is leaving the country. I can't quite see him there with the didgeridoos and the sloths but I'm sure he has his reasons. Ms. Patel has asked if it is okay with us that she take over our files, or whether, perhaps, (and she asks this so gingerly) we would prefer to transfer them to "someone from our own community." Put that way, of course, we almost have no choice in it, though I like her. I think she will be just fine.

"Do you want to walk a block or two?" Bridget asks.

It all seems so workaday around us. There is a construction crew fixing the sidewalk, people hurrying along carrying shopping bags, an occasional white man in a suit. Through the glass we see people eating in a restaurant, someone trying on shoes.

"Perhaps I'm not destined to be murdered on West Street between Gardner and Field," I say. "It would be too ridiculous."

"What I can't figure out is what you expected," Bridget says. "Running gun battles? People cowering in doorways?"

"No," I say. "But do you know that there are more murders in Durban in two days than there are in New York City in one year?"

She stops walking.

"If you do that one more time I'm not going out with you again," she says. "It's a crazy perspective. Everything's dangerous, flying's dangerous, but people accept the risks and they make whatever adjustments they have to. People are living their lives. Look around you."

Instead of responding I take her arm and we begin to walk. There are vendors on the sidewalk and one must weave about them, and the sound of the jackhammers digging at the edge of the road is deafening. There is dust everywhere. We notice that our driver is following us, inching along through the heavy traffic several yards to our left.

He looks anxious.

"Let's put him out of his misery," I say.

Sitting in the backseat of the car Bridget flips through her lists. Everything she has planned is contained in her little spiral notebook, pages of phone numbers and addresses and head counts, a chaos of scrawls and numbers and columns. Her notebook is, somehow, at the intersection of fantasy and reality.

"He assumed we were in touch with all these people," Bridget says.

"We have been," I say. "You wrote to them."

"That's not what he meant," she says.

"It'll be fine," I say.

"I've been calling people since I got here," she says, "the ones from Mom's address book that I sent invitations to, and everyone's being so vague about whether they're coming or not. Do you think it's this orchestra thing?"

"I don't know," I say. "What do they tell you?"

"They're all just vague," Bridget says. "Like I was trying to sell them something and interrupting them over dinner. They're polite, ask all the right questions, about us, about whether we have kids, about what we do, and then they just leave it, don't say exactly whether they're coming or not."

"I don't know," I say again.

"I feel like a character in *Our Town*," Bridget says. "Like one of the ghosts having to watch his family live their lives without him."

"Except that we're not dead," I say.

So much time has gone by and this belief in a stable circle of loving friends who went on with their lives after we had gone, went on but remembered us and felt the hole we had left, is beginning to seem, here and in the light of day, to be, perhaps, a myth.

"What if nobody comes?" she asks.

"People will come," I say and then, as if it hadn't been an issue, her doubt passes and she concentrates again on her plans.

"I do have another idea," she says suddenly. "Perhaps we can rope the rabbi into this. Persuade him to come and offer some sort of benediction."

I may pause for just a moment too long.

"Is that dumb?" she asks.

"Bridgie," I say at last. "Neither of us has been to a temple for twenty years. We don't even know the guy."

"I'm not suggesting you change your religious views," she says. "Just that there might be something symmetric in it. To say nothing of the added bonus of roping in another live body."

"Stop," I say. "Really. Just stop."

"I have his number," she says. "I actually called his office already and left a message. His secretary asked me to spell my name. Imagine that. I had to spell our name."

We approach the hotel and the driver swings the car under the portico. As we get out I see that Tibor has been waiting in a chair in the lobby, and he rises and begins walking briskly, almost running, toward us.

"You're not going to believe this," he says as he reaches us.

"I'll believe anything," Bridget says. There is an edge of defeat in her voice, a tiredness.

"You're still not going to believe *this*."

"Try me," Bridget says.

"Arnold's here," Tibor says, the most peculiar expression on his face. "In this hotel."

"Oh, come on," Bridget says, almost angry now, but something in Tibor's manner stops her in her tracks. "What do you mean 'Arnold's here'?"

"I saw him," Tibor says. "Right now. Here in this hotel."

"Here?"

"Checking in."

Tibor nods, smooths his hair.

"Did you talk to him?" Bridget asks.

"Of course not," Tibor says. "I saw him and I ducked."

"You ducked? The hero of the heist, Moishe Pipick, ducked?" Bridget says, but the seriousness of the news overwhelms her levity. "Was he alone?"

"Yes," Tibor answers. "And I'll tell you something else. He looks quite different than he did two years ago."

"How?'

"He's aged," Tibor says. "He walks with a limp. He looked pathetic if you ask me."

"What kind of a limp?' Bridget asks.

"What does it matter what kind of limp he has?" I say impatiently, and Bridget turns to me angrily.

"Don't take it out on me," she says. "I didn't bring him here."

"What I wonder," Tibor says, "is what he's doing here. I mean, it's not a secret that we're here. But what's he doing here?"

"What kind of limp?" Bridget asks again.

Tibor looks at her for a moment, realizes she really wants to know.

"Sort of like this," he says and begins to move. "Shuffle. Clump. Shuffle. Clump. Like something's wrong with his feet."

Leora, who has been exercising in the hotel gym, joins us.

"All right," she says, catching just the tail end of her father's performance. "What's going on?"

"Arnold's here," Bridget says. "In this hotel."

Leora looks incredulous and then, surprisingly, she smiles.

"I can only say," she says, "that life with you lot has no dull moments."

She turns and starts to walk to the elevator.

"I like it here," she says. "Let's stay an extra few days."

"Why would Arnold be here?" I say to Bridget and she, her face still drained of color responds: "Why would Arnold be here?"

18

A MESSAGE FROM THE RABBI returning Bridget's call awaits us. It is Friday and he has invited us to the Sabbath service.

"So let's go," I say. "I could be curious."

"Maybe I'll ask him when we're there," Bridget says. "Maybe. If it feels right."

"Let's discuss it," I say, my general religious antipathies interfering with what might actually be a good idea. With what my mother may actually have wanted.

We scramble to get ready, postpone our dinner plans, return to town at sunset, to the synagogue, on a mission now. We find a parking space where an African man with an official looking orange jacket tells us that for three rand, a quarter in real money, he will watch our rented car while we are inside.

"Do you think he's legit?" Bridget asks.

"We'll find out when we get back," I say.

We walk down Silverton Road to the Synagogue and pass a small group of people standing at the gate. The gate is new, as is the formidable security system through which we must pass, but nothing else has changed, not the building, not the driveway, not the gray linoleum tiles on the floor. I learned the Torah portion for my bar mitzvah here, once sat on these same benches beside my father on the High Holy Days. The place remains very familiar and yet nothing is the same. It has shrunk. It is older. It is darker. The sanctuary, coldly lit by fluorescent lights, is sparsely filled.

"They've recovered the seats," Bridget says. "They used to be beige and now they're brown."

There is an awkward moment as we realize that we have to separate, that Bridget, Tesseba, and Leora must go upstairs and sit with the women while Tibor and I remain downstairs in the main sanctuary. It is Tibor's first time in a synagogue. He sits beside me, earnestly wears the skull cap he has taken from a bin at the door. It is an incongruous sight, Tibor in his familiar brown jacket with a white satin *yarmulke* on his head. If my father were alive and still here, if things were just a little different, we would sit side by side as adults in this bank of seats on one Friday night and then another, watch time pass with calmness and acceptance, after each service walk from the building shaking hands and saying, *Good Shabbas.*

Tibor sees me looking and reaches up to his *yarmulke.*

"Do I have it on right?" he asks.

I feel suddenly protective of my brother-in-law. There is so much he takes on faith. He is so patient with us.

"It looks good on you," I say.

The neon lights suck color from the air, bleach the wood, wash the carpet in a thin, white glow. Upstairs Bridget has chosen, whether deliberately or by instinct, my mother's usual seat just as I have chosen my father's. It was here, on this spot, that I said *kaddish* for the first time, looked up to see my mother and Bridget, their heads together, watching. The service is underway and quickly becomes, for me, tedious. I am not a religious man, not at all, and I find myself looking around aimlessly, at the ark, at the raised *bimah,* staring at the brass lights that hang in small clusters from the ceiling. A man in the front row sways. The rabbi sits in his little box to one side of the ark. A senior member of the congregation sits beside him in another. I recognize someone, an elderly man sitting across the aisle from me. I think, though I am not sure, that he is the father of someone I once knew. He looks so gray, so stooped.

We have spent hours driving about the city, revisiting old places, but what had promised to be satisfying is over in a flash, reduced to an aimless meandering between places that once meant something, a peering over gates and between electrified fence posts, a pointing out of things to Tibor and Leora as they barely listen. Bridget and I prattle away—this house used to belong to these people, that house to those—some of the trees are the same, the grassy islands are the same, but in truth there is nothing from the past that is alive. An Indian family comes down the steps of the Epstein's house, a Japanese van sits where Carolyn Levy's father once parked his vintage silver Jaguar. I see that Bridget has made a mistake in her choice of seats. She has chosen the seat that once belonged to her. It is Tesseba who is in my mother's seat, sitting there where my mother once sat, her long hair in a braid, her face earnest and open, watching carefully. The cantor sings, and I gaze up at her. She is familiar, achingly familiar. I long for home, for a distant, unreachable home.

After the service ends we walk, Tibor and I, back down the long gray corridor to the stairway to wait for the women. I examine the photographs that line the corridor walls, synagogue trustees, benefactors, rabbis. I know many of the names. Some of these people were my parents' friends. Most are dead too. The air here is harsh, humid and warm, and some of the photographs are mildewed, have slipped free of their mountings and sit skewed against insect-stained glass. People pass us on either side, men in dark suits, talking, laughing, shaking hands. Nothing inside this building has changed, nothing has changed except that the one place that has not changed has become, instead, claustrophobic.

We are strangers in a strange, strange, land, Bridget and I and Tesseba and Bridget's Bulgarian husband, and we are also, here in the most familiar, the most unchanged, the most frozen spot in the city, almost, almost, Americans.

"Do you want to know what I think of trying to see the rabbi now?" Bridget asks.

I look at her expectantly.

"Screw it," she says. "We don't know him, and he doesn't know us. How impressive does this vaudeville act have to be?"

"It's not vaudeville," Tibor says. "You have a right to do this. You have every right."

"Sure I do," Bridget says. "But this tree's falling in an empty forest. I feel like I'm standing underneath it."

19

I SUGGEST TO BRIDGET that perhaps we might consider calling everything off. I have overheard her talking on the phone. She is being charming, laughing, chatting, but I can hear desperation in her voice.

"Why am I being made to feel that there's something off-color about this?" she asks. "That we're committing an indiscretion?"

"We could just pack up and go home," I say again.

"A hundred invitations is what stops us," she says. "This is beginning to feel like one of those dreams that won't move ahead or go away."

"Why are you saying the Madame's party won't be good?" Baptie asks. "I think it will be a blessing on you to do this thing for her."

She is wearing her Kangol hat.

"If all the people from the past days will be there," she adds. "I am sure it will be good.'

Bridget sighs, shakes her head.

"We've been gone for a long time," she says.

"People don't forget something so quickly," Baptie says. "Before, when you and Danny were left to the overseas and I was staying with the Madame in the beachfront, these people in Durban, these friends from before, they did not leave her alone they loved her so much. Sometimes I would watch and I would think: What must a person do for other people to love them like this? That was what my Madame had. You must not forget this."

Bridget looks puzzled and then lets it go, buries her face in her hands and rubs her palms over the top of her head like my father used to do.

"I don't know," she says. "I feel stupid for suggesting this whole thing."

"I know what you can do," Baptie says, and even Tibor looks up expectantly. "My Madame loved Zulu singing," she says. "She told me this, and my daughter-in-law, Julia, sings in her church choir every Sunday. People from everywhere ask this choir to sing, at school concerts, at other churches, everywhere. She can bring them, and they will sing prayers for my Madame, if you ask her."

For a moment the idea sounds ridiculous and the next moment it becomes perfect, exactly right. We begin feverishly working with her to get word to Eben at his office and through him to Julia, find ourselves following Baptie around like acolytes, asking for instant translations as she talks in Zulu on Bridget's cell phone.

"She says she can do it," she finally reports, "but she must speak to the other women."

"If they can't come will she sing on her own?" I ask.

"Danny," Baptie says, her tone once again one of suffering patience. "Why are you always in such a hurry? Sometimes you must let things happen when they are going to happen, not when you must make them to happen now."

"Don't try to make them to happen now," Bridget adds.

"Eben is here, you know, in Durban," Baptie says, and turning to me she adds: "He wants to speak to you."

20

It surprises me then, on the night before the event my sister has begun to dread, that the person with whom I find myself drinking tea on the veranda of the Oyster Box Hotel is not Rupert, but Eben. He has called to say that he is in town and has asked if perhaps, after dinner, he might stop by and have a few words with me.

"Of course," I say. "I'd like that," and then when he does arrive there is a moment of awkwardness as we stand side by side in the lobby.

"I don't need to keep you," Eben says, "but I just wanted to thank you for what you do for my mother."

Instead of responding I ask: "Would you like some tea? I never drink the stuff in Boston, but since I got here they've been force-feeding it to me and now I'm addicted."

Eben laughs, but behind his hand, modestly, like a young girl.

"I could have some," he says.

"Come," I say. "I know where we can go."

I hesitate outside as a group of African men ambles past us, hold back until they are gone, and then we cut across the parking lot, across a narrow lane and a patch of grass, and enter the lobby of the Oyster Box Hotel next door. The place is fully recognizable, hardly changed, but it has become very dated. Moisture has melted the edges of things. The carpets look sodden and threadbare.

"I haven't set foot in this place for a lifetime," I say to Eben. "I used to come here with a friend but they say it's about to be renovated and I expect soon enough nothing will be recognizable."

"I used to come here all the time, too," Eben says.

I look at him in surprise and see that he is teasing me, has made a joke.

"I'm sure you did," I say, and we both laugh. It is a relief to be laughing, he and I, even as I am not sure of the extent to which what we find funny would overlap.

"Yes," he adds. "The tea here is very good."

We walk through the lobby and the veranda is, indeed, exactly as I left it, the patterned tiles on the floor, the giant red lighthouse at the end of the lawn, the wicker chairs, the pool. Eben waits until I have selected a table and am seated before he pulls a chair closer and sits across from me.

"I just want to say this," he says, leaning forward, and then he says nothing.

There is an ashtray on the table and he begins to spin it slowly with long, slender fingers. We sit for a moment as he gathers his thoughts. It is clear there is something he needs to get off his chest.

"My mother was just a servant woman in your family's house," he says at last. "There is nothing that obligates you to do the things you do for her, and even if she doesn't say it herself, I know she is grateful. I know I am grateful."

"No," I say, *ja nee,* and I am somehow embarrassed by this, by his gratitude. "It's something we do gladly."

Eben watches me, continues fidgeting, and it is obvious that he is not done, that there is something else he wants from me. Finally he cannot restrain himself.

"Why?" he asks. "What is it that makes you treat her the way you do, that makes you see her the way you do?" He hesitates and then he adds: "I must confess I am curious about this."

A busboy approaches and wipes the table, but when he is done the surface looks grimier, less appetizing, than when he started. The air is thick with humidity, the smells of saltwater and seaweed. For the first sixteen or seventeen years after I left South Africa Baptie was not much more than a relic, someone with whom I exchanged occasional letters, mostly out of a sense of obligation and perhaps with a measure of curiosity. I always recognized her envelopes when I saw them in the mailbox, blue air letter cards, sometimes soiled, her handwriting large and uneven. I would make my way through them with difficulty, trying to glean snippets of information from her not always coherent descriptions. To me she had been nothing more than a servant woman, if the truth be told, until many years after she no longer was, and then as my mother's marriage became hellish for me to watch, as an edge of sadness about the past came to be a mark on everything in the present, Baptie changed too, or at least she did for me.

"Now that my parents are gone," I tell him, "she is all that remains of the past. I cannot think of her without thinking at the same time of a thousand other things, and now all I want is for her to be safe, to have the things she needs, to live out her old age in comfort."

Eben nods slowly, but he is not satisfied. He moves the ashtray to the center of the table, offers me a cigarette and when I decline lights one for himself. A waiter approaches, a tired old man in a starched white suit.

"What will it be?" he asks gruffly.

"I also think," I add, "that she tolerated things from me that no adult should have to tolerate. I wish I could change that, take some of it back, but of course I can't. Now I need her to be safe. That is all."

"What things?" he asks.

"You know how it was," I say at last. "You know."

Our tea arrives and we sit in silence. The beam from the lighthouse sweeps out to sea, across the grass at our feet, back to sea again.

"I know," Eben says finally. "But it was a long time ago. Everyone has moved on. What is done is done."

"I wish I had seen things differently when it mattered," I say suddenly. "I don't know why I didn't. I mean, shouldn't it have been intuitive?"

"I don't know about that," Eben says. "You are trying to stand on your own shoulders if you want to take what you know now, and say you should have known it before. Nobody can do that."

I look at him across the table, a cigarette in one hand, the other still touching the ashtray.

"You seem like a very calm man," I say. "I envy you."

He looks up, his turn now to be surprised.

"Calm?" he says. "If I am calm it is my wife who deserves the credit. And also my son, Danny is proof, if I needed proof, that looking back too hard, holding onto anger, or regret, or envy, is pointless. Those things are just a burden to the person who carries them."

"Nobody told us about Danny," I say. "I have asked Mr. Nerpelow to do what he can for him."

"I know," Eben says as if our assistance is a given. "Those lawyers will do what they can. But nothing can undo what sin he has committed."

"I'm not sure I would call it a sin," I say.

"It was a sin," Eben insists. "It can be repented for, but not undone. Violence against another is a sin."

"Given the way things were," I say, "it's a miracle there wasn't more violence."

"Violence against another is always a sin," Eben repeats and his vehemence catches me off guard. "Violence against another is *always* a sin."

I am not sure I fully agree. What of the Warsaw Ghetto? What if, in my bleak room in Liepaja, I had had access to a hand grenade? *Apartheid* for all its flaws wasn't systematic genocide but there is justice in self defense, isn't there? Either way this is not what I want to be discussing with Eben, not now on the veranda of the Oyster Box Hotel. And he has begun to look uncomfortable.

"In any event," I say, "I hope things are much better for you now. And for your mother too. They are better now, surely?"

He looks at me carefully.

"Believe it or not nobody has ever asked me that question," he says. "Maybe we are too busy, each with our own struggle. You can ask my mother yourself if you'd like, although I know for sure what she will say."

"What will she say?" I ask. "Sometimes your mother is a mystery to me."

Eben laughs, an easy, good natured laugh.

"She is not as mysterious as you think," he says. "My mother remembers those days at your house as her glory days, her golden days. She remembers those days, those *apartheid* days, with nothing but fondness. She grumbles about how things don't work any more, about how crime has made her life miserable, about the small corruption of government officials. She wishes the whites still ran things. What can you do?"

I shrug, and then I nod. The *goldene* memories that fill Baptie's rambling letters are something Bridget and I wonder about. Her letters are filled with yearning for the days when she lived in a dank little room at the bottom of our garden, and yet what is it that she could possibly want returned to her? Her little room? Being at our beck and call?

"You are right, though," Eben adds as if reading my thoughts. "There was a lot about those times that was very bad. Perhaps it is that memory is its own creature. It changes some things, leaves other things out, moves about our lives with its own paintbrush. Even with my son, Danny, his upbringing was quite easy compared to mine. He grew up in a good house, went to school every day, did not live with his nose pressed up against the glass, but his mind is filled with ideas that seem to belong to someone else. I try to understand, but on some days I come close to giving up."

I do not know for sure what Eben is referring to, but then I do not need to. Our own memories, I would have to say, are twisted enough, of golden Gordonwood, times that could not have been as simple, as blessed, as the ambiguities of adulthood, and our present situations, have come to make them seem.

"Yes," I say. "Memory can be mischievous."

In a warehouse in London are the relics of those times, as precious to me as any objects could be. What we have snatched from Arnold are reminders of what I have always kept in my imagination as pieces from an almost perfect setting, glory days indeed, though in the true light of day they are nothing of the kind. In some ways I don't want them at all, certainly don't need them, and yet I will move heaven and earth to get them.

"Things were very complex when you and I were boys," I add. "They were not happy times."

"I would think that you of all people would remember those as good days," he says.

"Maybe," I say, and there is a long silence.

Finally Eben cannot restrain himself.

"You say you did not understand us," he says, his voice raising. "It was you people who were hard to fathom. *Impossible* to fathom. You had everything. Your family in that big house with all those things, and you looked happy from what I could see, quite content to enjoy all those things that came from being white in those days, your swimming pool and your cricket and your *braaivleis* parties. And yet I know there was unhappiness too."

He is referring to my father. He must be referring to my father. I am suddenly so tired, so burdened with the complexity of it. Maybe one does need to just let things be.

There is a moment of silence but Eben has become quite voluble, eager to talk.

"Do you remember that one day you took me inside to see those things your father had? Do you remember that? I saw that you believed that if you were to touch my skin it would not feel like the skin of a human being. That is just the way things were."

He looks down as he finishes his sentence, almost as if he is again quite shy.

"I'm sorry to say this," he says finally.

"You have me wrong," I say.

"I think also," Eben adds suddenly, "that even after you left here and went somewhere else, because you were white and had money, everything was still easy for you."

The irony in his assumption is, of course, rich. I cannot take it on.

"Being white and having money does not guarantee happiness," is all I say.

"I have found," Eben says carefully, "that if money is not everything, it is almost everything."

He pauses.

"Yes," he repeats, nodding, and there is now an edge of aggresson in his voice, a hint of anger and directed at me, at me treating him to tea on the balcony of the Oyster Box Hotel. "I do believe that. I think for white people in South Africa everything is still more than okay, even if these days they complain about the way things are changing. But from where I am, where people have no money, where people go without food, and where there are no doctors no matter how sick you are, people are filled with disappointment and it comes down to money. Especially now since poor people think that the leaders made them promises and have not kept them, and then they see the rich ones in the city, blacks and whites, it all comes down to money."

I watch him, watch the light flash out to sea and back again over the grass.

"Money is important," I say.

"No," Eben insists. "Money is everything in a place like this. Without money there is only suffering, now just like before, people dying of AIDS, people who have no jobs and who go out to rob and steal just so they can eat, honestly, people from my own church who go and hijack cars, and I could say to them don't do it, stop doing that, and I know it is wrong, but the problem is that if they say: 'Okay, I will stop. Now where am I going to get money or a job?' I would have nothing to say to them. For white people who start out with everything change is nothing else but a threat, and we are all just one black sea that threatens them, not individual people at all. That is why they cannot tell who to be afraid of and instead are frightened by every change, by everything."

Something at the edge of the good feeling chills as he says this. The sea crashes against the rocks below us, the lighthouse continues to send its beam out and around in great, slow circles. You could say, one could always say, that against the problems he is referencing, our own problems, our own sadness, our maundering preoccupations, our feuds, are little indeed.

"I think people in America are very rich," he says suddenly. "Especially the Jewish people. Is that true?"

I look across at him and wonder what to make of this, how to respond to a question that rests on assumptions I could question all night.

"That's what I have heard," he adds. "It is the same here, in this country, too."

"I think you believe in a world of incorrect stories all your own," I say.

Eben sits forward and says quickly: "I didn't mean to offend you. That was not my purpose. I meant it, really, as a compliment."

I do not know if I will see Eben again after tomorrow. This is not what I thought it would be.

"You know," he says and his whole tone suddenly changes, "I asked to speak to you so that I could thank you, both for my mother and for what you have agreed to do for my son, and then I say something that offends you. I will try and make amends by answering your question honestly."

"What question is that?" I ask.

"About us. About what I thought of you, back then," he says. "And why that changed. Because the truth is that there was a time when I wanted to run in the streets looking for justice and waving an assegai, and in those days *yours* was the face I put on the unfairness of it all. Back then I dreamed with passion about the restoration of the Zulu kingdom, about Shaka's days, except that what I pictured when I thought those things was not Zululand at all, not me in Zululand, but me in that house, on that veranda upstairs, with all those things. You were long overseas then, but still I dreamed of dragging you from there, myself."

I nod.

"Oh," is all I can muster.

"Yo," he says, shaking his head. "I am ashamed even to say it, but I promised you the truth. Do you see how crazy people can behave? I will spend the rest of my life repenting for such thoughts. The rest of my life, truly."

We sit for a moment in silence.

"But things changed for me," he continues, "mostly because my wife's view of the world does not accept violence, and there is something almost perfect about how clearly she sees the world, if I say so myself. In her view of the world violence and anger have no place. You can be angry, and for good reason, but in the end it is you who pays for it. Only you."

He pauses, waits for me to say something, but I do not. I have nothing to say.

"Do you want to know the best part of it?" he asks.

"Please," I say.

"Sometimes your anger is wasted, just rubbish," he says. "All your ideas built only on sand. I discovered for instance that my son's hero, this supposed warrior after whom he has renamed himself, Shaka's bravest warrior, Mgobozi, never even existed. I heard this on the radio, some small program, and the next day I went to the library and saw that they were right, that there was never a person called Mgobozi, that this Mgobozi who my son has based everything on is a figment of some white historian's imagination. Let me tell you this, Danny," he says, and he leans forward and puts his hand on my knee, and I find this somehow touching, restorative. "Sometimes I think that's the problem, that half the stories we believe about ourselves and about others too aren't true." He pauses and then adds: "I can't say things like that in front of my wife because she thinks when I do that I'm talking about Jesus." He chuckles, and it is a gleeful, mischievous chuckle: "And maybe I am, at that."

It is late now, approaching midnight. I am finding his face increasingly familiar with each passing moment, and even as he has shown his anger, as we have watched it rise and fall of its own accord, I feel a tug of affection. Sitting on our wicker chairs in this hotel whose time has come and gone, listening to his words, seeing a deep brown face I have known almost all my life, I feel, suddenly, that there are no points to be made, not with Baptie's Eben, not now.

"Let's order something stronger to drink," I say.

If Rupert were here we would, once again, be going over old times, tracing the history of people and events, when things started, how we thought they would turn out, how they turned out. We would share black humor, speculate about people's fates, compare the styles of Bill Clinton and Tony Blair, analyze the sources of our parents' political beliefs, compare our lives abroad with what they would have been had we remained. We would, in short, have the same conversation here as we would have in London or Boston. But this, now, is different.

"You see, I am guilty of the murder my son committed because it was me who planted this dream in my boy of fighting for a new Zulu kingdom," Eben says, "but I have come to see that it is a ridiculous notion in these times. The government spends more money on the Zulu royal family than it does to fight AIDS in Kwazulu, and even that is the wrong kind of reparation, in my view. I look at the pictures of King Goodwill wrapped in leopard skins and leaning against a Range Rover and I feel halfway ridiculous myself. I mean," he adds, "in this day and age, who needs royals running around in Lear Jets with money taken from my pocket?"

"My mother wrote her Ph.D. thesis on Shaka, you know," I tell him, and he says: "My mother told me something like that, but I found it hard to believe."

He laughs: "You people were not always easy to fathom. And now, we are not easy to fathom either. We have our rights, but still, people have their flaws."

Rupert would want to be hearing this, I think, as Eben talks. Rupert would see, as I do, the other side of something we thought we knew so well, hear things that cast what we believe about ourselves in a new light. I was watched from behind a hedge, it seems, and though we didn't know it or ignored it if we did, we ourselves were emblems, rich with meaning, there as if from Mars to preempt everything, to possess everything, embodiments of a dispossession so vast and so comprehensive that nothing was spared, not even our servants' imaginations. Somehow I learn, at this point, that Baptie has not been getting the full pension Bridget had arranged for her. I don't know why, though I have my suspicions. A phone call in the morning will fix that.

We turn to look at the sea, the line of ships on the horizon waiting to enter the harbor. Tesseba, if she were here, would have made an origami swan from the napkin that lies on the table in front of me, placed it carefully in the middle of the table.

"Do you know what I think?" I say, and then without waiting for him to respond I say: "I think despite everything that may look different, we are as similar as brothers, like two brothers from the same broken home."

The lighthouse beam flits over our heads. The surf is unremitting. The shriek of the crickets is constant. Eben smiles and leans forward in his chair.

"Brothers," he says, and he laughs and laughs. I cannot be sure that he is not, in some small way, mocking me. If he is, I deserve it. "I do know that there was a time when you had more of my mother than I had myself."

He laughs as he says this. He is so clearly a good natured man.

"Yes, for sure. She was certainly nicer to you than she was to me, but then maybe she thought you were more worth the effort " he says. "But don't worry. I do not hold this against you. In fact, now I have my answer. Perhaps you take care of her because she is your mother too, because in the end we share a mother, and so I have my answer. You should take care of her. It is your duty. And so you do."

As we walk back into the hotel the thought occurs to me that of all the strange things that might happen in the world, few would be stranger, or more symmetrical, than if the tusks that once stood at Gordonwood were to end up standing in Eben's home in Zululand. I can't quite picture the place—it would be small, I'm sure, basic—but fake though they are, they would be back in Zululand where they theoretically belong, would have come full circle, have new meaning amidst people no one once imagined would ever be in a position to claim them.

"Do you remember those tusks that we had?" I ask instead, eager, for whatever other reason, to mention them.

"Of course," Eben says. "Of course I do. Those tusks. Where are they?"

"They're in London," I say. "But we hope to be bringing them home soon."

"To here?" Eben asks, suddenly animated.

"No," I say. "My home is in Boston."

"I would like to see them," he says, "just one more time in my life."

"Why is that?" I ask.

"I wouldn't know where to begin," he says.

"Come and see them in my home," I say. "Anytime," and even as I flirt for an instant, for just an instant, with telling him the truth, Eben who may have earned the right to the truth, I back away, decide against it.

Let everyone preserve their illusions.

21

HOW, ANY REASONABLE PERSON might ask, just how, given all that we have said and been through, how does it come about that Baptie gets left at the hotel on the evening of my mother's memorial? We are standing, Bridget and I, in the foyer of the Durban Jewish Club, Bridget fretting, me marveling at how little it has changed, when a woman comes hurrying up to us and says that there is an urgent call for Bridget in the front office. When Bridget returns she is laughing in a way that makes me expect the worst.

"Baptie's still in Umhlanga Rocks," she says.

"What do you mean?" I ask, looking about, expecting to see Baptie at any moment standing there in one of my mother's old dresses and waiting for us to lead her to where she is supposed to be.

"She's at the hotel," Bridget repeats. "I just spoke to her. The concierge wouldn't have even known where to reach us if someone hadn't overheard us talking."

"What's she doing there?" I ask.

"We forgot her," Bridget says.

Leora, who looks striking in a dark brown dress and sparkling earrings, overhears.

"You left Baptie behind?" she exclaims. "How did you leave Baptie behind?"

"I thought she came with Eben," I say.

"Eben took Julia to fetch the singing nuns," Bridget says. "I told you he was going to."

"You left Baptie behind?" Leora marvels and then repeats: "They left Baptie behind."

The Jewish Club is a symmetrical gray building one block from the sea. In the old days, before emigration forced the Jewish school to sell its premises and the club to jettison its bowling lawns and tennis courts, the club was a center of Jewish life. There were plays and lectures, sports events, public meetings. During the Six Day War when they needed blood in Israel the Red Cross set up a special collection site here, and when there was an emergency drive for money women brought their jewelry and fur coats to help raise what was needed. The men who started this club a century ago, newly successful men barred by their religion from entering the Durban Club, chose furnishings and decor that reflected that other place with its heavy wooden doors and cut glass windows. Now it feels to me, perhaps only to me, unspeakably forlorn.

"I told them to send her in the hotel car," Bridget adds.

"I'll wait for her at the door," Leora says and Bridget responds, her tone dull and distracted: "That's a good idea."

There are tables set up near the stage, a station with drinks, another stacked with enough *hors d'oeuvres* for a hundred people, a microphone near the side windows.

"It's early still," Bridget says as we all notice, can't help but notice, that the room, large and open, is almost empty.

"It must be the Philharmonic," I say. "People are going there."

I take Leora's hand as we wait in the room and I know what she must be thinking, how this all must look to her. Eben arrives with Julia and we greet him effusively, shake hands with the women who will sing, but who can fail to notice that Eben and Julia and her women, and we, outnumber our guests?

"The women want to know," Eben says, "what you would like them to do."

Bridget looks at me helplessly and then Tibor, realizing that the time has come for him to step in, says: "Perhaps they should check the microphone and make sure that they have what they need."

"Microphone," Julia says looking around with a puzzled expression on her face. "I don't think we will need a microphone for this space."

She walks off with one of the women and we wait, Tibor without expression, Bridget looking about in desperation. The time on the invitation arrives and there are perhaps eight or nine guests now in the large hall, and as I am trying to convince myself that somehow this is adequate two or three more come in, and then someone else, and then someone else. Bridget's greetings are hearty, but to me they sound forced. One might have said, on another occasion when one did not need to be charitable, that she sounds almost hysterical.

It starts to rain. I can hear the drops hammering down outside, a heavy, drenching downpour. I am inside but I can feel the drops even so.

"We should start," Tibor says and Bridget mutters, barely audibly: "Why bother?"

"For the people who came," he says. "It's not only the number that matters."

From behind the microphone I look out at the faces, all of them quite familiar though so much older than I had remembered, with skin like parchment, pouches under the eyes, wispy gray hair. The great hall really is empty, so sparsely filled that it feels entirely so, and the people who have come are now undecided as to where to stand, whether to sit, what to do next. I had assumed, in London, when people came to pay their condolences, that the frailty of my mother's contemporaries there was an artifact, something wrought by the cold English weather and the uncertainty of exile, not simply by time and not something that would have happened so markedly here too, where they are at home, in their element, in Durban. But time has ravaged everything, I see, even the eyes, especially the eyes which were once so clear and which are now milky, tremulous, uncertain.

"Good evening," I say, dispensing with the microphone, a glass of water in my hand. "For those who don't remember me, I'm Danny Divin."

There is a murmur, an echo in the emptiness that is only sporadically broken by faces that watch me expectantly, hopefully. In the back of the hall I see Morton Nerpelow come through the door. He is wearing a raincoat, looks like a fugitive alone there against the wall. He catches my eyes and nods. It is doubtless his first time in this club, and he is, one can sense it in the way he clings to the wall, here against his instincts.

"When my mother passed away in London," I say, "we did not think that her death would lead us back to Durban."

There is as I say this a loud clunk and I see that Baptie has come into the hall, and that Leora has not managed to prevent the door from slamming behind her. The click of her shoes on the floor fills the room. How could we have forgotten her? What must she think of it?

"After she died," I say, "it seemed to Bridget and me that there was one thing more we needed to do, and that was to come to Durban and to say good-bye for her, and that is why we are here."

It is my mother's palpable absence that makes everything feel so flat, so lacking in context and in charm, and my unease is now fed by a sense that we are meddling, Bridget and I, in things that do not concern us, going through my mother's private closet perhaps, rearranging where we have no business being. This myth of ours, the myth of a large and resilient and loving community for whom the memory of my mother is strong and fresh, is collapsing about us. There is only what we saw, the house in London, the nurse, the few frail visitors, our memories of other times, nothing else.

I feel so fatigued it is a wonder I can go on, but I do.

"We have decided to make several gifts in my parents' names," I say, and I list them, an old-age home, a hospital, several local orphanages, and there are smiles when I am done. But it is all meaningless. My heart feels like a stone.

Bridget moves from the audience and takes the microphone.

"We have arranged," she says, "for some music my mother would have loved."

She turns and nods to Julia who makes her way to the front followed by her women, but just as she does I hear Leora gasp and then everyone turns, and though I do not it is clear that something is happening.

"Oh, my God," Leora whispers. "It's Shuffle Clump."

I turn now as well and true enough Arnold has entered the hall. He has aged, Tibor is right, stands hunched over to the side, is wearing his trademark cravat, gesturing as he talks. He has lost weight, his neck is thin, he is wearing a shirt that is too large for him, not tucked in, that hangs about him like a badly made tea cozy. He looks about and it is clear that he is surprised by what he sees, by the flatness, the thinness, the sparseness. He pauses to shake someone's hand and then he fixes his eyes on us and determinedly begins to make his way across the room. Even Julia's women know that they should wait, and they do.

As he nears me, this intrusion of one thing into another, he extends his hand, masters a sympathetic smile, tilts his head.

"I think," he says, and his voice, though thin, is loud too, "that it's time we buried the hatchet, don't you think, you and I?"

I do not respond. There is something in me that recoils from overt conflict, that prefers a more subtle engagement. I can be sarcastic, I can spirit things away in the dead of night, but I recoil from scenes such as the one that seems set to unfold. I look at Bridget, she at me, but her face is blank.

"We are a family, you know, like it or not, we are a family, and this has all gone too far," he says. "I am not, in all sorts of ways you know nothing about, the ogre you have come to see me as."

I sense in the people around me that something in Arnold's tone is resonating with them, that whatever it is he is after, he must be heard out.

"And I'll show you that I mean what I say," he adds, standing now right before me, his hand still extended, looking me directly in the eyes. "I am prepared to let bygones be bygones and have instructed my lawyers to end the lawsuit we have against each other in London. I didn't like your methods, I didn't appreciate your methods, I don't think your mother would have approved of them, but I'm prepared to see your side of it and if the blokes here in South Africa can find a way to settle their differences, I don't see why we can't. If I have offended you I apologize, and here, in Durban of all places, let us agree that, in the end, life is too short to nurse grievances that last forever."

As he talks I realize that there is a moment of equilibrium in life, a moment when something can tip either one way or the other, and that we are at such a moment now. Though my body remains filled with something that feels like hatred, maybe there is something else in it too, a shared history, like it or not, a shared past with this man who, for better or for worse, was once married to my mother. I loathe this man, without a doubt, and for good reason, but maybe my fury masks other things far more serious, grief and guilt among them, and whatever else happens in the next five seconds my memory of his face at this instant will not allow anything to stay the same. Maybe then this is the gentlemanly thing to do. Certainly I can feel that everyone in the room wishes me to take his hand and to shake it. My mother would have wished it. Maybe there is something to the idea of forgiveness and reconciliation. All around us they have let go, or are in the process of letting go, of transgressions far worse than Arnold's. And the tusks, that business of the restoration, what Arnold knew and did not know: There is a possibility, there has to be, that he too, and for his own reasons, may have decided to protect us, or at least my mother, from the truth.

Who knows?

In short, I am wavering, but I do not reckon on Baptie who is standing behind me. She is standing still one moment and then the next she has sprung into action like a steam engine bursting a gasket, a mass of hissing and quivering, furious beyond measure, derailing once and for all any chance of reconciliation, any kind of peace.

I hear her before I see her.

"You," she says. "I know who you are."

There is a clearing of shocked silence, faces blank, everyone on edge.

"I know you," she repeats, "so don't you look away like I am a rubbish, someone you do not need to listen to, someone you can throw away because you have no use for me."

She pauses, glares at him.

"Do you hear me?" she asks, her tone menacingly quiet. "Do you *hear* me?"

Bridget, standing at her side, puts her hand on Baptie's arm, begins to say something, but Baptie shakes her off.

"I asked you if you hear me," she demands again. "Because there is something I want to say to you. I want you to leave these children alone so that they can forget you. Leave my children alone."

Now Arnold, suddenly alive too, raises his eyebrows in quiet contempt.

"Don't think that you can come in here and behave the way you people think you can behave outside," he says finally. "There are two sides to every story too, you know. I would have thought you were old enough to know that."

"Between you and my children I know who I must believe," Baptie spits. "And also I know everything about you, even if you think I know nothing. Leave my children alone."

"Can you believe this?" Arnold says, his face beginning to change, to whiten. "This is vulgar, setting the house girl loose to do the dirty work in this manner."

"I knew of you before the children knew of you, before my Madame knew of you," she says. "Do you think, Master, that we do not talk to ourselves because we are only your servants, that you can do anything you want, that you own everything, even people."

"Take it easy," Baptie, I say.

"This man," she says, looking at me, looking past me, "is no good. It is my fault that I did not tell my Madame what I knew, that first time, after my Master died when he came to visit her. I have felt bad for all these years that I did not tell her."

I do not know what she means, even if she is coherent. Most of all I wish this were not happening.

"I should have told her," she continues, looking now straight into Arnold's whitening face, "what the servants who worked in his house told me, that he used to go to the servant girls in their rooms in those passed days, when his first Madame was still alive, and sick. I should have told her. It is my fault that we are here like this. If I had told her everything we would not be here."

Suddenly she is quiet, shocked by her own daring.

"How dare you?" Arnold says, and then we lose track of it as Baptie steps forward and begins, forcibly, to push him to the door and people stand back, just part, magically, to clear a path.

Arnold turns, beckons to an African security guard who is standing nearby, breathes heavily.

"Would you please control this girl," he demands.

"She is not a girl," the guard says, and he could be Ambrose saying "Yes, Master, I will light the barbecue now," or, "We need to stop and get petrol," but he is not.

Our ceremony, our careful little charade designed to refurnish memory, to create memories that are not sullied, has been sullied, our efforts are in ashes. I see it in the faces of people standing about me, shocked, muttering among themselves, watching us all, me, Bridget, Tibor, speculating, commiserating. And it is then, at that moment, that what it is we have tried to do, and why it could never have succeeded, and why this does matter, becomes clear to me. Nothing we do, nothing we can do, can take us back to a time when things were whole, when we were whole, when my father was alive, and when Durban was just a city, just a dull, uninspired, city and not this cauldron of myth and dreams, when things were ordinary and we were whole. We are, Bridget and I and those we have dragged back with us, clinging to shadows here, standing on the stage of a play that has lost its interest, and in a theater that has long since closed. What audience is left is frail and flawed, beset by problems wholly unrelated to our own, and its views are of no continuing interest. There are no battles for me to fight except those at the fault lines of my own life, and these do not lie in Durban or in any place one can visit. We are here on a fool's errand.

"I remember everything," Bridget has said. "Even the door handles here are more familiar than any I see in America, and the light fixtures, the way curtains hang." But in the end, these are all very small things, these memories of ours. The world here has turned upside down but it has done so slowly and inexorably and those who live here, who have lived through it, have had time to adjust, to absorb things piece by piece so that no big decisions have been made, no big changes, just little ones, one after another after another, until nothing of the old, or almost nothing, remains. To those who have lived through it, change has been so stealthy it is almost as if it has not been noticed. But for us time has swept away everything that once was familiar and we are left to grasp at phantoms as unreal as the one that Shaka somehow belongs to us too, that the riches of the past lie in Durban, that it should be ours to visit and to share at will. A good portion of our beliefs, it seems, are not even genuine, not real, as fake as our blessed tusks, constructs of epoxy and nostalgia.

The guard's manner is gentle, but his voice is quite firm.

"She is not a girl," he repeats. "She is an old woman."

"Wait, wait, wait," I say. *"Wait,"* and immediately there is silence, an expectant, tense silence. Even Arnold recoils in uncertainty.

I extend my hand to him. For some reason a memory of Eben's quiet demeanor returns.

"Things can't be left like this," I say. "You were married to my mother. That is enough. Do stay. Please stay with us."

And at that moment we hear singing, Julia and her group of women on a stage at the other end of the hall, a chorus in Zulu with words we don't understand but with a melody and cadence that is unmistakable. This is the music we heard coming across the garden, over the swimming pool, from the servants' quarters, the music I once heard, standing in a tiny store in Greenwich Village with Bridget, both of us inexplicably confused, somehow dispossessed, on the verge of tears on a very cold January day. Everyone stops talking, turns to the women, listens as the music fills the great hall of the Durban Jewish Club. Their voices transcend everything, the jagged edge of things, the uncertainty, the sadness.

My father died and it all caved in, and yet we are here. There is still time left.

"These are the songs they sing in their church," Eben says quietly. "I think they have chosen the most beautiful ones they have."

Somewhere in it all I am aware of Baptie as she makes her way to the front and motions to Eben's wife Julia, of Julia as she gestures to the others to keep singing and walks over to where her mother-in-law is standing, of Baptie as she says something in her ear. When the song ends we see Julia caucus briefly with the women and then they begin again, but this time the music is different, more solemn, and we hear, interspersed with the words in Zulu, my parents' names, Helga and then Silas, once and then again, "*Inkosi ibenawe, ixolele ibusise, uHelga,*" God be with, may he forgive and bless, Helga, and bless Silas too, may he forgive all of us our transgressions, our many, many transgressions and I see Bridget standing quite still, clutching Baptie's hand, and Baptie, her manner resolute, standing with no trace of grief about her, a look of triumph, indeed, on her face.

When the music is over Arnold is still there, beside me, rooted to the floor, and there is something else too. Lined along the wall at the back of the hall are a number of people whom I do not recognize, Africans for the most part, and now they come forward to introduce themselves, representative of the various charities Bridget has contacted, gracious people, soft-spoken, holding our hands as they thank us for Bridget's generosity, compliment the choir on their music, and later, when we have moved toward the tables and eaten, on our choice of food. We remain in the hall, all of us, until the time we had reserved ends, before we part exchange e-mail addresses, hugs, embraces.

I wish we had left things undisturbed, exactly as they were and beneath whatever layers of silt had come to cover them, and yet I feel joy to be here.

22

SITTING ON MY SUITCASE in the foyer of the Beverly Hills Hotel and waiting for a taxi to the airport, I take a newspaper from the concierge's desk and there, on page four, I see a picture of Arnold Miro surrounded by three black men, all of them smiling. I read that Arnold may not have come to South Africa solely or even primarily to torment us, but that he has been brought out by the government, at its expense and with all due fanfare, to participate in some business venture that involves a great deal of public money. He has apparently teamed up with a group of black billionaires, men he would once not have allowed into his home, and been awarded a government tender. Because investment banking is my field, and because the article smacks of illogic, I read it twice and it is clear that something in the story is not what it seems. In the photograph Arnold seems to have just told a joke that everyone finds funny, and the Africans beam at him with pleasure, even with affection. I scrutinize the picture, look for ambiguity, a trace of irony in the smiling faces, and find none. I have seen all I need to see.

I tear the page with Arnold's picture from the newspaper and begin to fold it so that later I can show it to Bridget and the others, and then as I see them coming toward me, Leora with one arm around each parent, Bridget laughing about something, Tibor looking down at his daughter with an expression of bemused pride as she shows Tesseba something she has just bought at the gift shop. I decide not to interrupt our departure with this discordant image, tear the article into small pieces, and drop them in a bin meant for ashes and old cigarettes.

23

WE ARE GOING OUR SEPARATE WAYS, my sister and her family and Tesseba and I. They are going home, and we are going to Kenya, on a safari I have organized at the last minute. Tesseba loves animals, and she has been looking forward to this part of our trip since we left home.

Our farewells in the foyer of the hotel are surprisingly lighthearted, you could say almost joyful, and the feeling remains with us as Tesseba and I fly over Africa. I answer her questions, about Eben, about Baptie, about my father, and somehow against the backdrop of the last few days none of it sounds as tawdry, as ridiculous, as I had always imagined it would. She listens without comment, looks occasionally out the window at the endless expanse below. We land in Nairobi late in the afternoon and just as we clear customs I see a porter in a meticulous white suit carrying a Mount Kenya Safari Club sign with our names on it, "Mr. and Mrs. Daniel Divin, Boston, America," and it feels, strangely, as if we are finally free.

Over the next five days I see a side of Tesseba I have not seen before. She sits gleefully in the scout's seat of the Land Rover, leans out fearlessly to photograph any animal that ventures near us, eggs on the driver as he battles across rough ground toward a pair of cheetahs stalking their prey.

"Go, go, go," she says excitedly as the vehicle grinds over rocks and clumps of grass. "Just there. They're just there. Behind the *koppie*."

"I love this place," she keeps saying. "Promise me, promise me, that we can come back and back and back."

"I promise," I say.

As for me, there is something familiar about the old lodge, something I recognize in the grassy wind that blows into our bungalow each morning, something I know well in the shapes of the trees that grace the edge of every horizon. There is something about being in the lodge at night, momentarily safe from the menace of the African night, that feels quite familiar. The food is delicious. The quarters are sumptuous. We enjoy them all without guilt. We are visitors, and we are safe.

I also know the music that drifts from the staff's quarters each night. I know this place. It is as if I have been here before, though I have not.

24

RUPERT CALLS TO TELL ME that the judge in England has dismissed Arnold's suit, that Arnold has, notwithstanding everything, been true to his word. It is as if I have won, hands down, a battle of no importance.

"The court has awarded you costs," Rupert adds. "Over here we believe the loser should pay the winner for his troubles. Apparently Arnold didn't anticipate this when he agreed to back off."

"What's involved in it?" I ask. "What must he pay for?"

"Almost everything," Rupert says. "Lawyers' fees too, I might add."

I think of this, of piling on now and going after Arnold, extracting from him the tens of thousands of dollars that all of this has cost, and I have no stomach for it. There would be no satisfaction in it. I have even, if you can believe this, in the instant after Rupert relays the news that Arnold has not reneged on his promise, begun to feel sorry for him.

"Let it go," I say.

Eben was right, of course, when he talked about the mischievous nature of memory, because all of a sudden I feel something approaching compassion for Arnold. In short, my memories of him have changed, and something tells me it is more than mischief afoot. What we snatched from him are what I thought were the remains of our golden days, relics of paradise, but of course in the light of day they are nothing of the kind.

I go with Tibor to the shipper to fill out the various customs declarations and where one of them asks if we have anything that needs special clearance, anything that may violate, for example, the Endangered Species Act, like ivory, I write "No," and then I turn to Tibor and I say, "Tibor, those tusks are fake, you know."

Tibor pauses just for a moment, purses his lips, and then goes back to working on the form.

"Of course," he says softly. "Although I'm not sure what difference that makes."

We continue for a few moments in silence and then I realize that Tibor is right. The tusks are not real, perhaps, and I am not only not upset by it but somehow relieved, jubilant even. They were not Shaka's and they are not ivory, but they were my father's and wherever they came from they did end up in Africa, imposters like us and laying claim to things that could never be theirs. They have been at the center of so much, have held themselves out as so many things, and now they are coming to Boston too and they will mean something else again, all over again. Their provenance, like ours, is incomparable.

"Bridget would like one of them, you know," he adds, and he keeps on writing, his head down, his manner quite calm.

Without notice my vision of the tusks facing each other on either side of my travertine fireplace is under siege. I am suddenly furious, more than furious, at Tibor and his careful, studied manner—and who is Bridget to be usurping me now, to be laying claim to something I have thought so much about, worked so hard to bring home while she watched, indifferent, critical? Who indeed?—and then I realize that this is Bridget against whom I am railing, Bridget, *Bridget,* that I am on the verge of allowing these worthless pieces of plastic to emerge as a point of contention between me and my beloved sister. If there is rancor with her, the only constant in my life from the first day to now, and over pieces of wood and junk, then there is discord reaching into every corner of my life and we are back full circle, in Arnold's living room, having learned nothing.

"They're a pair," I say. "If you have the space for them, take them both."

"Are you sure?" he says, unexpectedly, but it is too late to back down and in any event I feel suddenly lighter for the offer, suddenly enlightened.

"I wouldn't say so if I wasn't," I say.

I am driven too sternly by memories of the past and it is time, as Eben says, to try and let some of them go. I can start with those ragged, fake relics. I look across at my brother-in-law as he works his way through a government form. Bent over the table, a smudge on one lens of his reading glasses, in a baggy gray sweater, he seems, for a moment, quite fragile. I feel like I did the evening I saw Tesseba sitting in my mother's seat in the synagogue. Maybe this then is what happiness is, those little moments when your heart opens, truly opens, and you feel as if you could weep for all the good feelings that flood in.

Of course Bridget and Tibor's home is the appropriate place for them, just out of reach, nearby, not mine. Memory may be mischievous but it is also remarkable, self-cleaning, creative, ultimately as magical as a prediction.

THE END

I am grateful to Franklin Dennis in New York
for his many contributions to this novel
and for his constancy,
to Nellie Somers and the Killie Campbell Library in Durban
for their hospitality,
to Claude Pretorius for his assistance
in Zululand,
and to the Ostroffs for their help with
the London settings.
Obviously all errors are my own.

GLOSSARY OF NON-ENGLISH TERMS AND WORDS

Page 23. **Toytn bankes.** *Yiddish* slang. Generally, as helpful as cupping—an archaic medical procedure—to a dead person.

Page 27. **Coloured.** In the South African context, refers to a person of mixed race, a distinct ethnic group.

Page 40. **Voetsak.** *Afrikaans.* Go away, often said to a dog

Vrek. *Afrikaans.* Die, referring to an animal.

Gey in drerd. *Yiddish.* Go into the earth (and die).

Page 48. **Meshugga.** *Yiddish.* Crazy.

Page 56. **Kraals.** *Afrikaans.* Pen for livestock, or stockaded enclosure for huts.

Page 74. **Schmuck.** *Yiddish* slang. Idiot: literally the removed foreskin after a circumcision.

Page 81. **Schmooze.** *Yiddish.* To make small talk.

Page 102. **Oseh shalom bimromav.** *Hebrew.* Start of the concluding stanza of the Jewish prayer for the dead.

Page 115. **Goldene yorren.** *Yiddish.* Golden years.

Page 141. **Sawubona.** *Zulu.* Hello.

Page 146. **Stoep.** *Afrikaans.* Porch

Page 159. **Braaivleis.** *Afrikaans.* Barbecue.

Page 218. **Bhansela.** *Zulu.* Gratuity.

Page 276. **Jou vok. Kaffirboetie. Jood.** *Afrikaans.* You fucker. Nigger lover. Jew.

Volk. *Afrikaans.* People, but here meaning something akin to a chosen people.

Page 290. **Nkulunkulu**. *Zulu*. God.

Nkosi. *Zulu*. God.

Page 307. **Panga**. *Afrikaans*. Large cutting tool that resembles a straight scythe.

Page 315. **Kaddish**. *Hebrew*. Prayer for the Dead.

Page 345. **Koppie**. *Afrikaans*. Little hill, especially on the African veld.

EMPIRE SETTINGS *was published in hard cover by White Pine Press in 2001 and in paperback by Plume in 2002. The book won the SUNY John Gardner Book Award in 2003 and was the South African* Sunday Times *Book of the Week. Here are excerpts from some of its reviews:*

"Thoughtful, affecting and skillfully constructed first novel."

—*Los Angeles Times*

"Unexpected, even unforgettable .... [an] artful battle against cultural and historical amnesia."

—*Washington Post*

"This artful, moving novel .... displays a sure touch with character, plot and atmosphere alike."

—*San Francisco Chronicle*

"Striking first novel [that] brings characters, family tensions and racial complexities alive in just a line or two."

—*Seattle Times*

"Finely crafted, deeply satisfying debut novel."

—*Boston Herald*

"Engaging and poignant account .... An altogether promising debut."

—*Publishers Weekly*

"Teaches us volumes about hello and good-bye, holding on and letting go."

—*Christian Science Monitor*

"A longing [for the past] Schmahmann elucidates with bittersweet grace."

—*Baltimore Sun*

"A marvelous and painful psalm to love of both people and places .... a book to share with people you care about."

—*Providence Sunday Journal*

"Beautifully written debut novel full of honesty and emotion; you'll feel like you're leaving friends when the last page is turned."

—*Elle Magazine*

"Vividly written. Anyone who has lived in Durban will be overwhelmed by it."

—*Sunday World* (South Africa)

"Evocative, lyrical and moving."

—*Sunday Times* (South Africa)

"Read it if only for the towering beauty of the prose."

—*City Life* (South Africa).